I went cold all over.

I closed the oak door firmly behind me before sprinting down the corridor toward the bride's dressing room. The door was slightly ajar, and a sickly hospital smell reached me as I tried to shove it open. An obstruction behind the door gave way slowly, and then held. I shoved harder and squeezed through.

The obstruction was Dorothy Fenner. She was tumbled across the rug like a rag doll, her permed silver hair askew, her breathing hoarse and wet. Beyond her was an old overstuffed chair, one of several in the faded, mismatched furnishings, piled high today with the bridesmaids' street clothes, their hairbrushes and lipstick cases and crumpled tissues. But this one chair had nothing on it except a satin shoe. One of Nickie's. Inside the shoe was a piece of lined white paper, a rough penciled note printed on it. Dazed, in slow motion, I picked it up. *We'll tell you what to do*, it read. *No police or you get her fingers in the mail.*

Veiled Threats

DEBORAH DONNELLY

A DELL BOOK

A Dell Book
Published by
Dell Publishing
Random House, Inc.
1540 Broadway
New York, New York 10036

For information, address Dell Publishing, New York, New York.

Dell® is a registered trademark of Random House, Inc., and the
colophon is a trademark of Random House, Inc.

ISBN: 0-440-23703-3

Printed in the United States of America

Published simultaneously in Canada

January 2002

10 9 8 7 6 5 4
OPM

This is dedicated to the one I love.

Acknowledgments

I'd like to thank my agent, Jim Frenkel, who defines the word "perseverance," and Diane Hall-Harris, true artist and true friend. Thanks also to Anne Bohner, an editor with an excellent eye. Last, but never least, heartfelt thanks to Frederick K. Dezendorf, patron of the arts.

Veiled Threats

Chapter One

WHY ON EARTH DO PEOPLE GET MARRIED? AND WHY, WHY DO I offer to help them do the deed? Why do I promise "Elegant Weddings With An Original Flair," as it says on my business card, when I know damn well how many things can go wrong at once? "Made in Heaven Wedding Design, Carnegie Kincaid, Proprietor." Tonight, the proprietor was ready to resign.

So far, on this rainy Sunday night in June, the florist's truck had had a flat, the groom's grandmother had had a fit, I was missing one waiter for the reception, and the four-year-old ring bearer had hidden the ring in her underpants. Twice. And now, moments before their procession down the aisle, one of the bridesmaids was sneezing. Explosive, rapid-fire, high-decibel sneezes. The other bridesmaids were smothering hysterical giggles while Diane, the bride, was developing a deer-caught-in-headlights stare. We were approaching meltdown.

The bride, the bridesmaids, the ring bearer and I were clustered outside the ballroom of Sercombe House, one of Seattle's Victorian mansions-for-rent. The mahogany doorway ahead of us framed a festive and expectant scene, with fluttering candle flames and masses of pale pink English roses, delivered dangerously late but lovely all the same. The string quartet played Haydn—loudly, thank God. The judge winked at the groom. The guests beamed in anticipation. And Susie, a plump little blonde gone very red in the face, kept on sneezing.

"I'm so sorry," she gasped. "I don't know what . . . aaahhh—"

"Here!" I shoved another handkerchief at her. "It must be your bouquet. Are you allergic to flowers? Don't try to talk, just give it to me. Quick!"

I examined the offending bouquet. English roses, stargazer lilies, stephanotis. No telling what was setting Susie off. I yanked the pink satin ribbon from around the stems, held back a spray of lilies, and pitched the rest of the bouquet in a nearby wastebasket. "Nickie, take the ring away from Tiffany and give it to me."

Nickie Parry, the maid of honor and my next bride-to-be client, gave me the gleaming gold-and-black enamel band so that I could thread the ribbon through it and tie a big loopy bow.

"Susie, you are now the ring bearer." I handed her the ring and bow, and we waited. Two more small sneezes . . . a couple of sniffles . . . blessed silence.

"Excellent!" I stooped to present the lilies to Tiffany. "Here you go, Tiff, now you're the flower girl. It's a *very* special job. And Michelle, change places with Susie so she ends up close to the bride, OK?"

"What*ever*." Michelle rolled her eyes and I imagined, not for the first time, strangling her with the bride's garter. She was a cousin of Diane's, in from New York, cadaverously thin and heavily sardonic. She'd made it clear that weddings, especially hick Seattle weddings, were a ridiculous bore, especially when it was suggested that she take out her nose ring for the occasion. Her boyfriend, a densely pierced and tattooed youth, obviously shared her opinions. As far as I was concerned, they deserved each other.

Michelle belched abruptly, and I guessed from the fumes that the bottle of champagne I'd brought to their dressing room earlier must have gone mostly down Miss Sophisticate's throat. I felt my back teeth grinding.

"OK, everybody line up. Susie, are you all right now? Great. You all look fabulous."

They did, too. Diane loathed what she called "those pastel jobs with bows on the butts," and I agreed—baby-blue chiffon is best seen on babies. So I'd had long-skirted evening suits made up in black damask, with pearly white blouses underneath the peplum jackets. In effect, a lady's tuxedo. Every man ever born looks good in a tux, and so does every woman, if she gets the chance.

The Haydn wound up, and the processional, the Bach Cantata BWV 140, began. I sent little Tiffany and then the first two bridesmaids down the aisle, then the glassy-eyed Michelle, then Susie, still flushed but no longer erupting, and holding the ring-and-ribbon with formal care, as if we'd planned it. Then the maid of honor, then the bride stepped forward . . . accompanied by a hideous ripping sound, so loud that the entire back row of guests craned around to look. She hastily sidestepped away from their line of sight. Another *rrrrip*. The beaded hem of her gown had snagged on a nailhead and torn free from the fragile silk of the skirt, leaving a two-foot length trailing along the floor.

"Do something!" Diane's already pale face had gone even paler.

"I'm doing it." I was already on my knees behind her, whipping out my pocket sewing kit. Had I replaced the

straight pins since the last time I'd used it? I had. I was pin-
ning frantically when I heard a soft, kindly, sickeningly familiar voice.

"Oh, dear. Yet another little problem. Can I help?"

I looked up and forced myself to smile at Dorothy Fenner.
Dear silver-haired Dorothy, the best-known wedding consultant in the Northwest. So aristocratic and yet so maternal. So
well versed in etiquette, so well connected to the rich and famous. So very similar in appearance to Meryl Streep. And for
three years now, so very successful at acing me out of potential clients. Nickie Parry's would be my first really big society
wedding, and dear Dorothy had only missed landing the contract for it because she'd been on a Mediterranean cruise for
the last month. She was strictly a guest here tonight, her husband being a colleague of the groom's father, but she kept
popping up and pointedly offering help as one thing after another went awry.

"There's no problem, Dorothy," I said gaily. "OK, Diane,
all set."

"But it's crooked!"

I stood up and glared. "All eyes will be focused on your ra-
diant face. Now go."

She went, but Dorothy didn't.

"Carnegie. I thought you should know." Dorothy always
pronounced my name as if it had quote marks around it. (My
late father was a big fan of Andrew Carnegie, having edu-
cated himself in the public libraries funded by the old robber
baron. As a kid, I'd hated my weird name, but now I figured,
why should a skinny five-foot-eleven redhead even try to be
inconspicuous?) "Carnegie, that Mary woman managed to
get in."

"Oh, hell."

Crazy Mary was a tiny, silent, bug-eyed old woman, dressed in charity clothes and lugging a shopping bag, who wandered the streets of downtown Seattle. Some people said she was secretly rich, and others that she was homeless, but everybody knew Mary's hobby: attending fancy weddings. She never said a word or caused a problem. She just appeared and disappeared, like a little bird seen from the corner of your eye.

"Well, she won't hurt anything, and she'll probably leave soon. Please sit down, Dorothy."

As she did, I checked the crowd for Crazy Mary. Sure enough, she was there near the back, hunched in her chair, the shoulders of her shabby jacket dark with rain. Who knew what weddings meant to her, or what memories lay behind those unblinking eyes? Dorothy Fenner had twice, to my knowledge, had Crazy Mary thrown out of weddings she was managing. I couldn't bring myself to do it, and I was sure Diane wouldn't mind her presence. As if she'd heard my thought, Mary turned, cocked her head at me, and smiled softly. I smiled back, nodding, and in unison we turned our gazes back to Diane, who had just reached the head of the aisle.

I love this moment. Young and trembling or calm and not-so-young, seed pearls or tie-dye, intimate ceremony or extravaganza, this first public appearance of the bride always makes me misty. There's all the romance that Western culture can bestow: the idea of the fairy princess, Cinderella, the one and only true love. Not to mention the sheer theater of making a solo entrance in a knockout costume. But it was the courage that caught at my never-married heart. To publicly say, He's the one; I pledge my life to his life. All the divorce statistics in the world can't tarnish that moment. That's the real reason why I help people get married. I'm a sucker for romance.

So I lingered while Diane, bright as a sunrise, took her place beside her chosen man. The candlelight gleamed on her gown and in her eyes, and Jeffrey looked, as all bridegrooms should, like the luckiest fellow on earth. I sighed, dabbed at a tear, and slipped back through the fine old oak-floored dining room into the mansion's kitchen. I had to track down a pair of antique crystal goblets sent over by the groom's grandmother this morning, thus setting off the old lady's tantrum. And I had to ask Joe Solveto, the caterer, where the hell that third waiter was.

The kitchen was crammed with hors d'oeuvres but empty of Joe or anyone else. My stomach growled fiercely at the fans of prosciutto-wrapped asparagus, ranks of crisp snow pea pods piped with velvety salmon mousse, and clusters of green grapes rolled in Roquefort. The wedding cake, three tiers of chocolate hazelnut glory, was already in the dining room, but the old marble countertop along the kitchen wall held a parade of cut-glass dishes piled with petit fours and chocolate-dipped apricots. Surely I could pluck just one apricot from its dish, one tiny cream puff from its pyramid, one oyster from its bed of crushed ice, without disturbing Joe's fearful symmetry. . . .

But no, first things first. I stepped out to the back porch and squinted into the drizzly night, hoping to see the waiter's headlights. Sercombe House sits high on a hill, with terraced flower beds stretching down the lawn. The parking lot behind the house had filled. Parked cars were now lined up nose-to-tail the whole length of the steep drive leading down to the highway, where a mossy old brick wall bordered the property. I could see my modest white van, nicknamed Vanna White, just uphill from Nickie Parry's candy-apple-red '66 Mustang.

The car had been a college graduation gift from Nickie's father. Douglas Parry owned several department stores, a few Alaskan fish canneries, and a good chunk of downtown Seattle. He was so very fond of Nickie that he'd said the three magic words about her wedding: Money No Object. Fifteen percent of Money No Object was going to put me firmly in the black, for the first time since I'd started Made in Heaven. I wondered idly if my parking brake was set—I'd hate to dent that Mustang—but I wasn't willing to brave the downpour to find out.

Someone else was out in the rain, though: a heavyset figure was striding downhill just beyond the Mustang. His long raincoat flapped as though he were shoving something into a pocket. Car keys, probably. But he was heading away from the house, not toward it, so he couldn't be my waiter. Well, we'd have to manage with only two. I turned my back on the hissing of the rain and went inside to find Grandmother's goblets.

I had better luck on this count. The crystal in question, facets winking in the light, had been unwrapped and set on a high shelf out of harm's way. Also out of reach, even for me, so I pulled over a wooden chair and stood on tiptoe. Just another inch . . . A startling blast of damp air lifted my skirt. Already off balance, I turned abruptly to see a handsome, frowning man enter through the porch door and shake the rain from his windbreaker. My third waiter. The chair wobbled, then tipped over with a clatter, sending me in a harmless but ungraceful leap to the checkerboard tile floor. I saved myself from sprawling flat at the cost of a cracked fingernail and my dignity.

He reached out a hand. "Are you all right?"

"Of course I am," I snapped, brushing off my dress. The

broken nail launched a run in my left stocking. Damn, damn, damn. "But you just barely made it. Where's your tie?"

He looked down at his heathery sweater, and then down at me. I'm over six feet tall in dress shoes, but he was six four, with wavy chestnut hair and the most distinctive green eyes I'd ever seen on a waiter or anyone else, the glass green of a breaking wave.

"This was the best I could do," he said coolly. "I just came from the airport."

"The best you could do!" I kept my voice low, but green eyes or not I was angry. "Black slacks, white shirt, black bow tie. I was very specific! Look, I need those glasses up there."

"Yes, ma'am." He mounted the chair, reached up, and handed the goblets down to me. He had broad, tanned hands, still chilly from the rain where they brushed my fingers.

"Thanks," I said. "Now let's find the others."

"Right here, Carnegie." Joe Solveto's cunningly mussed sandy hair and narrow, theatrical face appeared in the stairwell leading up from the basement-level pantry. He brandished an unopened champagne bottle. "We're popping the corks downstairs, but this is the special stuff for the happy pair. I see you found the goblets. Excuse me, sir."

Sir? Joe relieved me of the glasses and pressed on into the dining room, quickly followed by all three waiters, in their white shirts and black bow ties. Number Three must have arrived during Susie's sneezing attack. I felt a blush rising from the asymmetrical neckline of my jade silk dress. It was my one haute-couture rag, and my favorite outfit for weddings: gracefully appropriate for day or evening, generously cut to allow mad dashes to my van in case the best man forgot his tie or the maid of honor her lipstick, and equipped with pockets in which to thrust my hands when embarrassed. Which I was, and did.

"You're a guest. I'm very sorry. I—"

"My fault." He had a light tenor voice, surprising in such a large man, and slightly crooked front teeth that showed when he smiled and saved him from being male-model perfect. Not that one objects to perfect strangers. "Obviously I came in the wrong door," he was saying. "Have I missed everything?"

"Yes. No." Deep breath. "The ceremony is almost over, but you can slip in the back if you go through the dining room and to your right. I am sorry."

"No problem," he said, smiling as he walked by. "You can order me around anytime."

I stood bemused for a moment, muttering "Who *was* that masked man?"

Then I got back to work.

Chapter Two

WHEN YOU'RE WORKING, WEDDING RECEPTIONS ARE ONE LONG adrenaline rush. Make sure a table is set aside for signing the marriage certificate. Make sure the photographer knows where the table is. Make sure the string quartet knows their cue to switch from Mozart to the first waltz, and will adhere to their blood oath not to play the horribly overplayed Pachelbel *Canon*. Make damn sure everything is elegant, with an original flair.

A wedding coordinator is a sort of general contractor, a hardheaded business type who secures the services of printer, dressmaker, wine merchant, reception hall, bakery, clergy, ad infinitum. She's also an assistant daydreamer and amateur therapist, bringing fantasies to life and smoothing family tensions. At that moment, though, I felt like nothing so much as a Broadway producer with a hit on my hands. Diane, Jeffrey, and their guests filed into the dining room in a cheery chaos of laughter, hugs, and champagne, strobe-lit by flashbulbs and perfumed with roses and the honeyed scent of beeswax candles.

I paused to catch my breath and take it all in. This was my largest wedding yet and I'd done an excellent job, more than earning my percentage of the wedding budget and some invaluable word-of-mouth advertising. I allowed myself a moment of giddy optimism. Surely Made in Heaven would make it after all. Though we'd better do it soon. The bills were mounting up, my partner Eddie Breen was deferring his salary, and I was overdue on the start-up loan my mother had made me. She had a balloon payment on her mortgage coming up in September. Surely I could pay her back by then.

Back to business. "Where do the gifts go?" "Is there pork in the pâté?" "Can the violinist play 'Feelings'?" Upstairs, definitely not, and I'm *so* sorry but no, I replied, while directing the photographer, paying the judge, and flinging my last handkerchief on some spilled champagne before it stained the oak floor and ate into our damage deposit.

Suddenly I had company: Crazy Mary was on her knees, scrubbing at the spill with a napkin. Her hands were curled and knobbly with arthritis, just like my mother's.

"Why, thank you," I said.

She turned her startled eyes to me and spoke, in a voice like dry leaves. "She said I could stay, the bride did! She said I could have a piece of cake."

Good for Diane. "Of course you can. And don't worry about this. I'll take care of it."

"Terrible," she muttered, continuing to scrub. "People are terrible. Breaking things, stealing things. I saw him, you know. I saw him."

It was actually a woman who'd spilled the champagne, but I let it go. "It's all right, thanks for helping. They'll be cutting the cake soon."

"Terrible." Her head went on shaking, like a pendulum. "Terrible, terrible. I saw him."

Then the crowd shifted around us, and she was gone. I rose and waved across the room at the photographer to take her position near the cake. Oops. Just behind her, stepping aside from the knot of guests around Diane, was the green-eyed man in the heathery sweater. He raised an eyebrow and waved back at me, and I felt myself blushing again. Sometimes I hate being a redhead. He lifted his champagne glass in a private toast. Or was it an invitation to join him?

I would have joined him, too, but my way was suddenly blocked by 265 pounds of Slavic fury: Boris, the Mad Russian Florist.

"Kharrnegie! You rruined my bouquet! For what?"

Boris Nevsky was not really mad, not entirely, but my pal Lily had nicknamed him and the name stuck. He was huge and loud and brilliant with flowers, and the fact that I'd dated him a couple of times apparently gave him license to harass me at wedding receptions. The dates had stopped when I went to his family's place for a lamb barbecue, and the lamb was still alive when I got there. He thought I was prissy and squeamish, and I thought he was a barbarian. Besides, any more of his embraces and I'd have had broken ribs.

No one exactly invited Boris to their weddings, but once he delivered his flowers and arranged them with ferocious precision, he just never left. You don't ask a force of nature to go home. I explained about Susie's bouquet, quickly and quietly. Boris stared at me, his thick black eyebrows parting and rising like the Fremont drawbridge. His face seemed to contract, like a fist, when he was angry, and then expand like the full moon when he smiled. Just now he was expanding, and erupting in laughter.

"Sneezing? Sneezing! You should have put her in string quartet, for percussion! Kharnegie, you look beautiful tonight."

"Well thanks, Boris, but—"

But he was at it again, embracing me in a grizzly bear hug, then planting a big wet kiss. It was like being hit in the mouth by an affectionate truck. I pushed him away, and caught a glimpse of the green-eyed man, who was now heading for the bar. And there by the cake table was dear Dorothy Fenner. Bloody hell. She looked at me in a pained but sympathetic way, as you would at a four-year-old who's knocked over the orange juice again. Sighing, I headed for the ladies' room to regroup.

The Sercombe House cloakroom was sweet enough to induce diabetic coma: gilt cupids, blossom-and-ribbon wallpaper, and tiny china bowls of potpourri. But at least it was empty, giving me a chance to collect my straying wits while redoing my hair and lipstick. There. Lipstick on straight, eyeliner unsmudged. On the other hand, nose still beaky, eyes still an undecided hazel, and freckles still on parade despite foundation and powder. Ah, well. As I dabbed at my soggy dress—Boris must have been out in the rain—Nickie came in.

"Carnegie, can I talk to you?"

"Sure. What's wrong?"

Nickie was a pretty, curvy girl, full lips and full hips, with heavy waves of dark hair and fine olive skin. Just now she was close to tears, biting her lip and picking nervously at the spectacular double strand of baroque pearls at her throat.

"It's Grace. She's back from Chicago. But I haven't told her about the dress yet. I'm . . . I'm kind of scared to."

I was a little worried about the dress myself. Nickie's original wedding gown had recently arrived, two weeks late and two sizes too small. The couturier couldn't produce a replacement in time, and Nickie's stepmother Grace was out of town, so

Nickie and I had gone shopping. A chance detour into my favorite vintage clothing store turned up an Edwardian gown, a timeworn but lovely concoction of cream-colored lace. We both loved it, so I bought it, dispensing a hefty sum from the household checking account, which Douglas Parry had put at my disposal. But perhaps we'd been a wee bit impulsive. I hadn't met Grace yet, but I hoped to hell she was open-minded.

"And besides," Nickie rushed on, the tears overflowing, "Ray's family is all upset because of this new publicity about Daddy and King County Savings. They're so conservative and proper, and I never know what to say to them anyway—I keep thinking they don't like me because I'm not Japanese. But Ray thought I was criticizing them, and I thought he was criticizing Daddy, and now there are these anonymous letters, and then we had a fight on the t-telephone. That's why he's not here tonight, so I drove myself and brought Michelle and Sean."

"That must have been a pleasure," I said dryly.

She laughed, damply. "It was awful! She kept wanting to drive the Mustang, but I don't let anybody drive it, not even Ray." The tears overflowed again. "And now he's mad at me. Why does everything get so complicated? I just love Ray and I want everybody to l-leave us alone!"

Juliet, at bay between the Montagues and Capulets, might have been more eloquent, but no more sincere. I hugged her to me, letting her cry for as long as she needed, and hiding my own rueful smile. Youngsters keep falling in love and wanting the world to go away, and the world never does.

Then I frowned at myself for this remarkably middle-aged sentiment. Who was I, Juliet's old hag of a nurse while still in my thirties? Always a bridal consultant, never a bride. I had a sudden image of those sea-green eyes, and a sudden desire to star in my own romance. I set it firmly aside and pressed on to more serious matters.

"Nickie, I'm sure you and Ray will sort this out. Just give it time. But what's all this about your father? What letters?"

More tears. "Someone's sending him threats in the mail, and I think they're calling him, too! He didn't want me and Grace to know about it, but I saw one of the letters by accident. It called him a—it called him names, and said he stole people's life savings. It said if he didn't confess to the grand jury, that he'd be sorry for the rest of his life! Carnegie, he wouldn't do anything wrong, ever."

"Of course he wouldn't," I told her, thinking just the opposite. Douglas Parry didn't look like a crook to me, but then again I'd once been stiffed for nine hundred dollars by a baker who looked like Mother Teresa with a rolling pin. And the whole savings-and-loan debacle seemed so Machiavellian, so many deals within deals. How many of those wealthy, well-connected bankers were completely above reproach?

I knew only the outlines of this case. Douglas Parry had chaired the board of King County Savings, which went into receivership after heavy losses and allegations of securities fraud. During a seemingly endless federal investigation, the CEO, Keith Guthridge, had tried to shift the blame to Parry, but Parry claimed that Guthridge had misled him every step of the way. What made it really ugly was that the two men had once been close friends. Keith Guthridge was Nickie's godfather.

"The grand jury will sort it all out," I said, trying to sound brisk and knowledgeable. "After all, your father's just a witness. It's Guthridge who's the defendant, right? The letters are from some poor investor who got his facts wrong. Lots of prominent people get hate mail. Let's just concentrate on the wedding, OK? Grace is going to love your dress, I know she—"

"FUCK YOU!!"

Nickie and I stared at each other. The voice had come from the dining room, but it was more than loud enough to reach us here. A slurred, screechy voice. Michelle. As we rushed out of the cloakroom, Nickie's tears forgotten, we heard the smashing of glass, and more shouting. The string quartet faltered to a halt, then started up again, providing a lovely Strauss counterpoint to the appalling brawl now going on between Michelle and Sean, her leather-clad boyfriend.

"You bastard! I saw you looking down her dress, you bastard, don't lie to me!" Michelle was standing, or rather swaying, with her back to the cake table, while Sean backed away from her, muttering halfhearted denials and dark threats. A champagne flute lay in shining splinters at his feet, and another one was still clutched dangerously in Michelle's gesticulating hand. Both of them had the foolish, defiant look of misbehaving children who suddenly realize there are adults in the room.

Most of the adults tonight were looking shocked and uncomfortable, though I noticed the waiters grinning broadly. Jeffrey had his arm around his bride, as if to sweep her away to safety, or perhaps to keep her from murdering her cousin. And dear, dear Dorothy had one hand pressed to her proper bosom and was shaking her head in regret at this deplorable scene. This stuff never happened at her weddings, of course. I groaned and stepped forward.

"Look, Michelle, let's go talk about this somewhere private, OK?"

"There's nothing to talk about!" she hollered. The music had stopped again, and her words were piercingly clear. "I'm so fucking sick of all you people *talking*!"

With the last word she flung her arms wide. The glass flute went flying from one hand, but it was her other hand that did the real damage, smacking deep into the middle tier of the wedding cake and sending the top tier to the floor with a weighty, chocolatey splat. The bride shrieked, Sean snorted with laughter, and Michelle pulled her hand free and fled down the hall toward the bridesmaids' dressing room. Sean made to follow her, but I caught his arm.

"Leave her alone. I'll go talk to her. You go cool off." I pushed him into the custody of the blessedly sober best man, motioned the quartet to play on, and helped the waiters begin to mop up. I needed a minute to cool off myself, I was so furious. Then I headed down the hall, through the exclamations and the nervous laughter of the wedding guests. Poor Diane. Poor me! Poor Michelle, once I got my hands on her.

The dressing room was empty, and I heard the back door slam. *Idiot* girl, running around in the rain. I cut through the kitchen and stopped on the porch to let my eyes adjust. Headlights flashed past, blinding me with their glare. Michelle wasn't running; she was driving. She'd taken the keys to Nickie's Mustang and gone roaring down the steep, narrow drive toward the sharp bend down below.

"Michelle! Michelle, stop, don't—!"

I could no longer see the car, just the yellow cones of light from the headlights marking its crazy flight down the hill. I was still shouting when the Mustang tore straight across the bend and rammed full speed into the brick wall at the bottom. A crumpling, splintering crash, then the headlights died, and there was only darkness and the sound of rain.

Chapter Three

IT WAS WELL AFTER MIDNIGHT BEFORE I LEFT SERCOMBE House, moving in a slow-motion trance of weariness and guilt. There had been plenty of guilt to go around as the police cars came, and then the fire truck, and then the ambulance that acted as a hearse, because Michelle had died instantly. Young Sean felt guilty about the fight, of course, to the extent that he could feel anything at all beyond his shock. Diane felt guilty for letting Michelle guzzle champagne while they got dressed. Nickie felt guilty for leaving her car keys lying around.

"If I'd just put them away," she said for the fourth time, as we all stumbled out to our cars at last.

"Nickie, please, try not to think about it. Listen, shall I drive you home?"

"Oh. I guess I won't be driving, will I?" Her eyes were glassy, and she giggled, then laughed, on a rising, quavering note. "But Michelle won't be driving ever, will she? And I won't be driving the Mustang. God, I loved that car!"

She stopped herself, appalled. Jeffrey and Diane, their wedding night in ruins, stared at her. "I'm so sorry! I didn't mean that! I didn't—"

"Nickie, honey." I shook her gently. "You're in shock. It's OK." Thinking about her car at a time like this might seem callous, but then I'd been thinking about my business. This could be a disaster for Made in Heaven.

"I'll take her home." Dorothy Fenner was, for once, a welcome sight as she came down the porch steps. "I know the way."

I handed Nickie over and trudged down the graveled drive, grateful to be left alone. But then my own guilt rose up. Worrying about my business was a trivial sin. What if I could have prevented the accident altogether? I replayed it over and over on my mind's movie screen: the brief, crucial time between Michelle's leaving the room, drunk and rude and alive, and her turning the ignition key, doomed. If only I'd cared less about the broken glass and spilled champagne and more about talking to her. If only I hadn't been so angry at my spoiled reception, and had gone after her right away. If I'd run across the grass instead of hesitating on the porch. If, if, if.

I reached my van, one of the few cars remaining beside the emergency vehicles clustered down at the bend. The driver's door was sticking again, and as I circled around to the other side the revolving light from a police car flickered on something shiny just under the front bumper. Mechanically, I picked it up: a business card case, dropped by a departing guest. I always ran a little lost-and-found service after a wedding. I wiped off the mud and tossed the case into my tote bag, where it joined the disposable camera, the dangly silver earring, and the plastic sandwich bag of what I hoped was not dope. The odds were good that nobody would call me about the bag, but the card case looked expensive.

I'd sort it out tomorrow. Tonight it was all I could do to navigate the empty streets of Seattle. I drove slowly to the east shore of Lake Union and parked in the narrow lot reserved for houseboat owners, and for houseboat renters like me. I had lived alone since college, over ten years ago. Living alone suited me, but how many weddings can you watch without wanting to come home to someone? I'd had dates, I'd had lovers, I'd had six months of let's-live-together-and-see-what-happens. I hadn't had the nerve to marry someone, and most of the time I hadn't had the someone. Tonight I really could have used a someone.

I decided to leave all my stuff in the van until morning, and headed down the dock, my solitary footsteps echoing on the worn wood planks. I loved my houseboat dearly, and I hoped someday to buy it from my landlady. It was a shabby old place, with no closet space and a miniature kitchen and no heat in the bathroom, but it had two great virtues: a two-room second story that was now Made in Heaven's office, and a priceless location at the very end of a dock.

You passed a dozen or so houseboats to get from the street to my door, but on the lake side my only neighbors were ducks. I could sit on my narrow, splintery front deck, or retreat to the glassed-in porch when it rained, and see the whole lake, from the high-rises of downtown at the south end to the green slopes of Gas Works Park at the north. Speedboats and sailboats shared the waterways with flotillas of Canada geese, and sunsets flared across the lake above Queen Anne Hill and the Fremont drawbridge. When rain squalls burst and then faded, the water's surface changed from silver moiré to ruffled pewter to mother-of-pearl. Sometimes I spent whole evenings just watching the lake and breathing.

The dock was silent at this hour, the row of houseboats dark and sleeping. The few dim lampposts along the walkway cast tilted shadows of the flower boxes and hanging baskets and driftwood sculpture with which my neighbors decorated their porches. I picked up a fallen honeysuckle blossom from beneath one basket and twirled it between my fingers. The evening's showers had left the dock gleaming in the lamplight, looking not quite real, a stage set waiting for the hero's entrance.

But this was a tragedy, not a romance, and the heroine had to play the scene alone. I could hear the slow, hollow slapping of waves under the logs and foam floats that supported each house. Over the edge of the dock, heavy guy-wires and seaweedy ropes disappeared into the black water. Unlike most of my neighbors, I was no swimmer, and the cold depths under my little street of boats looked eerily opaque. I leaned over the water and dropped the honeysuckle. It touched lightly on the black mirrored surface and floated away, slowly rotating, to disappear into the swaying shadows. Michelle's life had just disappeared. I shivered in the night breeze and hurried to my door.

Once inside, I left a phone message for Eddie to hear in the morning. Then I crawled into bed and tried to hold off the gloom by thinking about the handsome green-eyed man. But that all seemed so long ago, and anyway I was soon drifting into exhausted sleep. The man in the sweater, coming in from the rain . . . the other man in the rain . . . the heavyset man walking down the private drive in the rain. But it was a *private* drive; it didn't lead anywhere but Sercombe House.

I opened my eyes in the darkness. Where had the heavyset man been coming from as he headed down the hill? He wasn't a wedding guest, or I would have noticed him leaving. Had he been—crazy thought—had he been somewhere near Nickie's car? Speaking of crazy . . . Crazy Mary said she'd seen someone "breaking things and stealing things." Maybe that was who she meant. He'd been shoving something in a pocket: a tool? Was Michelle so terribly drunk that she couldn't even hit the brakes, or was there something wrong with the brakes? I saw again the headlights slashing down the hill, and I wondered. The man in the rain, headlights in the rain, the car nobody drove but Nickie . . . I lay back, mind whirling, and surrendered to sleep.

Chapter Four

I LOVE TO SLEEP. I LOVE IT THE WAY SOME PEOPLE—INCLUDING me—love food or sex. I am a passionate sleeper, and I guard my mornings like a lioness guarding a dead zebra, so that I can gorge on sleep. The normal mornings, that is. The mornings when no one has died the night before. The Monday morning after Diane's wedding I slept in, but only by force of will, trying to stay unconscious because reality was so sad and messy and guilty.

I'd forgotten to switch my personal phone line over to the answering machine, and at ten-fifteen the one in the kitchen rang like a fire bell. I jammed a pillow over my head, waiting for it to stop, but it didn't. Ten rings, twenty rings, thirty—it had to be Eddie. No one else would be so rude, and Eddie was too prim to come downstairs and hammer on my door when he knew I wasn't properly dressed. In fact he never came downstairs, stubbornly behaving as if my residence were miles away from my workplace instead of separated by a dozen wooden steps. I'd given him my one spare house key, in case he wanted a snack from my kitchen sometime when I wasn't around, but he never used it.

After thirty rings I decided to fire him, and after forty I decided to face the day. As I crossed the kitchen the linoleum was chilly underfoot, but the faded yellow walls were neon-lit with sunshine. I perched on a stool by the phone. It had stopped ringing, but I knew it would start again, so I just sat there rubbing my eyes and trying to think. What was it that had seemed so urgent last night? That's right, the man in the rain. Pure fantasy, late-night paranoia.

On the counter before me was an antique toy I'd just bought: a miniature wood stove from the 1890's, five inches high and made of cast iron, right down to the nickel-sized skillet that sat on one burner. I swung the curlicued oven door open and shut, open and shut. I had planned on a leisurely breakfast while I cleaned off the rust and went over it with stove polish. What a silly, trivial little plan, made back when Michelle was alive. The phone clamored again. Time for a new plan.

"Good morning, Eddie."

"Mrs. Parry left three messages on the machine before I got here this morning." Small talk had no place in Eddie's repertoire. He got to the point and then prodded you with it. "Wants to see you at the estate ASAP, and she's pissed off."

"About what, the dress?"

"Yep. Get on over there."

"I'll come up first. I've got something to ask you about."

I hung up and fished the business card case out of my tote bag, but when I pried it open all I found was a soggy wad of cardboard, glued together with rain. Maybe some of the cards would be readable later.

As I showered I speculated about the cards and the other lost items, and then my thoughts wandered to the second Mrs. Parry. Was she a sharp operator like her husband, or a trophy wife who spent all her time shopping? Heaven knows she'd spent enough when she ordered Nickie's first wedding gown from New York: Even in a too-small size, the thing had been a positive snowbank of lace and beadwork, with a cathedral train and a fingertip veil. Nickie's lovely olive skin would have looked unpleasantly sallow against all those acres of stark white. I've always disliked that tired old notion that a snow-white gown is a symbol of purity, like the safety seal on an aspirin bottle.

I dressed quickly, in flats, and a pale lemon cotton sweater, and slacks. Grace Parry could live with me sans makeup and with my hair clipped back. She was from Chicago, I remembered now, and had gone back on business. So she did have a business. Probably antiques or art collecting or something else suitable for a tycoon's wife. I headed outside and upstairs, sparing a glance for my barrel garden on the deck, trying to focus myself on ordinary daylight instead of last night's darkness. The tulips and daylilies were past their prime, but the irises were still holding on, with nasturtiums curling at their feet. A couple of kayakers paddled by, their shoulders level with my front deck. I kicked some dried-up goose turds off the planking into the water. Canada geese are pretty, but their manners stink.

Upstairs, Eddie Breen was at his desk in the workroom, with his feet on the desk and a pile of invoices in his lap. He was a small, wiry man, tanned into a web of wrinkles, with lively gray eyes and fine white hair that was sparse enough to make his jug ears even more conspicuous. His standard uniform was as crisp as ever: khaki pants with knife-edge creases, spotless deck shoes and a white oxford shirt with the sleeves rolled back as precisely as origami. He looked more like a ship's officer than a CPA, though in fact he'd been both.

Eddie avoided weddings, on the principle that they led to the inherently undesirable state of marriage, and he avoided

our clients because he thought they were nuts to get married.
But though he never attended them, Eddie's penny-pinching
guaranteed that our weddings stayed on schedule and on
budget. He was cranky and critical, but an absolute wizard
with contracts, discounts, and taxes. He was also surprisingly
vigorous for a man of seventy-two, which was handy since I
wanted him to live forever.

This morning he looked up from his papers, chewing on
an unlit cigar. I loathe cigar smoke, so Eddie only lit up while
leaning out one of the windows. Windows made up most of
the office's western wall, echoing the glass sunporch downstairs. You entered the office through what we called the
"good room," the one with new paint and framed wedding
photos and halfway decent furniture, including a glass-
topped coffee table invitingly covered with bridal magazines,
etiquette books, and portfolios of gowns, cakes, and floral
arrangements. The workroom, through a connecting door,
was larger and messier, with both our desks facing the lake,
the secondhand computer on its stand in the corner, and a
couple of scratched gray file cabinets along the back wall.
With the door closed, clients saw only efficiency and elegance. With it open, as it was now, Eddie could easily bellow
across both rooms.

"You OK?"

He'd gotten my message, then. "Yeah, I'm fine."

But he could see that I wasn't. As I crossed the good room
and dropped into my desk chair, he came over to pat my
shoulder. Pretty good for a non-hugger like Eddie.

"At least Diane and Jeffrey have left for Paris by now, so
they'll have lots to distract them." I sighed. "Pretty grisly way
to start a honeymoon."

"Well, try not to dwell on it."

"But I *am* dwelling on it. I should have stopped Michelle before she ran outside. And now I've got this spooky thing I can't get out of my head. See, there was this man. . . ." I described the figure in the rain, the dead-end road, and my sudden suspicion that the Mustang had been tampered with. "What do you think?"

The cigar swiveled to the other side of his mouth. "I think I remember when you saw a suspicious fellow casing the houseboat, and it turned out to be a real estate agent."

"Well, he was lurking around!"

"And I remember you thought your friend Lily's new boyfriend was married, because he wouldn't show her his house, and it turned out he was just a lousy housekeeper."

"Didn't it strike you as funny when he kept putting her off?"

"No, it did not. What strikes me is that you keep playing Nancy Drew, when you should be drumming up new business." He lifted the invoices. "We are seriously behind this quarter."

"I know, I know, but really, don't you think I should tell the police?"

"Well, the police called this morning, as a matter of fact." He picked up a notepad and glared at it. "A Lieutenant Borden. Wants you to call him, but not 'til this afternoon. Says a Mrs. Fenner told him you were encouraging the bridesmaids to get drunk."

"What?! I was not! That bitch. OK, I brought them a bottle of champagne, but I always do that. They all have a little toast and—"

"Well, this Michelle kid had more than a toast, didn't she?"

"I know. I should have stopped her. I . . . I . . . Eddie, it was so *awful*—" Suddenly I was shuddering, and Eddie actually did hug me.

"Hey. Hey, I didn't mean to upset you. Carnegie, don't."

"Sorry. I'm OK, really." I took a deep breath, then took the slip from him with the lieutenant's number. A nasty thought occurred to me. "Eddie, if I tell the police I saw someone suspicious, they'll think I'm just avoiding this accusation about getting Michelle drunk."

"Well, they might. Honest to Pete, Carnegie, you do have a lively imagination. Why on earth would anybody try to hurt the Parry girl? She's only about nineteen."

"Twenty-two. Well, I don't know. Keith Guthridge must be pretty angry at her father, with his grand jury testimony coming up."

"Angry enough to kill Parry's daughter? Jesus, that would guarantee Parry's testimony against him. Doesn't make sense."

"No, no, of course it doesn't. Maybe I *am* just avoiding the accusation. I'll never give my bridesmaids champagne again."

"Worry about that later. Right now, worry about that faded old dress you bought the Parry girl. And about these bills. I've said this before and I'm going to say it again: You're undercharging for this wedding, and you're spending too much time on it instead of marketing for new business."

He was just trying to distract me, but I let him. "I'm only charging them our standard rate."

"Douglas Parry is not standard, for God's sakes. He makes millions off widows and orphans; you don't have to knock yourself out to hunt down good deals for him. Christ, we could charge him double on everything and he'd never notice!"

"Eddie, I see your point, I really do. But Douglas Parry hasn't been convicted of anything, OK? In fact he hasn't even been accused, not yet. Even if he is, it won't affect us. This wedding is going to establish our reputation. What's left of it after last night."

"Louise can't pay her mortgage with our reputation," he said. Louise was my mother, the widow of Eddie's oldest friend and a dear friend in her own right. "That payment deadline is coming up."

"Oh, Eddie, you're worried about her, aren't you? I'm going to pay her back soon, honest I am. If I have to I'll get another line of credit on the business. I won't let her down."

"I know you won't," he relented. "I'm just fussing. You get yourself over to the Parrys', and we'll take in a show tonight, OK? Get your mind off things."

Every couple of weeks the entire staff of Made in Heaven went out for a bad movie and a candy binge. Art films I saw with Lily. Eddie and I preferred science fiction, but we'd take natural disasters, gangsters, or spies, as long as it was loud, fast, and unbelievable.

"It's a date. Thanks, Eddie."

He made a shooing motion with his hands. Resisting an impertinent urge to kiss him on top of his silky white head, I took the notebook on Nickie's wedding out to Vanna. Maybe he was right, and I was being overimaginative about the man in the rain. Well, I'd tell Douglas Parry about the mysterious stranger, and he could tell the police if he wanted to, and that would be that. I put the van in gear and the transmission made a faint but ominous new noise. Soon, I promised my faithful vehicle. You'll get a tune-up soon.

I picked up a scone and a double cappuccino from Federal Espresso, my favorite caffeine pushers, and headed across the Evergreen Point Bridge over Lake Washington, admiring the whitecaps on one side of the span and the calm silvery water on the other. The Parrys lived in Medina, a semirural enclave of the rich and rustic on the east side of the lake. Just a modest little cottage with a quarter mile of shoreline, a view of Mount Rainier, and a staff of five. Just a place to hang your hat, dock your sailboat, and have the chauffeur park your Rolls. Ray Ishigura, the groom, was a middle-class military brat whose family lived in a split-level in Tacoma, near McChord Air Force Base. But Ray had the potential to be a pianist of international reputation, which must have helped his courtship in Douglas Parry's eyes.

I managed the scone just fine, scrounging on the floor for a tissue to wipe my fingers. But the coffee did me in just as I started up the Parrys' half-mile driveway. I swerved to miss a jaywalking squirrel, and a stream of hot brown splotches suddenly bisected the front of my sweater. I had nothing on underneath, and nothing in the van to change into. Great.

Swearing the way only children of the merchant marine can swear, I pulled up in front of the house, dabbed at the splotches, and walked past a line of cars that made Vanna look as downscale as her driver. Nickie's car was gone, of course, but there was Douglas Parry's splendid silver Rolls, and two sports cars, a hunter-green Jag and a blood-and-silver Alfa Romeo that looked fast standing still. I had some nail polish that color once, but it kept me awake at night.

As I stepped up to the front door, I remembered my first visit to consult with Nickie. In my infinite wisdom, I'd known exactly what the Parry estate would look like: mock Tudor, maybe a French baronial tower or two, stiffly groomed grounds, lots of antiques. Wrong, on all counts. The house was Northwest avant-garde, with a king's ransom in old-growth cedar in swooping curves and jutting angles and unexpected skylights.

My musings were interrupted by Theo, the chauffeur. He opened the door, stared coldly at my stained sweater, and lingered for just a moment before stepping aside to let me in. I'd been expecting Mariana, the housekeeper, and my cheery smile stiffened foolishly in place. Theo was about twenty-five, but his skin was as pale as a baby's, as if despite his spiffy sports clothes he'd never set foot in the open air. His hair, brows, and eyelashes were white-blond, giving him a colorless, raw look that I found unnerving.

"It's a jungle out there," I prattled. "I just got mugged by a cup of coffee."

No reaction whatsoever. "Mrs. Parry is in the master bedroom."

"Right." I edged past him. Inside, antique Persian rugs mixed with gaudy Central American textiles, and a dizzying number of mirrors reflected confectionery art glass and ceiling-high houseplants. The main stairway had alternating black and white marble steps, like piano keys, rising from a black marble hallway edged with tiled pools complete with water hyacinths. Got to have those hyacinths.

I ascended the stairs, and paused to admire the view from the landing. An immense ebony Doberman, as dark as Theo was pale, trotted out from a hallway: Augustus Caesar, guardian of the house and all within. Nickie called him Gus. Gus gave me a cold yellow stare.

"You don't fool me," I whispered. "I know your dirty little secret."

I leaned down to pull gently on his ears—a liberty I took with him only in private—and he closed his eyes in contentment. Outside the bay windows, Mount Rainier was in full glory, snow white and ice blue above its forested lower slopes. My next wedding after Nickie's would be at a lodge halfway up Rainier, and I wished I were already there, strolling the meadows instead of dealing with a dress crisis. But duty called. From the master suite down the left-hand corridor I could hear a woman's voice, calm but sharp-edged.

"I can't imagine what you were thinking of, Niccola. It's torn, for heaven's sake. And it's *dirty*."

I gave Gus a farewell tug and headed for the voice, through a foyer to a froufrou dressing room. Nickie stood in front of one mirrored wall, shoulders slumped and arms dangling, doing no justice at all to the Edwardian gown. Mariana, a wizened Brazilian woman, was standing quietly to one side without her usual sunny, gap-toothed smile. Beyond them, regally erect in a wicker fan chair, was Grace Parry, small, blonde, and elegant in a mauve silk suit and an out-of-season tan.

"You're Carnegie Kincaid." Her voice was low and smooth. I nodded, and she nodded back, slowly and thoughtfully. "You're fired."

Chapter Five

WE FROZE: NICKIE WIDE-EYED, MARIANA CAREFULLY EXPRES-
sionless, and me, I assume, with my mouth open. Nickie
flung herself into the conversational breach, her gaze switch-
ing rapidly between me and her stepmother. She looked very
much as if she'd been crying all night. Life went on, but no
one was forgetting what happened to Michelle.

"She's kidding, aren't you, Grace?" said Nickie. "It's not
Carnegie's fault. We can return the dress—"

"Actually, we can't," I said briskly. "And we won't need to.
I'll have it dry-cleaned, repaired, and starched, and once you
have your hair up, and the right accessories, you'll be lovely."

She was, in fact, lovely already. The dress was fashioned
from diagonal ribbons of glossy satin and bands of intricate,
rose-patterned lace, with a skirt that dropped from a high
waist to a scalloped hem that swept lower in back, forming a
hint of a train. Antique gowns are often tiny, but this one had
been created for a full-figured woman, and it fit Nickie like a
dream. The low-necked bodice and softly draped skirt followed her curves, and the color, not so much faded as bur-
nished by time, drew a golden glow from her skin. Standing
at the altar, shy and womanly, Nickie would be a bride from
another, more gracious time.

"There are only a few buttons missing. We'll have some

made to match, and the two panels of lace that are a bit discolored can be replaced." I crossed the room with my head high. "Nice to meet you, Grace. I'm looking forward to your ideas on Nickie's hairstyle and flowers. Unless I really am fired?"

She rose, with a single easy motion. "Of course not. Just a little joke."

Some joke. But she smiled at me warmly enough, looking up from her five-foot-four height, and shook my long narrow hand with her dainty, elegant one. Her cornsilk hair fell casually but perfectly back from her face, and her tawny complexion spoke of sunbathing, not mowing the lawn. Grace Parry looked about thirty-five, and as if she intended to look that way for years to come, no matter how much time or money it took. The one visible flaw was quite subtle: Her eyes were a pale, clear amber, but the gaze of the left one was angled ever so slightly out of true with the right. The effect was disconcerting, as if she were looking past me, or through me. Just now, though, she was clearly looking at my coffee stains. She arched an eyebrow. Bette Davis couldn't have arched any better.

"Would you like a change of clothes? Let's find you something. Nickie, we'll be right back." She drew me into the bedroom, but she didn't go looking for clothes. I knew what was coming.

"About last night," she said.

"Mrs. Parry, I'm so terribly sorry! I mean, we all are, but I just wish I'd stopped Michelle, or—"

"Call me Grace. And there's nothing you could have done, I'm sure. But Nickie's terribly upset, and I'm concerned about my husband's heart."

"His heart?" Douglas was a robust, bull-shouldered man

in his sixties, with faultless posture and an energetic stride. I'd come to like and respect him, as a hardheaded but enthusiastic client for Made in Heaven. "He has heart trouble?"

"Quite serious trouble." Her face took on a tight, determined look. "He had a damaging heart attack at Christmas. We were skiing in Switzerland, and he recuperated there. He doesn't want anyone here to know. But it's critical that he avoid stressful situations."

I took a deep breath. "In that case, I think I'd better tell you instead of Douglas. Last night I saw someone suspicious—"

A far door was flung open and Douglas Parry strode into the bedroom, waving a newspaper and breathing fire, with Gus trotting sternly along at his heels.

"I'll sue this bastard Gold, Grace, I swear I will! This article of his is libel, it's sheer—" He stopped abruptly and frowned past us into the dressing room at Nickie. "Pumpkin, is that your wedding dress? It isn't white."

Instantly, Grace, Mariana, and I joined feminine forces in the face of this monumental masculine gaffe. That the bride's father should see her gown before the wedding, let alone criticize it, was more than any of us could tolerate. I stepped in front of Nickie, Mariana put a protective arm around the girl, and Grace took her husband's arm and ushered him downstairs, cutting through his bluster with a stream of soothing words. With her father out of earshot, Nickie laughed, a little wildly.

"Maybe we should just elope! Only Daddy would want to carry me down the ladder, and come on the honeymoon to make sure we did everything right."

At that, Mariana and I both laughed, and tragedy gave way to romantic comedy, at least for the moment. Nickie slipped out of the gown and Mariana boxed it up so I could take it to a dressmaker's for repairs. As she got dressed, Nickie offered me a purple-and-gold University of Washington sweatshirt in exchange for my spotted sweater. Thus collegiately attired, I followed her downstairs, still hoping for a quiet word with Grace.

But Douglas was waiting for us at the foot of the piano-key staircase. His normally florid complexion was mottled, and his thinning, gingery hair was all askew. Nickie must have gotten her coloring and her heavy dark tresses from the other side of the family. The Parry divorce had gotten head-lines, but I'd never seen a photo of Julia Parry, Nickie's mother.

"Carnegie, good to see you again." Douglas had a low, gravelly voice and an air of focused concentration, as if he were weighing your every word. "Sorry for breaking in on you. There's a reporter who's been on my back about this King Savings case—"

"She doesn't need to hear about that, Douglas," said Grace. She was posed in the doorway to the living room, looking like a photo out of *Architectural Digest*. "Shall we have coffee?"

"Of course, of course." He turned to Nickie and tugged at a lock of her hair, a teasing gesture that he'd probably been making ever since she had hair. "Is there a problem about your dress, Pumpkin?"

Nickie hesitated, then busied herself pouring coffee as we took our seats around a low Chinese table. The burnt-orange lacquer surface set off a black bowl of perfumed freesias and other, more exotic blooms I couldn't name, though I'd seen them at Boris's studio. Outside the picture window, an emer-ald lawn flowed in artful slopes and curves down to the glittering lake, with a gardener here and there to ornament the scene. Maybe Eddie was right. Maybe we should charge double.

"No problem at all," said Grace. "Wedding gowns don't have to be a perfect white anymore, you know. Niccola will be stunning, but we're not going to give you a peek, are we, Niccola? You'll see the gown at St. Anne's, and not before."

Nickie brightened, and her father beamed approvingly at his gracious, warm-hearted wife. Grace was a smooth operator, all right.

"Fine, fine." Having resolved one point on the agenda, Douglas moved briskly to the next. "Carnegie, how's the balance holding up on the house account? Good thing I only have one daughter, or I'd need a tax shelter just for the weddings!"

Grace's coffee cup rapped down on its saucer. "The house account? Douglas, I thought the bills were being held for me to pay."

"Well, you were gone for so long, I just gave Carnegie here check-writing authority. Hal Jepsen at First Washington handled it all. This way Carnegie can go ahead and pay the bills for the shindig on Saturday, too."

"The fund-raiser?" Grace looked at me, a startling flash of anger in her mismatched eyes. "She's involved in our party for Senator Bigelow?"

"I forgot to tell you. That one caterer burned down or some damn thing, so I asked Carnegie to get us another. It's all taken care of."

Douglas frowned at his wife, and I watched, fascinated, as she visibly calmed herself. Power struggles are so interesting when you're not in them. But why didn't she want me on this particular job? Maybe she didn't appreciate my presence in general, or maybe she thought Nickie was getting too fond of me. Being a stepmother couldn't be easy, and being stepmother-of-the-bride must have its own pitfalls, especially for a stylish young stepmother who's used to being in the spotlight herself. And now with her husband in legal trouble, and nasty letters in the mail, not to mention a horrible car accident . . .

"Your original caterer had a fire at their kitchen," I explained to Grace in a deferential tone. Oil on troubled waters, that's me. "They're out of business for at least a month. I've hired Solveto's, the ones who are doing the wedding reception, but we're keeping the menu you selected, the grilled shrimp and the cucumber terrine. I'm sure you'll be satisfied with the results."

But Grace had other shrimp to fry. "Very well, but there's still no need for you to use the checking account. Just send me the bills as usual, and I'll review them before they're paid."

"Not necessary." Douglas frowned, and his voice went flat. "I have complete faith in Carnegie, honey, and I'm sure you do, too."

A brief, uncomfortable silence, while Nickie stared out the window and Grace gripped her coffee cup as if it might escape her.

"Of course," she said. "I'm really much too busy at the moment to be bothered with all these details."

It was a feeble parting shot, and Douglas let it go. "Now, there's been a change in the guest list for the fund-raiser. We're inviting the press after all." He touched his wife's shoulder and smiled, getting her back on the team. "I wasn't happy about it, but Grace convinced me that it's for the best. The senator needs the coverage, and maybe the reporters will leave King County Savings alone for a while and focus on him."

"Should I arrange a space for interviews and cameras?" I asked. "Solveto's will need to know if they can't use all the tent space for the buffet."

This tricky political decision on his part was just another logistical problem for me. Weather permitting, the fund-raiser for Senator Samuel Bigelow was to be a garden party, casual Seattle-style, with picnic tables scattered around the lawns down to the water's edge.

"Talk with Sam's PR people," he replied, taking a leather-bound notepad from his breast pocket and scribbling some names and numbers. "They'll probably use the terrace or the gazebo." ·

Nickie spoke up. "Daddy, I've been meaning to ask you— will Uncle Keith be there? I mean, I know he's close to Senator Bigelow."

"He'll be there," said Douglas, his voice grim at the mention of his former friend. "Sam insisted. Just as long as Guthridge stays sober and steers clear of me. And keeps his mouth shut around the reporters. They call it freedom of the press, and then they print all kinds of speculation, just to sell their damn—"

"You know," I said, groping for an exit line, "I'm heading downtown next, to the dressmaker's. Nickie, if you'd like to come with me we could have lunch and shop for the brides-maids' gifts, and then I'll bring you back."

Nickie bounced to her feet with a relieved smile. "Great!"

"Theo will be delivering some papers to Holt Walker's office about three o'clock," said Douglas, as we all rose. "Why don't you go over with Carnegie and then meet him there later on? He can bring you home."

Nickie ran upstairs for the gown, accompanied by Gus. Grace walked me to the front door and then, with a glance back to see that Douglas was heading for his office, came outside with me. Theo had the hood of the Rolls up, and there was a smear of grease on the chest of his mint-green polo shirt. He probably just threw them out when they got dirty, like Louis XIV using new dishes at every meal.

"You were saying something about last night?"

"I don't want to alarm anyone," I began, though of course that was exactly what I was going to do. "But last night, during the ceremony, I saw a man walking down the drive away from Sercombe House. He could have been somewhere near Nickie's car."

"Near her car. What do you mean?" Grace's mismatched eyes were intense and unblinking, and I began to flounder.

"Well, I wondered if he, if someone, might have done something to the Mustang. To, to make it crash."

Grace snapped her head around so fast that her hair whirled around her face. "Theo!"

He joined us on the front steps, moving heavily, like an overmuscled boxer.

"Theo, Carnegie thinks someone is trying to harm Nickie. Tried to kill her, in fact, by tampering with her car last night." Put like that, it sounded insane, but Grace was taking me very seriously. More seriously than I was ready for. "I want someone with her at all times from now on, and I want the car examined. By experts. Find an expert."

"No problem." Theo looked at me curiously, but continued to address Grace. "She saw somebody?"

"Just a man in the distance," I told him, "not to recognize, but I don't think he was a wedding guest. And it seemed strange that he was on foot." What had I started here? "Are you going to tell Nickie?"

"Only if it's necessary," said Grace. "And we will absolutely not tell Douglas, is that understood?"

"Understood," said Theo grimly. "If it's Keith Guthridge, I'll kill him. I'll—"

"Theo." Grace put a hand on his arm and he stiffened, like a snarling dog recognizing its master. "Theo, we don't even know if it's true. In fact I doubt very much that it is. I'll discuss it with Lieutenant Borden and perhaps he can help us with the car. Then we'll decide what to do next. Carnegie, thank you so much for telling me. I'm sure it's nothing, but I appreciate it all the same. You're a real friend of the family."

"All ready!" Nickie came breathlessly out the door, all smiles, with the dress box in her arms. She beamed at Theo, and his stolid expression warmed up at the sight of her. Nickie, I knew, sometimes referred to Theo fondly as her big brother. Surely Eddie was right. Who would hurt a girl like this? It didn't make sense.

Chapter Six

"I TAKE IT THE WEDDING IS STILL ON?" I ASKED NICKIE AS WE recrossed Lake Washington toward Seattle. Ahead of us in the west a barricade of leaden clouds obscured the Olympic Mountains that rise up beyond Puget Sound. Behind us a similar barricade loomed across the eastern horizon, blotting out the Cascades. Rain in the Olympics, rain in the Cascades, and maybe snow as well at the higher elevations, even in June. But here, in between, we drove under a portal of serene, oblivious blue.

She blushed. "It's still on. Ray called this morning. He was all worried about the accident, and we made up. I guess I was overreacting. I've been so worried about Daddy."

"About these letters, and his heart condition?"

"Did Grace tell you? Yeah, his heart, and now his testimony to the grand jury." She wound a strand of hair around her fingers and tugged at it. "He's really worried, I can tell. Uncle Keith must be feeling betrayed, but Daddy can't lie, can he?"

"No, of course not. Are you still on good terms with your uncle? I mean, with—"

"With Keith," she said firmly, like a child with a lesson. "Grace asked me to stop calling him Uncle, but I forget. It's pretty weird. Sometimes he calls me, wants to know if I'm OK."

"Have you talked to him lately?"

"What about?"

"Oh, your wedding plans, other things. About going to Diane's wedding?"

She shrugged. "He doesn't know Diane."

Although, I thought, if he's having her watched she wouldn't need to tell him. He'd know where she left her car. I changed the subject.

"So who's Holt Walker?" I asked.

"One of Daddy's lawyers," said Nickie, unaware that some daddies don't have any lawyers at all. "I thought you'd met him already. They're old friends, and Holt comes to the house a lot, especially since his wife died a few years ago."

I nodded, picturing a gray-haired family retainer with bifocals and a dry cough. "And what's all this about a reporter?"

She frowned, as fiercely as her gentle features would allow. "Aaron Gold. He's a reporter for the *Sentinel*. He writes about King County Savings in nearly every issue, and he's not fair at all."

The *Seattle Sentinel* was a weekly paper, livelier and more liberal than the stuffy dailies. It usually focused on politics and the arts scene rather than business, but tying the savings-and-loan scandal to a local magnate was pretty juicy stuff.

"Don't worry about it," I told her as I threaded through downtown and pulled into a parking lot near the Pike Place Market. "Nobody believes everything they read in the papers anymore, and even if they do they forget it the next day. I'm starving. Let's find some lunch."

The Market was bustling. Tourists and local lunchers crowded along the open-air concourse of produce stalls and craft displays, and inside the shops and restaurants that

purveyed everything from kites to sushi to collectible comic
books. Strawberries in ruby rows, painted T-shirts fluttering
on racks, whole crabs and gaping salmon, stacks of hand-
woven baskets, bundles of fresh herbs, tables of carved
wooden toys—everything looked appropriately wholesome,
quaint, whimsical, or just plain tempting.

The street entertainers were out in force: a bluegrass fid-
dler, a team of jugglers, a one-woman puppet show with a tall
cardboard box serving as a theater. I watched her for a moment, then I followed the heavenly aroma of cioppino waft-
ing from a fishmonger's kettle. Nickie and I loaded up our
trays and found a table set back from the sidewalk, out of the
breeze. I was grateful for Nickie's sweatshirt, though purple
was hardly my color. As we wrestled with our clams and
mussels and sopped up the broth with French bread, I asked
another, more personal question.

"Did you ever get an RSVP from your mother?"

Julia Parry had moved to New Mexico soon after the divorce, when Nickie was seventeen. That was all I knew about
her, except that her name on the invitation list had triggered
a family quarrel. Douglas put it there, Grace objected, and
Nickie, with a very adult bitterness in her voice, pointed out
that since Julia hadn't shown up for her high school or college graduation, or anything else, she certainly wouldn't
come to the wedding, so what difference did it make? End of
quarrel, and the creamy envelope with its stately calligraphy
had gone off to Santa Fe.

Now, Nickie rattled the ice in her empty paper cup. "Not
yet. She won't come. I know she won't."

"Would you rather she didn't?"

"I don't know." She tossed the cup at a garbage can,
missed, and got up to retrieve it. When she sat down again,

she didn't look at me. "She was an alcoholic, Carnegie. I don't know if Daddy told you."

"No, and you certainly shouldn't if you don't—"

"It's OK." She let out a long sigh, as if the truth had been trapped in her lungs. "They didn't tell me at first, but I knew. She went to a clinic for a while, and we thought she was better, but she wasn't. Then there was a car accident."

"Was she hurt?"

"We both were." She drew back her lips in a quick grimace. "That's how I got all these teeth capped. When she got out of the hospital, Daddy told her not to come home."

"Nickie, I'm so sorry. The crash last night must have been horrible for you."

She seemed not to hear me. "I've been reading these books, about adult children of alcoholics? About forgiving and letting go of anger and all that. Daddy says she doesn't drink anymore, and I think he misses her sometimes. But I don't know if I ever want to see her. She used to get pretty scary. And she made kind of a nasty phone call when he and Grace got married."

I thought about my own mother, so fussy and prosaic and always, always there when I needed her. And my father, my stern hero who often seemed to forget that he even had children, let alone that they needed him. I wanted to comfort Nickie, but she wasn't asking for comfort this time. She was trying to make peace with reality by explaining it to me.

"It's hard to forgive your parents," I said. "It's hard to allow them to be ordinary, or to have troubles of their own." She nodded, but I couldn't tell if she was listening to me. "There's so much we never understand about their lives—"

"Grace has been terrific, you know." Nickie was rushing her words as if to convince herself as well as me. "She's a financial genius, everybody says she's just brilliant, and she does investment counseling for elderly women. They love her. She's incredibly busy, but she's been really good to me. Just like a mother."

She reached for her tote bag. "Could we get going now?"

"Sure."

We spent two pleasant hours wandering through the market stalls and the shops nearby, finding just the right handcrafted thank-you gift for each bridesmaid. Rain clouds rolled in. I'd left my bride's-hairdo-protecting umbrella in the van, so Nickie and I ended up with wet shoes and hair dripping into our eyes, but we laughed it off. After last night's horror, it was comforting to laugh a little. Our shopping done at last, we ducked inside a café to warm up with espresso. Warm up and wake up, since neither of us had slept much.

Outside the café the light changed on First Avenue, and a horde of pedestrians hurried across toward our seat by the window. Touristy couples with maps. Young skateboarders with pants baggy enough for clowns. The usual perforatti, punk kids with pierced eyebrows, nostrils, lips, and God knows what else, though if God does know he can keep it to himself. Everybody hurrying, except one little old bag lady trailing behind, still in the crosswalk long after the Don't Walk had lit. Some bozo in an SUV honked at her, and I looked more closely. Crazy Mary.

Suddenly I was hearing her old, rustling-leaves voice: "*I saw him.*" Crazy Mary, who always rode the bus, would have walked up the drive in the rain. No headlights to warn anyone of her coming. What had she seen?

"Nickie, I'll be right back."

I scrambled through the door and out to the corner, just in time to intercept her dogged progress up the street.

"Mary? Hi, Mary, I met you at the wedding last night, at Sercombe House?"

She stared up at me without recognition.

"I was wondering if you could tell me, did you see anyone, um, anyone suspicious out on the driveway? You said something last night about someone breaking things and stealing things. Did you see someone doing that?"

She looked confused, almost afraid, and then her face brightened. "Cake!"

"I'm sorry?"

"The bride said I could have some cake. But it fell on the floor. No cake, no, no, no." She shook her head vigorously and began to march away, the crowd closing around her.

"Wait!" I tried to follow, but I was blocked by a field-trip flock of school kids, noisy as starlings. Then a hand caught my arm.

"Carnegie, Holt is here!" said Nickie's voice. She'd come out to the corner and was waving to a tall, familiar figure approaching us. "Holt, we were just coming to your office! This is Carnegie Kincaid."

I lost sight of Mary, and focused on Holt Walker. So this was the old family friend, the one I'd pictured as an elderly widower. Except that this widower stood six feet four and owned a pair of astonishing green eyes. My nonwaiter, quite properly dressed this time in a fashionable gray suit and wine-colored tie. Expensive wine, a tie with a vintage. He smiled at Nickie and then, a bit blankly, at me. His teeth were just as endearingly crooked as I remembered. I probably had fish scales in mine. I certainly had wet hair and clashing clothes. What a time to meet Prince Charming.

"Maybe you two met last night," Nickie was saying. The shadow of last night's tragedy crossed her features.

"Yes, we did," he said absently, shaking my hand. "In the kitchen."

"Listen, I apologize," I said. "I can't believe I thought you were—"

"It's terrible about the bridesmaid," he went on, as if he hadn't heard me. "Unfortunately, I'm late for a couple of meetings, so . . ."

"I'm supposed to meet Theo at your office, is that okay?" Nickie asked.

"No problem," he told her. Then, with another murmured platitude to me, he was gone. Some prince. And Mary was nowhere in sight.

"Carnegie, are you OK? You look upset. Is it about last night?"

"Try to forget last night, kiddo. You go on home. I'm going to drop off your dress and go to the movies."

Chapter Seven

I HAD FORGOTTEN TO CALL LIEUTENANT BORDEN—OR MAYBE I was avoiding the whole issue—so the next day he called me. He tried the office first, and Eddie gave him the number at Joe Solveto's catering office in the Fremont neighborhood. Joe and I were having lunch at his desk, sampling the latest Solveto's hors d'oeuvres. Eddie and I had eaten popcorn for dinner, so I was famished, but I would have made room anyway. The food was superb.

Joe combined the languid aplomb of Noël Coward with the competitive instinct of a great white shark, constantly tracking his competitors and refining his menus. He wore exquisite clothes, and styled his body at a health club the way some women style their hair. He also ventured out before dawn in howling rainstorms to go steelhead fishing, and he collected Lionel trains, "but only pre-1950, before they went plastic." Almost all the vendors I dealt with were pleasant acquaintances, but a few, like Joe, had become valued friends. He was well-respected in the business, and generous with compliments and wise advice. Right now, though, Joe was in goofball mode.

"Doesn't Eddie cover for you when the cops call?" he stage-whispered as he handed me the phone.

"Shhhh!"

"Lieutenant Borden, Ms. Kincaid." It was a deep voice, with no particular inflection. "Just wanted to verify a few details with you."

He walked me through that dreadful evening, from the bridesmaids' champagne consumption to the estimated speed of the Mustang as it careered down the hill.

"And apparently you saw a suspicious individual on the drive earlier that evening?"

"Grace told you about that?"

"What exactly was this individual doing?"

"Um, walking. Down the hill, away from Sercombe House. But see, the drive dead-ends at the house, so where was he coming from? I mean, he wasn't just passing through."

A pause. Joe was juggling two cherry tomatoes. The lieutenant sighed. "You saw a man, walking."

"Well, yes. He could have been walking away from the Mustang!"

"You didn't see him at the vehicle, you didn't see him tampering with the vehicle in any way."

"N-no."

Long pause. Joe added a third tomato. "Thank you for your assistance, Ms. Kincaid."

"But what about the Mustang? Did you check it over?"

"Thank you for that suggestion." The weight of his sarcasm almost made me drop the phone. "Yes, we did. We expended quite a few man-hours on that, though the vehicle was too badly damaged to reveal much. We found no evidence of any cause of the accident beyond reckless driving while under the influence."

"Oh. But I suppose there could have been evidence that was destroyed in the crash?"

Very long pause. A tomato hit the floor. Joe retrieved it

and hit a two-point shot in the wastebasket across the room. "Thank you for your assistance, Ms. Kincaid."

I replaced the phone and cradled my head in my hands. If only I'd caught up with Mary! Maybe then I'd have had something concrete to tell him. Or maybe not. "Joe, am I crazy?"

"On occasion. Pretty upset about the bridesmaid, aren't you? What was her name?"

"Michelle."

"Right. The police got to me yesterday, not that I could tell them much except she was drunk and raving. But you think something else happened?"

"No, I don't guess I do anymore. Pass the veggies, would you?" We munched in silence for a few minutes. When he wasn't playing the fool, Joe could be nicely silent. "These baby squash are wonderful. What's in the marinade?"

"Cumin powder and extraordinary skill," he announced, eating one himself. His shadowy blue eyes narrowed. "And how is the bride business?"

Joe never pried, ever. I could have answered, Business is just fine, and he'd let it go at that. But it wasn't just fine and we both knew it.

"Business *was* getting better, but Michelle's accident isn't going to help. I hate to be cold-blooded about it, but there it is. I'd probably lose clients in droves, if I had any droves to start with. At least Nickie Parry's wedding has a huge budget." I didn't mention the Keith Guthridge business, of course. Wedding consultants see a surprising amount of dirty linen, and discretion comes with the service. Just the suggestion that I gossiped about my clients would be enough to cut my business in half. "I'll need my whole percentage from Nickie to pay off a family loan, and I've only got three smaller weddings booked after hers."

Like a magician, Joe produced two wineglasses from a desk drawer, along with a half bottle of something intriguing. "Well, one step at a time. This is a freebie from the new wine shop on Pike. Join me?"

"Yes, please."

"So you're on the way to paying off your loan, but meanwhile you need to eat."

"Meanwhile I need to eat and advertise and pay Eddie and get the front end of my van aligned. Landing Nickie's wedding was a godsend."

Joe frowned into his glass of Vouvray. "Douglas Parry is in legal trouble, isn't he?"

"No! Well, not exactly. Not yet. Why?"

He took a sip before answering and swished the wine in his mouth. "Hmm. Nice. But not nice enough for the price. Carnegie, I wouldn't presume to tell you your business, you know that. But I hate to see you so dependent on someone as . . . unsavory as Douglas Parry. There are rumors—"

"There are always rumors, Joe," I said stiffly. "Nickie and Ray are very nice kids, and Made in Heaven has a contract to put on their wedding. Whatever Douglas may or may not have done in his career, I don't see why I should boycott his daughter."

"Of course not," said Joe. "I didn't mean that you should. I just . . . never mind, forget I said anything, please. Listen, can I ask you a personal question?"

I leaned forward. "Anything."

"Hussy. You charge fifteen percent, right?"

I sat back, startled. "Yes, I do. Why?"

He swished some more wine. "I didn't tell you this, but Dorothy Fenner charges ten."

"What?! How can she? How does she manage?"

"She manages because she got into Amazon.com on the

ground floor and then got out at the roof. She could run red ink out of her shell-like ears for months and not notice it."

"But that's not fair!"

"Don't even go there, Carnegie. Nothing is fair. *Nothing.*"

I suddenly wondered how well I really knew Joe Solveto.

"Well, hell. Do you think I should drop my rates?"

"Absolutely not! Or we'll all be lowballing each other. But now that you've got the Parry wedding, you're batting in Dorothy's league. So, forewarned, forearmed, that kind of thing."

"Thanks, Joe."

"You're welcome. Forget I said anything about the Parrys, OK?"

"It's forgotten. I still hate Dorothy, though."

"I do, too. She calls me 'Joseph,' and she's snotty to Alan. Look, here's to Made in Heaven, then." He raised his glass, and I touched mine to it. We looked like a TV commercial, the perfect couple, redhead and blond, relaxing after the perfect party. Except that Joe's cheekbones were prettier than mine. He drank off his wine and bowed to me.

"May I have this dance, mademoiselle?"

"Delighted, monsieur."

He waltzed me around the office, humming Strauss. My eyes half closed, I swayed in Joe's muscular arms and wondered if Holt Walker was a good dancer. He probably didn't have Joe's flair, but then he probably didn't have a lover named Alan, either. I hoped. Joe gave me a final dip and spin.

"So when's your wedding, Carnegie?"

This was a standard joke between us, and as I finished my wine I gave the standard reply. "Once I found out you were taken, Joe, I gave up the whole idea."

Chapter Eight

"WHAT DO YOU MEAN, THE CHECK BOUNCED?"

It was Friday of the same week, and I was meeting in the good room with Mrs. Schiraldi, the assistant manager of the Glacier View Lodge at Mount Rainier National Park. At least, I was trying to meet with her. Eddie had interrupted us, insisting that I take a phone call at my desk while he stalled my visitor. The call was from the proprietor of Excellent Vintage, the shop where I'd bought Nickie's lace gown, and he was not amused.

"Bounced," he repeated. "NSF. Not sufficient funds. And I understand that it isn't even your account, it's a Mrs. Grace Parry's. There was some confusion at the bank—"

"I have signature privileges. It's all perfectly legal," I assured him. "But there's got to be a mistake here. That account had almost twenty thousand dollars in it."

"Not as of last week, it didn't. Now, are you going to pay for this dress yourself, or—"

"I'll call you back in half an hour. Bye!" I was already flipping though my Rolodex for Hal Jepsen's number at First Washington. He picked up on the first ring.

"Ah, Ms. Kincaid, I was just about to call you. There was a misunderstanding involving Mrs. Parry's account."

"I'll say there was. How did it drop to zero overnight? I've been keeping a close tally—"

"It's been cleared up," he said. "Nothing to worry about."

"Maybe not for you," I snapped, keeping my voice down so it wouldn't carry into the good room. "I just wrote a rubber check for a wedding gown. That's not too good for my credibility. Now what happened, anyway?"

"It's been cleared up," he repeated stubbornly. "The merchant can resubmit the check and First Washington will clear it."

"Fine, but what happened?"

"Thank you for your patience, Ms. Kincaid." Click.

I stared at the receiver. So *that* was why Grace Parry got so bent out of shape about my using her account. She'd been drawing down the balance, unbeknownst to her husband, and my impulsive acquisition of the Edwardian gown had scraped the bottom of that particular barrel. She must have made a big deposit after I left on Monday, which wasn't soon enough to cover the check to Excellent Vintage. I grinned. How embarrassing for Grace. She probably went on a shopping spree in Chicago and used up all the grocery money on suede pumps. Tsk, tsk.

I called the dress shop back and returned to my meeting, where I soon lost my grin. Mrs. Schiraldi was an iron-haired personage who called me Miss Kincaid, and she bristled when I told her that Anita Reid, my bride-after-Nickie, had her heart set on a sunrise ceremony on Mount Rainier. Outdoors.

"Does she realize," demanded Mrs. Schiraldi, "that there could be a snowstorm, even in July? Or at least thundershowers? We're above five thousand feet, you know."

"I know." I also knew the real motive for her bad temper, and it wasn't the weather. It was the fact that the Glacier View's restaurant, in my professional opinion, couldn't handle fancy menus, and I'd hired Solveto's to prepare the wedding banquet. The banquet was a cart-before-the-horse affair; it would serve as the wedding reception, with dinner and dancing, but it was actually taking place the night before the ceremony. The ceremony was scheduled for six A.M. the next morning, and then the bride and groom would set off on a week-long backpacking trip. Up the road from the Glacier View was an area called Paradise, with a Park Service visitors' center, spectacular views of the mountain, and the start of the honeymooners' trail. Peter and Anita would spend their wedding night tenting in Paradise.

Mrs. Schiraldi, meanwhile, undoubtedly suspected me of getting a kickback from Solveto's. She was wrong. I hired Joe frequently, but because he was good, not because he cut me in or padded his invoices and split the surplus with me. Such things do happen, in any business, but not with Solveto's and not with Made in Heaven. Big catered events meant big money changing hands, but none of it stuck to Joe's fingers, or to mine, except for our hard-earned percentages.

"An indoor ceremony followed by a brunch would be much more reasonable," she said. "Our kitchen does a very nice brunch."

"They could have brunch in Seattle," I pointed out, with my best artificial smile. "Peter and Anita first met on a climb of Mount Rainier, so they want their wedding outside, on the mountain. The National Park lodge at Paradise can't block out as many rooms as they need, and the Glacier View is the only private hotel in the vicinity. But if it's not going to work out . . ."

"It will work out," she conceded. Bookings like this didn't come along every day. I smiled some more, and we settled the particulars, from the breakfast menu to parking to the condition of the path connecting the Glacier View with the meadow where the ceremony would take place. Then I gratefully turned her over to Eddie for the financial details.

But my gratitude was short-lived. Eddie had apparently been stewing about the arrangements for the Parry wedding, and after Mrs. Schiraldi left he boiled over.

"I thought I handled the payments around here," he said. "Now you're bouncing checks with our vendors?"

I looked over from my desk, shading my eyes against the momentary sun. The weather that day was quicksilver, slipping from windy brightness to sullen showers within each hour, and lending a spotlit, melodramatic air to our view of the lake.

"Of course you handle the payments, in most cases," I said. "But your signature won't work on the Parry account."

"It would if you had insisted on it in the first place."

"Well, I forgot to in the first place. I told you that. What's the big deal?"

"It's no big deal for you," he grumbled, not meeting my eye, "but it fouls up my record-keeping if I can't pay the bills straight out. Waste of my time."

I might have held my tongue if he hadn't lit his cigar. The weather was already playing havoc with my sinuses, and just one whiff of that tobacco was too much.

"Well, I pay you for your time," I said, with chill politeness, "and your record-keeping is too complicated anyway. I never know where anything is."

That was a low blow. I never knew because I never looked, and in fact I was shamefully ignorant about my own business's books.

"You never brought it up before," he said, puffing furiously.

"I never needed to," I said, "and you never smoked cigars in here before!"

"Well, I'll take it outside, then. Gonna drop off that earring at Diane's mother's house and then go home. I wish you'd let Sercombe House and the rest run their own goddamn lost-and-founds."

"It's part of the service," I insisted. "Listen, did anyone call about that business card case—?"

But he was already out the door. I could hardly object, since he was only supposed to work mornings, but I fumed just the same as I yanked open a desk drawer. The card case was still there, a heavy little thing, maybe even gold, with its soggy wad of paper inside. I'd already flushed the contents of the sandwich bag before Eddie saw it, to avoid yet another lecture on the younger generation. No one was going to claim the dope, and apparently no one was going to claim the case. Either the owner hadn't missed it yet, or . . . or the owner was the man in the rain. I slipped the case in my pocket and went downstairs.

Chapter Nine

BY THE TIME LILY SHOWED UP FOR OUR FRIDAY NIGHT DINNER date, I'd gotten the mystery cards peeled apart with tweezers, dried them out with my hair dryer, and laid them out on my kitchen table next to the rusty little toy stove. Only three business cards had survived the soaking: one for a gym called Powerhouse, another for a pool hall called The 418 Club, and a third for something called Flair Plus, which listed a street address but no indication of what kind of establishment it might be. My front door banged.

"Hey, girl."

"Hey, Lily. What can you tell about a person from the business cards they collect?"

"Depends on what they are. Is this a test from one of those trashy bride's magazines you read? Find Mr. Right by Stealing His Wallet?" She laughed, shaking me out of my Nancy Drewish study of the evidence. If it was evidence.

Lily James is a formidably handsome black woman, almost as tall as me, with a wide, sculpted face, a voluptuous figure that I envy, and a stiletto sense of humor. Not exactly my image of a librarian. I'd met her at the business desk at Seattle Public, back in the days when I spent every lunch hour devouring pamphlets on how to start a small business. We'd begun by having coffee together, and discovered a

range of common interests, like fine literature, liberal politics, and men. She was divorced, with two rambunctious little boys who called me Aunt Car.

Lily always recommended my services to her friends and
coworkers at the library, including Diane's mother, and
Diane had recommended me to Nickie. So at this point I
owed Lily my financial salvation, as well as a dinner I'd forgotten to cook.

"No offense, Carnegie, but it does not smell like roast
chicken in here."

"Oh, shit, Lily. I never even took it out of the fridge. I
found this card case after Diane's wedding—"

"Sorry about the accident," she said softly.

"Yeah. Me, too. If I'd just gone after her . . . Well, anyway,
I found this, and before that I saw this guy . . ." Once again
I explained about the man in the rain, but Lily was no
Lieutenant Borden. She was fascinated.

"So you think this Guthridge guy sent someone to kill
Nickie. And you think the killer dropped his card case after
he'd been fooling with her car—so now we just have to find
out who owns the card case!"

Her enthusiasm was a bit disconcerting. "Well, maybe.
That still wouldn't prove that the owner of the case was fooling with the Mustang. For that we have to find Mary."

"Mary who?"

"Crazy Mary, you know, the bag lady?"

"Sure. She's in the library a lot, checking the local papers
and planning her bus routes. She's kind of sweet."

"Yeah, she is. Well, that night, at the reception, she said
something about people breaking things and stealing things,
and she kept saying 'I saw him.' I thought she meant she saw
someone spill some champagne, but the person who spilled

the champagne was a woman. What if she meant the man in the raincoat? Maybe she saw him fooling with Nickie's car, and she thought he was trying to steal it? What do you think?"

"I think I'm starving. Where shall we go?"

We went to a noisy little Thai place in Fremont, not far from Joe's office, and pored over the cards between the phad thai and the coconut ice cream. As usual, Lily ate with a kind of wicked gusto, prompting other diners to crane around and see what she was having. Lily's like that.

"Well," she said finally. "You can't tell much from three cards, except the guy works out, plays pool, and likes Flair Plus, whatever that is. Why not give the whole thing to the police, or to Douglas Parry?"

"The police already think I'm a flake. And I did warn the family." I didn't mention Douglas's heart trouble. "Besides, the case might belong to one of the wedding guests who just hasn't missed it yet. Or to one of the poison pen writers that Nickie's worried about, and that could be anybody on earth. I should probably just wait a while."

"True. You know you're wearing your dinner again?"

She was right. I'd spattered noodle sauce on my blouse. "Damn! How do I do this? I'm not a clumsy person, am I?"

Lily grinned. "Your best friend wouldn't tell that, would she? So what else is up, besides the mystery man?"

I told her about the bounced check, and how I'd unintentionally embarrassed Grace with her banker and perhaps with her husband. "Grace could do me a lot of good in her social circles. Or a lot of damage."

"Isn't Parry the one who's been in the papers? Maybe it wasn't just a shopping spree that emptied that account. Maybe they're in a financial bind because of his shady deals."

"Oh, jeez, I hadn't thought of that. I'd better talk it over with Eddie. Maybe we could bill them in advance for some of the bigger expenses coming up, like the liquor and the rest of the yacht club's fees for the reception." I thought for a moment. "No, Eddie's so prejudiced against Douglas already, I'd better wait until I know more."

"Sounds like the story of your life right now. Wait till you know more."

"But I hate to wait!"

"Clumsy *and* impatient . . . Listen, Carnegie, if you decide to follow up on this whole thing, you call me, OK?"

I smiled. "You want to play detective, too, don't you?"

"Well, life's been kinda quiet lately. You're picking up the check, right? Or do you just want to owe me a chicken?"

When I got home the phone was ringing: Mom. I skipped all the bad news and told her about Nickie's dress instead. As I described it to her I took the cordless phone outside to the deck. The evening was cool and still, reflected lights wavering just a little on the black water of the lake.

"She looks just like an old portrait, Mom, or a cameo," I concluded, settling down cross-legged on the planks. "I wish you could see her. So, anyway, have you heard from Timmy?"

"He says Sue has morning sickness, but only at night." My kid brother Tim, who had chipped in for my loan, was in graduate school in Illinois with his newly pregnant wife. Another reason for big sister to pay her debts. "He sends you his love."

"Tell him he'll have his money back soon," I said, painfully aware that I'd said that before. I slipped off a moccasin and reached one leg down to dip my toes in the lake. Ouch. The water was much too cold even for dabbling. How could people swim in that stuff?

"Oh, Tim's not worried," Mom said. "Eddie told me last night how well you're doing."

"He did? I mean, good."

"He said the loan won't be any problem at all."

"Well, he's the money man," I said, sounding more confident than I felt, "so it must be true." I wouldn't see Eddie again till Monday, but then I'd have to ask him the source of this remarkable optimism. After my apology, of course.

"But Carrie, what are you doing home on a Friday night?" My mother was the only one who still called me Carrie, and the only one who thought I had a date every weekend.

"Well, Mom, I've got this big function tomorrow."

"Have you met anyone nice lately?"

Had I? I thought about it, while I said something noncommittal and my mother went on chatting. Did Holt Walker qualify as nice, or just handsome, successful, and up to his knees in money? I hadn't even mentioned him to Lily, let alone to Mom, because I didn't want to be interrogated. And face it, I was still smarting from the cold shoulder he'd given me downtown. Nice shoulders, though. But that way lies madness.

"Nobody special, Mom, but you never know. Maybe Mr. Right will be at the bash tomorrow. Just pray for sunshine for me."

She promised she would, and left me to my thoughts.

Chapter Ten

SOMETIMES A MOTHER'S PRAYERS ARE ANSWERED. WHEN I WOKE up Saturday, June had decided to impersonate July. The sun would shine on the senator, his supporters, and the ladies and gentlemen of the press while they ate grilled shrimp and drank moderately priced chardonnay, courtesy of a Republican wine merchant. And I wouldn't have to move the picnic tables inside. Wonderful.

But I couldn't decide what to wear. The jade silk? Too dressy for a picnic. Slacks and sweater? Too casual for the paid staff. I settled on a summery, pale-peach outfit with a soft skirt and a casual, unlined jacket over a white eyelet blouse. The gathered skirt made me look less of a beanpole, and the peach went surprisingly well with my red hair, not that anyone would notice. "Anyone" meaning Holt Walker, of course. Maybe he'd just been distracted the other day downtown. Maybe he'd find the shrimp and sunshine quite relaxing and romantic. Maybe pigs could fly. I checked my lipstick twice in Vanna's rearview mirror, and whistled "Some Enchanted Evening" through my teeth all the way across the lake.

If I were a senator, and somebody threw me a fund-raiser, I'd want it to look like the spread at Douglas Parry's that day. It was all postcard-perfect: the icy white mountain rising beyond the glittering azure lake, gala green-and-white striped tents on a vast emerald lawn, tables of food and buckets of wine, and the kind of well-wishers who arrive by sailboat and BMW. Once the Dixieland band struck up "Tiger Rag," I was ready to vote for the guy myself.

Joe Solveto had brought his best staff, dressed in old-time suspenders and straw hats, to serve the shrimp, tend bar, and park cars. Things went so smoothly that, after directing the buffet arrangements and helping to set up the podium and microphones in the gazebo, I actually had time to people-watch.

From the cedar railing of the back terrace, I watched the picnic tables rapidly filling. People were all decked out, the way Seattleites do when the sun finally shines: garden-party dresses on the older ladies, and linen suits on the older gents, nicely mixed with avant-garde play clothes in the most trendy of shades. The senator himself, who enjoyed the distinct political advantage of resembling John Wayne, was working the crowd. He was trailed by two bright young staffers with instructions to fend off reporters until after the speeches, which would come after supper.

At this rate, I could even eat supper myself. My purse was on a side table in the living room; I stepped through the French doors to stash my clipboard there, too, and ran into Holt Walker. Physically. There was a lot of him to run into, and he kept me from falling with one hand, as if I weighed nothing at all. At this rate, I wouldn't need any wine. The sense of his body so close to mine went right to my head.

"Sorry! I didn't see you, the sun's so bright out there." I sounded like a nervous teenager. "It's going really well. Don't you think?"

"Very well," he said, picking up my clipboard and handing it back. "Thanks to you, no doubt."

He was wearing new-looking jeans, neatly pressed, with a tattersall check shirt, and my flat shoes made him seem even taller than he had at Diane's wedding. His eyes were still green. I couldn't remember whose turn it was to speak.

"Are you busy?" he asked. "Of course you are, but do you have time to eat? I could get us both a plate."

"That would be fine," I said, put suddenly at ease by his simple courtesy. "But don't you have to go meet and mingle?"

He shrugged those nice shoulders. "I'm off duty today. I've already sent Sam a contribution, and I don't feel like answering legal questions on a Saturday."

"How about nonlegal questions?" I found myself saying.

He narrowed his eyes curiously. "Such as?"

"Such as, when you arrived late to Diane's wedding, did you see anyone else in the parking lot or along the drive?"

The green eyes grew wary. "No. Was I supposed to?"

Here we go again, I thought. I'm going to sound paranoid to him, too. And I really, really don't want to do that.

"No, not at all, it's just that . . . it's just that I found this card case, and I'm wondering if one of the guests dropped it." I rummaged in my purse and produced the card case. He took it, looked at it idly, and handed it back.

"Looks expensive. No one's claimed it?"

"Not yet. But I'm sure they will."

"Well, then, how about some supper?"

"Wonderful."

We went back out on the terrace, and he crossed the lawn with a long-legged stride. I saw him wave to Nickie, who was holding hands with Ray at a table full of younger people. A contribution to Sam, I thought. Samuel Bigelow. Could I date a Republican? Could I date a Republican with those eyes? No need to be narrow-minded, after all. It's the two-party system that made this country great.

Further political musings were interrupted by Grace Parry, coming up from the lawn, with Dorothy Fenner in attendance. Grace was wearing a tropical-print silk blouse over slim white pants and tiny white sandals. Her toenails were painted coral, probably by someone else. Dorothy looked proper as ever, in a linen sheath and a hat that would have done the Queen Mother proud.

"Carnegie, there you are!" said Grace. "I've just been raving about you to Laura Simone. Her oldest girl just got engaged. . . ."

I felt a wave of relief. No hard feelings about the bank account, then.

"Dorothy here has a few suggestions," Grace was saying, "and I told her you'd be glad to hear them."

"Of course," I lied. "What's the problem, Dorothy?"

"Oh, goodness, Carnegie, no problem at all. But the parking area is getting full, so you should tell the attendants to use both sides of the drive. Some of the waiters are pouring the wineglasses too full, and the bar nearest the lake has run out of lime wedges."

"Heaven forfend," I muttered.

"Pardon me?" She raised those goddamn eyebrows at me and smiled that goddamn smile.

"I'll take care of it," I said.

Dorothy departed for the ladies', and Grace crossed the room to survey the scene outside, shielding her eyes with one hand. She wore a diamond ring the size of a golf ball. "Oh, Holt, thank you! I haven't had a minute."

Holt had returned, a heaped plate in each hand and two napkins hanging out of his shirt pocket. Before he could speak, Grace took a plate from him and perched prettily on a wrought-iron bench on the terrace. "Here, there's plenty of room. I haven't seen you in ages."

He gestured to me with the empty hand. "But—"

"I've got work to do," I said. "Shall I send a waiter up with some wine?"

"Thanks," he said, and winked. "See you later."

Content with that for the moment, I was starting down the steps for the limeless bar when Grace said, "Who's that?"

She was on her feet, pointing down the lawn to the first buffet table.

"Who's who?" I asked.

"With the bad haircut and the dreadful jacket."

"He has a press badge," Holt remarked, squinting into the sun. He had smile lines around his eyes, and gold highlights in his chestnut hair.

"That's what I thought," said Grace. "That's Aaron Gold from the *Sentinel*. They were specifically told to send someone else. For God's sake, get him out of here before Douglas sees him."

Holt set down his plate and began to get up, but Grace put a dainty hand on his arm and produced a smile.

"I meant her, not you, silly. Solving these little problems is what you're paid for, isn't it, Carnegie?"

"It certainly is," I said, holding onto my temper with both hands.

I don't usually work as a bouncer, but getting rid of Aaron Gold clearly took priority over limes and wineglasses. I kept him in sight as I plowed through the crowd, until Douglas Parry entered the gazebo and tapped the microphone. People gathered to listen, and when the way cleared a bit, Gold was gone. I spotted Theo and worked my way over to him as

Parry introduced the senator. The crowd laughed and applauded on cue, giving me plenty of cover to tell Theo the problem.

"In a minute," he said flatly, not looking at me. "I've got another situation over here."

He nodded toward a trellised gate that marked a path to the famous rose garden. The roses were the one thing Douglas Parry hadn't changed when he had the old house torn down, and I'd heard that he had hired a special gardener just to care for them. The gate was twined with clematis vines, the feathery leaves and starry white flowers nicely framing the couple conversing beneath: Nickie Parry, looking dismayed, and a gaunt, gray-haired man in a three-piece suit, looking drunk.

"Who's that?"

"That is Keith Guthridge," said Theo, "and I am going to evict his ass."

"Well, do it quietly," I said. "I'll go with you and see if Nickie's okay, and then you go look for Gold, all right? I have to get back to the waiters."

"Fine."

Nickie saw us as we crossed the lawn to the gate, but Guthridge was absorbed in telling her his troubles. Like Grace Parry, he had splendid clothes and a perfect haircut, but money would never revive his ashen complexion, or still the palsied tremor of his hands. Keith Guthridge looked like expensive hell. Did he look like a man who would have Nickie killed? Of course not. Then again, what would a man like that look like?

"I never meant to upset you, sweetie, you know that," he was saying. His voice was old and slurred, and his lower jaw dropped slack, like a puppet's, between phrases. "But your father has hung me out to dry. I can't let him do that, can I? I can't let him ruin me. What do *you* want?"

This last was directed at Theo and me.

"Can I give you some help to your car, Mr. Guthridge," said Theo. It was not a question.

"No, you cannot," Guthridge began, but I cut him off with a placating smile. Crook or not, I felt sorry for him.

"Excuse me, Mr. Guthridge, but Nickie's fiancé is looking for her." I took her arm and guided her away, leaving Theo to his evicting. Senator Bigelow's amplified voice said something about values, and everyone applauded again.

"You didn't have to do that, you know," said Nickie, stopping and shaking off my hand. "He has the right to talk to me."

"Well, yes," I said. I could hear Guthridge behind me, calling Theo a thug. "But I thought it would be better if—"

"And I have the right to talk to him." She turned back toward her godfather, and I was suddenly weary of the whole family.

"So talk to him! But if your father sees you together . . . oh, hell."

Her father had seen Guthridge already. He was striding around the edge of the crowd, getting redder in the face with each step. Theo moved away from Guthridge with the now-you're-in-trouble smirk of a schoolyard tattletale.

"Keith, I will thank you not to bother my daughter." Parry kept his voice down, but I could see that a few people at the edge of the crowd were being distracted from the senator's speech.

"I would thank you to tell your daughter the truth!" roared Guthridge.

Parry, his face a dangerous dark crimson, took a step forward, as if to stifle this intolerable noise. Guthridge raised both mottled hands in alarm, forgetting that one hand held a drink. The wine splashed up along his sleeve and flicked drops into his eyes. Theo laughed.

"You're going to regret this, Douglas, I swear to God." Guthridge was shaking. He pulled out a handkerchief and dabbed at his face, as if the wine were tears.

"Gentlemen, there are reporters here." I stepped between them, wondering if I was about to get slugged by a banker. "You're both going to regret this conversation if it shows up in the papers tomorrow."

As if on cue, the applause rose and fell, cameras flashed near the gazebo, and a woman's voice called out, "Senator, what about unemployment in the rural counties?"

Parry closed his eyes for a moment to compose himself, and just then Ray Ishigura arrived like the Seventh Cavalry in a Beethoven sweatshirt and mirror shades. He beamed at each of us impartially and took Nickie's hand, blissfully unaware of the tension or, more likely, determined to ignore it.

"Want some dessert, sweetheart?"

Nickie had used up her bravado. "Sure. Bye, Uncle Keith."

Guthridge watched her go with dull pain in his eyes.

"I never meant to upset you," he repeated softly. OK, I thought, either this man is the world's best actor, or somebody else tampered with the Mustang. Or, of course, nobody did. Maybe I should forget the whole thing. But forgetting about Michelle wasn't going to be easy.

An impassive young woman, evidently from Guthridge's staff, came up and spoke to him in an undertone. He followed her back to the driveway, Theo slipped away, and I was left with Douglas Parry.

"She invited him to the wedding," he said, shaking his head. "God*damn* the man." Then, searching for another topic, he said, "But today is going fine, Carnegie, just fine. And Nickie says she loves the dress you found her."

"It suits her perfectly," I told him, as we walked back to the terrace. A high white haze was beginning to obscure Mount Rainier and soften our shadows on the grass. "She'll be lovely."

"You should have seen Julia on our wedding day," he said quietly. "She was a picture."

Not Grace, but Julia. Interesting. I couldn't find an answer to that, but he didn't seem to need one. We walked past the buffet tent, where the waiters had cleared away the shrimp to make way for the ice cream and strawberries. The guests were lining up for dessert and more wine, leaving the senator to his interviews.

"Have you eaten?" Douglas asked me, weary but courteous.

"I'll get something from the kitchen, thanks."

"Fine, fine." He was focusing on the senator, gauging the tone of the press questions. Guthridge was forgotten, at least for the moment. I climbed the terrace stairs, past the now vacant bench, and went around to the side door to the kitchen. I heard Mariana laughing inside, and cheered up at the thought of some food and some uncomplicated company. But then I opened the screen door and lost my appetite.

Leaning against the refrigerator, drinking beer and speaking a foreign language and obviously charming the socks off Mariana, was Aaron Gold.

Chapter Eleven

WHEN IT COMES TO MEN, THE FIRST THING I REGISTER IS height. Aaron Gold was shorter than me by a couple of inches, and probably younger by a couple of years. His crow-black hair was not so much badly cut as infrequently, and his lightweight tweed jacket fought a losing battle with the plaid of his shirt. Baggy corduroys and grass-stained sneakers completed the ideal party-crasher's ensemble.

"You must be the wedding lady," he said, in a fast-paced East Coast accent. His smile showed neat, perfectly white teeth below chocolate brown eyes and a hooked nose. He took a swig of beer and smiled again. "Mariana told me you had beautiful red hair."

What's a bouncer supposed to do with a remark like that? Mariana giggled and carried a dinner tray out of the kitchen and down the hall to her apartment.

"I'm Carnegie Kincaid, and I'm helping to run this event," I said coldly. "And if you're Aaron Gold, I've been asked to escort you out of the house. You were not invited."

Gold held up his hands in mock surrender. "Guilty as charged, Your Honor. But it's society's fault, not mine. I had an unhappy childhood. So how's the fund-raising going?"

"None of your business." After putting up with Grace all day, it was a relief to be rude. "Are you going to leave, or—"

"Or what?" he said. "You'll call the cops?"

"Something like that." I thought fondly of Theo and his muscles, and not so fondly of the scene Gold would cause if he put up a struggle. "Look, be reasonable. Your newspaper was specifically asked not to send you."

He shrugged. "They didn't get the message. What a shame. Are you on the staff here? What does Parry pay for a full-time hostess?"

"I'm not on the staff. I'm a wedding and special events consultant. What does the *Sentinel* pay you for invading people's privacy?"

"Touché. But Mariana invited me in, you know. I wasn't interrogating her. Just having a friendly chat about Brazilian cooking."

I knew I should cut this off, but my curiosity got the best of me. "You speak Portuguese?"

"In my part of Massachusetts, there are more Azoreans than there are left in the Azores. Those are islands off the coast of Portugal, you know."

I didn't know. "You sound like New York to me."

He rolled his eyes heavenward. "You people! Everything east of the Continental Divide sounds like New York to you. So what exactly do you consult about? The daughter's getting married soon—is that your job, too? Wait, where are my manners. You want a beer?"

"I want you to stop asking questions and leave!" I did want a beer, and some shrimp, and some peace and quiet. "I'm trying to do my job."

"And I'm trying to do mine." He sat down at the butcher block table and pulled out a notebook. "Give me your phone number so I can call you later. Or are you in the book under Wedding Lady?"

Fortunately, the screen door opened at that point. Unfortunately, it was Grace Parry. She looked at Gold, then at me, with equal disdain.

"I asked you to get rid of him, and you're serving him drinks."

Gold stood up and smiled. His nerve was astonishing, or maybe chutzpah was a better word. "Mrs. Parry, nice to meet you. Aaron Gold, from the *Seattle Sentinel*. I wonder if I could ask you a few questions about your husband's role in the Guthridge trial? He hasn't returned my calls."

Grace might have been deaf. "You're needed at the dessert table," she told me. "As soon as possible."

She left the kitchen, and the temperature rose back to normal. Gold drummed the tabletop with his fingers. I hate fidgety men. "Have I gotten you in trouble?"

"It could have been worse," I said. "You could have gotten Mariana fired."

"Is old Grace really that much of a bitch?"

"Grace is hell on wheels. But she's not that old."

He shrugged. "Fifty ain't young."

"Fifty? Grace Parry? She can't be."

"Fooled you too, huh?" He grinned and tipped back the last of his beer. "She makes a big deal of being Parry's younger second wife, and dressing like the daughter, what's her name?"

"Niccola."

"Yeah, like Niccola's sister. But the little-known fact of the matter," here he consulted his notebook, "is that she'll be fifty-one next October. Gossip says she's vain about her age, faithful to her husband, and she didn't object to signing a restrictive prenuptial agreement because she's so good at making money herself."

I shook my head. "Fifty, that's amazing. But why are you collecting gossip?"

"I'm not. I'm just following the Guthridge case, rounding up stray facts, and seeing a lot of strange stuff along the way."

"Such as?"

"Such as two old friends threatening each other at a garden party. What was that all about, anyway? To testify or not to testify?"

"More or less," I said, then caught myself. That's right, Carnegie, chat with a reporter about your client's personal affairs. Aaron Gold may have struck out with Grace, but he was insinuating himself into my confidence with embarrassing ease. "It was just a conversation. A private conversation. And now you'd better leave."

I opened the screen door and waited. He walked past me, the top of his head level with my eyes. When he paused on the terrace, I looked nervously around for Douglas Parry, but everyone seemed to be down on the lawn.

"Don't you care whether Parry is a criminal?" Gold asked me.

"Of course I care! But he's not. And for all I know, Keith Guthridge isn't, either. What about innocent until proven guilty?"

"Let me tell you something, Wedding Lady. Keith Guthridge has connections with some very guilty types of people." Aaron Gold smiled and cocked his head. He might have been talking about the fine weather, or paying another glib compliment. "You think that organized crime just stood back and let the civilians make all the money in the savings-and-loan scams? Parry is blowing the whistle on a dangerous man."

"Are you saying Guthridge is involved with organized

crime?" His old man's voice echoed in my mind: *You'll regret this, Parry, I swear to God.* Suddenly the anonymous threats Douglas had been receiving seemed far more ominous, and the car crash seemed anything but accidental. Why hadn't I held on to Crazy Mary?

"I'm not saying anything until I can prove it. But I'll prove it. Meanwhile, can I use a phone? I came by cab."

"There's a pay phone at the general store down the road," I said, and escorted him resolutely around the house to the front entrance. To keep him from lingering, I walked with him down the front drive, past the luxury cars and SUVs and luxury SUVs under the colonnade of madrona trees. Some of the guests were leaving, and they roared past us without a look.

Gold strolled after me, hands in his pockets. "Do you always walk so fast?"

"I've got work to do."

"Must be tough, helping rich girls get married."

I halted and faced him, feeling all the aggravations of the past week coming to a head, and more than a little upset by his talk about crime and criminals. "Where do you get off criticizing my job? I'm planning Nickie Parry's wedding, and she's wealthy, so you assume that she's a spoiled brat and that I—"

"That you get paid to pick out cakes and flowers? Well, don't you?" The little twerp smiled. I'd risen to his bait.

"Yes," I said carefully, "yes, I do, among other things. And I'm good at it, and a number of people, not all of them wealthy, appreciate my help. The general store is that way. About a mile." I glanced up at the early-evening sky, which was not going to rain on him. Too bad. "Have a nice walk, Mr. Gold."

He sighed and set off, but turned back almost at once. "One last question."

"What is it?"

His teeth showed white. "How did you get more freckles on one side of your face than the other?"

"*What?*"

"I like it. See you later."

Not if I can help it, I told myself, and went back to work. I wasn't really needed at the dessert table, but there was plenty to do. I ate my supper standing up, answering questions, directing the breakdown of tents and tables, and dispersing well-earned tips to the waiters. The June daylight lasted until past nine o'clock. The setting sun threw a sudden wash of rosy gold against low, soft-edged clouds, and a gusty breeze came up, whipping dropped napkins along the ground and snatching at the brims of departing ladies' hats, turning the tents into billowing monsters that had to be wrestled to the ground. As the sunset faded and the people disappeared, the view from the terrace was transformed from a bright blue-and-green snapshot to a somber oil painting with just a few touches of color against the silver lake and the dim grass.

One vivid touch was a splash of fuchsia-purple beneath a huge old hemlock tree, on the edge of the narrow belt of woods that separated the lawns from the rose garden. I wandered down toward it, gathering up abandoned napkins and a couple of wineglasses as I went. I might as well save someone's jacket from the dew, and stretch my legs before the drive home.

Behind me on the terrace, Grace, Douglas, and the senator were moving inside with a select circle of late-staying guests. Including Holt, I supposed. Now that I knew her true age, Grace's coquettish air with her husband's young attorney seemed a bit pathetic. She'd probably complain girlishly about how incompetent I was, letting a hostile reporter invade the house. Or maybe they just talked money, or vacations in Bali. Or, to be fair, Douglas Parry's legal dilemmas.

As I picked up the purple jacket, lights went on in the house, casting pale rectangles down the lawn and deepening the shadows from gray to black. I could hear fragments of laughter, and the rumble of Solveto's trucks pulling away. A reasonably successful event, despite Keith Guthridge and Aaron Gold. I'd had enough of them, of their threats and accusations. I wanted to return to my world of white dresses and string quartets and chocolate-dipped apricots.

And roses. I'd had a quick glimpse of the Parry rose garden earlier in the spring, but rosebushes are downright dull when they're not in bloom. Twilight was my favorite time for gardens, and a stroll through the roses would be just what I needed to put myself to rights. I set down my armload of debris—let it spoil Grace's perfect view in the morning—and draped the abandoned jacket across my shoulders as I stepped further into the shadows between the trees. I could have gone around to the clematis arbor and the proper pathway, but these woods were only a few hundred yards deep, and I was sure I could find my way.

Within minutes, I wasn't so sure. The towering hemlocks and firs blocked out the sky, creating a sudden midnight. Their wind-swayed branches murmured around me as I walked. I stopped abruptly, listening. Were there voices murmuring ahead of me as well? Then I heard a girl's laughter. Of course, I hadn't seen Nickie and Ray go inside with the others. They must be lingering down here, away from the older generation's small talk. I hesitated, torn between the lure of the roses and the possible embarrassment of intruding on an

intimate scene. I must be close. I could smell flowers on the
evening air, sweet and spicy, strong enough to be almost unpleasant. Discretion won out, and I turned back.

And screamed. Almost invisible against the night, a dim
figure stepped out from behind the black column of a tree
trunk, arms upraised. I could sense violence, malice. I
jumped backward, but a root caught at my foot like an animal trap. Panicked, I pulled free and whirled around to run.
A cracking pain at my temple, a rush of nausea, and then
darkness.

Chapter Twelve

I WAS ONLY OUT FOR A MOMENT. THEN THERE WERE VOICES around me.

"She's awake!" A girlish voice, breathless and agitated.

"Don't move her until we know what's wrong." A young man, speaking calmly.

"Jesus, I didn't mean to scare her." Another man, loud and indignant.

Nickie, Ray, and Theo. I identified the voices, and then the faces, ghoulishly lit by a flashlight in Theo's hand. I was lying flat on soft, scratchy ground, with the three of them kneeling around me in the darkness like surgeons over a stretcher. I tried to sit up, but my skull tried to explode, so with Ray's help I settled for slumping against a tree trunk. Nickie knelt beside me and lifted my hair gently.

"It's not bleeding," she said, "but it's swelling up. We'll call a doctor."

"No, call the police." My memory sprang into focus: the dark figure, his arm raised to strike. "He's getting away!"

"Who's getting away?" asked Nickie.

"The guy who hit me."

Ray chuckled, then stopped himself when Nickie glared. "Sorry, it isn't funny. But nobody hit you, Carnegie, except this tree here. Theo saw you fall."

"No, a man jumped out—I think it was a man—"

"It was me." Theo's flashlight moved, making the shadows on their faces quiver. The wind stirred the scent of cedar bark on the damp air from the lake. "Mrs. Parry sent me down to look for Nickie. I didn't see you till you yelled and fell down. Listen, I'm really sorry. Mr. Parry is going to kill me."

"It wasn't your fault," said Nickie kindly. "We don't have to tell him."

"Of course we'll tell him," said Ray.

"But he has so much to worry about already—"

"Could somebody worry about me for a minute?" I snapped. Nickie touched the rising lump of pain at my hairline and I pulled away. "No, my head's all right, I'll be fine. But I'm telling you, somebody attacked me. I think?"

I looked uncertainly at Theo. He wore jeans and a dark sweater, so he would have been dark against the shadows. And he was more or less the size of the figure I saw. But surely I would have recognized his pale hair, his bleached-out face? Maybe not. And was it definitely a man, or could it have been a woman? The memory was blurring. And besides, I thought suddenly, if someone was stalking me, maybe it would be better to pretend I didn't know it.

"I'm really sorry," said Theo. "I must have come up right behind you before I saw you were there. You fell sideways and hit your head. You hit pretty hard. You want an ambulance?"

"No, of course not. Honestly, I'm not dizzy or concussed or anything." I stood up, with six arms aiding me, and took a step, then another. All systems go. "I just want to get out of these damn trees."

Nickie brushed the fir needles from my back, and Theo

picked up the purple jacket, its color pallid in the flashlight beam, and handed it to me.

"My jacket!" said Nickie. "I knew I left it somewhere."

I tried to pass it to her, but she insisted that I keep it on as we set off for the house. Halfway up the lawn, Theo excused himself with another apology and headed for the garage. Ray offered me a shoulder to lean on as I walked. It was almost unnecessary, but not quite.

Soon I was sitting in the kitchen, with Mariana providing tea and sympathy, and Nickie preparing an ice pack for my aching head. Nothing else ached, except for a scrape on my left arm where I'd slid along the rough bark. Ray might have been right, of course: I could have glimpsed Theo, mistaken his own startled response for a threat, and fallen. Maybe.

I had begun to apologize for all the fuss when Grace Parry entered with Ray on her heels. She still wore her gaily-colored party clothes, but her lipstick was gone, and she looked a bit faded, a bit closer to her true age.

"Carnegie!" No hint of archness now. She was clearly upset. "Ray told me what happened. Are you sure you're all right?"

"I'm fine, really, thank you. It's just a headache now. I'll be ready to drive home in a minute."

"Absolutely not!" she said, with Nickie echoing her. "What if you felt faint on the way? I'd never forgive myself. Theo will take you."

"No!" I said, too loudly. No way was I getting into a car with Theo. I was willing to pretend it was an accident, for the moment, but I wasn't suicidal. "I mean, I'm fine to drive, honestly. I don't want to cause any more trouble."

The women started to protest, but Ray made a placating sweep with his long pianist's hands. "I need to go back anyway. I'll drive Carnegie home in her van, and take a taxi to my apartment. You can drive my car into Seattle tomorrow, okay, Nick?"

Nickie gazed at him as if he'd just discovered DNA, and I had the distinct feeling that Grace and I had become invisible. "That's perfect! I'll walk you out to the van. Carnegie, don't get up until you're sure you're all right."

"Don't worry," I said. At this stage in their romance, it would take at least fifteen minutes to kiss good-bye.

"Run along," said Grace. "Mariana, thank you so much, but I'll make more tea if Carnegie needs it. Good night."

So I was left alone with Grace Parry. Closing my eyes, I could hear far-off sounds of the party winding down in the living room and library. I wondered if Holt had left yet. Grace smelled faintly of cigarette smoke and brandy, entwined with her own perfume. Her scent triggered something, a fragment of memory. Roses, the smell of roses, back there in the woods. But had it been roses, or something else, something odd . . . ? Something cold brushed my leg and I jumped. It was Gus's inquisitive nose. He nuzzled my hand for a moment, just checking in, then padded away to follow Nickie.

"I need to ask you a favor." The urgency in Grace's tone made me look up abruptly. She refilled my cup from the delicate china teapot. One of her coral fingernails was broken, the jagged edge not yet filed smooth. "If you're sure you're not seriously hurt, I'd rather not tell Douglas about your accident. This whole affair with Keith Guthridge has been very upsetting, of course, and then the car crash. He's having chest pains again. So if you don't mind—"

"Oh, I see. No, of course I don't mind. It was my own fault, anyway. I probably scared Theo just as much as he scared me."

She smiled in obvious relief and her features softened, her asymmetrical eyes just a slight, humanizing flaw in a pretty face. "Thank you, Carnegie. Shall we see if the lovebirds are ready?"

They were. Ray piloted me home, keeping me amused on the way with a long, silly story about a famous soprano, a piano tuner, and a flooded basement at a New Year's Eve party. It was the first time Ray and I had been alone together, and I liked him better by the mile. For the first time, it occurred to me that his easygoing compliance in all the wedding plans didn't make him an easygoing man. A concert pianist, after all, needed more than talent. He needed single-minded determination, and a healthy ego. No doubt Ray had both. When he pulled up at my dock, I invited him in for a drink while he waited for his cab.

"Actually, I'm going to walk. Nickie thinks the city is dangerous at night, so I don't tell her."

I looked at his face, handsome but misleadingly bland, profiled against the driver's side window. He kept his hair short and brushed forward a bit, very trendy, like his wardrobe. I had never been attracted to an Asian-American man, probably because I towered over most of them, but I could see the appeal for Nickie. And not just in his looks. The world might judge that Ray Ishigura had caught himself an heiress, but the heiress was a lucky young woman herself. "Anything else you don't tell her?"

"Well," he said solemnly, "I don't actually care whether we have orchids or dandelions at the reception."

I laughed, and even though it made my head hurt it felt good. "Ray, there's never been a bridegroom yet who truly cared about half the details of the wedding."

"Just so long as Nickie is happy."

"I'm sure she will be," I said, and meant it.

Chapter Thirteen

THIS TIME I UNPLUGGED BOTH PHONES, AND SLEPT LONG AND hard all Saturday night and half of Sunday. When I woke up, my temple was the size and color of an overripe plum, but I was otherwise sound. Physically, anyway. While I artfully prepared a gourmet breakfast of toast with toast—I'd have to go shopping soon—I puzzled over yesterday's events.

Keith Guthridge was murderously angry at Douglas Parry, that was plain, and Aaron Gold believed that Guthridge was dangerous. Two hours after Gold told me that, someone attacked me in the woods on the Parry estate. But Theo said the someone was himself, and there was no attack, just an accident. Anyway, Theo obviously saw Keith Guthridge as the enemy, so how could he be involved in Guthridge's threats? And I'd smelled an odd sweet scent in the woods, but I'd been around Theo enough to know that he always smelled like plain soap. Besides, why would Theo or anyone else attack me? Putting on a wedding for Douglas Parry's daughter hardly qualified me as a target, for disgruntled investors *or* imaginary mobsters.

Lots of questions, but only one thing for sure: I was going to check out those business cards. To hell with waiting. I poured another cup of coffee and called Lily.

"Somebody clobbered you on the *head*?" she said.

"I think so. I'm pretty sure."

"And you think it was Theo."

"Well, it certainly could have been. He was right nearby. And if it was somebody else, why would Theo say it was an accident?"

"Good point. OK, what do we do next?"

"Well, I think we go to the Powerhouse and the pool hall and that Flair place, whatever it is, and try to find out if Theo is a customer. He's so weird looking, it shouldn't be hard. Also we try to track down Crazy Mary, so we have something definite to tell the police. But listen, Lily, are you sure you want to get involved in this? What if it gets dangerous?"

"Oh, shut up. The library's got a list of Seattle women's shelters; I'll start calling them about Mary."

"Great."

We made a date to check out the gym the following Tuesday afternoon, then I put on jeans and a sweater—June had reverted back to April, with a fine, silvery drizzle—and went upstairs to the office to check the answering machine, my head pounding with each step. Just one new bride, let there be a message from just one possible, potential new bride. The machine was recording as I unlocked the door, with a man's voice amplified through the staticky speaker.

"This is Holt Walker, Carnegie, we met at the Parrys? There was no answer at your home number, so I'm trying your office—"

I dropped my keys and sprinted. "Hi, this is Carnegie."

"Oh, you're there! How's your head?"

Better than my heart, I thought inanely, but said, "Fine. I mean, a headache, but fine. I guess someone told you what happened. Not Douglas, I hope? Grace didn't want him to worry."

"No, Grace is the one who told me. To be honest with you, I called her to get your phone number."

"You did?"

"Well, she mentioned yesterday that you're single, and that we might have a lot in common."

You being gorgeous, I thought, *and me being a fan of gorgeous. Thank you, Grace, you wonderful client, you.*

"I enjoyed talking to you yesterday," I said. "Brief as it was."

He laughed. Nice laugh, to go with the shoulders. "Would you like to have dinner, and talk at length? How's Wednesday night?"

He didn't sound too doubtful about my answer, but then he didn't have to be. I made a pretense of checking my calendar.

"Wednesday's fine."

"Five-thirty?"

"That's a little early . . ."

"Indulge me," he said. "The restaurant I have in mind is a bit out of town."

"Okay. Wednesday at five-thirty."

And that was how I discovered a miracle cure for headaches. I called Lily back, just to share my medical breakthrough.

"Guess what? Our long national nightmare is over. I've got a date."

Lily laughed at me, but then she often does. "OK, who is he?"

I told her about Holt. I tried not to gush, but I must have tried too hard.

"Let me get this straight," she said. "He's not actually handsome, he's just tall and curly-haired with amazing green eyes. And he's a hotshot lawyer, but that's nothing special. And he asked you out for dinner, but of course he's not really interested in you. Have I got that right?"

"Okay, he is handsome, and maybe he's sort of interested. I just don't want to get my hopes up."

"I can understand that." Lily sighed. "I've been burned before. So I don't suppose you want me to look him up in Martindale-Hubbell?"

"Oh, could you?"

She laughed again. Martindale-Hubbell is a Who's Who of attorneys. It couldn't hurt to know something about Prince Charming's background. "I'll call you from work."

Librarians are so great. Lily called me Monday morning, right after Eddie and I had muttered our apologies for that childish argument on Friday afternoon.

"No word yet on Mary," she announced, "but Holt Walker is hot stuff. Rhodes scholar, Harvard Law School, with a year at Oxford at some special international program. Practiced in Chicago, now here—he's migrating west—both times at big corporate firms. He's thirty-eight, has a penthouse apartment downtown and a time-share condo on Maui. Goes rowing on Lake Washington every morning for exercise, does pro bono work for a senior citizen group. And half the women at Voigt, Baxter, McHugh have a crush on him."

"It says all that in Martindale-Hubbell, does it?"

Lily guffawed. "Well, it just so happens that the legal librarian at VBM is a friend of mine."

"Lily! You didn't tell her why you were asking?"

"Are you kidding? I said I'd been referred to a Harold Walker, a really boring old guy who writes wills, and she spent fifteen minutes telling me why Holt Walker couldn't be him. Smart, huh?"

"Brilliant. What else did she say?"

"Well, he's a widower. His wife died in a boating accident a couple of years ago and he hasn't really dated much since then, except for taking female friends to benefits and office parties. Lots of women at VBM would like to help him back to the land of the living. Are you still there?"

"Hmm?" I was off in a reverie. So Holt had been solitary since losing his wife, keeping up a good front but not getting close to anyone new. And now he'd taken a chance and asked someone out: me. I was flattered, and touched.

"Listen, Carnegie, I've got to get back to work. See you tomorrow, okay?"

"Okay. Thanks, Lily. You're a peach."

"You bet I am," she said.

Chapter Fourteen

WITH WEDNESDAY NIGHT BECKONING ON MY CALENDAR, Monday and Tuesday flew by in a blur of checklists. The lists were designed and printed out by Eddie and then covered with my scribbled notes about typefaces, foreign postage, bridesmaids' hats, videographers, ring engraving—someday I'd have to count up how many decisions and telephone calls go into a wedding. Three or four hundred, anyway. Eddie noticed the lump on my temple, but I played it down as a minor fall at the Parry estate.

Nor did I mention that curious remark my mother had made about the loans. If Eddie wanted to reassure her with his pumped-up confidence about Made in Heaven's financial future, that was fine with me. Peace at any price. When Eddie gave me a list of checks he needed for Nickie's florist, liquor distributor and so forth, I wrote them up without a murmur. This wasn't standard procedure—he would normally give me the invoices themselves—but I wasn't going to challenge him. I'd resolved to go over our books with him later in the summer. Meanwhile, he was the accountant. If he gave me the numbers, I'd write the checks, no questions asked.

I even let him win an argument. Eddie had scheduled me to make the two-hour drive to Ellensburg, east of the

Cascades, on an upcoming Friday for some preliminary arrangements on a country-western-type wedding. That would have been fine, but he wanted me to spend the night, meet with the pastor after breakfast, and then drive back to Seattle on Saturday morning.

"Eddie, that's the day of Anita's reception at the Glacier View! I can't drive back from Ellensburg that morning and down to Rainier that afternoon!"

"Why the hell not?" he demanded. The younger generation's lack of fortitude was a pet peeve of Eddie's. One of many. "Are you going to call Fay Riddiford, one of the only four clients we've actually got at the moment, and tell her to cancel her plans because you're too feeble to drive five whole hours in one day?"

I sighed, and drew some arrows on my big desk calendar. "All right, all *right*. Lily's got friends in Ellensburg. Maybe she'd like to come with me and we can share the driving. Satisfied?"

"I'd be more satisfied if you'd do some marketing instead of—"

"Time out!" I held up a hand. "Tomorrow and Friday, I will faithfully call every single one of our past brides and ask them for referrals, *and* I'll reserve a booth at that bridal show in Tacoma. I'll even get working on our Web site. OK?"

"OK," he said, mollified for the moment. Then, in his own gesture of peace, he tossed me the newspaper. "There's a laugh for you, halfway down on the business page."

I read it, but I wasn't laughing. The headline said "Wife of King County Savings Chair Linked to Insider Deals?" and the byline was Aaron Gold. A former colleague—and obvious ally—of Keith Guthridge was suggesting some nasty things about Grace Parry. No outright accusations, libel laws being what they are, but the implication was that Douglas Parry had made a practice of discussing King County Savings' loan customers with Grace. And that Grace just might have used the information in her securities trading, to her own and her clients' advantage. Near the end of the story, Gold sketched in Grace's background as Parry's second wife, a prominent socialite, and, in the words of one anonymous employee, "hell on wheels" to work for.

I dropped the paper on my desk and groaned. Hell on wheels. *I* said that, *I* was the anonymous employee—how dare he quote me without my permission? What if Grace figured out who was talking behind her back? Damn Aaron Gold, and damn my trusting nature. This was my own fault, but that didn't stop me from calling the *Sentinel.* I got a receptionist, and then the unmistakable flat, East Coast voice.

"Hi, this is Aaron Gold's voice mail. Leave me a message and I'll call you. Don't talk faster than I can write, OK?"

The beep sounded and I exploded, even angrier because I didn't have the satisfaction of doing it in person.

"This is Carnegie Kincaid, and what the hell do you mean quoting me as an anonymous employee, you snoopy son of a bitch? That was an offhand, flippant remark and you know it. Don't you have any ethics at all? And anyway I'm not an employee, I'm a consultant."

I stopped for air, and then slammed down the phone. What else was there to say? Eddie was leaning back in his chair, hands behind his head, deck shoes up on the desk.

"You said that about a client? To a reporter?"

"Eddie." I closed my eyes. "Eddie, it was a dumb thing to do, but I don't want to talk about it, all right? I'm going to go run a couple of errands. If Aaron Gold calls back, tell him to drop dead."

My first errand was the trip to the Powerhouse, but I wasn't going to tell Eddie that. He thought I'd put the Mustang crash out of my mind. Lily and I met in Ballard, a Scandinavian neighborhood that was once a hardworking little fishing and sawmill town in its own right. Seattle had spread out to engulf Ballard long ago, and lately the rising tide of Seattle's well-paid software types had discovered its low real-estate prices. Now the old brick business district was an uneasy mixture of ancient taverns and new vegetarian restaurants. There was even a hair salon and day spa. I remembered Eddie sneering about that. He lived in Ballard, where he'd been going to the same barber for twenty years.

"OK, what's the plan?" In honor of the occasion, Lily had worn running shorts and a zippered sweatshirt. She was fiddling with the zipper as we hesitated above a set of cement steps leading down from the sidewalk to an unappealing door marked Powerhouse Gym. The afternoon sun illuminated the shards of a broken beer bottle and some nasty-looking stains. "Who says what? Do we just ask right out, does a guy named Theo come here?"

"Something like that. I thought I'd—"

"S'cuse me, ladies." A small, tough-looking man wearing Eau de Sweat came out of the gym and held the door open for us. A moment passed, then another, but he still stood there. Chivalry was not dead in Ballard. Lily looked at me, round-eyed, and we plunged down the stairs.

Inside was not nearly as off-putting as outside had been. A perky receptionist smiled at us from her glassed-in cubbyhole, and beyond her an array of weight machines, treadmills, and stationary bikes were in use by a mix of fit and not-so-fit Seattleites, mostly men. Over it all blasted that staple of gyms everywhere: really loud, really bad seventies arena rock. At present we were being favored by Foreigner playing "Hot-Blooded," but at any moment I expected REO Speedwagon or even, heaven help us, Lynyrd Skynyrd doing "Free Bird."

"Hi, I'm Mindy. You guys want to look around?" Mindy wore shorts and a thin white Powerhouse T-shirt stretched to the breaking point over a lacy black bra.

"That would be great," I said. "We're thinking about joining—"

But she was already bouncing through the place, rattling off her sales pitch. None of the customers even glanced up, and Mindy seemed to be on automatic pilot herself, almost shouting over the music.

"All the usual stuff, free weights, Nautilus . . ."

"Well, I'm hot-blooded, check it and see"

"No swimming pool, that's why our fees are so cheap, I mean reasonable . . ."

"I got a fever of a hundred and three . . ."

Lily clutched my shoulder as we trotted along behind. "If they play 'Free Bird,' I am out of here."

"Shhhh!"

"Locker rooms are down there if you want to check 'em out. I'll be up front, OK?"

"I was just wondering if a friend of mine ever—" But she was gone, in pursuit of a ringing phone, before I could bring out my carefully rehearsed inquiry about Theo. I made to follow her, but Lily stopped me and pointed to an open file box on a counter, in the hallway leading to the locker rooms. It held an alphabetical set of cards that the customers used to record their day's rounds on the weight machines. And at the top of each card was a name.

"Bingo!" said Lily. "What's Theo's last name?"

Theo's last name. As far as I knew, it was Driver, and his middle name was The.

"You don't know, do you?"

"Well, no."

She rolled her eyes, but I grabbed half the cards and handed her the other. We shuffled through them, turning our backs nonchalantly when anyone came down the hall past us. I had the back of the alphabet: McFadden, Ogura, Palmer, Quillen, Stern, Thorpe, Vandenack, Wignall, Wyble . . .

"For I'm as free as a bird now,
And this bird you cannot change."

I heard Lily groaning, but I was busy staring at one particular card, out of order at the very end.

"Hey, what are you doing? Cut it out!" Mindy was bearing down on us. Lily dumped her cards and retreated through the nearest door. I followed, fast.

Lily had a radar for men, but this was ridiculous. She had entered the men's locker room, where a naked and dripping gentleman was glaring at her in horror, his towel out of reach. For once, Lily was at a loss for words. Not me, though.

"Hi!" I burbled. "Channel Eight Newsbeat! Sir, how do you feel about the proposed city ordinance on unisex locker rooms?"

He bellowed, Mindy hollered, and Lily and I fled along the hallway and up the stairs to the street, leaving scattered cards and Lynyrd Skynyrd behind us. We ran down the block and around the corner, gasping and snorting with laughter. Then I sobered up.

"Lily, did you recognize any names?"

"Nope. No Theos at all. How 'bout you?"

I raked my disheveled hair back from my face. "No Theos, but I did see a Boris."

"Boris *Nevsky*?"

"Yeah."

"You think Boris is the bad guy? Wow. Well, he *was* at Diane's wedding."

"No, of course I don't think that. But maybe we could ask Boris if Theo goes to that gym. We could tell him some story—" "Story" rang a dim bell. I checked my watch. "Lily, where are my brains? It's Tuesday! I'm due at Kidsplace."

"OK, but call me later, promise?"

I promised and drove off, thinking about Boris Nevsky.

Chapter Fifteen

KIDSPLACE WAS A DAY-CARE PROGRAM FOR LOW-INCOME WORK-ing mothers, where I did a story hour once a week. I parked by the scrawny hedge surrounding the little playground, full of kids running riot in the sunshine, and rummaged in the van for my stash of storybooks.

"Hey, Wedding Lady!"

That East Coast voice again: Aaron Gold, standing by the playground gate and smiling like an old friend. He had traded the tweed sports coat for an ugly tan windbreaker, and he held a battered steno notebook in one hand.

"What do *you* want? More quotes?"

"How come you're so worked up about one little anony-mous phrase? Is old Grace going to fire you on suspicion of having a big mouth?"

"Forget it, just forget it." He'd hit much too close to home. I did talk too much, and I knew it. "Are you following me around? How did you know where I'd be, anyway?"

"Your partner Eddie told me."

"*Eddie* sent you here?"

"Well, he mentioned the name of the center, so I looked it up."

"Bully for you." I said. "Now please leave me alone. I'm running late, and I have absolutely nothing to say to you, about Grace Parry or anything else."

The Kidsplace supervisor appeared at the door of the building, a train of kids in tow. "Carnegie, I thought we'd try the story hour outside today, all right? And Mr. Gold can watch."

I turned back to him. "Mr. Gold?"

"I'm doing a story on day-care kids," he said, utterly deadpan. "Single career women who volunteer as storytellers seemed like a perfect lead."

It was not my finest story hour. The kids ranged from wide-eyed kindergartners to world-weary fourth graders, so it was always a challenge to hold everybody's attention with the same tale. The presence of "Mr. Gold" didn't help.

"Who's he?" demanded Nathan, a pugnacious nine-year-old stretched out on his belly next to me.

"He's a newspaper reporter," I said. "He wasn't invited, and he's leaving very soon, but right now he's going to sit quietly and listen to this next story. Isn't he?"

"Sure," said Gold, grinning. "What's it about?"

"Unicorns," I replied, and began to read. Unicorn stories were a sure-fire hit with the girls, and I figured the boys would sit still for this one because it included a dragon. But Nathan was bent on showing off for the stranger.

"There's no such thing as unicorns," he pronounced loftily, his plump chin resting on two plump fists.

"Are, too!" Latoya, a unicorn fan who favored pink dresses, was adamant.

"Are not, Mucus Face," said Nathan. "They're just made up, aren't they, Carnegie?"

"Nathan, I've talked to you before about name-calling."

"But aren't they just made up?"

We'd been through this once at Christmas, when I'd sidestepped the Santa Claus question. I began to frame an answer, but Latoya made a face at Nathan, and he retorted by throwing a pebble at her, which made her cry. Throwing things was verboten at Kidsplace, so I comforted the victim and marched the perpetrator inside to cool off. When I returned, all eyes were on Aaron Gold.

"Now how about you, have *you* ever seen a unicorn?" He was asking Stephanie, the little girl on his left. Apparently he'd gone around the whole circle. Stephanie shook her blond head solemnly.

"Not even taking a bath in your bathtub? Or nibbling on your socks for breakfast?"

"No!" she shrieked, and the other kids giggled in delight.

"Me, either." Gold sighed. "So who knows if they're real or not. But this is a pretty good story, isn't it? Who wants to hear how it ends?"

There was a chorus of "Me, me!" and he looked up smugly. "Over to you, Scheherazade."

"Thanks."

"You're welcome," he said. "I hope the dragon gets it in the neck."

The dragon did, and I finished the hour with a sing-along story. After his show of charming the kids, Gold lost interest and wandered over to the van, flipping through his notebook. I wondered if he actually liked children, or if he was just softening me up for more questions. Or maybe he really was doing a story on day-care programs.

"How about a lift home?" he asked when I was done. "I'm right near you."

I threw the books in the back seat and got in. The van was hot and my head was aching, distracting me as I tried to think of an excuse for turning him down. "Don't you drive?"

"No car," Gold replied. He walked around to the passenger side and climbed in, taking my hesitation for consent.

Damn him anyway. I gave up and started the engine. "OK, where do you live?"

"Lakeshore Apartments."

"That figures."

The Lakeshore was an eyesore, a tacky stack of cheaply built, overpriced units two blocks south of me, much resented by the homeowners whose view it spoiled.

"Yeah, I knew you'd be thrilled." He dug a pack of cigarettes out of his windbreaker and began to pat his pockets for a match, the way men do. "You can come in for a beer."

"And give you more quotes? No, thanks." I had to speak up over Vanna's racket. "And please don't smoke in here."

At close quarters, the cigarette smell on his clothes was bad enough. He shrugged and contented himself with tossing the pack from hand to hand. You'd have thought he was oblivious to everything else, but then he looked at me sharply. He did have nice eyes.

"What happened to your head?"

My bruised temple was facing him. I pushed a lock of hair over it. "I fell down."

"Funny spot to fall on."

I didn't answer. Traffic was especially heavy, and I was anxious to return to the office and sort out my notes for Fay Riddiford's country-western wedding. I only half listened as Gold ran through his theories about Guthridge and the Parrys. His rapid-fire speech got on my nerves, and I tuned him out until we got hung up at an intersection.

"—So it's almost a certainty that Parry knew about the MicroTech stock split before the fact," he was saying, "and old Grace just might have used that info to hit the jackpot for two of her clients. I'd love to get my hands on her files, if she hasn't shredded them already. Does she ever talk about her investment business?"

"No." I craned around, trying to see if the idiot truck driver two cars ahead was stalled or just trying to make a left turn.

"How about Douglas Parry? You worked with him on Bigelow's fund-raiser, you saw him argue with Guthridge. Any idea how seriously he's taking Guthridge's threats?"

"No." The truck was stalled. I slipped past and down the hill just as the light turned red again, then made good time on the freeway.

"Any theories about what kind of beans Parry is going to spill when he testifies?"

"No."

"No, no, a thousand times no. Your lips are sealed?"

"That's right."

I drove past my own dock to the Lakeshore: three identically hideous buildings projecting into the lake, with blue-gray siding and alternating blue and gray balconies for the upper units. The lower apartments had sliding glass doors out to a common deck that wrapped around each building at lake level. I pulled into the parking lot and left the engine running.

"Is this close enough?"

"Yeah, that's me right there, lucky thirteen." He pointed toward a first-floor apartment in the nearest building. One curtain rod hung askew, giving the windows a forlorn air, and the potted azaleas flanking the glass door were brown skeletons, long dead of thirst. "No place like home. So Parry thinks Guthridge is bluffing, huh?"

I clenched the steering wheel. "Look, for the last time, my only interest in the Parrys is making sure that Nickie's wedding goes off well. Don't you understand that?"

"No, frankly, I don't. An intelligent person like you can't be all style and surface, there's got to be depths underneath, right? So how come we can't have a conversation about Douglas Parry?"

"This isn't a conversation, this is the third degree! You want to pump me about my clients, and I'm not going to be pumped."

"I just thought you'd be interested in truth, justice, and the American way, that's all."

"Trial by media, you mean," I put the van into gear. "You got your ride home. Good-bye."

Gold got out, but leaned back in through the open window, a cigarette already in his mouth, a lighter in his hand.

"All right," he said, "be that way. But be careful, would you? Real life is not just orange blossoms, and these are not nice people."

"No, according to you they're all gangsters," I snapped. If he hadn't spooked me with his talk about criminals on Saturday, I wouldn't have run from Theo and brained myself on that tree. "This isn't Sicily, for crying out loud."

He rolled his eyes. "Sicily? Do you ever read the news part of the newspaper? Ever heard of the Russian Mafia?

"The *Russian* Mafia?"

"Yeah, money laundering, big-time corruption, people getting killed, little stuff like that? There's a sizeable Russian community over in the Eastside suburbs, you know."

I did know. That was where Boris lived. And Boris had been out in the rain the night of Diane's wedding. . . . This was insane. Pretty soon I'd be suspecting myself.

"Look, I'll concentrate on weddings, and you concentrate on writing about day-care, OK?"

He straightened up to light his cigarette, and I drove off. Real life—give me a break. Maybe he thought that Made in Heaven was a hobby, that I could afford to lose my best clients just to be his inside informer. I stomped up the walkway to the houseboat, muttering as I went, and saw Eddie coming down the office stairs.

"Eddie, do you think I'm all style and surface?"

He paused to consider. "You've got terrific style. Why?"

"No, I mean do I concentrate too much on superficial things like cakes and flowers, and not enough on real life?"

"Listen, sister, the world is full of people who concentrate on real life. Stick with what you know."

"Oh, never mind. See you tomorrow."

I went inside to call Lily, and we puzzled over the possibility of Boris as a hit man.

"He *could* have tampered with the Mustang," I said. "It could have been him I saw down the road. But . . ."

"Yeah, but," said Lily. "But can you imagine dear old crazy Boris deliberately hurting someone? I mean, so what if he's Russian?"

"I can't imagine *anyone* deliberately hurting someone," I said. "But people still get hurt, don't they?"

"Well, let's check out the pool hall. The gym could be just a coincidence."

"OK." We made a date for the 418 Club, then considered the other half of our plan. "Lily, how are you coming with calling the shelters? Want me to help?"

"No, thanks, it's no problem. But I'm almost through the list, and no one's seen Mary. I'll keep checking."

Finally it was Wednesday afternoon, and time to get ready for my evening with Holt. I'd bought a new dress, on the spurious grounds that I really needed another stylish outfit to alternate with the jade silk at clients' weddings. The color was lovely, a deep rich red with no pink or orange tinge to jar against my hair, and the fabric was smooth and fluid on my skin. I slipped it on and spun before the mirror, as a woman might if she were dancing with Holt Walker, and the skirt lifted and whirled, showing lots of leg. And yet, when I stood demurely still, the effect was proper enough for an afternoon wedding. Perfect.

Even with a long shower, I was ready early. I put some more makeup over the fading bruise on my temple. Polished my black pumps. Changed purses, to a little black clutch bag. Tried putting my hair up: too formal. Tried pulling it back: too severe. Brushed it all out loose: too everyday. This is everyday, I chided myself. Go do something useful.

So when five-thirty came I was washing the dishes, with my elegant scarlet sleeves pushed up over my elbows, and frowning at a small open motorboat zooming toward my dock. I never went boating myself, being a martyr to motion sickness, and I had no patience with the seagoing cowboys who roared around the lake to show off. They were supposed to slow down near the houseboats; the speed lanes were out in the middle. And this one was coming in too close, as well. I left the dishes and crossed the living room and porch to the sliding glass doors.

"Hey!" I stepped on the deck, which was rocking slightly from the motorboat's wake, and shielded my eyes against the afternoon sun.

"Hey, yourself." The boat's driver cut the power and spun the wheel, coming to rest neatly against the deck's edge. I looked down into green eyes.

"Holt!"

"In person." He bowed gallantly, and his bright yellow slicker flapped in the breeze. Underneath it he wore a tuxedo. "Ready for dinner? Let me take you away from all this."

Chapter Sixteen

NOW, I'M JUST AS WILLING AS THE NEXT WOMAN TO BE SWEPT off my feet, but not off dry land. I get seasick at the drop of a deck. Holt didn't know that, of course, and he looked so pleased with his swashbuckling arrival at my back door that I couldn't bring myself to spoil it. So I grabbed my purse, smiled bravely, and took his offered hand. The boat bobbed and swayed as I stepped aboard—an ominous gap of dark water loomed beneath my feet. Holt slipped his arm around my waist to steady me. Strong arms, broad shoulders . . . maybe I could manage not to throw up on them.

"You look gorgeous!" he called over the din of the motor, whose fumes were already making my stomach roil. "You should always wear red."

"Thanks," I said weakly. "Um, are we making a long voyage?"

"You'll see." He wrapped a second slicker around my shoulders and revved the motor, tearing me away from the safe haven of my dock and out onto the lake. It was probably a fine June afternoon, and I bet the sunshine was pretty as hell on all the sailboats and cruise ships around us, but I didn't notice. I was praying to the gods of nausea to spare me, just this once. We headed west, across the width of the lake toward a seafood restaurant I'd been to before. Fine, I thought, I'll be stationary in minutes.

But no, we cruised past the restaurant's decks and picture windows, past the marinas and boat repair facilities, and fetched up against a dock next to, heaven help me, a float plane. As Holt tied the boat up I could see that the logo on the back of his slicker matched the one on the plane: "Eagle Air, We Get You There."

Holt looked back at me, the hotshot lawyer transformed into a ten-year-old kid shouting *Surprise!* "How does dinner in Canada sound?"

"Wonderful," I croaked. "Just wonderful."

And it was wonderful, despite the occasional lurch and swoop. I closed my eyes during takeoff, reminding myself that I was rarely motion sick on airliners, and this was just a miniature airliner that happened to be slamming along over the waves. The pilot, a beefy young guy in an Eagle Air T-shirt, made a wide circle over the city and the lake. Holt reached past me to point out my houseboat, a toy house with a toy dock, and the bright confetti specks of my barrel garden. We lifted higher, and Seattle fell away to wider views of Puget Sound: green islands crouched on silver water, white ferries cutting white wakes, and the Olympic Mountains standing guard to the west, echoed by the Cascade peaks to the east.

"I love this place," Holt said. "I'll always come back here."

Back from where, I wanted to ask, but the engine noise was too much, so I just smiled and relaxed, letting the sights distract me from my uncertain stomach. The flight took less than an hour, but offered a new and spectacular view every minute: the San Juan Islands below, cloud towers on the horizon, Holt's profile inches away. All too soon we were descending to Victoria, British Columbia, and a final test of my equilibrium—the landing. The pilot brought us in smoothly

to a floating dock, and I thanked him with real gratitude as
Holt opened the plane's door and jumped down.

I paused in the plane's doorway. Looking at him from
above, I realized that crooked teeth weren't Mr. Walker's only
flaw: In the middle of his wavy chestnut hair was a bald spot,
a small but stubborn harbinger of things to come. I smiled,
thinking ruefully of the crow's-feet that were sneaking up on
me. Holt glanced up, saw my smile, and passed a self-
conscious hand over his head, so I looked away as he helped
me down and steered me to Customs.

"Holt, this is wonderful! When you say out of town, you
mean out of town."

Victoria harbor was bustling with boats, from sleek cabin
cruisers to tall-masted sloops to chunky little workaday tugs.
Across the water, joggers and dog walkers and families were
enjoying the sunset from the promenade along the north
shoreline, and in the pretty little bit-of-Britain downtown, sightseers were window-shopping beneath the flower
baskets that hung from every lamppost. The stately old
Empress Hotel presided grandly over the holiday scene, its
ivied walls rising up to cupolas and mansard roofs and the
jaunty red maple leaf of the Canadian flag. Sea gulls wheeled
and called, as if in celebration, and I knew just how they
felt.

"I'm glad you're pleased," said Holt. "We can walk a bit
before dinner if you'd like."

"I'd like."

We walked to and past the Empress, our long strides
matching, and over to the grand facade of the Provincial
Museum. A lovely city, just foreign enough to be charming.
And a new red dress, a handsome man in a tuxedo, and the

prospect of food in the near future. What more could a woman ask? Especially a woman who's all style and surface, like me.

"Why the frown, Carnegie?"

"Just something in my eye. It's gone now. You were talking about Voigt, Baxter?"

"Yes, but I can't imagine why. I'd much rather hear about Made in Heaven. Are you ready to eat and tell me the story of your life?"

I laughed. "Well, ready to eat, anyway."

He led us down a narrow, quiet street, its windows glowing in the twilight, to a door with a gay blue awning and a brass plate inscribed *Les Oiseux Blancs,* The White Birds, and below that, *Bienvenue.* Inside, past a tiny vestibule, a tiny woman with silver hair and bright black eyes greeted Holt with a torrent of French. He answered in French, just as rapidly, and then introduced me.

"Mme. Lamartine, the owner of this establishment."

"Mademoiselle!" She cocked her head, quite birdlike herself. "M. Walker requested a special table, special menu, and I can see his reason before me. Come in, come in."

Special was hardly the word for that dinner. We sat in a secluded corner screened by a planter box of gardenias, their leaves dark and glossy among the pale blossoms. On the table, an oil lamp like a silver teardrop shed a steady glow over the pink linens and bright crystal. Between sips of pale wine and bites of crusty bread, Holt and I observed the room full of smartly dressed diners, making silly comments about them and laughing like old friends. He didn't ask about my head, and I didn't mention the accident, or the Parrys. All that was far away. When our dinner arrived, we turned away from the others and withdrew into a sense of perfect privacy. And perfect food: roast pheasant with chestnut purée, tiny new peas, and dark, earthy wild mushrooms.

"A toast." Holt raised his glass. "To entrepreneurs like Carnegie Kincaid. I really do want to hear all about your business."

"But why?" His fast-track legal career and my faltering sole proprietorship seemed worlds apart.

"Because I admire people who make their own way. And you're obviously so good at what you do. Nickie says you're the best."

"She's a pleasure to work with. Some brides aren't."

"I'll bet. Tell me some horror stories."

So I told him about the temper tantrums over napkin colors, the mother-daughter spats, the Byzantine seating arrangements needed to keep the groom's hard-drinking, twice-divorced father away from the bride's disapproving aunt. Holt laughed at all the right moments, and poured more wine. The waiter brought salads, each as perfect as a corsage, and Holt asked about the business end of Made in Heaven. I explained the marketing and financing and other nuts and bolts, including Eddie's crucial role.

"He keeps track of the billings, and our percentage from each product and service that we handle. It's a lifesaver for me. I hate paperwork, and he's really sharp about getting good deals for our clients. I just sign where he tells me to."

"How does that work out with a big wedding like Nickie's? Do you put up your own money and get paid at the very end?"

"No chance! Nickie's dress alone would have wiped us out." I almost told him about the Parrys' household account, and the mix-up with the bounced check, but I held back. Too much chatter, Kincaid. "Do you really want to hear all this?"

"Of course!" he said warmly. "I've never met a bona fide wedding planner before. Or is it wedding consultant?"

"Doesn't matter. It's a pretty loose occupational title, you know, not like attorneys or electricians or whatever. Lots of part-timers with an office at home, and some people whose real business is selling wedding gowns or invitations. They steer their customers to a brother-in-law who's a florist, and a cousin who's a deejay, and then they call themselves bridal consultants."

"And that bothers you."

I laughed. "Did I sound bothered? I guess I'm a little defensive sometimes, when people think that all I do is pick out a bouquet and order a cake. A wedding can be such a complicated, expensive event, like a business conference or a theater production. And yet it should also be a lovely, meaningful ritual for two people, and two families. Eddie and I cover all the bases, or at least we try."

"Looks to me like you succeed."

We paused a moment, while the waiter cleared our places.

"You know," I said, "this is exactly what I've been needing."

Holt looked up from the dessert menu. "White chocolate mousse with fresh raspberries?"

"No. Actually, yes, that sounds wonderful. But I mean telling you about my work. It's giving me a sense of perspective again."

"Which you were losing?"

"Losing my mind is more like it." I sipped the hot, aromatic coffee that Mme. Lamartine had personally poured for us from a scrolled silver pot. "One headache after another, petty anxieties, the trees instead of the forest. I really love my work. I love making a beautiful occasion for people like Nickie and Ray, being efficient about the business details and creative about the ceremony."

"Which wedding has been your favorite?" asked Holt.

I thought that over, luxuriating in his interest, his focus on me and my work. "Marty and Carol's, I think. Marty is a paraplegic. Carol's father wanted to walk her down the aisle, but she was afraid Marty would be self-conscious, waiting for her up front in his wheelchair. I don't think Marty cared, really, but Carol was really worried about it."

"So you did something brilliant."

"You flatter me, sir. But I did have an idea that made everyone happy. I rented an antique, this beautifully carved oak chair. Carol's father gave her away, and then she sat next to Marty on the antique chair and they were married sitting down. Everyone cried. Now I know that's just a little detail, some people might think it's superficial—"

"No one with any sense of romance," said Holt. "Or any sense of you."

Our eyes met, and I swear the table rose and tilted like a Ouija board at a séance. Holt took my hand and asked the fatal question.

"Would you like to hear some music?"

Music. Dancing. That was all I needed to go down for the third time. Holt paid the bill, called a cab, and whisked me away to a sophisticated little jazz club, where it seemed that a very special trumpet player was coming out of retirement to jam with his old combo, this week only. Holt had planned it all in advance, bless his heart.

There was just one little detail he didn't know. I *loathe* jazz. I know it's un-American of me, but anything except the most corny of Dixieland tunes makes my back teeth ache. The trumpet slides around queasily, the piano wanders so far from the melody that you'd need a Saint Bernard to fetch it back, and the drums hover sadistically close to a recognizable rhythm without actually settling down to one. And you can't *dance* to the stuff. Jazz makes me feel restless and unsophisticated and irritable, and the prospect of two hours of that followed by possible airsickness was enough to drive me to the club's sophisticated little ladies' room, close to tears.

"All right, Kincaid," I said sternly to the mirror. "He planned this as a nice surprise for you, you can grit your teeth for a while and try to enjoy it. Maybe there'll be a fire. Or an earthquake."

Holt welcomed me back to our table with another raised glass, this time a brandy snifter, and we sat back and listened. The set lasted a couple of centuries, with Holt nodding appreciatively while my eyes glazed over and I drank my brandy too fast. The piano player wore a toupee, and I tried to concentrate on how well it clung to his skull while he attacked the keys. At last the band took a break, and I applauded in gratitude.

"Well, what did you think?" Holt asked.

"Remarkable. Just . . . remarkable." I'm a poor liar, so I hastened on to safer ground. "And dinner was delicious, and the plane ride was great. But you know, what I really appreciate most is your interest in my work. You're a good listener. I can see why your clients trust you completely."

He stared down into his brandy, then drank it off with an abrupt movement that seemed unlike him.

"Carnegie," he began, and then faltered. "There's something I want to talk to you about, but I don't know how. I—"

"Another round?" The waitress startled us both. Holt frowned and shook his head. The silence stretched on, and I began to dread the arrival of the musicians. If Holt was feeling what I was feeling, it was time to get out of here.

"Could we go for another walk?"

"I'm sorry, have I made you uncomfortable?" He lifted his

hands in apology. "I don't want to take you away from the music."

"I don't mind, honestly I don't. Let's go walk by the water somewhere."

So we did, in silence at first and then in conversation that strained to be casual. Meanwhile, I was getting angry at myself. First I sit through a lot of music I hate, and then I let him do all the floundering when we reached the delicate subject of sex. Was that any way for a modern woman to behave? We came to a little park near the harbor and sat on a bench, the wrought iron chilly to the touch even in the warm evening. He put his arm around my shoulders, and I took the plunge.

"Holt, I think I know what you were trying to say, so why don't I say it instead?"

"But—"

"Would you like to spend the night together?"

His arm withdrew, he shifted away from me on the bench, and I knew on the instant that I'd made a bad mistake. Completely misread the situation. Put my foot in my mouth. Screwed up, big-time. Holt took a deep breath, then let it out and said nothing. A car drove by behind us, and from a boat out in the harbor a radio blared and then cut off abruptly. We both spoke.

"I didn't mean—"

"I shouldn't have—"

We stopped, and I tried again. "I'm sorry, I was rushing things, wasn't I? Forget I said that, please."

"It's not that I'm not attracted to you," he said. "God, I sound like a teenager. I can't explain—"

"You don't have to." His wife, I was thinking. He can't explain how much he still misses his wife. It was a big step for him to get romantic with me at all, and then I tried to blunder right into his bed. Such tact, such sensitivity. I wanted to jump into the harbor, but instead I stood up.

"How about some more strolling until we meet our plane? And this time I'll let you finish your sentence."

He agreed, but as we walked he changed the subject, and never returned to his difficult statement, whatever it was. Something about Douglas Parry, maybe? Or something about not saying stupid things to reporters? Of course, that was it: Douglas knew or guessed the source of Aaron Gold's quote, and Holt, as his attorney, was supposed to warn me to be more discreet in future. Should I take Holt off the hook by mentioning the gaffe myself? The more I thought about it, the more mortified I felt. In the middle of being warned not to shoot my mouth off, I charge right in and do it again.

"You mentioned a mountaintop ceremony," Holt said at length, as we reached the door of Eagle Air's little office. We were a few minutes early for our return flight, and a second beefy young guy checked us in and showed us the waiting room. Holt continued, "Don't tell me someone's climbing Mount Rainier on their wedding night?"

I explained Peter and Anita's plans for a backpacking honeymoon, and he told me about the ice climbs he'd done with a mountaineering club. He seemed determined to keep the conversation light and bright, so I followed his lead, and we both began to relax. Maybe my gaffe hadn't spoiled everything after all. By the time our plane took off, I had described the reception at the Glacier View Lodge, and by the time we landed on Lake Union I had invited Holt to join me there. Why not? My clients often asked if I wanted to bring a date to their weddings, often on the assumption that I was married myself. Peter and Anita certainly wouldn't mind if I had a friend for company at their prewedding dinner dance.

"Sounds great," he said, as we clambered into the motor-boat. "I'll have to check my calendar."

The lake was dead calm, and his voice had a faint almost-echo, as if it came to me from far over the water. As he started the engine I had the sudden illusion that the rest of the world had vanished in the darkness, that the shore lights falling behind us were just more stars in the night. Then we were across, and the moment was gone. Holt cut the engine, and I took the precarious step up to my deck, making it clear that I didn't expect him to follow. But I was still curious if I had guessed right about his interrupted message.

"It was a wonderful evening, thank you. And if you ever want to talk about, well, whatever it was you started to say—"

"Forget it." Holt's voice was cold, his face in shadow. Then he leaned forward into the homey light from my kitchen window. "Really, Carnegie, it wasn't important. Sleep well."

"You, too."

I watched the boat slide into the darkness, then unlocked the glass door from the deck. Once inside, I glanced across the living room, automatically checking for the little red light on my answering machine in the kitchen. It glowed steady, no calls. I turned away from it but then I stopped, motion-less, not even breathing.

Someone else was in the house with me.

Chapter Seventeen

THE EVIDENCE WAS INVISIBLE BUT CLEAR, AT LEAST TO ME: A faint scent in the air of my living room, sweet and spicy, but acrid somehow, bitter. I sensed it, and then, with a cold shudder, I recognized it. I had caught the same scent just before losing consciousness near the Parry rose garden. Not the soft perfume of roses, after all, but something sharper, something I couldn't identify but that I would never forget. The person who attacked me that night was here, now.

I bolted. I ran for the front door, for escape to my neighbors or the lighted parking lot, anywhere away from the trap that my house had become. Across the living room, through the empty kitchen, to fumble with the front door lock, tugging desperately at the stubborn knob. The door swung open and I stumbled outside. And smack into Eddie Breen.

"Jesus, Carnegie, what's the matter?"

"There's someone in there! Don't go in—"

But he already had, leaving me vacillating on the doorstep. The image of that dark figure in the woods had all the power of a nightmare, but if he hurt Eddie . . . Through the windows to my right, the bedroom light came on, then the bathroom light. I rushed back into the kitchen and down the hallway, grabbing a skillet from the wall above the stove as I went.

Eddie was standing in the living room, looking concerned, alert, on the job. My hero. "Nobody here now. Did you see him or just hear him?"

"Well, neither."

"What?"

"Wait a minute!"

I brushed past him to check the bedroom and bathroom myself, then looked around the deck outside. Except for the slamming of my heart, everything was dark and quiet, undisturbed. No receding footsteps on the planking, no roar of a car from the parking lot. I came back in. No unaccustomed scent in the air anymore, except for Eddie's aroma of cigars. I sat on the couch, still holding the skillet. Eddie took it from my hand and placed it carefully on the end table. Then he sat next to me.

"Carnegie, if you didn't see anybody or hear anybody—"

"I smelled him, Eddie."

"You smelled him." His expression was courteous and neutral, the face you show a small child while she tells you about the dragon under her bed.

I closed my eyes. "It's a long story, and it's late, and— What are you doing here, anyway?"

"Forgot something in the office. Have you been drinking?"

"What if I have!" I got up to put the skillet back in the kitchen, trying to walk away from the fear and embarrassment that were fighting it out in my mind. Eddie followed me.

"You better tell me what's going on, sister. I don't know whether to call the cops or a doctor. Is your head still hurting?"

"No, but it wasn't an accident, Eddie, I'm sure it wasn't. Somebody attacked me after the fund-raiser, either Theo or somebody else, and whoever did it was here tonight. He must have gotten away just before I came in."

"And you know that because you *smelled* him?"

Quickly, I explained about the bittersweet scent. I began to relate Aaron Gold's warnings about Keith Guthridge and his criminal connections, and to speculate about Theo's role in all this, but Eddie turned away from me to pick up the phone.

"What are you doing?"

"Operator, I need Douglas Parry, P-A-R-R-Y, in Medina."

"Eddie, I've got that number upstairs, but why—"

"Shh! We've got to do this fast." He nodded to himself as the operator gave him the number, then called it. "Hello, Parry residence? I need to talk to Theo, your driver. It's urgent. . . . Well, can you give me his number? No, it can't wait." A pause, more nodding, then he hung up and dialed again. Just as I realized what he must be doing, he held the receiver to my ear.

"Hello? Hello?" Theo's voice, blurred with sleep, then angry. "Who is it? What the hell—"

Eddie hung up the phone and looked at me, his snowy eyebrows lifted. "It takes, what, forty minutes to get to Parry's place from here? Say half an hour, speeding with no traffic. A little more than that to fall asleep. So unless this mysterious smell lasted all that time, I don't think Theo was here tonight."

"But somebody was!"

"You sure? Is anything stolen? Let's look around, check the office, and then we'll sit down and talk this over, OK?"

"OK."

We searched, Eddie skeptically and me with grim determination, for some sign that a stranger had invaded my home or the offices of Made in Heaven. We found nothing. No valuables gone, nothing out of place. I thought I caught the familiar scent upstairs in the workroom, but one window was open a crack to let in the breeze, and I couldn't be sure. My head was aching with a vengeance. It was two in the morning. We went downstairs without speaking, and I dropped onto the couch.

"Eddie, I don't know. Do you think I'm crazy?"

"I think you're scared, but I don't understand why. If you really think somebody attacked you the other night, you should go to the police. If you don't . . ." He shrugged.

"I don't know what I think, anymore. Aaron Gold's got me jumping at shadows."

"The reporter?"

I nodded, and told him about Gold's warning. It all sounded silly and melodramatic to me, and obviously to Eddie as well.

"Tell you what," he said finally. "I'll get my stuff from the office, and lock up tight. Then I'll come down here and sack out on the couch, how about that? You get a good night's sleep, and—"

"Eddie, thanks so much, but I feel ridiculous enough without needing a baby-sitter. You go on home. I must have been imagining things. If anything else happens, anything at all, I'll call the police and then you. I promise."

But nothing sinister happened, nothing at all. I overslept and woke up with nothing worse than a hangover, and called Eddie in the office right away.

"No more trouble?" At least he wasn't laughing at me.

"No trouble. I'll be up soon. Make the coffee strong, OK?"

I considered calling Holt as well, but why? He didn't know about my mysterious nonexistent intruder, and I certainly wasn't going to tell him. Upstairs, Eddie made no further mention of the night's adventure, and by midday I had just about put it down to brandy and nerves. Still, I wasn't giving up on my search for the owner of the gold card case. Next stop, the 418 Club. That evening Lily and I had our delayed chicken dinner at my place, then set off.

Compared to the Powerhouse, the 418 Club was a cinch. For one thing, they weren't playing bad music, or any music at all. For another, we were rescued before we did anything too ghastly.

I guess I was expecting a tavern, with beer signs and crowd noise. In fact, the 418 was quieter than most libraries. The large, low-ceilinged room, upstairs from a dry cleaner in Ballard, held about two dozen pool tables in orderly rows stretching off into the cigarette haze. Each was lit with a single low-hanging light fixture, with near darkness in between. Lily and I, hesitating at the entrance, could hear the occasional murmur of men's voices and the click of pool balls, and not much else. A sign near the door said "Please No Excessive Whistling. No Noise." I immediately resolved not to whistle, not a single note.

"How much time, ladies?" A weedy, round-shouldered man drummed his fingers impatiently on a glass display case holding pool paraphernalia, T-shirts with the club's logo, and a selection of cigars.

Lily was quicker on the uptake than I was. "What's the minimum?"

"An hour."

Our plan this time, after the gym fiasco, was to hang out for a while, maybe come back a couple of times, and then begin to ask around about Theo. We paid for an hour, and he handed us a black plastic tray of balls. "Table nine."

I almost asked for cue sticks, till I realized that dozens of them were ranged in racks around the walls. Table nine was in a remote corner near the restrooms. As we walked over, a few of the other patrons, who were all men, glanced at us in a less than friendly way. Judging from clothing, they ranged from bankers to panhandlers, but in this setting Lily and I were the odd men out. So to speak.

We selected cue sticks, cunningly going for straight wooden ones, then surveyed our table.

"Can you play pool?" Lily murmured.

"Well, no, but I've seen *The Color of Money*. We rack up the balls like this . . ." The pool balls were surprisingly heavy in my hand, and made a satisfying thump as I dropped each one into the triangular rack. I scooted the wooden frame forward and back to align the balls, and they clicked like M&M's do when you scrabble in the bag for them at the movies. "Then we lift the rack away and break with the white ball, like *this*—"

Unfortunately, I'd only seen the movie once. When I stroked the cue ball it popped off the green surface like a dolphin leaping from the sea. Lily lunged for it, but it sailed to the floor to land with an echoing crack. Lots of stares, a few laughs, and then a familiar voice.

"Christ on a crutch, Carnegie! What are you doing here?"

It was Eddie, just emerging from the men's room. He scooped up the still-rolling ball and handed it back to me, glaring indignantly through a little cloud of cigar smoke.

"Just trying something new," I said lamely. "Do you, um, come here often?"

He snorted.

"No, really, are you kind of a regular?"

"I guess so, yes. Why?"

"I was just wondering, do you ever see Theo in here?"

"You've got Theo on the brain lately. What's this all about, anyway?"

I glanced at Lily. She was studying her shoes. "Uh, Lily and I were thinking of taking up pool, kind of in private, so we wondered if we'd run into anyone we know here. Like you, or anybody else we know. Joe Solveto, or Theo, or anybody."

"Never seen either of them. The only familiar face I see around here is your friend the flower guy. The Russian."

"*Boris* comes here?"

He looked at me curiously. "Yeah. So what?"

"So . . . so I guess Lily and I better be going. See you tomorrow, bright and early."

"Good. We've got work to do."

Chapter Eighteen

THERE CERTAINLY WAS WORK TO DO, ON EACH OF OUR UPCOMing weddings, as well as marketing for new ones. I supervised the second fitting of Nickie's gown; Eddie met with Joe to wrangle over a contract for the reception dinner; and the two of us made what seemed like hundreds of phone calls, concerning everything from mosquito repellent to basque waistlines to exactly what kind of sippin' whiskey would suit Fay's kinfolk at her rootin' tootin' reception. Eddie and I worked well together, conversing in a brisk shorthand and making jokes about the latest dumb movie we'd seen. In between calls, I thought some more about Boris. About Boris and that unfortunate lamb.

One incoming call was from Lily, who reported no luck in trying to track down Crazy Mary through her list of homeless shelters. And on Friday morning, Holt called to say his calendar was clear for the party at Mount Rainier, and would it be all right if he booked a room for the night at the Glacier View?

"I won't actually come to the wedding in the morning," he said hastily. "I don't want to get in the way. But as long as I'm down there I'd like to hike around a little, and then I could ride home with you."

"That would be fine," I told him, swiveling my chair away

from Eddie to hide my ridiculous smile. "I'm out of town the night before, but I'll be back in plenty of time. Actually, I'm sure you'd be welcome at the ceremony, too. I'll mention it to Anita."

"Great. Where are you Friday night?"

"Ellensburg, setting up a wedding. I'll be back by noon at the latest on Saturday. So we could leave from here about one o'clock?"

"I'll be at your place at one. Well, I'd better let you get back to work."

"Yes. You, too." I could picture him, sitting in the high-power offices of Voigt, Baxter, McHugh with his thoughts straying off to alpine meadows. "Bye."

I hung up the phone, humming, then stopped when I saw Eddie's sardonic eye on me. But all he said was, "So when do you see the Parry girl next?"

"Eight A.M. tomorrow. She leaves at noon for a trip to Portland with friends. We're doing an RSVP count and a final run-through on the flowers. She keeps coming up with more relatives to pin corsages on, so we'd better order a few extra."

"That's your department, you and Boris. Just remember to ask her if she wants special champagne for the bridesmaids' deal."

"Luncheon, Eddie. Bridesmaids don't have deals. Oh, and Fay Riddiford changed her mind again about the barbecued ribs. . . ."

Finally it was closing time. I pushed aside my paperwork and took a minute to leaf through an antique etiquette manual, a recent gift from Lily. "Eddie, listen to this. Not only are white wedding gowns a recent invention, but they used to dress baby boys in pink and girls in blue! Pink was considered a stronger color, and blue was delicate and dainty."

"Just like you," Eddie snorted.

I stretched and yawned, not at all daintily. "Anything else for today?"

"Nope. Have a good weekend." He paused at the door-way to the front room, unlit cigar in hand. "Carnegie, about the other night. You never found anything missing, did you?"

I blushed and shook my head.

"Everything was OK up here, too," he said. "So we're agreed that it was just . . ."

"Just my imagination? Yes."

He nodded, then went on almost gently. "So you're not worried about it anymore, not feeling nervous?"

"No. Thanks for asking, Eddie."

"No problem."

What a sweetheart he was. Driving to the Parry estate the next morning, I marveled at my good fortune in having Eddie for a partner. Too bad most of my clients never met him, al-though he didn't always show well on short acquaintance. Nickie would like him, though, if he didn't growl at her. She was certainly happy to see me. She met me at the front door in a short terry cloth robe, her dark hair still wet from the shower, practically dancing with excitement.

"Carnegie, I've got this great idea! We could have the bridesmaids' luncheon in the rose garden instead of a restau-rant! Wouldn't that be elegant?"

She looked so young, and so inelegant, that I laughed aloud. "It would, but is there room for a table? I still haven't seen the rose garden, you know."

"Oh, that's right." Her face went solemn as she remem-bered my injury, and she led me inside. "Is your head OK?"

"It's fine, don't worry about it. Let's get started on the guest list."

"Couldn't we look at the rose garden first? I'll get dressed, I'll be right down. There's rolls and stuff in the living room."

In the Parry household, "stuff" consisted of Mariana's scones, still warm, and homemade blackberry jam. I was about to help myself when Douglas Parry came in, dressed informally but well, the lord of the manor on his day off. He had a sheaf of papers in his hand, and a frown on his ruddy face.

"Ah, Carnegie, I had something to ask you about." He seemed uneasy, running a hand over his thinning hair. "Is Nickie here?"

"She's upstairs. Is there a problem?"

"I hope not." He cleared his throat. "Are you associated in some way with Aaron Gold?"

"No! I mean, I've spoken with him, but associated, no. Why do you ask?"

"I, ah, have been able to obtain some of his articles before publication. This one is innocuous in itself, but since you're mentioned in it . . ."

I looked down at the printout he handed me. The headline read, "Seattle's Day Care Kids: The Economics of Motherhood." I sighed in relief. There were no direct quotes from me, only a reference to the valuable work of volunteers like Carnegie Kincaid, the storyteller.

"Just a coincidence," I said firmly. Not quite the truth, but close enough. "I met him briefly, that's all."

"You know that he's been causing me trouble? All my employees are under orders not to talk to the press, especially Gold, after he came snooping around at the fund-raiser.

You're not on my staff, of course, but I'd like to know that I can rely on your discretion."

"You can," I said, returning the printout. "My clients' privacy is important to me." *Too bad freedom of the press isn't important to you,* I added silently.

"Thank you." Having conducted his unpleasant business, Parry became a genial host, even overdoing it a bit. "Would you like some scones? Coffee? I'll have Mariana make a fresh pot."

"Maybe later. Nickie wants to show me the rose garden. Would you mind if we had the bridesmaids' luncheon out there?"

"Not at all, not at all." Parry beamed at his daughter as she skipped down the marble staircase. "I'll go out there with you two. We're five to eight degrees cooler here than in the city, Carnegie, so the growth cycle runs a little behind, but I've got quite a show by now."

He continued to talk roses as we descended from the back terrace and took the path under the clematis arbor. It was a cool, fresh morning, with the sun growing brighter behind an uneven, silvery mist. The mist, and my unfamiliarity with the place, confused me for a moment when we left the path and passed through another ornamental gate. I saw uprooted bushes, jagged holes in raw earth . . . was this a new section being added to the famous rose garden?

Then an eddying breeze cleared the air, so I could see the details of the destruction around us, and the naked shock on the faces of Nickie and her father. Every rosebush had been dragged out of the ground and trampled, or hacked off to a stump. What must have been a serene, geometric pattern of glossy green foliage and neat pebbled walks was now a chaos of dirt and twisted roots and splintered branches. The roses, in their silky hundreds, had become handfuls of tattered rags, the gay crimsons and seashell pinks and buttery yellows all fading now to withered brown.

At the heart of the ruined garden, a stone reflecting pool was fouled with mud and wilted foliage. Lying in its center, on a cruel bed of thorns and drowned flowers, was a sodden lump of something that had once been alive.

Chapter Nineteen

"GUS?" NICKIE'S WHISPER ROSE TO AN INCREDULOUS WAIL. "Daddy, it's Gussie!"

Her father tried to hold her but she darted forward to the stone lip of the pool, then crumpled to her knees. The dog's head had been smashed, his noble profile savaged into a mess of blood and bone. There was a moment's silence, then Douglas Parry began to swear in a cold, furious monotone. Nickie turned aside and retched. My own hands went clammy and my throat closed up as I held her shoulders and fumbled for a handkerchief, my thoughts plunging in a sickening spiral: such a sweet dog, this insane violence, they must have done it in the night . . . In the night, like the night when I came through these woods, the dark figure lifting his arms. *They could have done this to me.*

Slowly, horrified, I turned back to look. Douglas Parry had pulled off his jacket and was leaning out from the stone ledge to lay it over Gus, soaking the cuffs of his monogrammed shirt as he did. It was an absurd, generous gesture, and I loved him for it. I lifted Nickie to her feet and guided her back to the house, leaving Douglas standing in the sunshine among his dead roses.

An hour later I was still at the house, feeling much calmer and embarrassingly hungry. The tray of scones still sat on the lacquer table in the living room, but I could hardly dig in under the circumstances. Over and over, I'd watched the same series of emotions play across a different face: first Mariana, then Theo, then Alice the cook, then the maid and the gardener, and lastly Grace Parry herself, back from an early tennis date. Each one of them heard what had happened to the roses and to Gus, and each one reacted with incomprehension, shock, disgust. And finally, fear. Except for Theo, who went absolutely blank with outrage, we all showed fear.

Grace took it hard. Douglas met her at the front door, and I watched them from where I sat in the living room with my arm still around Nickie. They murmured together, outlined by the June sunlight that sparked and flared across the black marble floor of the hall.

"What?" Grace was incredulous, angry at the bearer of bad news. Or perhaps angry at him for permitting the squalid outside world to come so near. "What are you talking about?"

Douglas clearly wanted to spare her the sight of the destruction, but she pulled away from him and strode past me to the terrace, her tennis dress crisply white against slim, tanned legs. Her husband began to follow, then the doorbell rang and he let her go.

A dead dog in an ordinary neighborhood might have merited a single cop, but Douglas Parry's dead dog brought us Lieutenant Borden, the officer who had interviewed us about the Mustang crash. He was a barrel-chested, slow-moving man with an immense bald head and no expression whatsoever. He dispatched two uniformed officers to the garden and then settled himself ponderously into the largest chair in the room and began to ask questions. Nickie and I were dismissed quickly enough, and as I took her upstairs I heard him begin on the staff. Any strangers in the neighborhood lately? Any noises in the night? Did the dog usually sleep outside?

Nickie began to cry again, thinking about Gus's empty bed in the kitchen. I stayed with her until Mariana joined us, and then told her I'd call her Monday. Her trip to Portland had been postponed, and Ray was on his way over. We didn't mention the bridesmaids' luncheon. And I didn't mention Boris Nevsky, to the police or anyone else. Not yet. Not till Lily and I found Crazy Mary.

Grace Parry returned, her knees and sneakers dirty, like a tomboy who's been roughhousing in her party dress. But the look in her eyes was far from girlish. She must have knelt down, as her stepdaughter had, to look at Gus, and her face was still pale under her tan. On my way toward the front door, I heard Douglas Parry say the name that was on everyone's mind.

"Keith Guthridge," he said. "No question about it. He's responsible."

Lieutenant Borden said carefully, "Well, Mr. Parry, you may feel certain about that yourself, but this kind of vandalism—"

"Vandalism!" Grace Parry's voice, barely in control, cut across her husband's reply. "Is that what you call it? This isn't a broken window, for God's sake! We've had death threats!"

"Grace, stop it!"

At the sound of Douglas's voice I paused on the staircase, the chrome balustrade slick and cold under my hand, arrested by the tableau in the living room. Borden was immobile and impassive in his chair, with a young black policeman standing soldier-straight behind him, taking notes. Douglas

Parry sat across from them on the sofa, leaning forward, reaching out to calm his wife. Grace was on her feet, one hand pointing dramatically toward the lawn outside.

"Of course it was Guthridge!" She was nearly shouting. "He sent his, his *goons* onto our property, our private property, to scare us with this sickening—"

"Grace, stop it." Douglas stood and took her arm. "Lieutenant, my wife is upset; anyone would be. Could you excuse us for a few minutes?"

I hastened across the hallway and let myself out. The sunshine was bright now, almost hot, the sky a flat, faded blue. A car pulled up behind my van: the blood-and-silver Alfa Romeo I'd seen at the house two weeks before. The top was down, and Holt Walker was at the wheel.

"What a nice surprise!" he called to me. "I've been taking Grace's car for a test drive. She's trying to sell it to me. What do you think?"

I looked blankly at him, then at the car. "Yes. Yes, it's a nice car. Holt, something has happened . . ."

I described the havoc in the rose garden, and Nickie's discovery of her butchered pet.

"Oh, Christ, the poor kid." He looked at Lieutenant Borden's discreetly official gray sedan, and then up at the house. "How's Grace?"

"Pretty shaken up. She thinks Keith Guthridge did it, I mean had it done, to scare Douglas."

"She could be right," he said grimly. "He's up to his neck in King County Savings, and Douglas's testimony is going to sink him. That *bastard*. And the police won't find a clue, I'd bet money on it. Look, Carnegie, I don't want to butt in on them now, I was just dropping off the Alfa till I make up my mind. Could you take me back to town?"

We were silent for most of the drive, Holt in contemplation of the news, me in my own private quandary. Was my injury in the woods that night an accident or not? If not, then Theo was lying, and was actually working for Keith Guthridge. Could Theo be that good an actor? Could he be the one, with his weight lifter's arms and his lifeless eyes, who beat Gus's skull in?

"Carnegie, you're white as a sheet. What's wrong?"

"I, I . . ." I clutched the wheel and tried to concentrate, but it was no good. As soon as we were off the floating bridge I pulled over to a side street and brought the van to a clumsy halt in front of a run-down convenience store. I couldn't stop shaking.

Suddenly Holt was outside, opening my door and urging me over to the passenger seat. "I should have driven in the first place. You've had an ugly shock, and I bet you've been taking care of Nickie all morning."

I just nodded, my eyes closed. When I opened them we were entering the parking garage of one of the new waterfront condominium towers near the Pike Place Market.

"Come on up," Holt said. "You need a drink."

"I'm all right," I told him, but as I got out my knees began to buckle and I had to steady myself against a concrete column that said "Reserved" in yellow paint. "Actually, I need some breakfast."

"Lunch," Holt said, steering me to the elevators. "At this time of the day we call it lunch."

Feast would have been a better term, a small but exquisite feast. Holt's condo was twelve floors up, with a view that swept from the Market directly below to the islands in the Sound to the icy wall of the Olympics on the horizon. The terrace was just big enough for a table for two. He left me there in the sunshine with a glass of sherry while he brought out French bread, a crock of paté, a dish of plums, artichokes in olive oil. I gazed at it all, bemused, while he went back to the kitchen for coffee and a quick phone call to the Parrys.

"The police have left," he announced, setting down a glass *café filtre* pot and two mugs that said "Harvard Law." "Douglas has gone for a walk to blow off steam, and they've got a team of gardeners coming in to salvage the roses. And someone from a security firm. Douglas is hiring body-guards."

I pictured muscle men in sunglasses flanking the father of the bride at the wedding. Should I order two more bouton-nieres? I giggled.

"Carnegie," said Holt gently, "eat something."

I ate everything, remembering to compliment the cook only at the end, as I polished off a slice of pear tart.

"No cooking involved." Holt laughed. "I can barely boil water. I just wander around the Market stalls and buy what-ever looks good, one day at a time."

"Well, you did some fine wandering today." I set aside my untouched wine and took a sip of coffee. It was tepid. He really couldn't boil water. I put the mug down. "Holt, can I talk to you about something? In confidence? It involves the Parrys, but I don't know if I want to tell them about it. In fact, I don't know if there's anything to tell."

"Of course," he said. "Shall we go inside?"

His living room was spare but comfortable, with Scandi-navian furniture in teak and pale green cushions. All the drama and color was on the walls: framed, oversized photo-graphs of zebras through savanna grass, mountain peaks cloaked in storm, a purple dawn over endless sand dunes. And one collage of snapshots showing Holt and various other smiling, suntanned travelers, with those same exotic locales in the backgrounds. I sat down, almost sleepy from the food and sun, and told my strange little story. It took a while, but Holt was patient and encouraging.

"So you see," I concluded, "Theo couldn't have been at the houseboat Wednesday night. He was home in bed. But if some-one was there, and the same someone attacked me in the woods, then Theo must have been lying. He claims I caught a glimpse of him in the dark, panicked, and hit my head when I fell. And if Theo's lying, maybe he's involved in . . . in what happened to Gus."

"And working for Guthridge behind Douglas's back? Not possible." Holt shook his head. He was wearing a spotless white sweatshirt with his jeans, and he pushed the sleeves up over tanned forearms as he spoke. "Theo is completely loyal to Douglas, I know that for a fact. And he hates Guthridge, for Douglas's sake. He told me so himself, and I can't believe he was putting on a show for my benefit. So if we leave Theo out of it, then where do we stand?"

I liked the way he said "we." This was much better than Eddie's fatherly disbelief. We tackled the puzzle from every angle, with occasional digressions about Nickie's wedding, Holt's close relationship with the Parrys, and Theo's choice of wardrobe. We talked about Crazy Mary, and what she might or might not have seen. But after a while we were talk-ing in circles.

"So maybe there's no mystery at all." I sighed. "If Theo re-ally is telling the truth, then I really did fall in the woods. In that case, I must have just imagined the mysterious scent. And in *that* case, there was no one in the houseboat Wednesday night." I looked at Holt accusingly. "Which means it's all your fault. You poured me one too many brandies up in Victoria."

He leaned forward across the coffee table between us, and I did the same. "How can I possibly make it up to you?"

It's not easy, kissing across a coffee table, but it's not that hard, either. And if you push the table out of the way and find a delightfully thick, soft carpet underneath it, well, there you go. We took a long time to kiss before we shed our clothes. First his sweatshirt and then my blouse, his jeans, my skirt, and then he tossed one of my shoes over his shoulder. It landed out on the terrace with a slap that brought me to my senses for just a moment.

"Holt, I have to ask you something."

He looked down at me solemnly. "You want to know if we'll be seeing each other again."

"That, too," I said. "But right now I want to know if you have a condom around."

"Coming right up."

"Well, I can *see* that."

We were still laughing when he returned from the bathroom. Then we held each other close, and the laughter stopped. I traced my fingertips along his temple, his jawline, watching my own reflection in his green, green eyes. He kissed me, hard, and a wave of passion drove us against each other with a force that was close to violence. He was crushing me, I was clawing at him, pulling him to me, demanding to be crushed. It was over very quickly, like a wave breaking, a rising, racing curve that smashes into spray and thunder and disappears. I lay cradled in Holt's arms, listening to his heartbeat become heavy and slow against my heart.

The telephone woke us. Holt grabbed his jeans and went to answer it, leaving me chilled and befuddled on the carpet. It was obviously a client. Holt's voice was all business. I groped for my clothes and found my way to the bathroom. It was late in the day, clouding over, and I was suddenly anxious to be back in my own home before dark. As I washed and dressed, the sight of Gus's blood-soaked fur kept appearing in my mind, and the memory of Nickie's tears this morning clashed in an ugly way with the laughter and the passion of this afternoon. Sex with strangers and crimes in the night, I thought, struggling for humor to combat a mounting sense of depression. Enough of this. I want a cup of tea and a nice cozy chat with Lily.

But when I emerged, the man on the terrace holding my shoe was hardly a stranger. He was Holt, familiar again in his white sweatshirt, a respectable attorney, a friend of a client. And a genuinely nice guy. When he saw my forlorn expression, he made me laugh by dropping to one knee, a parody Prince Charming, to offer me my quite unromantic moccasin. It was very silly, and very charming.

"Size six glass slipper, my dear? I'd know you anywhere, you're the dame who's always leaving dances at midnight."

"Nine and a half narrow to you, mister," I retorted, and leaned on his bent shoulder for balance while I put on my shoes. "And now I've got to go back to my own castle."

He rose. "Are you all right, Carnegie?"

"Yes. A little shaken up, that's all."

"Me, too." He put his arms around me, offering comfort, asking for nothing. "God, it sounds so trite, but I haven't felt this way about anyone in a long time."

We stood quiet for a moment, and then the phone rang again.

"The machine will get it," Holt said. "I'm sorry I jumped up like that before. It's just habit."

He continued to hold me, but I could sense him listening, and when Nickie Parry's voice rose from the answering machine I stepped away.

"Go ahead and talk to her. I'm sure the family needs you. I've got to go." As I began to let myself out, I could hear Prince Charming changing back into the family lawyer.

"Nickie, hello. I heard about the garden and the dog, and I'm just . . . When? Where are you, which hospital?"

I turned back, my hand on the doorknob. Holt covered the mouthpiece and stared at me.

"It's Douglas," he said softly. "He's had another heart attack."

Chapter Twenty

"HE WAS JUST TAKING A WALK," NICKIE TOLD ME WHEN I TELE-
phoned her a few days later. I hadn't wanted to intrude, but
there were some wedding details that couldn't wait, and I
knew from Mariana that Douglas's condition had stabilized.
"He started having chest pains, and when he got to the general store they called Medic One." She stopped to yawn,
sounding like a drowsy child saying very adult words. "Sorry,
I've been sleeping at the hospital most nights. The doctor
said myocardial infarction, and then arrhythmia leading to
cardiac arrest. And they broke a rib, doing CPR at the store,
but thank goodness they knew how to do it at all. Everybody
was really great, at the store and then at the hospital."

Are they greater, I wondered, when the patient is one of
the wealthiest men in the state? But then I remembered my
father's final weeks, back in Boise. Not an important man, in
the eyes of the world, no matter how precious he was to my
mother and me. But the nurses and aides had treated him
gently and well. I shuddered, recalling my own nights spent
in waiting rooms, the medical smell and the unread magazines and the vending machine coffee in white Styrofoam
cups. At least my father hadn't needed bodyguards.

"I'm so sorry, Nickie. Is he, that is, will he be able to come
home soon?"

"A week, they think, maybe less. He's doing really well. He says he'll be at the wedding with bells on. But if the angioplasty doesn't hold, the little balloon thing he's already got in one artery, then he'll have to have bypass surgery." Her voice turned bitter, close to tears. "I just hope Uncle Keith is proud of himself. This is all his fault."

"Have the police found out—"

"They say there's no evidence, but who else would do something like that? Oh, Carnegie, the trial isn't till the end of August. What's going to happen between now and then? And poor Gus . . ."

I murmured my sympathy, but I glanced at the master calendar on my desk while I did it. Dress fittings and limousines seemed irrelevant at a time like this, but if the wedding was to stay on schedule I had to think about them. Douglas Parry's wife and daughter certainly wouldn't want to.

"Nickie, do you want to cancel the bridesmaids' luncheon?"

"Oh, God, I forgot about that. Grace says to go ahead with all the plans, so Daddy doesn't feel like he's spoiling things, and Ray says so, too. Could you postpone it?"

"Sure. I'll call everyone and set up a new date, at a restaurant." We sure as hell couldn't use the rose garden.

"Fine, whatever. Is there anything else to decide right now? I want to get back to the hospital."

I scanned my checklists quickly, and we ran through a couple of items including the final dress fitting. "I think you can skip the fitting, actually, but there is one thing. We forgot to have you try on your pearl necklace with the gown. The dressmaker wants to see the pearls so she can adjust the neckline to match. I could drive over and pick them up, if you want."

"Don't bother, Carnegie. I'll have Mariana send them over to you by taxi."

"I'm not sure that's safe," I said in alarm. It would have seemed risky even to transport the necklace myself, but dropping several thousand dollars' worth of jewelry on some cabbie's front seat was just asking for trouble.

"It's all right," Nickie assured me. "I'll send the fakes."

"The fakes?"

"Daddy has all our jewelry copied, for when we travel. The real ones have a platinum clasp, and the fakes have gold. I can't tell them apart myself, except for that."

"Oh." I'd never had my rhinestones copied, so this was news to me. "OK, send them over, then. I'll be in the office all day."

The necklace arrived at mid-morning, in a velvet-lined cloisonné case. Teal-blue butterflies danced across the white enamel surface, and ruby-red flowers rose up on golden stems. Inside the case, on teal-blue velvet, lay the necklace, gold clasp and all. The pearls certainly seemed real, each one a little marvel of curves and captured moonlight. The gold clasp was a tiny, ornate work of art all in itself. As I lifted the double strands with a fingertip I heard the outside door open, and I called out without turning around. "Hey, Eddie, you're late! Forty lashes."

"Sounds kind of kinky, but I'm willing to give it a try."

I turned. Aaron Gold, with a cardboard box in his hands and a smirk on his face. I closed up the pearls, dropped the case in my purse, and joined him in the good room, wrinkling my nose at the cigarette aura that hung around him.

"Don't you ever make an appointment, or call ahead?"

"Not when I'm doing a good deed." He dropped the box on our glass-topped conference table and began pulling out the contents. "Remember that supplement the *Sentinel* did on kids' books? Sure you do, you're a loyal reader. They were getting rid of all the review copies, so I snagged some for your story hour. I got mostly little-kid books, but there's a couple of teenage romances, too. Lots of bondage scenes, probably. You'll love 'em."

I smiled in spite of myself and looked over the loot. Fresh new books with bright colors and intact covers, not like the battered volumes I got from the library and Goodwill. "Well, thank you. Thanks a lot."

"No problem." He put his hands in his pockets and looked around. "So this is Wedding Lady HQ. Nice."

"We like it."

He glanced into the workroom. "Very professional looking, computers and all. How's the Parry shinding coming along?"

"Just fine." I could see what was coming. *Goddamn you,* I thought. *Goddamn you for living off other people's troubles.*

"I heard Douglas Parry is in the hospital." He jingled some pocket change. "Is he OK?"

"Mr. Gold, are all your bribes this cheap?"

"What?" He looked like I'd slapped him, which I very much wanted to do.

"Well, it's pretty obvious, isn't it? A stack of books that didn't cost you a dime, and I'm supposed to give you all the dirt on my clients. Or maybe there's a fifty-dollar bill at the bottom of the box? Do you get an expense account for this kind of thing?"

I expected an argument, a snappy retort, but Gold just set his jaw and stared at me. He walked to the door, stood with his back to me for a moment, then turned.

"Where do you get off, being this rude to me? Who do

you think you are? I was asking after the man's health, that's all." He began to say something else, then stopped himself. "To hell with it. The books are for those kids. You can throw them in the lake for all I care."

He passed Eddie on his way out the door.

"Nice-looking couple," Eddie said. "New customers, I hope?"

"Couple? What couple?" I went to the door and looked down the staircase to the dock. Gold was walking toward the parking lot, his arm around the shoulder of a pretty brunette in shorts and a baseball cap.

"I didn't meet her," I said. "But he's Aaron Gold, the reporter who called the other day. He was . . . I don't know. He was dropping off some books."

Eddie shrugged and went back to work, and so did I. Business was picking up, or at least inquiries were. We'd had four prospective brides call in response to our ad in a regional wedding magazine, and each one would get red-carpet treatment when she came in for her free consultation. Later on, if there was a later on for Made in Heaven, we'd charge for consultations, but right now we just needed to get people in the door. I tried to focus on that, and forget about Aaron Gold's unfair rebuke. He was completely out of line, and even if he wasn't, there was no harm done. I wanted him to stop pestering me about the Parrys, and now he would. Good riddance.

Meanwhile, we had just under two weeks until Nickie's extravaganza, and pages of single-spaced checklists to work our way through. A backup generator for the dance band's power source and the rental chandeliers, check. Gray silk ribbon, not black, to wrap the stems of the ushers' heather-sprig boutonnieres, check. Separate dessert stations for the

wedding cake, lemon sour cream with a bittersweet chocolate glaze, and for the groom's cake, a *mogador* of rum-soaked
chocolate genoise filled with raspberry preserves, check. And
a new item: a wheelchair stashed unobtrusively at both
church and reception, in case the bride's father had need of
one. Check.

There were a few snags, of course. Nickie's future in-laws
didn't like the reception dinner menu, and one of the flower
girls had chicken pox. Those were the routine problems. The
unexpected acts of God, or of Douglas Parry's enemies, were
another matter altogether. Every time the phone rang, I
braced myself for more bad news, but none came. No more
heart attacks, and no more ugly incidents in the night.

And no more bounced checks. Eddie grew positively
cheerful as the Parry invoices came in and the payments
went out, while our fifteen-percent fees piled up.

"We should specialize in rich people," he told me on
Saturday morning. We were both in the office for a couple of
hours. "A few more society weddings like this and you can
pay your mother's mortgage and buy her the house next
door. What about the Parry girl's bridesmaids? Are they all
heiresses?"

"No, she's disgustingly democratic in her choice of
friends. Come to think of it, though, one of them is a cousin,
so there might be money there. I'll try to fix her up with one
of the waiters at the bridesmaids' luncheon. Whirlwind
courtship, big wedding. Happens all the time."

Eddie chuckled. "That's the spirit. You have a good weekend. See you Monday."

The phone rang just as he left, so I was still smiling when
I picked up the phone and heard Holt's voice. We'd been
trading phone messages since our tryst on his carpet, always

just missing each other, but confirming a date for dinner tonight at my place. I was planning gin-and-tonics on the deck. And then barbecued salmon for the main course. And then me for dessert.

"Holt! We meet at last. I'm getting to know your secretary better than I know you. What time are you coming?"

"Carnegie, I can't make it tonight." His voice was subdued. My smile faded.

"Is something wrong? Is it Douglas?"

"Douglas? No, he's doing remarkably well, and the angioplasty is holding. Tonight I'm just tied up with a client matter, nothing to do with the Parrys, but I'm not sure when I can reschedule. It's going to be hectic for the next week or so, maybe longer. In fact I'm at the office now. I should go in a minute."

"I understand." And I would have, too, if only his voice hadn't been so stilted. I was busy myself; I'd had to cancel dates once in a while. But I also knew a brush-off when I heard one, or thought I did. "Well, I'll just see you when I see you, Holt. Bye."

"Wait, wait! I'm sorry, I don't mean this to sound . . . the way it sounds. We're still on for the trip to Mount Rainier, aren't we?"

"Are we?"

"Yes," he said, some warmth returning to his voice. "We are. And I'll call you before then."

Maybe he will, I thought, after we chatted a bit more and hung up. And maybe he won't. I am not, repeat not, going to waste time wondering. On that resolute note, I went downstairs to make myself a gin-and-tonic and fire up the barbecue. I had my own little feast, and went to bed early. With a book.

Chapter Twenty-one

I WAS JUST DOZING OFF WHEN THE PHONE RANG.

"Carnegie, it's Lily. I think I've found Mary!"

"Terrific! Where?"

"Well, it's not definite, but I talked to someone at the First Avenue Mission. She said Mary comes in most nights."

"What's the address? I'll go right over."

"No, wait. They're already full for tonight, so if Mary does show up in the next few minutes she'll be put on the van that goes to an overflow shelter. It's a church up in the Greenwood neighborhood. I'd go with you, but I've got to put the boys to bed. . . ."

"No problem. Just give me the address of the church."

Greenwood Presbyterian was a long, low brick structure on a quiet side street, deeply shadowed by maples. I parked near the back entrance, where a plump gray-haired woman stood under a streetlight checking her watch. Lily had told me to look for her, but I would have guessed who she was. She had the wise, weary expression of a career volunteer.

"Hi," I said. "Are you Irene?"

She nodded, and waited. I took a deep breath.

"My name's Carnegie Kincaid. I heard from the First Avenue Mission that a woman named Mary might be here tonight. I don't know her last name, but it's important that I speak with her. . . ."

"Why?"

I was afraid she'd ask that. "It's a long story, but she may have been a witness to something that happened at a wedding a couple of weeks ago, and I just need to ask her about it."

She frowned. "Are you from the police?"

"Well, no, but—"

"We try to protect the safety and privacy of our guests, Ms. Kincaid. Their lives are difficult enough, and this is the one place where no one bothers them. I wouldn't want to distress Mary—"

"So you do know her!"

She smiled, ever so slightly. "I know a Mary whose hobby is weddings, yes."

"That's her." I hesitated, but I couldn't resist asking. "Do you know *why*? Why she goes to weddings, I mean?"

Irene smiled. "She told me once it was for the cake. She likes cake."

"Bless her heart, I'll buy her a wedding cake myself. But tonight, if I could just speak with her for a moment? I mean if she's willing. Really, it's very important."

"All right, but only if she's willing. There's the van now."

The driver, a boyish young woman, hopped out and handed Irene a set of keys. I stood aside while she unlocked the doors to what looked like a vacant rec room in the lower level of the church. Light flooded from the entrance, illuminating the van's passengers as they filed inside: fifteen or so women of all ages, several of them black, two who looked Indian, all of them carrying everything they owned in life in their two hands. Plastic bags, knapsacks, even a small wheeled suitcase like flight attendants use, pulled by a brisk fortyish blonde in a navy pantsuit. She glanced at me and then away, and I wondered what her story was. I also wondered where Mary was, because she wasn't in the van. I followed the blonde inside and immediately Irene came to bar my way.

"She isn't here."

"I can see that. But if she does show up one night, could you possibly call me?" I held out my business card. "I could come right over, and I wouldn't bother her if she didn't want to talk to me. Honestly, Irene, it's terribly important."

She contemplated the card. Behind her, the homeless women were pulling foam sleeping mats from a pile in the center of the bare room, and blankets from a huge duffel bag in the corner. A few of them chatted, a few glanced at me, but most just made up their impromptu beds on the brown linoleum, settled their belongings beside them, and lay down in silence. One elderly woman cradled a teddy bear. I wanted desperately to go home.

"Please?"

Irene took the card. "All right."

"Thank you so much. She must be at one of the other shelters tonight—"

She laughed grimly. "Not necessarily. She could be sleeping in a doorway, or under a freeway overpass, or on a park bench. We do an annual count. The latest one showed about a thousand people living out on the streets downtown."

"Including old women? I'd hate to think—"

"Including two dozen children," Irene said. "Think about *that*."

I thought about it a lot that night, and the next day too, until Lily came to pick me up for our foray to Flair Plus. It turned out to be a white cement-block structure a few feet back from the traffic on Aurora Avenue, with a huge pink-and-black plastic banner draped across the front: "LIVE, LIVE, LIVE! 100'S OF PRETTY GIRLS AND 2 UGLY ONES!"

We sat in Lily's car and watched a fat guy in a narrow black tie taping a bunch of balloons to the front door, along with a cardboard sign saying "Now Open at Noon!" Then he went back inside, so we sat looking at the balloons.

"No point asking around in there," said Lily, finally.

"Who's going to give out anybody's name in a place like that?" I agreed.

"And besides . . ."

"And besides," I said, "we don't want to go in there."

"No. We sure don't. Let's go home."

Chapter Twenty-two

WEDNESDAY OF THAT WEEK WAS THE FOURTH OF JULY. IN PAST years I'd thrown parties, with beer and barbecue and front-row seats for the fireworks that went up from a barge moored out in Lake Union. This year I was in no mood to play hostess, but I was determined to take a day off. No paperwork today, and no pondering mysteries either. Maybe I'd bathe in sunscreen and spend all day on the deck with a novel. Or gorge myself on popcorn at the matinee of a scary movie. Or get out that Thai cookbook I'd been meaning to try, and make myself a fiery feast to eat while I watched the fireworks display. I thought of inviting Holt to share it, then banished the thought. Let him call me.

The phone rang.

"Ms. Kincaid?" An unfamiliar voice, crisp and confident. "This is John Hyerstay, Douglas Parry's special assistant. Could you meet with me downtown this morning?"

"Today? It's a holiday. Why do you need—"

"This is an urgent matter, Ms. Kincaid. Urgent, and private. I'm at our main office on Sixth Avenue."

"Has something else happened?" I had visions of Gus in that muddy pool. Who was next?

He ignored the question. "Would ten o'clock be convenient?"

"All right. But—"

He hung up.

By nine forty-five I was in an elevator, rising to the thirti-eth floor of a gray glass tower downtown. The Pike Place Market and Westlake Park had been festive with locals and tourists enjoying the sunshine, but farther south the finan-cial district was almost deserted. A security guard had unlocked the lobby doors to let me into the building.

"Not many people working today," he said with a sympa-thetic smile. "Sign in here, please."

I'm not working, either, I thought, as the elevator hissed open to the headquarters of Parry Enterprises. *I don't know what I'm doing.* The reception area was empty and silent, and my footsteps disappeared as I stepped from the zigzag par-quet floor onto a vast pink-and-moss-green Oriental rug.

"Hello?" I ventured.

"Good morning." John Hyerstay was about twenty-eight, and he looked like he'd been on top of the world for at least twenty-seven. He had curly brown hair and a trim mustache, and he wore a fashionably garish tie, Gauguin on a bad day. His left hand was dominated by a massive gold ring with two diamonds set off-center in a flat onyx field. He was not smil-ing. "In here, please. I'll be with you in a moment."

"In here" was a walnut-paneled conference room with tall windows overlooking the city. Eight chairs in wine-colored leather surrounded an oak table, and surrounding them on the walls were recessed alcoves displaying Kwakiutl and Inuit artwork—red and black wooden masks, intricate baskets, a carved soapstone polar bear padding along an icy shore above its own soapstone reflection. Classy.

"Ms. Kincaid, this is Sally Kroger, from the Parry legal de-partment. You know Mrs. Parry, of course."

Of course. Grace took a chair, elegant in her gray slacks and a paler gray silk sweater. Sally Kroger was a hawk-nosed woman of fifty or so, with short unruly hair and dark, level brows. I sat down across from them, more and more confused. Legal department?

Sally Kroger opened a folder. She kept it tilted away from me, but I caught a glimpse of Made in Heaven letterhead.

"Mrs. Parry has asked me to handle this matter," she began, in a low, husky voice. "We want to minimize any effect on Mr. Parry's health."

"I'm afraid Mr. Hyerstay didn't explain the purpose of this meeting," I said, mustering my most professional manner. "What matter are we talking about?"

She looked at me. What a poker player. "Surely you know, Ms. Kincaid. The matter of overcharging Mr. and Mrs. Parry approximately"—she glanced at the folder,— "twenty-three thousand dollars for goods and services related to their daughter's wedding."

"What?!" I was so stunned that when Grace spoke it was difficult to focus on her words.

"That's the total so far," she said. "Who knows what other phony invoices she's got floating around."

"Phony invoices?" I actually laughed. "Made in Heaven charges a fifteen-percent fee on everything we handle. That's stated in our contract and clearly itemized in our billing. I'm sure I can explain any misunderstanding."

"There's no point taking that innocent tone," said Grace.

"What tone? You show me one single invoice that isn't legitimate."

Sally Kroger put two pieces of paper on the gleaming oak surface in front of me. One was a photocopied bill, marked "Paid," for the French burgundies and Bordeaux served at

Nickie and Ray's engagement party at the Parry estate back in April. The other was a Made in Heaven invoice for the same wine, with our percentage added to the subtotal. But the subtotal, which should have matched the wine merchant's bill, was four thousand dollars too high.

After that came bills for tent and furniture rental, the florist's deposit, a couple of checks made out to cash for miscellaneous expenses. All of them altered in some way, to bring more money into my firm than we had paid out. My hands trembled as I paged through the evidence. This couldn't be happening, it wasn't possible, it was crazy. *Unless . . .*

She put down the final sheet of paper. It was a photocopied news clipping, almost ten years old. A St. Louis paper. I saw the name Breen, Edward V. Breen, and the words "tax fraud" and "decertified" and "agreed to plead guilty."

Unless Eddie had cooked the books. Eddie, who insisted I was undercharging the Parrys. Who had been so worried about my mother's mortgage, but was lately so optimistic. Who handled all our invoices. Eddie, who wrote the checks, or told me what checks to write, knowing there would be no questions asked. Who had lost his CPA license because he cheated on his taxes.

Eddie, who had shown up at the houseboat suspiciously late on the night of my date with Holt, with a flimsy story about leaving something behind in the office. Something incriminating, like a doctored invoice that I might notice in the morning before he got there to hide it?

"Well?" Sally Kroger took the papers from where I'd dropped them and gathered them into her file. "You mentioned an explanation?"

They looked at me, Grace triumphant, John Hyerstay suave, playing with his ring, Sally Kroger stern as a judge. I stared at the soapstone polar bear over Grace's shoulder, and I thought about Eddie. I couldn't imagine him lying to me, but the proof was right there on the table, the unimaginable was there in black and white. It was a nightmare.

"I need some time," I stammered. "I'll have to look into it, talk to my partner—"

"So you can confirm that your partner is responsible for this?" Kroger leaned forward, hungry for a culprit. "He seems to have had practice. . . ."

"No! No, I just meant that I'll have to go over the paperwork with him, and—"

"And what?" said Grace. "Concoct more lies? You should both be arrested."

"Ms. Kincaid," said Hyerstay smoothly, "our primary concern here is to shield Mr. Parry from any more disturbance. We are prepared to settle this matter quietly, today." Grace sniffed indignantly but let him continue. "We've prepared a document which terminates your contract, and which specifies that you will immediately surrender all paperwork and material relating to Niccola's wedding, as well as any undispersed funds." He glanced at Sally Kroger. "At Miss Nickie Parry's insistence, and very much against our advice, you will not be required to repay the money already misappropriated."

I didn't answer. I was concentrating, miserably, on trying not to cry. I took one long breath, and then another. "I need some time—"

"If you refuse," Hyerstay said, his voice rising as he slid a single typed page across to me, "criminal charges will be filed against you and Mr. Edward Breen. And of course we would be obliged to warn your other clients of the, ah, situation. You can take your chances in court, or you can sign the agreement. Now."

I pictured Fay Riddiford and Anita Reid being warned about embezzled funds. They wouldn't believe it, would they? Embezzled, what a bizarre word. I closed my eyes. I couldn't think, I had to talk to Eddie. But what could I say to him? Certainly I could say nothing *about* him, not to these cold-eyed people. They thought I was a thief, greedy enough to abuse Nickie's trust. Absurdly, I scanned my mental list of Things Still to Do for her wedding. Who would manage the rehearsal if I wasn't there? Who was going to revise the reception dinner menu to suit Ray's mother, and proofread the ring engraving, and order space heaters for the tents if the weather turned cold? Who had lists of last-minute violinists and a pocketful of straight pins and three handkerchiefs?

Sally Kroger offered me a pen. I could take it, and sign, or I could walk out of the room and into a new and ugly life as an accused criminal. My career as a wedding consultant would be over, my name would have a permanent addendum. I'd be Carnegie Kincaid—you know, the one who cheated Douglas Parry. And worse, far worse than that, would be the choice facing me: to plead guilty, or to condemn Eddie. I might, if I was lucky, be able to prove that he had deceived me as well as my clients. I might succeed in sending my father's friend, my own dear friend, to prison. If I was lucky.

I took the pen. Then I asked a question, sounding just as humiliated as I felt. "No publicity?"

"No," said Grace with obvious contempt. "For my husband's sake, and for Nickie's, no publicity."

I signed my name and walked out, my face hot and my lower lip trembling, the third-grader leaving the principal's office. Theo was there, leaning insolently against the reception desk. He stared at me, a pale smile on his pale face, as I waited for the elevator. I was damned if I'd let him see me cry, and that determination carried me out of the building, back to the van, and eventually to Eddie's doorstep in Ballard.

I drove north out of downtown, along the lake and over the ship canal, then west on Market Street, past the old brick storefronts. I breathed hard and slow as I drove, trying to contain my shock and shame and anger. How could he do it, I kept repeating to myself. How could he, how could he.

I pulled up in front of the tidy brick house with its severely trimmed shrubbery. I had only been there once or twice before; Eddie liked his solitude. A pair of ship's running lights stood guard at the front steps, red to starboard, green to port, or was it the other way around? *I've lost my bearings,* I thought foolishly. *No compass anymore.* I stepped wearily up to the front door, which had an old ship's wheel bracketed to the wall above it. I knocked and waited, then knocked again.

"Carnegie!" Eddie appeared at the corner of the house, a plastic flowerpot in one hand and a trowel in the other. For once, his clothing wasn't immaculate. He wore dirt-smeared khakis and an old cotton undershirt with crescents of sweat under each arm. "Is something wrong? More invisible bogeymen?"

His humor put an angry edge on my words that I didn't intend. "For God's sake, Eddie, this is serious."

"Well, go on inside," he grumped. "It's not locked. I've got to turn the hose off back here."

The door opened on a small square living room almost bare of furniture. Two chairs, a rag rug, a large television set. A brown glass ashtray on a metal stand. I sat on the scratchy plaid upholstery of a swaybacked recliner, and propped my

forehead in my palms. I could hear Eddie coming in through
the back door and washing up at the kitchen sink. Then he
stood in the doorway to the living room, folding back the
sleeves of the flannel shirt he had just put on. Making himself decent for company. His hands were old and gnarled,
seaman's hands like my father's.

"Now, what's so serious?"

"We've just been fired, Eddie. For faking our bills and
cheating Douglas Parry."

"That's nuts!" he sputtered.

"I just saw it, in black and white." The chair, and the
whole house, stank of cigars. I felt sick and disgusted, and I
wished I hadn't come. What was the point?

"Wait a minute, what did you see?" Eddie demanded. He
was standing over me, hands on his hips.

"Inflated invoices. Evidence of embezzlement." He
dropped into the only other chair, a monstrosity of avocado
green vinyl. I told him about my trip downtown, the grim
lawyer and the slick "special assistant," and Grace Parry's
sneer.

"So they won't sue, and they won't tell anyone. Not that
our good reputation will help much if we don't have any
weddings to do."

"Never mind our reputation. How did this happen?"

I looked up at him. "That's what I came to ask you,
Eddie."

"Ask me? Why would you ask me? Carnegie, you're not
making sense." He was indignant, concerned, fatherly.

Don't pull that on me, I thought. *You're not my father. My father wouldn't have cheated and then let me take the blame.* "I'm
asking you because there's only two of us in the office. And I
know *I* didn't fake any bills."

Silence, for just a heartbeat, and then the storm broke.

"You're accusing me? *Me?* Christ almighty, I've been keeping you in business for your mother's sake—"

"And what else have you been doing for my mother's sake?" I was on my feet now, raising my voice, saying everything I meant not to, doing it all wrong. "How come you're so upbeat all of a sudden about our finances and her mortgage? And how come you never told me you were a crook back in St. Louis?"

"That was all a mistake!"

I shook my head. "Eddie, we've got to talk this over calmly. I know you meant well, but—"

"Get out of my house."

"Eddie!"

"You heard me." He hauled open the front door. He was breathing hard, and his face was scarlet. "Get out of my house."

I left, and sat in the van for a long time. Then I drove to Morry's, a tavern near the houseboat with no view and no wine-colored leather chairs and no nautical memorabilia, and began to drink beer.

Chapter Twenty-three

MORRY'S IS NOT A BAR TO WRITE HOME ABOUT. ON THE ONE hand, it doesn't have seventeen brands of microbrewed local ale, or salsa made with fresh cilantro to dip your chips in. On the other hand, it doesn't have colorful whiskey-soaked characters and grimy linoleum and the midnight-at-noon atmosphere that makes white-collar workers feel like they're seeing real life. It's just a bar. The glasses are clean, the peanuts are cheap, and a woman can weep quietly at a table by the wall without being bothered.

For a while, anyway. I replayed my scene with Eddie over and over, trying to make it come out right, trying to make him not have tried such a stupid, dangerous scheme in the first place. I wondered whether Grace would keep her word about no publicity, or whether I'd start losing clients the minute she got on the phone to her friends. And I wondered whether Holt Walker knew about the accusations, or believed them, or would ever speak to me again.

I was on my second beer when Aaron Gold came in and took a seat at the bar. He ordered coffee and a corned beef sandwich—he still sounded like New York to me—then spun slowly on his stool, looking over the clientele, acting like he owned the place. I tried an experiment to see if the human body can be rendered invisible by the power of wishful thinking. It cannot. Gold brought his cup and his plate to my table and stood there, wearing cutoffs and a black T-shirt that said "Do Not Play On Or Around." He still needed a haircut.

"I owe you an apology," he said. "The kids' books *were* a bribe. That was stupid, and I'm sorry."

"OK." Little did he know how little I cared, at this point.

"I won't try to pump you anymore, I swear."

"OK."

"So can I sit down?"

I sighed. "Look, I'm having a very, very bad day. I don't want to talk about it. I don't want to talk about anything."

"Me, neither," he said earnestly. He snagged a newspaper off a nearby table and made a great show of settling down to read it while he ate. I didn't have the energy to leave, or ask him to. I just sat there, sipping beer and watching him read the paper. The silence between us recalled some highbrow French film, significant and yet boring. At one point he pulled out his cigarettes, then put them away.

"Go ahead and smoke," I said, "I don't care. In fact, give me one."

His left eyebrow shot up, but he lit us both cigarettes. I took a deep drag and recalled my brief, embarrassing college phase of dramatic melancholy.

"This tastes worse than the beer," I said, and kept smoking.

"You *are* having a bad day."

"One of the baddest. One of the very, very most bad." I wasn't drunk—I was painfully sober—but I was feeling numb and detached, at a distance from the unpleasant world. "Don't ask me why."

"How about if I ask you out to lunch?"

"You just had lunch."

"Well, an early dinner, then." He stood up and clattered a tip on the table. "I saw your van outside. Can you drive?"

"Who's taking who?"

"You drive, I'll navigate. Trust me, Wedding Lady, you'll feel better where we're going."

Since I could hardly feel worse, and since I no longer gave a damn for Douglas Parry's directives about consorting with the press, I went with him. We drove north on I-5, out of Seattle and up toward the pulp mills of Everett. I could think of a dozen better things to be doing, but they all involved Eddie or Holt or Nickie, so I just drove, trying to stay numb. Gold was quiet for a change, whistling softly to himself or making brief comments about the glorious weather.

Rain would have suited me better, but it would have interfered with Gold's plans. He had me take the exit to Everett Stadium.

"We're going to a baseball game?"

"Now, don't judge too soon. It's minor league baseball. A-ball. You'll like it. Real grass and free parking, genuine Americana. Not the Red Sox, I admit, but perfect for the Fourth of July."

He chattered on, vastly pleased with himself and his surprise, as we joined the steady stream of fans flowing into the little ballpark. A high-school band was just marching off the infield, their Independence Day concert completed. The sun shone on the trumpets and the tuba, on the advertising posters lining the outfield fence and the green foothills of the Cascades beyond the freeway. It was Americana, all right.

We sat in the bleachers, where Gold cheered and heckled and gave me a running explanation of the first three innings. I barely heard him. I was busy brooding about Eddie. How could he have done this to me? And how could I have thrown it in his face like that, practically guaranteeing that he'd deny everything just to defend himself? He was a fool; I was a fool.

"You fool, you idiot!" Gold shook his fist at the home team's manager, then addressed the heavens plaintively. "Why didn't he call for a hit-and-run? Why?"

"Because the runner on first is Tino Rodriguez," I said crossly, "and Tino Rodriguez runs like a chair with a broken leg. He couldn't steal second if he started the night before."

Gold stared at me.

"Your mouth is open," I remarked.

He closed it, looked away from me, and then back. "If I say, 'You didn't tell me you follow minor league baseball,' are you going to say, 'You didn't ask me'?"

I smiled, for the first time all day. "Probably."

Aaron Gold began to laugh. He dropped his head back and bared all his white teeth and *laughed*. By the time he was done, I was laughing myself, the people around us were laughing, even Tino Rodriguez was probably laughing. Lose a client, gain a friend, I thought. Maybe life isn't so bad. Maybe Eddie and I will work things out somehow.

"What else do you do that I don't know about?" Gold demanded. He wiped a tear from his eye and coughed a little, still chuckling. "Lion taming? Smoke jumping?"

"Just wedding planning," I said. "When I can."

He put his head to one side. "Is that the reason for the very bad day? You don't have to answer."

"I'd rather not. Let's just watch the game."

"OK, but no more of this silent treatment. Who's up here? Ryan? Can he hit?"

"In his dreams. Let's get a hot dog while he strikes out. It'll take him a while."

I enjoyed that game, and the drive back to Seattle, even though the traffic was already near gridlock with fireworks fans jockeying for positions to view the spectacle. I had to flash my resident's ID to get past a traffic cop who was rerouting cars away from the lakefront.

"Do you mind walking from my parking lot?" I asked. "I don't want to drive any farther in this mess."

"Of course not. Though I was hoping for an invitation to watch the big show from your deck."

"Well . . ."

"You've got people coming. No problem."

"No, it's just that the fireworks won't start for hours and . . . Well, sure, I could use some company. Quiet company?"

He raised a solemn hand. "You won't know I'm there."

He was as good as his word. In fact, he took a nap on my couch while I went upstairs and pulled all the files marked "Parry." I could have sifted through them, looking for more evidence, but what would be the point? I wanted the files, and the pain, out of the way as fast as I could manage. I stuffed them all savagely into the box that Aaron Gold's books had come in, and scribbled myself a note to call a courier service first thing in the morning and have it delivered to Grace.

Poor Nickie. No one is irreplaceable, wedding planners included, but she was going to have an anxious time of it for a while, picking up the pieces that had just been struck from my hands. Well, it would distract her from her father's problems, and she'd still end up marrying her own true love and bringing him a couple of million bucks as dowry. Meanwhile, I told myself resolutely, I'd do a wonderful job for Fay and for Anita, and Made in Heaven would succeed in spite of this fiasco. If only Eddie and I could make peace. If only I could trust Eddie, ever again.

I taped the box shut, lugged it into the good room, and went back to tidy up my desk. The answering machine was blinking patiently. Holt? I hesitated, then tapped the play-back button. Just one message, brief and bitter.

"Carnegie, it's Eddie. We've got a new client, name of Ogden. Rush job, so I booked a function room at the Four Seasons. Rest is up to you. The paperwork's on your desk. Also, consider this my letter of resignation."

That tore it. I went downstairs, woke Aaron Gold, and told him my troubles, at length and with frequent angry, tear-ful digressions. I didn't even ask him if it was off the record. Lily, or even my mother, would have made a better choice of confidant, but Gold was right there, and he had the sense to keep his mouth shut for the whole wretched story. If he had made a wisecrack at that point, or even given me advice, I'd have pushed him overboard.

Story told, I went out onto the deck and stood glaring at the boats jamming the water, one raucous floating party after another, everybody enjoying the long summer twilight while they waited for the big show. Gold joined me, and put a hand on my shoulder.

"I'm sorry, Carnegie. Eddie means a lot to you, and he dragged you into this. You must feel like hell."

"Yeah." I ran a hand through my hair. "Thanks for listen-ing, anyway."

"No problem."

"And please don't tell anyone about this."

"No problem."

Then he kissed me. It was a tentative kiss, made more so by the difference in our altitudes. He had to lift his face to me, and I didn't take my cue and bend gracefully down. I'd spent all of high school trying to look short by slumping, and I had promised myself long ago not to do it again. I took the kiss on the side of my chin and stepped away.

"Aaron, please don't."

He stood his ground. "Why not? I've been wanting to do that all day." He grinned. "Except for a few minutes at the ballpark."

"It's just that I'd rather be friends."

"Well, I'd rather not. So what are we going to do about it?"

I walked back into the living room. "Look, I just don't think—"

"What don't you think?" He followed me, smiling but implacable. "You're single, right? And you're not involved with somebody or else you'd have been crying on his shoulder, not mine. Or am I jumping to conclusions?"

I thought about Holt. Grace must have told him about the meeting this morning, but he hadn't called. If he believed in me, surely he would have called. I glanced at the answering machine on my personal phone. The little red light glowed steady, no blink, no message. No loyalty to the one-night stand.

"Am I?"

"What? No, you're not jumping to conclusions." I sat down, suddenly weary. "Actually, yes, you are. You're concluding that you can interrogate me about this, and I've had all the interrogation I can take for one day."

He sat beside me, still smiling his cocky smile. "OK, Freckles, my sense of timing stinks. But you've got to admit, we make a great couple."

"No, we don't!"

"Why not?"

Because great couples don't look like Mutt and Jeff, or Boris and Natasha, I wanted to say. Because you're nosy and you talk too fast and you dress badly and you're *short*. You're a little guy, and tall women like me don't fall for little guys like you.

What I actually said was, "Because we're . . . different, and I'm just not comfortable about it."

"Different, how do you mean different?"

Sheepish and defensive now, I stammered out, "I don't know, our points of view, our backgrounds . . . I can't explain."

"You can't explain. I see." He stood up, with an expression on his face that I was much too tired to decipher. He put his hands in his pockets and shrugged. "Never mind, don't try. Just forget I said anything, all right? Have a nice life."

He closed the door quietly as he left. I watched the fireworks alone, which suited me just fine.

Chapter Twenty-four

THE NEXT FEW DAYS WENT BY IN A MISERABLE BLUR. I PUT Aaron Gold out of my mind easily enough, but I did need a shoulder to cry on. Unfortunately, Lily had houseguests, and Joe Solveto had gone fishing for a week. But then I figured that the absence of my friends was just as well. Instead of wallowing in my ill fortune, I had to go back to work. I still had a business to run, and no one to run it but me. And with the flow of fees from Nickie's wedding abruptly cut off, Made in Heaven was facing a very uncertain future. So I holed up in the office for the rest of that week and the weekend, sorting out paperwork and planning a direct mail campaign to generate more business. I also crossed off my calendar all the items related to Nickie Parry, and got in touch with Claire Ogden, my new client. Her afternoon wedding at the Olympic was the same day as Nickie's evening ceremony. Well, it would keep my mind off the Parrys, and off Dorothy Fenner, who had graciously, not to say greedily, stepped in as my replacement.

Lieutenant Borden called me late on Monday afternoon. I had a moment's fright that Grace had gone public with her charges of embezzlement after all. But instead the lieutenant asked me a strange question.

"Have you received anything unusual in the mail lately, Ms. Kincaid?"

"In the mail? Like poison pen letters?"

"What makes you say that?"

"Nickie told me about some threatening letters. Have there been more?"

"We're just checking with friends and associates of the Parry family," he replied, with the practiced ease of a man who asks questions rather than answers them. "Have you received any unusual packages or unpleasant phone calls?"

"No, not a thing." *Associates*. So no one had told him I'd been fired. The knot in my stomach eased a bit, but then relief gave way to alarm.

"Packages of what? Like letter bombs?"

"No, nothing like that. But there has been a reference to the violence in Mr. Parry's garden."

"What kind of reference, Lieutenant?"

"It's not important for you to know—"

"*Please*, Lieutenant. I care about these people."

"Someone sent Douglas Parry flowers at the hospital. A bunch of dead roses. Tied up with a dog collar."

My hands were cold as I hung up the phone. Perhaps I was well out of it, at a safe distance from the Parrys and their troubles. Unless his condition had changed—and who would tell me if it had?—Douglas was due home from the hospital in a few days. Would there be more threatening incidents at the estate, even ringed as he was with security guards? Like Nickie, I was unfairly angry at the police for failing to stop Keith Guthridge's campaign of intimidation. And couldn't Guthridge see that he was only hardening Parry's resolve to testify against him? Unless, with his damaged heart, Parry had lost his spirit for the fight.

The phone rang again. I told myself, for the hundredth time, that it wouldn't be Holt, and it wasn't. It was my mother.

"Carrie, you sneaky thing, you!" She sounded almost girl-ish, laughing with excitement. "I just opened my mail!"

"Mom?"

"Here you've been sounding so concerned about money, you thought I couldn't tell but of course I could, and then this! I'm going to march right in to the bank first thing to-morrow morning and tell them to hand over my mortgage! Or wait, it's a cashier's check, do I have to deposit it first in my own account?"

"Um, I'm not sure—"

"Of course, dear, Eddie handles the money for you, doesn't he? He put the sweetest note in with the check. Why don't you two drive over here for a visit, some weekend when you're not too busy? I'm so proud of you, Carrie, for making a success of your business."

"Mom, Mom, wait a minute. Back up. How much is this check for?"

"Twenty-five thousand, of course. The full amount of your loan."

"Of course." I sat down at the kitchen table, with Sally Kroger's husky voice echoing in my head. *The matter of over-charging Mr. and Mrs. Parry approximately twenty-three thou-sand dollars* . . . Eddie must have thrown in two grand of his own. Big of him.

"Are you there, Carrie? Is something wrong?"

"No, nothing's wrong, Mom. I, ah, I'm just heading out the door for a meeting, and I'm late. I'll call you later, OK?" I couldn't, I just could not destroy her exhilaration with the ugly truth. Later, I told myself as we hung up, later I'll tell her that Eddie and I have parted ways. But I won't tell her why.

I did head out the door then, but only to pick up my mail. A familiar stiff, creamy envelope stood out above the magazines and bills, but instead of the hired calligrapher's elegant loops, my address was scribbled in hasty ballpoint. I tore it open as I climbed the stairs to the office. Inside, beneath the familiar, formal "Mr. and Mrs. Douglas Parry request the honor of your presence," and so forth, was a highly informal message.

Carnegie, it read, *I hate what happened, but I don't care whose fault it was. Would you come to the wedding? My mother will be there and I want you to meet her. I miss you. Love, Nickie.*

Attending Nickie's wedding would be a mistake, I knew that. Her parents would be furious, for starters. They might even risk a scene and ask me to leave. And did I really want to watch while Dorothy Fenner carried off the gala event that I had planned down to the last detail? Every note of music, every morsel of food, every inch of lacy ribbon fluttering from the bridesmaids' bouquets had come into being through my hard work. And Douglas Parry's money, of course. But now the money was gone, dishonestly buying me my mother's gratitude, and I had nothing left to show for the work but a crossed-off date on the calendar and Eddie's empty chair.

I tore the invitation in half and went back inside.

Chapter Twenty-five

IT WAS A MIXED MARRIAGE: SHE WAS CATHOLIC, HE WAS Klingon. Or something. The "rush job" Eddie had committed me to was a Star Trek theme wedding. I hate theme weddings, and Eddie knew it, the bum. In this case, the bridal couple and their science fiction friends had done most of the planning themselves, except that their choice of site had fallen through. There wasn't really that much for me to do, since Eddie had lucked into a cancellation for a small function room at the Four Seasons Olympic. I was only attending the ceremony at all because Lily insisted we go.

Lily, of all people. You think you know somebody, and then she turns out to be a Trekkie. I called her to complain, and all I got were eager questions.

"Whose wedding are they doing?" she demanded. "Worf and Dax? Tom and B'Elanna? Or maybe a new one, like Kirk and Uhuru . . ."

"Lily, I have no idea what you're talking about. All I know is, they're being married by a Universal Life minister who's going to wear Spock ears. And they wanted me to dress as someone named Jane, but I said no."

"Captain Janeway—that would be so cool!"

"No, Lily, that would not be so cool. I admit that their photography idea is cool: The guests are being given digital cameras, and they're going to post all the pictures on a Web site. That's given me all kinds of ideas for the future. But I am *not* dressing up for this deal and neither are you, all right?"

"Oh, all right. I'll meet you in the lobby at three."

As I drove downtown I couldn't help wondering about Nickie's wedding. Had Dorothy kept to my schedule, and gotten the formal photographs done ahead of time? It was so hard to take posed shots after the ceremony, when everyone wanted to cry and hug and rush off to the reception. And how had the studio shoot come off? Nickie planned to give her father a hand-tinted black-and-white portrait of herself and Ray, to set beside his treasured memento of his own parents' wedding day. What about the scruffy young videographer; had Dorothy gotten him into some decent clothes? And was Joe Solveto personally slicing the smoked salmon over at the yacht club, as he'd promised?

I shook off my regrets as I pulled up to the hotel. If I ever got married myself, I sometimes thought, it would be downtown at the Four Seasons Olympic, a gorgeously restored grande dame of a hotel from the 1920's. In the huge, three-tiered lobby, fluted gilt columns rise to a barrel vault ceiling, and the ornate chandeliers overhead are echoed by ornate flower arrangements below. All larger than life, and much more elegant.

Lily and I were heading up the marble stairs to the mezzanine when Alan Palmer, Joe Solveto's partner, waved at me from some easy chairs near the entrance to the Georgian Room restaurant. I was running a little late, but I always had time for Alan. Especially when he's chatting with the mayor's wife. Besides his chief career of being devastatingly handsome, Alan was a media buyer for a local ad agency, and a networker par excellence. Joe had recently suggested that Alan put me in touch with some families in need of my services.

"Lily," I said, "let's go schmooze. That's Vivian Wyble, and she's got unmarried daughters."

The two of them rose at our approach, and Vivian met my friendly smile with one of her own as Alan made the introductions.

"So nice to meet you," I said. "I met your husband recently, at Senator Bigelow's fund-raiser."

Well, I hadn't so much met the mayor as showed him where to park his car, but all's fair in love and small business. I just hoped she wasn't a pal of Grace Parry's.

"Yes, he told me how well it went. And Alan was just saying what a lovely job you do with weddings."

"That's kind of him. I'd love to talk with you sometime about . . ."

Alan was staring over my shoulder with the oddest look on his face. Vivian Wyble was staring as well, and she backed up half a step as if in fright. I began to turn around, but doom was already upon me.

"Kharrnegie!"

I got the full Boris bear hug, made additionally painful by a huge metallic sash he was wearing across one shoulder of an outlandish gray-and-black uniform. He also wore a bizarrely misshapen skull cap, a long shaggy wig, and fangs. Lily, at least, loved the whole look.

"Boris! You're Lieutenant Worf!"

"Affirmative!" he bellowed, putting me down. "Come, we must drink our fill of blood wine!"

Mayors' wives are a gallant breed. Vivian ventured a courteous smile, while Lily swallowed a giggle and Alan remained tactfully deadpan. I could hear the spirit of Dorothy Fenner snickering. Boris clapped a gorilla-sized arm around Lily's shoulders, grabbed my hand, and towed us upstairs to a room that had been transformed into somebody's idea of a spaceship. Or something.

Lily was in heaven, pointing out Starfleet officers and various aliens, and explaining that her mother used to watch the original Star Trek series and now her boys watched the latest one. The ceremony itself was mercifully brief, involving very down-to-earth gold rings. After scanning the crowd for Crazy Mary—would she like outer-space cake?—and downing a glass of "blood wine," a.k.a. merlot, I dragged Lily away. She stopped in the ladies' room, so I sat in the lobby and leafed through a copy of the *Seattle Times*.

When she returned I was weeping.

"Carnegie, what's wrong? Are you sick?"

I offered Lily the newspaper with hands that were suddenly cold and sweating. Crazy Mary's death got half a column on page two of the local news section. Well-Known Fan of Weddings Victim of Hit-and-Run, it read. Died instantly. The car in question located by police. Stolen, no fingerprints. Mary's last name was Jaeger. She left no family. Lily read the article, then sank down in a chair beside me.

"Oh, God, Carnegie. You think she saw someone that night, and now they've killed her?"

I nodded. I couldn't speak.

Lily folded the paper and clutched it tightly, taking deep breaths. "Carnegie, listen. I know I volunteered to look into all this with you, but now . . . I have to think about my boys. They don't have anybody but me. This is too dangerous. It's too dangerous for both of us!"

I held up a hand. "I understand, Lily. Listen, can you take a bus home?"

"Sure. What are you going to do?"

I stood up, unsteadily. "I'm going to crash Nickie's wedding."

Chapter Twenty-six

THE SIDEWALK IN FRONT OF ST. ANNE'S EPISCOPAL CHURCH was empty, and the arched double doors were closed. I parked Vanna in a handicapped spot and sprinted up the stairs. I had no plan: I just had to tell Douglas and Grace that their daughter was in danger.

But I'd have to do it after the ceremony. As the door banged behind me, echoing in the vaulted space, I could hear the sweet, precise notes of flute, cello, and violin scattering down from the musicians in the balcony, and the anticipatory murmuring of the guests. The candelabra were lit, and solemn young ushers were already escorting family members to the special pews marked with garlands of white ribbon and stephanotis blossoms. I slipped into a rear seat, trying to slow my breathing. I'd catch the Parrys before the reception, and convince them that Nickie and Ray should escape to the airport right from the church. Or should I actually try to stop the wedding? I couldn't decide.

"You must be Carnegie. Nickie described you to me. You've done a lovely job."

The woman beside me was in her fifties, with no cosmetics to soften the wrinkles around her tired brown eyes and the rough, uneven coloring of her cheeks. Her dark, heavy hair was as long as a girl's, and pulled simply back in a style that disregarded the many streaks of iron gray. She wore a plain sand-colored dress with a long full skirt, and her only jewelry was a heavy turquoise-and-silver necklace in a squash-blossom design.

"I'm Julia Parry."

How brave of her to come, I thought, when all Douglas's friends know the story of how she left Seattle, a drunkard, a bad mother, disgraced. And then I thought, with wild irrelevance, why did Dorothy seat her all the way back here? Well, I knew myself that divorced parents, especially estranged ones, make for interesting but perilous points of etiquette.

Julia was still speaking. "Your assistant was so helpful at the rehearsal last night. I realize that it's awkward, having to fit in ghosts from the past."

I looked at her more carefully. There was a glint of humor in that last remark, but also a somber dignity in her eyes. This woman had lied to herself for a long time, and now she lived quietly with truth.

"Dorothy's not my assistant," I whispered. "She's my replacement. Grace and Douglas thought I was cheating them. I wasn't."

"I see." She smiled, and I could see Nickie in her weathered face. "Well, then, we're both a bit superfluous, aren't we?"

I smiled in agreement, and glanced past her at an inconspicuous oak door near the end of our pew. The door, I knew, led to an enclosed corridor which ran the length of the church, from the dressing rooms at one side of the main entrance all the way down to the vestry near the altar. Ray and his best man would be waiting in the vestry now, and Nickie and her bridesmaids would be fidgeting in the dressing room. They would enter the church down the main aisle, but Dorothy could move unseen along the corridor between the groom's preparations and the bride's, or through the dressing room's outside door to the service parking lot where the dresses and flowers had been delivered.

The delivery vans would be gone now, the corridor empty, and Dorothy would be putting the finishing touches on the bride and her attendants. I imagined the scene: the flower girl would upend her basket of rose petals, someone would lose an earring, and Greta, the photographer, would take a snap of the bridesmaids clowning around that would later be one of Nickie's favorite memories. And Dorothy Fenner would be doing a fine job of orchestrating the whole affair, and no one would miss me in the least. Well, better to fret about that than think about poor old Mary, lying on the pavement somewhere. I should have asked Lily to call Lieutenant Borden. But what did we have to tell him, really?

A few late arrivals were still finding seats. Julia and I shifted down our pew, and I directed my attention toward the center aisle, trying to distract myself. Ray's brothers were both acting as ushers, just now escorting his parents and sisters to the front. Mrs. Ishigura's hair was still a gleaming ebony, but her husband's was a distinguished pepper-and-salt mix. They didn't look at all disapproving today, just quietly proud. I could see Holt, up front, sitting with the bride's family. Douglas Parry was already seated, next to Nickie's uncle and aunt; so he wasn't walking his daughter down the aisle after all. As he leaned across them to speak to Holt, I could see why. Douglas must have dropped twenty pounds since the heart attack, and his gingery hair only emphasized the slack pallor of his face. At least Keith Guthridge had had the grace to stay away tonight, and not upset him further.

The music changed tempo, and Grace Parry entered, moving regally past the guests on the arm of the handsomest

usher. She wore a wrap-front dress of palest green silk. It se
off her cornsilk hair and slender legs to perfection, and wher
she glanced up at her young escort with those strange ambei
eyes, the back of his neck turned crimson. Somehow I'd have
to get Grace alone, away from her husband, to tell her abou
Crazy Mary.

The ceremony began. The Reverend David Allington, silver
haired and spry, mounted the steps to the chancel and turnec
to face the congregation. Ray Ishigura and his best man, ;
lanky, curly-haired French horn player named Ted, were
debonair in their cutaway coats and gray ascots. The ushers
filed to the front and made a handsome line to the right, mosi
of them even remembering to stand up straight. The flute
trilled to a close, and the trumpet soloist stepped to the balcony rail and began the processional. Purcell's *Trumpet Voluntary in D,* an oldie but a goodie. Now, I thought automatically
First bridesmaid, step out now.

She did, right on cue, and there were smiles and sighs for
her lilac peau de soie gown and her bouquet of tulips and
narcissus and her nervous, lovely smile. The other bridesmaids followed, all of them so young and so pretty, enjoying
their moments in the spotlight. Then the maid of honor
Nickie's cousin Gloria, with her more elaborate flowers and
her impish smile. There was a pause while the attendants
arranged themselves on the chancel steps, and then we
waited, ready to ooh and aah over adorable little Piper, the
flower girl with the yuppie name.

And we waited. The *Trumpet Voluntary* went on, joyful and
inexorable, while our smiles of anticipation became fixed
and then faded. A long minute went by, then two. Indulgent
chuckles broke out here and there: Nickie's nervous, people
murmured, or the little girl is acting up. Reverend Allington

frowned, and then smoothed his face into patient benevolence once more. The trumpet wavered. My pulse was pounding. The murmurs grew, loud enough to cover the childish voice that reached me from a crack in the little oak door.

"The lady fell down," whispered Piper, peering around the edge. She was crying huge, silent tears. "I'm scared."

I went cold all over. I stood up, thrust Piper into Julia's comforting arms, and closed the oak door firmly behind me before sprinting down the corridor toward the bride's dressing room. The door was slightly ajar, and a sickly hospital smell reached me as I tried to shove it open. An obstruction behind the door gave way slowly, and then held. I shoved harder and squeezed through.

The obstruction was Dorothy Fenner. She was tumbled across the rug like a rag doll, her permed silver hair askew, her breathing hoarse and wet. Beyond her was an old overstuffed chair, one of several in the faded, mismatched furnishings, piled high today with the bridesmaids' street clothes, their hairbrushes and lipstick cases and crumpled tissues. But this one chair had nothing on it except a satin shoe. One of Nickie's. Inside the shoe was a piece of lined white paper, printed roughly in pencil. Dazed, in slow motion, I picked it up.

We'll tell you what to do, it read. *No police or you get her fingers in the mail.*

Chapter Twenty-seven

I STOOD HOLDING THE VICIOUS LITTLE NOTE FOR ONLY A moment, but it seemed like forever. I was strangely reluctant to release the paper from my hand, as if doing so would release a flood of events that must be held back at all costs. I had no sense of disbelief, no futile thought that this wasn't real, couldn't be happening. I didn't look wildly around the room to convince myself that Nickie was gone, or run frantically to the street door to try to catch a glimpse of her abductors. The deed was done, the terror and the grief would be all too real. But not until I opened my hand, and let the paper fall.

Then Dorothy Fenner stirred, and the trance was broken. I dropped the note and knelt beside her. The sickly smell was strong on her face and her silver hair. The door pushed open again and Julia Parry's face appeared above me, concerned but calm, responding sensibly to what she assumed was a minor crisis.

"Has she fainted? I can take care of her. I left the little girl with the woman sitting next to us. But Nickie had better hurry up." Then her face changed as she took in the rest of the room. "Where—?"

"She's been kidnapped." The word was spoken now, the flood had begun.

Julia went white. "Oh, my God. Oh, Nickie."

I was afraid she'd faint herself, so I gave her no more time to react. "Help me with Dorothy. I think it's chloroform or something—you can smell it."

I swept some clothes off a sofa and we lifted Dorothy onto it. She moaned and coughed, but her breathing was regular. Did she need a doctor, and would a doctor notify the police? The penciled words came back to me, and a nightmare image of a mutilated hand. I was almost grateful when Grace Parry walked in.

"What are *you* doing here?" Grace might have meant Julia, but she was glaring at me, her mismatched eyes narrowing like a furious cat's. I expected her to hiss and spit. "Where's Nickie?"

Julia told her.

"No. No!" Grace ran, as I hadn't, to the street door and pulled it open. Brick stairs led down to empty gravel. The service drive curved around the corner of the church to the street beyond. We could hear cars passing, but only the normal, indifferent sounds of everyday traffic. Julia's daughter, Grace's stepdaughter, had vanished into that traffic like a stone into the sea. Invisible, irretrievable.

"No, no, no." Grace slammed the door. "You're wrong, it's a mistake. It's *her* fault, she's trying to ruin the wedding."

Her words hit me like a slap. "Don't be stupid, Grace. There's a note there by her slipper, read it yourself."

I was sorry the minute I'd said it. Grace snatched up the white paper from the chair, and cried out in near hysteria as she read the last line. Julia read it too, and turned away, one hand pressed to her mouth.

"Julia," I said sharply. "Julia, can you stay here with Dorothy? She's waking up." She nodded, mute, and took my place at the sofa. I crossed the room to Grace and shook her by the shoulders. Her body was rigid, a beautifully dressed mannequin. "Grace, listen to me. I'm going to go get Douglas. Don't let anyone else in here, understand?"

She pulled away from me, but I could see that she was trying to control herself. I gave her a handkerchief, and shut the door behind me. But I didn't have to go far. Douglas Parry was coming along the corridor, impatience turning to anxiety as I watched. *His posture is shot*, I thought irrelevantly. *He walks like an old man. I don't want to tell him about his daughter.*

"How dare you come here?" he demanded. "How dare you interfere—"

"Never mind that. Douglas, something has happened to Nickie." His heart, I thought, how can I say this without endangering his heart? Parry was staring at me, but I could tell that I'd become invisible to him. "She's missing, and I'm afraid that—"

"Guthridge," he said hoarsely, and shoved past me toward the dressing room.

I slumped for a moment against the paneling. I had to tell Ray, and Holt. Surely Douglas would want Holt's advice. But no one else. The more people who knew what had happened, the more danger there would be to Nickie.

People. Now that I listened for it, I could hear the wedding guests buzzing like puzzled bees on the other side of the corridor wall. There were four hundred people out there, speculating wildly on the events backstage. I straightened up and smoothed back my hair. The Parrys saw me as an intruder, but they needed my help, and they'd get it. I hurried along the hallway, through the vestry, and up the chancel steps to where Ray Ishigura stood waiting for his bride.

Ray was too polished a performer to betray embarrassment before an audience, but his face was wooden with the strain of being left at the altar, even for a few minutes. He started slightly when I touched his arm. Reverend Allington was glaring at me, and the bridesmaids and ushers were gaping. Quietly, I told Ray that he was needed in the bride's dressing room, and he left at a dignified pace. Then I faced the congregation and held up a hand. People began shushing each other, craning to see me. I gave them a moment to quiet down.

"Ladies and gentlemen, I'm sorry to tell you that Niccola Parry has fallen ill. The wedding will not take place today. The ushers will show you out, beginning with the front pews. Thank you all for coming."

A babble of voices, blank looks from the ushers, questions from the maid of honor and the groom's father and everyone else. I wanted to scream, but professional habit came to the fore: I smiled brightly and politely, and ordered everybody around. For a few minutes, I almost had myself convinced that the bride really was ill, and that my only concern was smoothing out the resulting confusion. Just another Things to Do list to start checking off. The musicians, bless them, began to play the recessional, which helped me get the ushers into action. They stepped uncertainly to the first pews, and after some hesitation the guests began filing out. Most people are docile enough when someone takes the lead. The Parry and Ishigura family members stood their ground, however, and Reverend Allington bore down on me, a stern old eagle with his white head and black plumage.

"Miss Kincaid—?"

"Oh, Father, could you stay with the families for a few moments? I know they're worried, but there's nothing to be alarmed about."

I turned my back on him firmly and addressed the bridesmaids, who were twittering like flustered sparrows.

"Girls, I'll bring your street clothes and your purses out to
you in a little while, but we need the dressing room for
Nickie until she's well enough to go home. Where's Ted?"

"Right here. What's the matter with Nickie?"

"We're, ah, not sure yet. Listen, use the pay phone in the
foyer and call the Heron Bay Yacht Club. Get hold of Joe
Solveto; he's the caterer. Tell him the reception is canceled
and he should dismantle the tents and send everyone home.
Oh, and hang on to the wedding ring, don't lose it."

"Canceled? Why?" said a warm tenor voice.

I looked up at Holt, and the prospect of crying on his
shoulder almost cracked my facade of brisk efficiency. I
didn't let myself touch him. "Come with me."

I explained the situation as we went. The dressing room
door was locked when we reached it, but Ray heard our
voices and let us in. His hands were trembling, his jaw
clenched tight. Dorothy Fenner was sitting up on the brown
velvet sofa, looking queasy and upset, but uninjured. Julia
had brought her a glass of water from the adjoining bathroom, and was urging her to take small sips. Theo had arrived, and was looking around the room as if he wanted to
break something. Or someone.

Grace, still the angry cat, was stalking back and forth. If
she'd had a tail, she would have lashed it, back and forth,
back and forth. Douglas, in contrast, sat absolutely motion-
less in the overstuffed chair, holding the slipper in one hand
and the kidnappers' note in the other. His face was gray, his
eyes dull with shock.

There's nothing for them to do, I realized. *Here is this
calamity, this horror, and there is nothing whatsoever they can do*

except imagine Nickie terrified, Nickie screaming in pain, Nickie dead. The cold cruelty of it made me feel sick.

"Holt," said Douglas, and his voice broke. "They took my girl."

Holt took the note from him and stared down at it, then pulled over a straight chair and sat knee to knee with his old friend.

"They won't hurt her, Douglas," he said, trying to make it true, make Douglas believe it. "They said this to scare you. If we keep it quiet, we'll get her back safely. Now, first, are you all right? Do you need Dr. Fischer?"

Douglas shook his head, and seemed to become conscious suddenly of the other inhabitants of the room. "No, I'm all right, no angina. But Dorothy there was attacked by those bastards, those—"

"Take it easy." Holt considered the gray-haired woman on the sofa. "We can get a doctor if you need one, but . . ."

"I understand," Dorothy said weakly. "You have to keep this a secret. I'm so *sorry*. I didn't even see them. I came back to hurry Nickie along, but when I opened the door something covered my face, a cloth with a horrible smell . . ."

She shuddered, and Julia murmured something soothing and stroked her shoulders. Dorothy Fenner would have her share of nightmares from now on.

"And Carnegie, you found her unconscious?" Holt asked me. "What made you come in here in the first place?"

I had been standing quietly by the door, half forgotten, but now all of them fixed their eyes on me. Dorothy nodded gratefully, and Julia was still my ally, but Douglas, Grace, and Ray looked at me coldly, joining forces against the outsider. Even Holt seemed to withdraw from me somehow, an uneasy emotion stirring in his eyes. Was it the beginning of a doubt, a faint suspicion taking shape? I was a disgruntled ex-employee, after all, a discredited consultant who had conveniently shifted the blame for embezzlement onto her absent partner. A business owner whose business was failing. A woman who had been overeager to become intimate with a wealthy attorney.

"It was just by chance—" I began. But then there was a sound behind me, and Holt rose abruptly, upsetting his chair. Everyone's gaze had swung away from me and toward the doorway. Little Piper was standing there, her tears long gone, innocent but determined curiosity on her freckled face. Looped around her neck, hanging low on the bodice of her lacy little-girl dress, was a grown woman's necklace.

"Nickie's pearls!" Douglas barked. The child flinched, and he softened his tone. "It's all right, honey, I didn't mean to scare you. Where did you get the nice necklace?"

"From that lady's purse." Piper lifted one tiny hand, and pointed straight at me.

Chapter Twenty-eight

"IT'S NOT WHAT YOU THINK—" I BEGAN, BUT HOLT WAS AL-
ready at my side. I thought he was moving to defend me, to
physically stand by me against their suspicions. Then he
clutched my arm above the elbow, hard enough to hurt, and
shook that pitiful illusion right out of my head.

"Where did you get the necklace? Where's Nickie? *Where
is she?*"

"I don't know!" I pried his hand away, scratching him
fiercely with my nails, trying to hurt him back, drawing
blood. Grace rushed to us and seized his arm.

"Stop it, Holt!" she snarled. "Leave her alone! She doesn't
know anything!"

We've all gone mad, I thought. *This has to stop.* I held up
both palms and took a breath.

"That necklace is a fake, a copy," I said. "The dressmaker
was using it to alter the neckline of her gown to match the
real one. I haven't had a chance to return it yet." That was a
stretch; I hadn't even remembered it was in my bag.

"But why are you even here?" Grace demanded.

"Nickie invited me." No point telling these frightened, furious people about a bag lady run down in the street. Not
now, anyway.

Douglas was glowering at me. I had become the lightning

rod for all his impotent rage over Nickie. Ray was poker-faced, reserving judgment. Holt had gone very still. His distrust was almost a tangible thing, a cold wind that licked against my skin, trying to reach my bones, my heart.

"Piper told me Dorothy was sick," I rattled on. "That's why I came in here in the first place. I left Piper with Julia, and then Julia came to help me, and Piper must have found my purse under the pew."

"Of course she did," said Julia. "Don't be absurd. Carnegie's purse has been out in the church all this time." Her impatient, no-nonsense tone rebuked their suspicions and also my defensiveness. She rose from the sofa and knelt in front of the little girl, who was absorbed in playing with her new toy, indifferent to our adult bickering.

"This looks very pretty on you, Piper," Julia said gently, lifting the necklace over the gingery curls. "But it's time to give it back."

Still kneeling, she held the strand out to Douglas. He took it cautiously, as if to guard his daughter's possession as he had failed to guard his daughter. The pearls gleamed like moonlight in his ponderous hands, and he slid his fingers along them to touch the gold clasp.

"She's right," he said. "These are the imitations. Nickie's still wearing the real ones. Unless . . ."

Unless her kidnappers have torn them from her throat. The same image came to all of us, you could almost see it in the air: Nickie unconscious, in a windowless van or an anonymous motel room, blindfolded and gagged, with men's hands groping roughly at her body. I folded my arms across my chest, an involuntary and useless shield against the thought of violation. Douglas flung the necklace, clattering, into a metal wastebasket.

"Let's get Piper back to her mother," said Julia, smiling for the child's sake but warning us with her eyes. "Do you need me to help you find her, dear?"

"I *know* right where she *is*," said the girl scornfully. "She's at the front with the priest man. They keep talking and talking and it's *boring*. Where's Nickie?"

"She's in the bathroom," I said quickly, when the others hesitated. "She and Mrs. Fenner both got sick; isn't that too bad?"

"It certainly is," Julia said. "Piper, I expect your mother is ready to take you home by now. Run along."

"OK. But I'm still bored."

Julia locked the door behind her, then leaned her shoulders against it. Her graying hair had come loose on one side, drifting across the broken veins on her cheek. "What should we do, Doug?"

I'd never heard anyone call him that. Suddenly I saw them as Doug and Julie, twenty years ago, the young parents of a baby girl.

"What *can* we do?" Grace's voice sliced between Nickie's mother and father like a blade. She came to stand by Douglas, hand on his shoulder, at once claiming her place and barring Julia from it. "We have to wait for these horrible people to contact us, so we can pay them and get Niccola back."

"Pay them!" Douglas stood up, ignoring her touch, and suddenly he was in charge again—not Nickie's desolate father, but the head of Parry Enterprises. "This isn't about money. This is Keith Guthridge. He wants me to lie for him."

"Will you do it?"

It was the crucial question, but I hadn't meant to say it aloud. I wanted no more of their cold stares.

Douglas scowled. "I don't see that it's any of your goddamn business. You shouldn't even be here! Of all the nerve—"

Ray spoke up then, for the first time. "Carnegie has been
trying to help, Dad. She smoothed things over out in the
church." He looked at me, the stylish young bridegroom in
his traditional clothes and his trendy haircut, asserting himself with the older man. Of all of us in the room, he was the
calmest, the most single-minded. But his hands were still
trembling. "I do think you should leave, though, Carnegie.
Can you take Mrs. Fenner home?"

"Yes, of course. I'll go and get my purse." I reached for the
door, but Holt's voice stopped me.

"Before anyone leaves, we have to get one thing straight."
He sounded authoritative, self-possessed, as if he'd been in
control of himself and the situation all along. A trickle of
blood slid down his hand where I'd scratched it, gathered in
a bright bead at one knuckle, and fell, landing on the toe of
Grace's elegant little high-heeled shoe. Neither of them noticed. "We have to be sure that no one outside this room
hears about what's happened, for Nickie's sake. If Douglas
decides to bring anyone else in—"

"No police," Douglas said quietly. "No matter what."

"Agreed," Holt replied. "And no rumors, not one word that
might reach the kidnappers and force their hand. But your
house staff may need to know, so they can cover Nickie's absence at home. In any case," here he looked at each of us in
turn, as if we were members of a jury, "in any case, Douglas
decides who to tell, is that clear? It's imperative that everyone
else keep silent. Dorothy, are there any reporters here?"

She closed her eyes wearily. "The social columnist from
the *Sentinel*, I believe."

You shouldn't "believe," I thought. *You should know.*

"I'll go talk to her," Dorothy went on, but when she stood
up she swayed, and went even paler.

"I'll do it," I said firmly. "I've already made the general announcement, so people will assume that I'm working with Dorothy."

Holt looked at Douglas for confirmation, and he made an irritated, brushing-aside gesture with one hand. "Whatever is necessary. Just get everyone away from the church so we can get out of here. We'll take care of Dorothy."

"All right," I said. My mind switched gratefully from the ugly reality to the polite fictions, the created perceptions that were sometimes needed in my work. I addressed Grace, my former employer. " 'Niccola Parry came down with a violent case of the flu this morning. She thought she could go through with the ceremony, but regrettably it was not possible. Her parents will announce the new wedding date at a later time.' Is that all right?"

"Yes." Grace nodded, her cornsilk hair swinging smoothly. "Yes, that will do."

It took me less than half an hour to get the church cleared out. Julia and I ferried the bridesmaids' belongings out to them, and I assured the musicians and the photographers that their fees would be paid despite the cancellation. Reverend Allington wanted to see the ailing bride, but I explained that she was still sitting on the toilet with severe diarrhea, and he was so embarrassed that he swooped off to berate the altar boys for not extinguishing the candles.

Corinne Campbell from the *Sentinel* was no problem, not at first. She was a transplanted Southern belle, a sort of perpetual debutante who had carefully preserved her looks and her drawl. Her looks were remarkable, too: a waterfall of fair, curly hair, and a spectacular cleavage. Like the old vaudeville joke, she had a balcony you could play Shakespeare from.

Corinne accepted the flu story without a question. She

tucked her notebook away in her snazzy alligator bag, and plucked a wavy blond hair from the lapel of her snazzy pink suit. Then she went hunting for juicier meat.

"What a shame, after y'all did so much work." We were standing on the front steps, and she gestured prettily up at the church facade as if I'd had it built for the occasion. "But Carnegie, I am confused. I thought that Made in Heaven was no longer employed by the Parrys."

"Dorothy Fenner handled the final details," I said blandly. "We're working together."

"And why is that?" Corinne cocked her head flirtatiously. "Why couldn't you handle it all?"

"Well, a society wedding like this one is such a big job, as I'm sure you know. Dorothy has been invaluable, she's got so much experience with formal events." I took her by the arm and steered us both down the steps, just a couple of good old gals sharing a special moment.

"But didn't I hear that there was a *tiny* bit of trouble between you and the Parrys?"

"Now, Corinne, where would you hear a thing like that?" I silently consigned Grace Parry to the circle of hell reserved for liars and backstabbers. But then I remembered—how on earth could I forget?—the hell she was already in over the fate of her stepdaughter. So what if she gossiped a bit.

"Look, Corinne, I've got a lot to do, and Nickie needs my help." I dropped her arm. "I don't mean to cut you short, but I have to go back inside, OK?"

She smiled an icy Southern smile. "Just one more thing—"

"Oh, look, it's Boris!" I'd never been so pleased to see him, at least not since well before the lamb episode.

"Corinne, have you ever done a story about Boris? He's absolutely the florist to the stars, you know. Boris, over here!"

I left them standing on the steps together, like a grizzly bear grinning down on a poodle, and returned to the dressing room. Only Julia was left. She was picking up a hand mirror, framed in tortoiseshell plastic, from the floor near the sofa. Someone had stepped on it, making a spider's web of cracks.

"It's mine," I said. "I loaned it to the bridesmaids earlier on."

She handed it to me, and I gazed at my splintered reflection. Two haunted hazel eyes, more crooked than Grace Parry's, looked back at me from the crazed surface. I could hardly recognize myself. And I doubted Holt could either, now that my reputation was shattered. Would the seven years of bad luck be inflicted on the owner of the mirror, or only the person who broke it? Oh, lord, maybe Nickie broke it, or her captors, as they fought to steal her from her family and steal her wedding day from her. I went to drop the mirror in the wastebasket, but paused when I saw Nickie's pearls, the sad counterfeits, coiled at the bottom. I lifted them out, resolving to keep them against her safe return, and let the mirror fall. It made a muffled clang and a tinkle of glassy shards.

"Have they gone?" I asked, for something to say.

"Yes. They brought all the cars around back here, in case anyone was watching, so it would seem like Nickie was getting into one of them. Such a strange charade, isn't it? They're going to tell Mariana what happened, and the driver, I don't remember his name—"

"Theo."

"Yes, that's it. But no one else, and they'll give the rest of the staff some time off."

"How much time?"

She shook her head bleakly. "That's what we don't know, isn't it? Doug and . . . and his wife will wait at home until they hear something."

"But you're not going to wait with them?"

She looked at me, not defenseless but bravely undefended. No makeup, no hair dye, and no illusions. "I wasn't welcome. And this is hard enough for Doug without any additional strain."

"She'll be all right, Julia. She'll come home."

"I hope so. Dear God, I hope so." Finally, with my arms around her, Julia Parry allowed herself to weep.

Chapter Twenty-nine

THAT NIGHT, THE FIRST NIGHT OF NICKIE'S CAPTIVITY, MY SLEEP was invaded by the hands of silent, faceless men. Again and again, in my dark dreams, their hands tore fragile roses from the earth. Smashed a stone into the bloody carcass of a dog. Clamped a poisonous cloth over a gray-haired woman's face. Grabbed at a young bride, hurt her somehow, carried her off away from her family. And then, in a final apparition, the men's hands seized one hand of the bride's, pulled off her diamond ring, spread her fingers flat, and brought a chopping knife whistling down, faster and faster—

"No!" I sat bolt upright in bed, my own fingers clutching the sheets that tangled around me and draped to the floor. Panting and shuddering, I looked at the coldly glowing numbers on the clock radio: 5:07 A.M. Better to get up and face the demons of the day. The strain of waiting for news, and the lesser tensions involving Eddie and Holt and my business, were far preferable to those hands in the darkness.

As I stared out the kitchen window at the lake I wondered if I would actually hear the news when it came. In the melting, misty light, a flotilla of geese arrowed across the smooth water, their rippling silver wake stretching far behind them to the tarped-over sailboats and the silent docks. It would be a cloudy day, cool and still, a long, shadowless progression of hours to wait through until nightfall. Would Holt call me when they heard from the kidnappers? And should I tell him my suspicions about Crazy Mary's death, or did any of that even matter now?

Perhaps Julia would keep in touch with me, or Ray, but it was Holt I yearned to hear from. I wanted him to tell me that I had imagined the doubt in his eyes, that he had simply lost his temper in a moment of stress. That now, on reflection, he couldn't possibly imagine any link between me and Nickie's disappearance, even if he could imagine me as a cheat. And I swore to myself that I would not call him. I was ashamed of myself for thinking about him at all, at a time like this, but at least I wouldn't call him. Not today, anyway.

And I wouldn't call Eddie, either, much as I wanted to. What was there to say? My fury at him had shrunk into a hollow sourness. Sure, he was in the wrong and I was in the right, but I would have given anything to have my old Eddie back. Even more than Holt, I realized, I missed Eddie.

The teakettle screamed behind me, and I tried to get on with my morning. After letting one cup of tea, and then another, go cold while I stared absently out the window, I turned to my one reliable sedative: housework. Scouring the kitchen floor would be especially therapeutic, I decided, so I got down on my knees and stripped off the old wax, scrubbing ferociously in tight, hypnotic circles, and used an old butter knife to scrape up petrified spills that had lain undisturbed for months, maybe years. The helpless anger I felt over Nickie's plight transformed itself into an absurd determination to clean that damn floor. Finally, I sluiced it with clear water, mopped it dry, and spread the new wax with scrupulous care, as if it mattered. As if it would help.

Then I vacuumed the hell out of the rugs, and dusted

every horizontal inch I could reach. I even thought about nailing up a shelf to display the miniature cast iron stove. But I would have had to leave the houseboat—and the telephone—for the wood, so I set the little toy on the kitchen table, centered just so on one of my grandmother's crocheted doilies. I spent hours cleaning and arranging and fussing, and the phone never rang. Had Douglas heard anything? Would he break down and call the police?

I could picture Grace and Douglas in their living room, Julia at her hotel, Ray and Holt at their apartments, all staring at their telephones, waiting. Or had they gathered at the Parry estate, to pass the time in assuring each other that Nickie was far too valuable a hostage to harm? I wondered, with stubborn, morbid curiosity, what was happening to Nickie right this minute. She must know that her father would do anything to get her back. *Hold on, kiddo.* I clenched my hands and sent her my thoughts, wherever she was. *Hold on, don't despair.*

Finally, in late afternoon, I took a long hot shower, telling myself that if I stayed in long enough, the telephone would break its endless, unrelenting silence. Sure enough, when I twisted the faucets shut I could hear it ringing in the bedroom. Had it just started, or was that the final ring? *Wait, don't hang up.* Naked, scattering droplets everywhere, I ran to answer. Maybe they'd found her, maybe she was already home—

"Carnegie, this is Aaron Gold . . . Are you there?"

I sank down on the bed and pulled the coverlet around me. "What do you want?"

"Nice to talk to you, too. Don't worry, this is strictly business." He spoke quickly, getting it all in before I could stop him, but I didn't have the strength. And his voice, aggravating as it was, made a change from the silence. "Listen, I wouldn't be calling you at all, but the Parrys won't talk to me and that Fenner woman isn't at her office or her house. I just need to verify some facts. Can we do that?"

"Maybe." I was light-headed from skipping lunch, and from the hot water. I lay back on the bed, feeling my hair soak the pillows, and closed my eyes. "Stick to yes and no questions, all right? No multiple choice, no essays. No quotes."

"OK, then, Niccola Parry's wedding was canceled, right?"

"Right. Well, postponed."

"Postponed," he echoed. "Until when?"

"No date yet."

"And the reason for the postponement was the bride's flu?"

"Right."

"Nothing to do with Douglas Parry's health? Or a bomb threat from the people connected with Guthridge?"

"*Bomb* threat? Jesus, where do you guys get this stuff?"

"We pull it out of the ether. You have to admit, it makes you wonder. Here's Parry the dangerous witness, up against a guy like Guthridge and his backers, and then here's a church full of people being sent home all of a sudden. What's the real story, Wedding Lady?"

"There isn't one." There had better not be, for Nickie's sake. "The bride had the flu, period. Corinne Campbell was there at St. Anne's. Why don't you ask her?"

"Yeah, well, there's this slight problem of Corinne being a moron. She believes anything anybody tells her, and she's never heard of Keith Guthridge or King County Savings. Probably keeps her money in her mattress."

"No comment."

He chuckled. "By the way, how come you were at St. Anne's? Did the Parrys unfire you?"

"No comment."

"OK," he said, his voice turning chilly, "excuse me for caring. I'll forget that you used me as a crying towel on the Fourth of July."

I winced. "You haven't repeated any of that to anyone?"

The temperature dropped some more. "I am not quite the scum you think I am. I have not sold your personal life to the tabloids. And I hardly ever kick children or dogs."

"I'm sorry, it's just that—"

"What sorry? This is strictly business, remember? So— there was no emergency, the old man is healthy, the kids are still planning to get married, and everything's normal?"

"Completely normal," I lied. And I would keep on lying, to anyone about anything, for as long as it took to get Nickie home safe. Having a reporter around this situation was like pointing a gun at her head. "So there's no story."

"There's still the Parry story," Gold countered. "I've been digging up some interesting things about—"

"Look, I've got to go. I'm expecting a call—"

"Let me guess, from a lawyer named Holden Walker?"

"Holt Walker," I said automatically. Then I sat up, my hair slapping coldly against my bare spine. "What do you know about Holt?"

"Not a thing, except Corinne says he's romancing you, and that he's the quote catch of the century unquote. Oh, and of course my shrewd journalistic guess that he's tall, dark and Gentile."

"What?"

"Forget it. Stupid thing to say. None of my business."

"Boy, you've got that right." I banged the receiver down so hard that it stung my fingers. Then I got dressed, reheated some soup and ate it, and sat by the telephone with a book that I never opened. The phone didn't ring again that night.

On Monday morning I pulled myself together. I could stare at the telephone spinning nightmares about Nickie for the rest of the year, and it wouldn't do her or me one bit of good. Better to stick with my normal routine, both to keep myself occupied and to convince anyone who happened to care that nothing much had occurred Saturday at St. Anne's. If a headline hunter like Aaron Gold got even a hint of the truth, the police would find out within hours and Nickie's safety would be forfeit. I was hardly Gold's best lead, I knew, but I had nothing else within my power to help her. Business as usual, I told myself. My partner is an embezzler, and my lover thinks I'm capable of committing a heinous crime. And Thursday I'm supposed to do a perky, upbeat interview with *Washington Women Entrepreneurs* magazine, with a focus on Nickie Parry's wedding. Business as usual.

The first item of Monday's business was to call Joe Solveto. Someone owed him an explanation, however falsified, about the canceled reception. So I told him about Nickie's dreadful flu, and while I was at it, that Eddie had resigned because of poor health. End of both stories.

"This is going to cost her father a fortune, you know," said Joe. "The booze can go back, but all that food has to be paid for. I donated everything that didn't spoil to the Fremont Food Bank, but I'm not running a charity."

"I know, Joe. Dorothy Fenner will sort out the details with you later on. She's not feeling too well herself right now."

"That's the next question. Who's running this wedding, you or dear Dorothy? I'm getting, as they say, mixed messages."

"Dorothy is. I just helped out with a few things at St. Anne's. She has the account from here on."

"But how—"

"Joe," I said hastily, trying for a diversion, "Can I talk to you about Made in Heaven? Things aren't going well, and I could use your advice."

"Of course."

I briefly laid out the assets, liabilities, and prospects of Made in Heaven, concluding with, "I only have three other committed clients, and damn few potential ones. I've got cash flow problems, accounting problems, and maybe public image problems. Have you heard any unpleasant rumors?"

"Just a few snide comments here and there. Nothing too bad."

"But nothing good?"

"Well, people are saying you had a personal problem with Mrs. Parry, personality clash, that kind of thing. Did you?"

"You might say that. I resigned the account at her request."

"But nothing that would carry over to your work with other clients? I have a good reason for asking."

"Absolutely not."

I could hear him thinking it over.

"The reason is, I'd like to invite you to work for me. One of my assistants is pregnant. Cheryl, you've met her. She's quitting in September, and I need someone who can do large-scale event planning. You'd have to come up to speed on the food side, but your organizational skills are sharp, and you're good with society types. Cheryl's always been intimidated by them. I need someone more like me."

"Joe, I'm flattered." A job. A paycheck. Safe harbor after all the storms. But no more Made in Heaven. My brain wouldn't hold all this and Nickie, too. "I, um, I need some time to think about it."

"Of course you do. It's a big decision. You might want to fight it out on your own, and if you do, more power to you. Let me know."

Maybe it was selfish, but my time out from thinking about Nickie had done me a world of good. I worked my way through the day, and at dinnertime I even ran out for some pizza. When I got back, there were two messages on the office machine. The features editor of *Washington Women Entrepreneurs,* sounding ever so diplomatic, had called to tell me that my interview had been postponed indefinitely, what with the cancellation of the Parry wedding and, well, circumstances in general. Circumstances, I thought. What an interesting term for the mud being slung at my good name.

The second message banished that thought, and everything else. It was Ray Ishigura, asking for my help.

Chapter Thirty

I BARRELED DOWNSTAIRS TO THE KITCHEN AND MISDIALED twice before I got through to Ray's apartment.

"It's Carnegie. What happened? Have you heard from them? Is she—"

"Nothing. Nothing's happened yet." His resonant voice was taut and strained, a cello string stretched to the breaking point. "I just need to talk to you about something. Would you mind coming over? I don't want to tie up the phone."

"Of course." I scribbled down the address he gave me. "I'll come as fast as I can."

"Don't run any red lights with that fine machine of yours."

His attempt at humor made my heart ache. "I'll keep it under eighty. See you soon."

The evening traffic was maddeningly slow as I drove under the freeway and up the backdoor route to Capitol Hill. Past the Lake View Cemetery and the stately landscaping of Volunteer Park, the "millionaires' row" of mansions from the Hill's hey-day long ago, and the old brick buildings near Group Health Hospital, where I'd once had a studio apartment myself. I thought Ray lived in one of them, in fact, but his address turned out to be a ramshackle house on the east side of the hill, where it slopes down to the poorer neighborhoods along

Madison Street. Garages are rare on that part of the hill, and
the average life span of an empty curbside parking space is
measured in seconds. I finally found a spot several blocks
away.

Ray's apartment was a box with a piano in it. The gleaming Steinway seemed to take up the entire living room, making it clear that the tiny, clothing-strewn bedroom and the
even tinier and grubbier kitchen were mere annexes to the
musical life. Presumably Nickie would furnish their new
home. If they ever had one.

"Thanks for coming," said Ray. He glanced around as if to
offer me a chair, and seemed puzzled to realize that there
wasn't one.

"The floor is fine," I said, and he smiled slightly.

"That's what we've been using."

"We?"

"Hello, Carnegie." Holt Walker stepped out of the
kitchen. He wore summer slacks and deck shoes, and a loose
cotton shirt with blue and white stripes. He was carrying two
glasses of iced tea, like the perfect host at a patio party. I
wanted to hit him. *You don't trust me,* I wanted to scream. *I
was falling in love with you, and you doubted me, first about the
fraud, and then about the kidnapping. Who do you think
you are?*

I looked at Ray. "You didn't tell me—"

"I asked him not to." Holt handed one glass to Ray and
offered me the other, but I shook my head. "I was afraid you
wouldn't come. We treated you so badly—no, *I* treated you
so badly at the church. We were all upset, but still it was in-
excusable. I can't defend myself, Carnegie, but you have to
remember that Douglas and Grace were still angry at you.
They don't know it was really your partner—"

"Never mind how anyone acted," I said flatly. "Ray, why did you call me? Did the kidnappers finally contact Douglas?"

He sighed, looking very young and very weary. "No, not yet. But people are bombarding the house with phone calls about the wedding. It's getting crazy, and Holt thought I should call you."

"What about Dorothy Fenner? She's the one getting paid for all this." I was ashamed of myself the minute I said it. After all, as far as Ray knew, I'd lost the job through my own greed. But he didn't seem to notice.

"She's been in bed since the . . . the attack. Nickie's mother is staying with her."

"That's good." Julia Parry would be a calming, capable nurse, and Dorothy would be able to talk freely about the kidnapping. Maybe she'd talk it out of her system and her sleep would be more peaceful than mine.

"Yeah, it's a big help. But we need someone to talk to the press and the bridesmaids and the country club and everyone. To put up a good front." He looked bewildered at the tempest of attention that a rich girl's wedding could generate. "Grace wanted to do it herself, but Douglas needs her. He's feeling pretty rocky. It was Douglas who agreed that I should call you."

"I bet that took some persuasion," I said wryly.

Ray nodded. "He's still pretty bitter about, uh, that other business. That's why he didn't call you himself. But the woman from the *Sentinel* keeps calling, and then Lieutenant Borden showed up—"

"The police came?" said Holt sharply. His iced tea lapped over the rim of the glass and splashed on the floor. "No one told me that."

"It was after I talked to you this afternoon," said Ray. He

sat on the floor and leaned against the wall by the phone. I followed his example. Holt stayed standing.

"What did Borden want?" he demanded.

"It was about Gus, and the garden and all." Ray ran his hand, the one that should have borne a wedding ring by now, over his glossy black hair. "Mariana let him in, she's terrified of policemen. I think she's afraid if she causes trouble, they'll deport her or something. Anyway, Grace got rid of him. He didn't ask about Nickie at all."

Holt seemed to relax. He sat down across from me, but near enough to touch, and I wondered if he was remembering that afternoon on his carpet. I certainly was. I blushed, angry at my body for turning traitor on me, and hastened back to business.

"Ray, I'll do absolutely anything I can to help." I quickly reviewed the week's schedule and began to think out loud. "Friday I'm supposed to drive over to Ellensburg, to make arrangements for a wedding. I was going to stay there overnight, and then Saturday there's this reception on Mount Rainier, but I'll make up some excuse—"

"No." Holt set his glass down. "We need a day or two of your time, Carnegie, but that's all. We don't want you to jeopardize your business. Stick to your schedule."

He knew, only too well, how precarious my business was at the moment, and I had to appreciate his concern. But where was his concern at St. Anne's, when he saw the necklace and found me guilty until proven innocent?

"All right," I said, shaking off the thought. "Ray, I'll leave you the number where I'm staying Friday night, and at the Glacier View over the weekend. If there's any news—"

"I'll call you." The haunted look on Ray's face made me pray for news, good news, much sooner than Sunday.

"I talked to the caterer earlier today," I went on. "First thing tomorrow, I'll call everyone connected with the wedding and give them an update on Nickie's flu. In fact, maybe we should announce a new date for the wedding, just to make it plausible."

"Whatever you say," Ray answered, then added, with a wistful show of faith, "After all, we're going to need another date."

"Of course you are." I wanted to hug him. His nightmares must have been darker, and his empty hours longer, than any of ours. Instead, I pulled out my pocket calendar and a notebook. "Let's pick one out, and get a list started of people for me to call."

We worked on the list for an hour or more. Aaron Gold's name didn't come up, but we talked in general about getting the *Sentinel* off the track, and negotiating with the many vendors involved in the ceremony and the reception. We even discussed the etiquette of keeping or returning wedding gifts. I realized, partway through, that the two men must be as grateful as I was for the sense of purpose that these incongruous tasks were giving us. Anything was better than idle waiting. Finally, I got up to use the bathroom, and when I came back Holt was alone.

"I asked Ray to take a walk around the block. He needs it, anyway."

I crossed to the window and watched Ray stride down the front walk. "Poor kid."

"He's a strong young man," Holt said. "He'll hold up all right until he gets her back."

I turned to face him across the piano. "What if he doesn't get her back, Holt? What if they kill her?"

"They won't." He set his wide brown fists on the polished wood. "They won't. Douglas would never forgive Guthridge if they so much as hurt her, and Guthridge can't afford that."

"So you're sure it's him?"

"Of course." He slipped his hands in his pockets, the perfect host once more. As if he'd never misjudged anyone in his life. "Who else could it be?"

"Someone who's just desperate for money. Me, for instance." He flinched, and the movement gave me a perverse pleasure. "Or am I off your list of suspects now?"

"You were never on it."

"Don't give me that. All along, you've been so ready to believe the worst of me. First you thought I was a white-collar criminal—"

"I explained all that!"

"—and *then* you thought I had stolen Nickie's pearls, and maybe her, too!" My voice was rising to an unreasonable pitch, but I didn't care. "Why? Is it because I'm not wealthy like you, so I must be after something? Just one more gold digger trying to become the next Mrs. Walker? Or because I don't live up to the memory of your sainted wife?"

I stopped, shocked at my own words. Holt had gone white around the mouth. He drew his hands from his pockets. I held my breath. Then he stepped forward, and pulled Ray's piano bench out from beneath the keyboard.

"Oscar Wilde," he said carefully, "or maybe it was Chekhov, or somebody, said that you can change tragedy into farce by sitting down. Would you sit down with me, Carnegie?"

We sat, as far apart as the bench would permit. He brushed the fingers of one hand against the keys, making a soft ripple of notes in the dim, quiet room, and I recalled the touch of his fingers on my skin.

"I'm not the most trusting person," he said. "I'm sorry. I do have my reasons."

He pressed a single key, then another. The wrong one, apparently, because he went back to the first key and tried the sequence again. Another false note, but then he had it. *Blue moon,* the piano sang, in its lovely, mellow voice. *You saw me standing alone. Without a dream in my heart—*

Holt brought both hands down on the keyboard in a single discordant jangle, then let them fall to his lap. When he spoke, his warm tenor had flattened to a bitter monotone.

"My sainted wife married me for money. Except that I never made enough to suit her. We fought like animals, and when she drowned all I felt was relief. I never cried a single tear."

There was a long silence, and then he picked out the melody again. *Blue moon . . .*

I laid one hand on his, and he bent his head and kissed it. I stroked his hair, my fingers pale in the gathering darkness. Then he straightened up and looked at me with grief fathoms deep in his shadowed green eyes. "I'm so sorry, Carnegie."

I meant only to embrace him, to offer comfort, but the embrace became one kiss and then another, hard and intense. He slid his hands down my spine and then stood, half dragging me up with him, and we pressed against each other as if the heat of our desire could fuse us together.

"I want you," he said hoarsely, his lips against my throat. "Christ, I want you, I love you, I—"

The apartment door opened, and we broke apart so fast that I barked my shin on the piano bench. Ray stood swaying in the doorway, staring down at a small package in his hands.

"It was in the mailbox," he whispered. "It looks like the printing on the note, the note about not calling the police or else, or else . . ."

Holt reached over to take the package, but Ray wouldn't surrender it. Instead he set it on the piano and carefully, almost reverently, began to pull apart the wrapping. The sound of tearing paper was painful, but Ray's groaning cry was worse. Inside the paper, limp and heavy, lay the silken waves of Niccola Parry's hair.

Chapter Thirty-one

THAT NIGHT, AND FOR MANY NIGHTS AFTERWARDS, THE FACELESS men came again. But this time their groping nightmare hands were reaching for me. Over and over again I ran from them, calling out to Holt. But he couldn't find me in the darkness, and when the alarm went off I was more exhausted than ever. By Friday, the day of my trip to Ellensburg, I was dead on my feet.

Fortunately, Lily volunteered to do the driving, so that I could review my paperwork on Fay's wedding. Not that I could concentrate on anything but Nickie. I hadn't seen Holt since Monday night, when he dropped me at my van before driving Ray and that horrible package over to Medina. Both of them were spending most of their time at the Parrys' estate now, to provide moral support and wait for the kidnappers' next message.

So I spent the two-hour drive over Snoqualmie Pass staring at checklists and contracts without really seeing them, while Lily hummed along to the van's radio. Once in Ellensburg, we checked into a motel and parted ways until dinner. Lily went off to see her friends and I spent the day taking care of business and restraining myself from calling Holt until seven P.M., our prearranged time. The hours crept by, and finally I was back in the motel, hunched over the phone, listening to it ringing at the Parry estate.

Holt grabbed it on the second ring. "Carnegie?"

"Yes. Any news?"

"They finally made the ransom demand." He paused. "They want two million dollars, and a promise from Douglas that he won't testify against Keith Guthridge."

"So it *was* Guthridge!" I said. "Will Douglas go to the police now?"

"He doesn't dare. He told them he won't pay unless he hears directly from Nickie that she's all right, but he's already getting the money together. It's the business about the testimony that will really be hard on him. He'll have to keep silent, though. He'll never be able to let Nickie out of his sight again if he doesn't."

"I wish there was something I could *do*."

"We all wish that," Holt said ruefully. "But all we can do is keep up the appearance of normal behavior. The kidnappers knew that Lieutenant Borden had come to the house—that's why they cut her hair—so we know they're watching."

"So I should still go down to Mount Rainier tomorrow?"

"Absolutely. In fact, I'll still go with you. I'm beginning to think I'm doing more harm than good around here, because Douglas is embarrassed about being seen when he's so upset. I'm going back to my place tonight."

I cradled the phone with both hands, wanting to hold him. "I can't wait to see you. It's so crazy, trying to act as if nothing's wrong. I miss you terribly, Holt."

"I miss you, love. I'll be at the houseboat at one o'clock tomorrow afternoon, OK?"

"One o'clock." Just a few hours, really. But how many hours would it be until Nickie came home?

I met Lily at a steakhouse recommended by her friends. Ellensburg is a ranch town, and this was a restaurant where cowboy boots were footwear, not a fashion statement. We ordered steaks and a pitcher, and I nodded and smiled while Lily chattered. Nickie had been held hostage, a piece of merchandise with a price tag on her, for six days. I wondered if she was getting enough to eat, and when my steak came I couldn't touch it.

So I had another beer instead, and then another, while Lily switched to coffee. The country music began to throb inside my skull, and the laughter of the men at the pool table seemed cold and malicious. Damn them all, damn everything. Lily said something to me about checking in with her babysitter in Seattle, but her face was lopsided and her voice was far away. Another burst of laughter, and someone lit a cigar that smelled like Eddie's. What if I never, ever saw Eddie again? My wonderful, darling Eddie . . . I drained my glass and stumbled to the ladies' room.

Lily found me leaning by the sink with a wad of wet paper towels pressed to my forehead. "Carnegie, I've got to go back to Seattle. Ethan's got a fever and—Hello? You're drunk, aren't you?"

"Yes. Yes, yes, yes. Stupid thing to do, stupid to be here. I shouldn't have come. . . ."

"Well, you had to come, Carnegie, but your brain is sure somewhere else. Do you want to talk about it?"

"No." I made the mistake of shaking my head, and the room whirled around me. "No, I'm sorry, it's just . . . maybe another time. Wait, you said Ethan's sick?" Ethan was her four-year-old cherub.

"Yeah." Lily smiled mechanically, but even in my beery fog I could see the strain in her eyes. "No big deal. I'm sure it's only the flu. I just want to be with him."

"Of course. Let's get going."

"What about your appointments tomorrow morning?"

"I'll come back over next week. It'll be fine. Let's go home."

I paid for dinner, we checked out of the motel, and within half an hour we were driving into the darkness with Lily at the wheel, back over the mountains on Interstate 90, westward toward Seattle. Sagebrush ridges rose steep and black against the starry sky, pine trees marching across their crests in silhouette, like soldiers to some ghostly battle. I fell asleep just before the summit of the pass, and didn't wake again until Lily roused me.

"Carnegie, we're here. Do you need help getting inside? Have you got your house keys?"

"In my purse," I mumbled, sitting up. I could hear familiar sounds, water lapping against pilings, the houseboats swinging and bumping gently at their moorings in the darkness. I rolled the window down and the night air swept in, damp and chilly after the dusty sunshine of Ellensburg. My neck was stiff, and my tongue tasted like a bar towel. "But wait, I have to drive you home."

"No way," she said. "I'll bring Vanna back in the morning. Do you need your tote bag from the back?"

"No." I just needed more sleep, preferably horizontal. "Lily, I'm sorry you had to drive—"

"Hey, look, we all have our crazy times. You get some rest."

"OK. Love to Ethan."

I unfolded myself from the passenger seat. Lily handed me my purse, and I tottered down the dock as she drove away. The van burped and backfired, then all was quiet. I was queasy and shivering, grateful to duck inside my dark, familiar home. I left the lights off, in deference to the headache building up behind my eyes, and went straight to the answering machine. No blinking light, no messages. No word about Nickie.

Well, what had I expected? That my sudden return to town would miraculously bring her freedom? I slumped, defeated, onto the couch, and waited for the energy to take a shower and go to bed. Up and at 'em. But even hunting up some aspirin seemed too great a task, and the longer I sat the farther away the bathroom became. Beer, fatigue, and disappointment chopped away at my resolve like axes at a tree trunk. I swayed, and I fell. *Timberrr.* Tomorrow morning, I promised myself. Tomorrow morning I will get up and go straight to bed. Meanwhile I nestled into the cushions, hung my too-long legs off the too-short couch, and slept.

The key turning in my front door lock was a delicate sound, fitting neatly into a dream of my mother's house in Boise. In my dream the sun was shining, lighting up the gay pinwheel blooms of the dahlias that crowded her backyard. It all disappeared as I opened my eyes in the darkness. A creaking door, and footsteps. I yanked myself upright, my heart banging like a loose shutter in a windstorm.

Two men. I could hear them muttering to each other in the hallway off the kitchen, as if they had the house to themselves. Of course. I wasn't supposed to be here. There was no van outside; I was supposed to be out of town. That's why they could stand muttering inside my front door. Oh, Jesus, the door. The only door out, my only line of escape, and they were standing there in the shadows blocking it. Faceless men, men with hands that groped at me in nightmares, the men who took Nickie, who slashed off her hair.

I should have shouted, I suppose, screamed for the neighbors or called the police or something rational like that. But I wasn't rational. I was groggy with alcohol and half asleep and strained to the snapping point with the tensions of the last several days. I had one thought, and one only: *They don't know I'm here.* And if they didn't know, if I could hide and listen, maybe I could find out what had happened to Nickie, and whether Theo was involved.

But could I hide? What if they searched, what if they cornered me in a closet with knives in their hands? They were moving into the kitchen. I could hear their heavy steps; they'd be in the room with me in another moment. I could slip into the bedroom and out the window to the dock, but would that window open wide enough? Windows, doors . . . of course! There were doors just behind me, the always-open door to the sunporch and the sliding glass door from the porch to the deck outside.

I rose with the thought, crossed the room in a split second, then glanced back and saw my purse. It was lying on the coffee table, screamingly visible even in the faint illumination that fell across the room from the urban night outside. Advertising my early return, and my presence on the premises. I bit my lip and took another endless second to cross back and snatch it up, the patterned leather slipping in my trembling hands. *They don't know I'm here, don't let them know, hurry, hurry, hurry.*

Onto the porch; slide open the glass door; thank God it ran smooth and quiet in its metal track. Out to the rough old planks of the deck. I pulled the door closed behind me and gulped the cool air, but I was no safer, not yet. As soon as they stepped into the living room they would see me through this glass wall, silhouetted against the lights across the lake just as clearly as those pine trees against the stars. Which way to run? To the right, past the uncurtained kitchen windows and around to the dock? Or—

A flicker of movement caught my eye from inside. In a single simultaneous motion, as if the intruder's movements governed mine, overruling conscious thought, I dropped softly to the deck and slipped over the edge into the slick black water of the lake. My jeans soaked through in an instant, my shirt filled and billowed around me. I hung suspended, holding the splintery wood above with the fingers of both hands, while the cold water gripped me like a ruthless fist, squeezing the breath out of me in a single, painful gasp. My purse floated away, invisible in the shadows under the deck. I had to follow it, to disappear as well, but I hated like hell to let go.

Footsteps, vibrating through the wooden deck. I let go, sinking down and then bobbing up, desperate to keep the water out of my nose and mouth. I lunged forward and reached blindly into the darkness. My hand met something thin and hard, slimed over with algae. A wire cable, one of the many that secured the houseboat to the log floats beneath. It felt revolting, and smelled worse, but I clung to it like a child to its mother, trying to fight the vertigo. Trying not to imagine the murky depths beneath my dangling legs. Black depths of choking water, drawing me down, closing over my face . . . I forced myself to breathe, slowly and silently, through my mouth. There was barely enough fetid, dripping space for my head to lift clear of the surface, but that space was my only sanctuary. My hair drifted around me like seaweed. I held on, and waited.

Footsteps again, huge and hollow on the planking just inches above my upturned face. One of the men had come out on the deck. Had he seen me, heard me? Did he notice the telltale ripples that were spreading away from my hiding place under his feet? Silence. He shifted his stance. Then another set of footsteps, and the second man's voice, half-whispering, furious.

"Get rid of that, you asshole! She knows the smell."

No answer. But a tiny red-gold ember arced into the water and sputtered out, close enough for me to touch. And to smell. A spicy, acrid scent, the one I had recognized in my living room weeks ago, the one I had caught just before my fall near the Parrys' rose garden. So there *was* an attacker that night, and a real, not imaginary, intruder in my home when I came back from Victoria. He was here again tonight, and he smoked clove cigarettes. The discarded butt drifted toward me on the water's surface, level with my chin and my chattering teeth.

I clenched my teeth and closed my eyes against a greater vertigo. It wasn't the cigarette smell, and the revelation it brought, that held me paralyzed with shock. It was the sound of the second man's voice. A light tenor voice, which I'd heard so recently, murmuring words of consolation and love.

Holt Walker's voice.

Chapter Thirty-two

IT WAS ANGER THAT SAVED ME. AT FIRST THE SHOCK OF BE-trayal almost loosened my hold on the cable, and forced Holt's name aloud from my throat. But he and his companion would have hauled me out of the water like a hooked fish, and then what? The other man had attacked me once already, that night in the garden. The smell of his cigarette brought it all back: the dark swaying trees, the chilly wind, Nickie's jacket around my shoulders . . .

Nickie's jacket. Of course. I held tight to my stinking, slippery lifeline, and cursed myself silently for a fool. The man on the deck with Holt Walker had mistaken me for Douglas Parry's daughter there in the dark woods, and my supposed fall was really an attempt at kidnapping her. Nickie's abductor was standing directly over my head.

Along with his boss. That much was all too clear from the next words Holt spoke. "Andreas, what are you doing out here? We've got work to do."

"Thought I heard something." The reply was sullen, with a guttural German accent, inaudible to anyone farther than a few feet away. "Listen."

They listened, while I held my breath and made the ugly, mortifying connections, step by step. If this man Andreas had kidnapped Nickie, and if he took orders from Holt, then

Holt had planned it all from the beginning. Had deceived us all from the beginning. Not just when he let poor Ray open that package in the moonlight. Not just when he feigned alarm and outrage at St. Anne's, comforting Grace and Douglas in their grief. But before that, when he took me back to his apartment the day I found Gus butchered among the roses. When he made love to me—

That was when the adrenaline hit. *You made love to me, you bastard! You listened to all my little theories and you nodded sympathetically and then you put it to me, right there on the carpet. And I let you! In fact I came back for more, and all the while you were laughing at me.*

Fury, sheer humiliated fury, gave me a lifeline then, as distasteful but as solid as the cable I clung to. Holt and his buddy weren't going to haul me out of the water, because they weren't going to know I was there. I'd wait them out if it took all night. Above me, their footsteps shifted, then moved back inside. I slid gingerly along my cable, flinching as a sliver of wire bit into my palm, and strained to hear them. What work was there to do in my house, and how was it connected with Nickie?

I couldn't think. My feet had gone numb, and the long bones of my legs were throbbing with cold. The silence from above stretched out, minute by minute, and with each minute the prospect of holding out all night grew more remote. Surely if I paddled away now, they wouldn't notice the ripples on the dark lake?

The floats beneath the houseboat swung and creaked. From inside, it had always been a familiar, homey sound, one that formed the background of my dreams each night. But from where I hung now in the water, helpless and sodden, it sounded ominous, almost alive, a beast moving in a watery cave. I'd have to swim *under* the floats at some point, to reach the dock itself and work my way along it to the parking lot and the street. If I lost my bearings under the houseboat, if I ran out of breath and tried to come up before I reached clear water, hit my head or tangled myself in the wires and ropes—

Something nudged my shoulder and I whipped my dripping head around. A piece of unidentifiable garbage, caught in the backwater made by the floats. Just like my corpse would be, if I didn't get out of here soon. *Don't think about it, just move.* I continued hand over hand along the cable, away from the deck edge and further into the darkness, trying to get up my nerve to dive under the houseboat. Then I had a better idea. What if I swam *across* instead, to the end of the next dock? Once I got there, I'd have more cover from their searching eyes, and less chance of alerting them with the sound of my escape. But I also ran the risk that they would glance out the kitchen windows and see me as I crossed the gap between the two docks.

"Vat about in here?"

The German voice again, from the study window. I couldn't make out the words of Holt's reply, and I didn't wait to hear more. The study was a tiny room beyond the bedroom, the entire length of the houseboat away from the kitchen. If they were both in there now, I had at least a minute or two in which to cross the open water between the docks. I pried my aching hands from the cable and dog-paddled along the weedy log that rose up at my shoulder. *Anyone can swim.* Lily had tried to teach me once, at a hotel pool in Vancouver. *The human body is naturally buoyant. Just relax. Stroke and kick.*

I stroked and floundered, one hand and then the other lifted to ward off the treacherous wires, straining to keep my

head up, straining to move quickly but silently. The edge of
the deck was in front of me, a low black line against a strip of
paler black water. Once I passed that edge, I'd be visible. I
could see a dinghy moored alongside the houseboat opposite. I knew that dinghy. In the daytime it was cornflower
blue, a cheery detail in the view from my kitchen. Five yards
away? A dozen? I'd never thought about it. Now it was a
washed-out gray hull rising up from my eye level, and it
seemed impossibly distant. My feet, still in sneakers,
dropped lower in the water, and I wanted to let my whole
heavy body follow them. I was too tired, it was too far.

Another creak above me. Were they coming? I sucked in a
lungful of air, squeezed my eyes shut, and dove down and
across toward the dinghy. I barely kicked, afraid of splashing,
but I pulled myself along with low sideways sweeps of my
leaden arms, growing weaker with each stroke. My chest was
burning, but I stayed under. Hold on, keep going, hold on.

Finally instinct conquered will and I shot to the surface
like a panicky cork, rearing my head up to gulp the air. Along
with the air, I got a glancing crack on the back of the skull. I
went under, sputtering, then came up grabbing for a handhold. My fingers jammed painfully into a rough metal ring,
and I pulled myself to the surface and hung on with both
hands as the water drained from my mouth and the stars
cleared from my vision.

The ring was one link of an iron chain, rough with rust,
wrapping a log float. I had passed under the dinghy, and
come up beneath my sleeping neighbors' houseboat. Invisible at last to Holt and his henchman, and almost giddy with
relief, I thought about shouting for help. But the ruckus
would alert Holt before it woke the neighbors, and whether
he fled or the police stopped him, where would that leave

Nickie? No, I had to think this over. But first I had to get out of the water.

Wearily, I made my way along the length of the float. My hands barely obeyed me, and my legs trailed uselessly behind, heavy and numb. A hissing noise grew louder as I reached the farther edge of the houseboat: rain, slanting needles of cold rain pocking the surface of the lake and masking my escape even further. I considered climbing up and using the walkway, but there was still a chance that I'd be seen. So I stayed in the water, paddling and scrabbling from handhold to handhold: a rope, a chain, a guywire, the edge of a canoe that rocked wildly when I grabbed it.

I lost track of time. The rain stung my eyes and clattered on the water, blurring sight and hearing. The handholds seemed to grow farther apart, and the effort of abandoning the security of one to lunge for the next was almost overwhelming. By the time I reached a small wooden ladder, and hung gasping from it, I was too dazed to understand why the water ahead of me was lapping against concrete instead of logs. Then I realized: It was the landward end of the dock. I'd made it.

Streaming with water and shivering from cold, I lifted myself up the slippery rungs to the top of the seawall. I sprawled flat, and the cessation of effort felt so good, the reprieve so welcome, that I nearly fell asleep on the spot. Then the wind picked up, drilling the rain even harder against my skin, and the shivering became a hypothermic shudder, uncontrollable and alarming.

I thought about Lily, but she had bowed out of this whole tangle, and with good reason. It wouldn't be fair to drag her back in. There was Eddie, too, but with my cell phone in my purse at the bottom of the lake, I'd have to find a pay phone.

And besides, why would Eddie even speak to me? No, I had
to get inside somewhere, get warm, and very soon. My im-
mediate neighbors on the dock were so close that Holt might
hear my efforts to roust them out of bed. And there was no
one I knew living in the apartments and condominiums
within walking distance.

Wait a minute. Yes, there was. I sat up, then stood up, my
legs unsteady and my feet uncooperative, and looked
around. The after-midnight, before-dawn darkness was broken up with streetlights here, and through the haze of cold
and fatigue I knew just where I was. The parking lot was in
front of me, the docks behind. That meant the Lakeshore
Apartments, where Aaron Gold lived, were somewhere off to
my right. Too exhausted to look for pursuers, or even to care,
I started walking.

Chapter Thirty-three

"WHAT THE HELL?"

A man in an intensely plaid bathrobe was staring at me from the open doorway of apartment thirteen. Lucky thirteen. Aaron Gold. The man in the robe was Aaron Gold, and he was going to help me. But help me with what? I had forgotten, somewhere back there in the rain, stumbling past the silent homes and the empty cars. Mind and body were both numb, my bleeding hands and banged-up skull so distant that they might as well belong to someone else, someone who had to reach apartment thirteen. Now that I had arrived, my purpose in being there eluded me, sinking from sight like a stone in deep water. In cold, black, bottomless water—

"Don't cry! Carnegie, come in, don't cry. I didn't recognize you, that's all."

He put an arm around my waist, and at the touch of his hand I crumpled like a puppet with cut strings. There was a clumsy tangle of limbs, a lifting and lurching, and then I was slumped across a sofa. I could hear water dripping onto the floor. Maybe there was a leak in the roof. Or was it me? Must be me. Gold was talking, his irritating East Coast voice growing nearer and then fading out, but the words didn't make any particular sense. Not that I cared. I was drifting in a heavy, pleasant torpor. Even the shuddering didn't bother me anymore. If only that troublesome voice would go away. Then I could sleep, drift to sleep . . .

"Your lips are blue! Here, let's get a blanket around you, you're like ice. And you're soaked. Is it raining that hard? Carnegie, wake up! Was it a car accident? Is anybody else hurt? Answer me, dammit!"

"No!" My own voice was weak and whiny. I coughed and tried again. "Nobody else. Just me."

"Where's your car?"

"There isn't any c-car," I said petulantly. My teeth were going like castanets. "Why do you keep t-talking about cars?"

"OK, never mind that. Do you need a doctor?"

I shook my head, most of the motion lost in shuddering.

"You sure? All right, wait a sec."

He disappeared, and I heard the rubbery squeak of a faucet and the gush of water drumming in a bathtub. Oh God, a hot bath. Clear, shallow, hot water. The thought roused me just enough to realize how cold I was, cold to the bone. It took a few minutes to marshal my strength, then I staggered to my feet. A fringed chenille bedspread fell from my shoulders and tangled around my knees, but I kicked it away with a sob and followed the gushing sound down a short hallway to a small, brightly lit bathroom. Aaron Gold reached out to me. I pushed past him and stepped into the half-filled tub.

"Most people take their shoes off first," he said mildly.

I didn't reply. I was busy scootching down, as deep as I could manage, into the bath water. As the tub filled, the mud and scum from my clothes turned the water to greenish murk, but it was hot murk and that was all that mattered. Kneeling by the edge, Gold shoved back the sleeves of his robe and lifted my ankles, one at a time, to pull off my sneakers. They came free with a sucking sound. My feet were wrinkled and fish-belly white.

"Wait a minute," he said. "You didn't get this wet just in the rain. Were you in a boat accident? Or do they go in for midnight swims around here?"

I was almost capable, now, of rational speech. "Give me some time, would you? There's . . . there's a lot to explain."

"No kidding. I'll get you some dry clothes. You want help getting out of those jeans?"

"No!"

He raised his hands, all innocence. "Just checking. Your womanly virtue is safe tonight. No offense, but you smell like low tide."

He left, pulling the door half shut behind him. I picked at the buttons of my shirt, but the sodden cloth resisted my numbed fingers, so I gave up and plunged my hands back into the filthy water. The heated current from the faucet swirled below the surface around my bare feet, and the steam drifted up, veiling the turquoise tiles around me. I ceased, for a time, to be conscious of anything except the painful pleasure of getting warm.

I was warming up to rational thought as well, and as the feeling stole back into my fingers and toes, I thought about Holt Walker. Smooth, suave, professional Holt must be working for Keith Guthridge, or for the men behind him. How convenient to kidnap Douglas Parry's daughter, if you had Douglas Parry's closest friend on the payroll! But why had Holt broken into my houseboat tonight?

Come to think of it, he hadn't broken in. He'd used a key. I could clearly recall the sound of it turning in the front door lock. But I hadn't given him my key, and no one else had an extra. *No one except Eddie.* I sat upright in the tub, the water sluicing off me in smelly rivulets. Surely not Eddie. That was crazy; I was crazy even to imagine it. Embezzlement was one thing, but conspiring in a kidnapping? It was unthinkable. Just as unthinkable as my smoldering, green-eyed Prince Charming chopping off Nickie's hair. Or had Andreas done that part? And what else had they done by now?

"I don't have anything wedding-colored, Wedding Lady, so you have to make do with this stuff." Gold poked his head around the door and dumped some clothes on the toilet lid. "Hey, your eyes are all the way open, that's good. You want some hot soup, hot coffee, hot something?"

"Coffee," I said absently.

"Coming up."

I pulled the plug and stood up. Unbuttoning the shirt was impossible, so I peeled it over my head and dropped it on the floor, then struggled wearily out of my jeans. Something chinked when they hit the floor. My keys were still in the pocket, where I'd shoved them after Lily dropped me off. I smiled grimly. If Holt and his sullen friend had locked the door behind them, I could still let myself in. But what would I find when I did?

I shook my head in angry confusion. A hot shower and a lot of soap; then maybe I'd be able to think straight. I didn't see any shampoo, so I used the soap on my hair, then rubbed myself briskly dry with a threadbare blue towel and got dressed. Of the heap Gold had left me, only the socks fit. The gray sweatpants stopped well short of my ankles, and the paint-spattered navy sweatshirt left my wrists bare. But it was all clean and dry, and so was I. I wrapped the towel tightly around my hair, binding every damp curl up and out of the way, and then I made the mistake of swiping away a clear spot in the steamed-over mirror.

The face in the mirror was frightful. Thin, deadly pale, with huge bleak eyes and bloodless lips, and an open cut above one temple, from which a thread of blood was tracing its way over my cheekbone like a brilliant red scar. I cleaned off the blood with a tissue and unwrapped the towel, shaking my hair loose over my shoulders.

"All style and surface," I muttered to my reflection. But at least I looked less like a skull.

"You all right in there?" Gold called. "The coffee's ready."

I could smell it as I came down the hallway, a dark, welcoming aroma mixed with the reek of tobacco. My host, now wearing jeans under his appalling bathrobe, was perched on a stool at a pastel-blue Formica counter, stubbing out one cigarette and lighting another. The counter separated the living room from a kitchen that was much like the rest of the apartment: clean enough, roomy enough, utterly impersonal. A small saucepan on the stove was crusted with soupy remains that matched, in color and state of decay, the remains on a bowl and spoon in the sink. Sitting in solitary splendor on the countertop were an expensive-looking coffeemaker, its glass pot filled with the darkest of brews, and an open bottle of Scotch.

I took the other stool and lifted my waiting cup greedily. There was almost as much liquor in it as coffee, and the mixture chased every lingering chill from my body, right down to the wrinkled soles of my feet. I drained the cup and held it out for more. And I don't even like Scotch. Gold, amused, blew out a mouthful of smoke and said, "You're welcome."

"What? Oh, I'm sorry. Thank you. Thanks for everything."

He reached behind him for the coffeepot. "My name is Aaron."

"Thank you, Aaron."

He nodded, pouring. With his unshaven stubble and his dangling cigarette, he looked like a second-string tough guy in an amateur play. "You're welcome, Little Mermaid. Now, what's the deal here?"

I took a deep breath. Where to start? Now that I had an audience, the story seemed so unbelievable. And so humiliating. Stick to the facts, I decided, and leave the feelings out of it. Keep it impersonal. "It's about Holt Walker. He's Douglas Parry's attorney, and—"

"And your boyfriend, I know. What'd he do, push you off his yacht?"

"No," I snapped. "No, as a matter of fact, he arranged to have Nickie Parry kidnapped at St. Anne's last Saturday."

Aaron Gold's cigarette fell from his lips and drowned itself with a hiss in his coffee cup. "*Kidnapped?* Are you sure?"

"I found the ransom note myself."

"She was kidnapped last week, and now this week she's blithely rescheduling her wedding date? Wait a minute. Wait just one minute." He skittered into the bedroom, came back with a small tape recorder, tried to start it, cursed at its dead batteries, and then grabbed a pencil and a legal pad from a drawer under the wall telephone. It was the telephone that alarmed me the most.

"No, you wait a minute!" I protested. "I didn't come here because you're a reporter! You can't write about this, and you can't call anybody! You have to promise me that, or I won't tell you another word."

Gold sat down again and looked at me, completely deadpan. No hospitality now, no quips. Just a narrowing of the dark eyes below the tousled black hair. "Listen, Wedding

Lady, I *am* a reporter. And you don't *have* to tell me another word. I can go out the door this minute and investigate the shit out of what you just said. Also I can boot you back out in the rain where you came from. This isn't the Salvation Army. It's my apartment, and I was asleep. Now if you didn't come here to give me this story, why the hell—"

"I came here to hide!"

"From who?"

"From Holt Walker and—and some thug he hired to do the kidnapping! He attacked me once already, and now they're searching my houseboat. And don't yell at me. I hate it when people yell at me!"

"Holt Walker attacked you?" Gold came around the end of the counter and took me gently by the shoulders, staring closely into my face. "There's blood on your forehead. That son of a bitch. That son of a *bitch*."

I shook him off. "Would you listen, please? Holt didn't attack me, this other guy did, but it was back at the fund-raiser for Senator Bigelow. I was wearing Nickie's jacket, and it was dark. Theo told me I just fell against a tree, but . . . Oh, my God. Theo must be in on it, too, or he wouldn't have lied."

"Who's Theo?"

I closed my eyes and swayed. The whiskey was doing its job too well. "I have to lie down. Now."

"Sure, of course. In here." He led me to the bedroom, where the chenille spread no longer covered the tangle of wilted white sheets on a double bed. There were no pictures on the wall, no personal mementos on the dresser, not even a bedside lamp. Just a pile of newspapers on the floor weighted down with an overflowing ashtray and a tiny portable television set. The carpet was apartment-building green, the drapes apartment-building beige. I fell facedown onto the bed, waiting for my queasy stomach to settle. Gold sat on the edge and brought out the inevitable cigarette.

"Do you have to smoke?" I said thickly, into the sheets.

"No, I don't have to. I like to."

But he returned the cigarette to the pack and took the ashtray out of the room. I used the moment to sit up against the pillows and sort out my thoughts, something I should have done before I spilled the beans about the kidnapping. And to a reporter, yet. But now that I had, what was best to do? I blinked at the glare from the overhead light. Could I use what I knew about Holt to help Nickie somehow, or would it be safer to remain silent? What Holt had done to me was mortifying, but unimportant. The important thing was Nickie's safety. So, enough whining. I had learned the truth about Holt by chance, and now chance had given me an ally, wrapped in a plaid bathrobe. When Gold returned, I was ready for him.

"Look," I said, in the voice I used to tame ferocious mothers-of-the-bride. "Later on, when this is over, you can have my exclusive story, all right? Eyewitness to heinous crimes in high society, any kind of garbage you want to print. But if you tell anyone now, you could kill Niccola Parry. Do you understand?"

"Of course I don't understand," said Gold. He sat cross-legged on the foot of the bed, his feet bare and his robe gaping open. "I thought the Parry girl was sick at home. Corinne Campbell said so."

"I lied to Corinne. I've been lying to everybody. Nickie's being held for ransom, and the note said that if the police hear about it, the kidnappers will cut off her f-fingers." I stumbled over the words, and felt tears rising. I blinked them back and went on. "Her parents are frantic. Douglas is going to pay the ransom, but they haven't told him when or where. And his closest friend is in on it!"

"Holt Walker?"

I nodded.

"Pretty nasty for you, finding that out."

I nodded again.

"Well, tell me everything, from the beginning." He shifted on the bed, and his hands moved restlessly, as if groping for a cigarette. Or a pencil.

"First you have to promise me to keep it secret until Nickie is safe. If you don't, I'll call your editors and tell them you're lying. I'll—"

"Whoa!" He leaned forward and captured one of my hands in both of his. "I promise. Swear to God. One lousy little quote out of context doesn't make me a monster, OK? Of course I'll keep it a secret, if the girl is in danger. Just tell me exactly what's going on."

I told him everything I knew or guessed, from the scent of cloves in the woods, five weeks back, to the sound of Holt's voice in my houseboat just hours before. And everything in between, from Nickie's pearls to the three business cards to Eddie's house key to that frightful package.

"When you think about it, the business cards sound like somebody from out of town, learning his way around," he pointed out. "I mean, do you carry cards for your favorite places in Seattle?"

"No, of course not. I didn't think of it that way." All that snooping around and suspecting Boris, when it was really Andreas, the man from out of town, who had tampered with Nickie's car. The man Holt imported to help with the dirty work.

Gold interrupted this dismal thought. "How much is the ransom?"

"Two million dollars, and the promise that Douglas won't testify about King County Savings. So you see, Keith Guthridge must be behind the whole thing, and Holt is working for him. Guthridge threatened Douglas. I heard it myself."

"That argument they had at the fund-raiser?"

"That's right. It seems so long ago. Guthridge must have decided to get back at Douglas in the most hurtful way he could imagine. You know that he's Nickie's godfather?"

Gold shrugged. "People do ugly things when they're cornered. And don't forget, Guthridge isn't his own man anymore. You don't do business with organized crime and then walk away. Somebody up the line probably thought this up, and used Guthridge and Walker and whoever else they needed to get it done. Including this guy Theo. Who's he again?"

"The Parry's chauffeur. He said he saw me fall, there in the woods. But I didn't, I was hit from behind by Andreas. So Theo was lying. Holt had me convinced that it was all my imagination, and that Theo would never do anything for Keith Guthridge. But Holt was lying, all along." I blushed as the unwelcome memories reeled through my mind like a movie, a steamy sex farce with a diabolical leading man and a comically naive ingénue.

Gold stared at the floor, perhaps out of courtesy or perhaps just lost in thought. My affair with Holt was apparently just another piece of the puzzle to him. I wished I could see it that way myself. I finished my tale, and Gold frowned and rubbed a hand across his eyes. My own eyelids were drooping, and my head kept rolling heavily back against the pillows.

"You realize that some of these connections are pretty tenuous?" Gold began. "Theo must be a criminal because you smelled clove cigarettes in the woods. Walker must be a kidnapper because he's rummaging around in your study with a man with an accent. Eddie must be an accomplice because he's the only one with your house key—"

"I didn't say that!"

"You implied it, Carnegie. I'm not saying you're wrong, but let's review the facts for a minute. Just the hard facts, not what you guess or suspect. Number one, Keith Guthridge threatened Douglas Parry about his testimony. Number two, Parry's daughter was kidnapped by persons unknown. Number three, Holt Walker was on your houseboat tonight, for reasons unknown. Number four . . ."

Maybe it was the Scotch, or the drone of Gold's voice, or just being warm and safe after being cold and terrified. Whatever it was, somewhere between numbers four and five, in the midst of puzzling out the most extraordinary and harrowing events of my entire life, I fell asleep.

Chapter Thirty-four

I WOKE TO THE SOUND OF SNORING, DISTANT BUT UNMISTAK-able, like a tractor idling in the next field. I sat up and groaned, head in hands. Judging by the state of my body, the tractor had run over it with both wheels on the way to harvest the haystack that used to be my hair. My body was one big charley horse, and my hair felt like I'd soaked it in molasses instead of Lake Union.

The lake . . . Aaron Gold . . . Holt. Reality flooded in, far harsher than the sunlight filtering through the beige drapes across the room. It was Saturday morning. I was in Aaron Gold's apartment, and Holt Walker was due on my doorstep at one P.M. for our romantic trip to Mount Rainier and Anita Reid's wedding. A scenic drive to the mountain, a gala evening, and a night of sensual delights with the man who had put his best friend through hell and threatened to mutilate an innocent girl. I levered myself stiffly out of bed and scanned the room for a clock. A wristwatch with a scuffed leather band lay curled on the dresser.

I picked it up. Eleven-thirty.

"No. Oh, *no!*" I hobbled down the hallway to the living room, wailing as I went. "How could you let me sleep this late?"

Aaron—somehow in the night he'd become Aaron instead

of Gold—Aaron coughed in mid-snore and jerked upright on the couch. His bathrobe, laid over him as a blanket, slid to the floor. He was still wearing his jeans. "Huh? What?"

"It's eleven-thirty!"

He yawned, screwing his eyes shut and scratching his bare chest with both hands. "So what?"

"So Holt Walker is going to show up at my place in ninety minutes! He doesn't know that I know. Only I'm not sure what I do know. Why did you let me sleep? What am I going to—"

"Stop."

"But—"

"Stop!" He held out one hand like a traffic cop. "Stop yowling. Wait here."

I stopped. Aaron stood up and shook his head slowly, then vigorously, like a horse with a horsefly. We were both barefoot, but he seemed even shorter than usual, and certainly more befuddled. His left ear and cheek were waffle-patterned from the sofa cushion, and on the other side his hair stood out in horizontal cowlicks. Some ally. He shambled past me into the bathroom and shut the door. I started the coffeemaker while I waited, and when he returned I headed for the bathroom myself. My hair was past remedy and so were my clothes, still lying in a damp, smelly heap on the tiled floor. I kept his sweatpants and sweatshirt on, and contented myself with splashing cold water on my face and forcing my feet into my cold, misshapen sneakers.

When I emerged Aaron was in the kitchen, wearing a baggy red T-shirt with a Boston Red Sox logo. He looked me over without enthusiasm. "You've got a date with Walker today?"

I nodded anxiously. "At one o'clock. I'm doing a wedding

at Mount Rainier tonight, and he's supposed to come with me."

"Then you'd better go home and change. You look like hell."

"What are you talking about?" I sputtered. "I can't go anywhere with Holt. He's a kidnapper. He's dangerous!"

"Not if he goes on believing that he's got you fooled. Look, I was thinking about this after you conked out. If Walker is in on the kidnapping—"

"What do you mean, if?"

"Just listen. If he's in on it, then it's important not to let him know that you suspect him. Right?"

"Right."

"And I take it you don't want to call the cops and have him followed?"

"Absolutely not." If Nickie was still alive—how dismal it was, to admit the existence of that "if"—then I didn't dare endanger her by overruling her father and involving the police.

Aaron handed me a coffee cup, sans Scotch, and half a bagel. "They wouldn't believe you, anyway, is my guess. What about telling Douglas Parry himself?"

I chewed on the question for a moment, and then on the bagel. It was stale, so I dunked it in the coffee. "I don't think so. He doesn't trust me anymore, and he does trust Holt. Holt could just say that he suspected *me* of being one of the kidnappers, and he was searching my place for evidence."

"Good point. So where does that leave us?"

I sat down on a stool, defeated. "It leaves us trying to find out what Holt really was searching for last night, without tipping him off."

"And the only way to do that is—?"

"Is for me to take him to Mount Rainier, and keep an eye on him."

"Exactly."

"But—"

"But what?"

"Nothing." I was silent then, watching Aaron's dark, stubbly jaw crunching up and down on his bagel and thinking, quite irrelevantly, that he must have to shave twice a day. His plan made sense, but why did I feel so aggrieved, so abandoned? Perhaps an ally wasn't really what I had wanted. Perhaps I'd stumbled through the rain last night looking for a champion, a knight in shining armor to slay my dragons for me. Or just John Wayne. "I cain't let you face that varmint, little lady. You just stay here in the bunkhouse and I'll gun him down for yuh." Instead I had this unshaven Bostonian bum, calmly advising me to change my clothes and walk right back into danger because it made sense.

"What are you going to do, meanwhile?" I asked peevishly.

"Snoop around, ask questions, check records. If Walker really is hooked up with Guthridge, there must be some trace of it somewhere. The more we find out now, the more we'll have to tell the police after they let Nickie go. And if you find out anything, you can call my pager and I'll go to Douglas or the cops or whatever."

I looked up sharply. "You think they'll let her go, then?"

Aaron turned aside to pour more coffee. When he spoke, he didn't look at me. "I covered a kidnapping once, back east. Spent a lot of time talking to a security consultant. This guy makes a fortune advising high-risk executives. According to him, the longer a hostage is held, the worse the odds are for a safe release."

"How did it end? The case that you covered?"

He unplugged the coffeemaker. "We'd better get going."

It was five to twelve when we reached the houseboat. Fortunately for my reputation as a snappy dresser, the dock was deserted. That was unusual for a Saturday, but I figured everyone was out enjoying the weather. The rainstorm had exhausted itself during the night, and now the last shreds of clouds were disappearing eastward, leaving behind a rinsed blue sky and a balmy breeze. The houseboat barely rocked as we stepped onto its deck, and the sun-spangled water all around us hardly looked like the nightmarish abyss I'd been floundering in just a few hours before. I unlocked the door and hesitated, but Aaron strolled right in.

"Nice place," he said, loud and overcasual. "OK if I look around?"

I realized that he thought Holt or his foreign crony might still be inside. I shook my head in a wild negative, but Aaron ignored me and set off through the living room for the bedroom and study. He returned in a moment and shrugged. "No bears around, Goldilocks. Can you tell if anything's missing?"

I made a quick survey with one eye on the clock. If I'd come back from Ellensburg this morning as planned, I would never have guessed at the invasion of my little domain. There was no scent of burning cloves, this time. And, just like that other night, there was nothing out of place.

"What on earth were they looking for?" I said, more to myself than to Aaron. I flopped down on the couch and looked helplessly around at my normal, pedestrian possessions. My eyelids began to lower like a theater curtain, soft and heavy. The hours I'd spent in Aaron's bed had been fitful, and too few. With the slightest of nudges I could have keeled over and gone back to sleep. Aaron prowled in and out of the room, full of restless energy.

"It must be something they didn't find the first time Andreas was here," he said, drumming his fingers on tabletops and chair arms. "Something of Nickie's, maybe? No, that doesn't fit; they've already convinced Parry that they have her. You don't suppose Walker really was searching for evidence that you're the guilty party?"

"Which would make him innocent?" I tried to keep my voice level, and conceal just how urgently I wished that were true. "But the first search was well before the kidnapping. Unless—"

"Unless what?"

I closed my eyes to concentrate. "What if Andreas is a private detective, and Douglas hired him to investigate the embezzlement? Then, after Nickie was taken, he came here again, with Holt this time, to try to link me to the kidnapping? How does that sound?"

"Pretty flimsy. Why search your apartment for evidence of embezzlement, when all your records would be in your office? And why wait till last night if they thought you were the kidnapper? For that matter, why investigate you at all, if Douglas Parry just wants to pay the ransom and get his daughter back, no questions asked?"

"Maybe Douglas doesn't know about the investigation," I said. I was grasping at straws and I knew it. "Maybe Holt is trying to track down the kidnappers himself, and rescue Nickie before the ransom is paid?"

Aaron snorted at this fairy tale. "And he just happens to suspect his own girlfriend?"

"I wish you'd quit talking about boyfriends and girl-friends," I said hotly. "We're not teenagers."

"So what's a better word?" he shot back. "Lovers?"

"None of your business!" I was close to tears again. "Look, it's twelve-twenty. If I'm going to go through with this stupid charade, I have to get ready."

I stalked off to the bedroom and went to pull out my overnight case. Which, of course, was still in the van. Which was still, presumably, at Lily's place. I slammed the closet door in vexation, then took a few deep breaths before picking up the phone. This was no way to begin my debut as an actress.

Lily wasn't home, and her answering machine wasn't an-swering. Wonderful. I took the world's fastest shower, just to get my hair into manageable shape, and laid on enough makeup to get me a job at a cosmetics counter. I still looked a little ragged, but nothing like the scarecrow I'd seen in the mirror last night. I was certainly better dressed, in white slacks and a dressy blouse under a navy jacket. I slipped my jade silk into a soft suitcase along with some lingerie, and strapped on a trendy watch with an oversized, easy-to-read face. My flats would work with both outfits, and their rubber soles were essential for looking elegant while running up and down stairs. How bizarre, to be thinking about clothes for my date with a kidnapper. I called Lily every two minutes. No answer.

I carried the suitcase and my second-best purse into the living room. My first-best was on the bottom of the lake, along with my wallet and my credit cards. At least Lily had my van key, and I always kept an emergency stash of twenty-dollar bills tucked away in my jewelry box. Aaron was gazing out at the lake with his hands in his pockets.

"I'm ready," I announced, "but Lily still has the van, so I'll have to ask Holt to drive me to her place. I'll see you tomorrow."

"No, I'll come by tonight," he said. "We'll compare notes and decide what to do next."

"I won't be here tonight. I thought I told you: It's a sunrise ceremony. I'm spending the night at the Glacier View."

Aaron frowned. "With him?"

"No, with the Queen Mother. Of course, with him. We have separate rooms, though."

"Will you expect you to . . . I mean, are you—?"

"Yes," I said flatly. "Yes, we were lovers, yes, he'll expect me to. I'll put him off." Then I added, quite maliciously, "If I can."

We glared at each other, the length of the room between us, with the tension rising in waves like a heat mirage on a desert highway.

Aaron looked away. "This is crazy. Call him and cancel."

"It's too late for that. Besides, what about not tipping him off and keeping an eye on him and so forth?"

"All right, I'll follow you down. You stall him, and drive slowly, and then—"

"You don't even own a car! And he's seen you before; he knows you're a reporter. Fat lot of good that'll do Nickie, if he sees you following him and he panics!" I was suddenly furious. "Anyway, how come it was all right for me to spend the *day* with a dangerous criminal but it's crazy for me to spend the *night* with him?"

"So I was wrong!" he shouted. "So sue me! But I'm not going to let you—"

"*Let* me? You're not letting me do anything, buster. Who do you think you are?"

At that high point in our civilized discourse, the doorbell rang.

Chapter Thirty-five

"HE'S HERE!" I WHISPERED.

"I'll *rent* a car," Aaron whispered back.

"No!" I rushed over to him, almost tripping on the suitcase. He smelled like an ashtray, but I leaned in close. "You stay here and snoop. I mean it! You talked me into this, but it's a good idea and I'm going to see it through. Don't endanger Nickie, and don't patronize me! All right?"

Another stare-down, briefer this time. His eyes were a dark, polished brown.

"All right. But call me tonight, deal?"

"Deal."

He slipped into the bedroom, and I opened the front door with what I intended to be a carefree smile.

"Hi!" It was Lily. She was all in green today, with dangly earrings shaped like parrots in flight. "What's wrong? You've got the strangest look on your face."

"What? Oh, nothing. Nothing's wrong. How's Ethan?"

"Much better. We probably could have stayed over there, but you know how mothers are." She glanced over my shoulder. "Sorry to interrupt your, um, conversation."

"What conversation? That was just the radio."

"Sure," she replied. "I see your radio is a Red Sox fan."

I turned around. Aaron stood in the kitchen, displaying his version of the same smile.

"Hello," he said. "Aaron Gold. I was just leaving."

"Lily James. Me, too. Leaving, I mean." She held out the key to the van and my tote bag, which I tucked into my suitcase. "And don't offer to drive me home, Carnegie. Vanna stalled twice on the way over. I'll take the bus."

"Jeez, I'm sorry about all this driving, Lily."

"No problem. I'm just sorry you had to cancel your meeting."

But I wasn't listening. A flash of red had caught my eye from the far end of the dock: a blood-and-silver sports car pulling into the parking lot. I heard the distant slam of a car door, and whirled toward Aaron.

"He's here!"

Aaron grabbed my free hand and pulled me back into the kitchen, suitcase and all. "This is perfect," he muttered. "If anything happens, Lily is a witness that Walker left with you today. Nothing's going to happen, anyway, but let her know what route you're taking. Be careful, Sherlock."

Then he gave me a brief but unequivocal kiss, pushed me out the doorway again, and shut the door between us. Lily grinned.

"Not that it's any of my business, Carnegie, but would you rather that the guy coming toward us didn't know about the guy inside?"

"Lily . . ." I said. My mind went blank. Was it possible that I'd kissed him back? "No. I mean, yes, I'd rather he didn't. Hold these a minute, would you?"

I handed her the purse and suitcase and turned around to secure the door, but as I touched the knob I heard a small, metallic click. Aaron, on the other side, had slid the bolt home. I tapped "shave and a haircut" on the weathered wood, and he rapped out "two bits." I *had* kissed him back.

"Carnegie! Am I late?"

Holt Walker, big as life, in razor-creased chinos, shiny new loafers, and a creamy shirt open at his smooth, tanned throat. His wavy chestnut hair lifted in the breeze, and his sea-green eyes caught the sunlight. He looked like he was running for president. He greeted, I introduced, and Lily responded. And all the while I thought, *You bastard. You lousy, lying bastard.* Because there was no doubt in my mind, and never had been since I'd hung shivering from that slimy cable under the deck, that Holt Walker was as far from innocent as he could possibly be. That easy smile, those expansive gestures, the smooth assurance of the large, handsome American man, the dominant male, they were all part of the lie. A lie that he was enjoying to the hilt.

"What a great day for a drive," he was saying, beaming down at Lily with his charm set at Medium High. "We're going to Rainier for a wedding in a meadow."

"At the Glacier View Lodge, down the road from the visitors' center at Paradise," I chimed in. "We're taking the freeway south to Tacoma, then Highway Seven around the south side of the mountain. You know, through Elbe and Longmire?"

"Whatever," Lily said. "Well, you guys take umbrellas. It's supposed to rain again tonight. Carnegie, I'll put this stuff in the van on my way to the bus stop. You've got your hands full already."

"What did she mean by that?" Holt asked as she walked off.

"Who knows?" I said lamely.

"And who cares?" He moved closer. "I just want my hands full of you."

And before I could dodge him, Holt pressed me up against the door and began to kiss me hungrily, his hands moving down my body as if he owned it. I could hear the wooden panel creak as I leaned away from him, and I swear I could hear Aaron Gold gritting his teeth six inches behind my backbone. It would have been funny if I hadn't wanted to scream. I got my hands up to Holt's shoulders and pushed him gently away.

"Hey, save that for later," I said archly, sounding like a soap opera vamp. "I've got to get to work, you know."

"We've got time," he insisted, his voice husky. "Let's go inside for half an hour."

"No!" I linked my arm in his and walked away from the door, tugging at him and forcing a laugh. "No, then we'd never leave. And honestly, there isn't a minute to spare. I've thought of a million more details to check out at the Glacier View, and I'll barely have time as it is."

He fell into step with me down the gangplank from my deck to the walkway, leaving Aaron farther and farther behind. I chattered all the way to the parking lot, and continued while he transferred an expensive little leather suitcase from his sports car to the van and climbed into the passenger seat.

"Lily and I had a nice time," I said. "It was good to get away, but I drank too much beer and I'm kind of a wreck today. You've never seen me before a wedding, I get so keyed up about everything that could go wrong. Well, you did see me before Diane's wedding, but that was really *at* the wedding, wasn't it? It's beforehand that I get really nervous, like now, but—"

"Carnegie, you don't have to pretend."

"What?" I froze with the key halfway to the ignition. "Pretend what?"

"That you're not worried about Nickie. We all are. But there's good news." The tenor voice that I'd found so intriguing rang hollow and sanctimonious now, like a bad actor's. But Holt Walker was an excellent actor, as he was about to demonstrate.

"What's happened?" I demanded.

"Douglas got a phone call late last night, and we heard Nickie's voice for the first time. It was on tape, and she seemed sedated, but she said she was wasn't hurt, and she read some headlines from yesterday's newspaper."

"Thank God!" Relief mingled with disgust at the man's hypocrisy. I almost rebuked him for withholding the news while he made a pass, but I was afraid that once I started I wouldn't stop, and the scolding would end in screaming accusations. Better to play it straight and follow his lead. "But what about the ransom? When are they going to let her go?"

"Soon. They want Grace to deliver the money the day after tomorrow."

"Grace!" I exclaimed. Not Douglas himself, then, or their accomplice Theo. No, Theo would stick close to his distraught employer, to make sure he didn't break under the strain and call the police. "Why are they waiting so long? And what's to keep them from kidnapping Grace as well?"

Holt sighed and grimaced, the very picture of a good

man rendered helpless in the face of evil. "Nothing, but I don't think they'll get anywhere near her. Once they call, she's supposed to start driving, and then they'll give her directions on her car phone to leave the money somewhere and keep going. Douglas wanted to go himself, of course."

"Of course. Was it all right with Douglas, your being away tonight?"

"He knows where to reach me, and he wanted me to have some time to myself. And I wanted to be with you."

He stroked my hair and then my cheek with one broad hand, and I tilted my head down to meet it, afraid my racing thoughts would show in my eyes. Surely the phone call really was good news. Nickie was alive, and once Holt's minions had the ransom in hand, there would be no reason to harm her, no reason at all. She'd be there in Grace's car, unconscious perhaps, drugged, but alive. Or would they lead Grace to some remote drop-off point, and leave Nickie in another spot far away? And how did the phone call relate to the search of my houseboat?

I slid out from under Holt's hand and reached forward to start the van. That was the one comforting factor in this harebrained scheme: At least I was driving. If things got too strange I'd pull over and run for help, or hit my flashers to signal a highway patrol car. As long as I was behind the wheel, I'd have some control over the situation.

I turned the key. Nothing.

"Happens all the time," I said lightly, and muttered dire threats at Vanna as I tried again. Still nothing. I checked that the gearshift was in Neutral, twisted the key a third time, and got absolutely no response.

"Maybe it's a fuse," I ventured. "Or maybe—"

"Doesn't matter," said Holt, all brisk masculine efficiency. "You've got no time to spare, as you said, so there's only one solution."

"Oh?"

"We'll take the Alfa."

Chapter Thirty-six

HOLT DIDN'T GO ANYWHERE NEAR HIGHWAY 7. HE STAYED ON the freeway only until we were out of the city, then he cut off toward the suburbs of Renton with a quick, almost absent-minded swerve of the wheel. I pulled a Washington map from the glove compartment. A state highway did lead from Renton down to Mount Rainier, but it ran along the unpopulated eastern edge of the national park before looping west again toward our destination on the far side of the mountain. Instead of farmlands and small towns like Elbe and Longmire, the security of people and telephones and police stations, we'd be driving through forty miles or more of deep, lonely evergreen forest.

Holt Walker was taking the long way around to Paradise.

"Won't this route make us late?" I had to raise my voice against the wind created by the convertible's speed, and clamp a hand across my forehead to keep the tendrils of hair from whipping into my eyes. I felt just as captive as my suitcase, strapped onto the trunk lid behind me. If only I hadn't made a fuss about being in a hurry, if only the unsuspecting Aaron hadn't still been in the houseboat, I could have called a mechanic to resuscitate Vanna. As it was, I'd been swept into the Alfa and out of town before I could plausibly object.

In answer to my question, Holt just smiled and hit the gas.

The car sprang forward with a rising snarl. Strip malls and car lots flashed by us in the sunshine, and soon we were in open country, south of suburban Maple Valley on the way to the old coal-mining hamlet of Black Diamond. After that would come the town of Enumclaw, and then the forest. I tried to imagine, or maybe to will into existence, long lines of tourists' cars stretching along the highway, bustling roadside restaurants, motels with bored, eagle-eyed desk clerks who would report the suspicious behavior of a panicky redhead in a sports car. But all I could picture was a dark wilderness of trees, and Holt's large, muscular hands, and the passion that had bordered on violence the first time we made love. If he enjoyed lying so much, and the mock-battle of lovers, what else would he enjoy?

"Black Diamond!" I exclaimed. The volume required to make myself heard gave a stagy, artificial air to everything I said. "There's supposed to be a great bakery there! Why don't we stop for lunch?"

Holt's hands tightened on the wheel. "What happened to 'not a minute to spare'?"

"Just a quick snack," I amended, rummaging in my purse for my sunglasses. "Or some sweet rolls to go." Anything to get me in a room with other people so I could regain my equilibrium, and maybe sneak a call to Aaron. Anything to stop feeling like a helpless victim, so that I could start acting like Holt's blissed-out lover.

"I always eat too much when I'm nervous," I said, with a girlish, self-deprecating lift of one shoulder. "I keep thinking about Nickie—"

"Forget about her!" He, too, was half-shouting, but he quickly softened his tone. "Just for now, darling. There's nothing we can do but wait. She'll be all right, you'll see. Think about us instead."

Ready or not, that was my cue. I leaned across the gear shift and nuzzled my head against his shoulder. Briefly. Thank God for bucket seats, or I would have had to stay there. "I've missed you so much, Holt."

He kissed my forehead, and when I straightened up he laid his arm across my shoulder and kneaded the back of my neck. His fingertips were icy. I pretended not to notice.

"Mmm, that feels wonderful." With my eyes hidden by sunglasses, it was easier to say.

"That's just a free sample," he assured me. "Tonight you get the full-service massage, front and back."

"I can't wait." I should have kissed him on the wrist, but I couldn't, I just couldn't, and at last he moved his hand away to shift gears. I had a sudden sensation of falling, as if the bright, empty highway ahead was Alice's rabbit hole and we were plunging down it, not into Wonderland but into a nightmare, falling faster and faster—

I bit my lip. Too much excitement, I told myself dispassionately, and too little sleep. Don't fantasize, just think. At least Holt had plans for tonight, which implied an uneventful trip to the Glacier View. That made perfect sense for a man who was just killing time while his confederates arranged the ransom delivery. There was no reason for him to harm me, as long as I didn't let my imagination stampede me into vertigo and melodrama. Just stay in character until tomorrow, when I could report back to Aaron. Maybe we should go to the police after all. Would they be discreet enough not to tip off Holt and Theo? No, Douglas was right. Wait quietly, pay the ransom, and get his daughter back. Then I could go to him and Grace and tell what I knew. For now, all I had to do was go along for the ride.

I tried to focus outward on our surroundings. As we

slowed to a decorous, legal speed through Black Diamond, Mount Rainier rose vastly into view. Rainier is an extinct volcano, a massive cone of rock and ice with a rounded top where the original summit blew off eons ago. At fourteen thousand feet, it's an arctic island in an alpine sea, surrounded by other mountains but a mile or more higher, and far more immense.

Lily was right about the possibility of rain. There were long, feathery plumes of cloud sweeping up from the southwest, moving high and fast. A sky like that could portend a storm, but it could just as easily blow itself clear. For now, the mountain glistened snowy-white against the luminous blue, its attendant foothills dark green with forest or checkered earthy brown with clearcuts. It would take us another hour to pass through those hills and the higher ridges beyond, and then miles of twisting road up the flanks of Rainier itself before we reached the lodge. Maybe Anita would luck out with her sunrise ceremony, and we'd really see the sun rise. That was something normal to think about: orchestrating her reception this evening, and making alternate bad-weather plans for the morning. In between the two, through the hours of this summer night, I'd find a way to deal with Holt.

"There's a sign for the bakery!" I said, trying for gaiety. *Stay in character.*

Holt drove past. "Let's make some time first."

"Sure." Was it really in character to be so compliant? How would I be acting if I hadn't heard him on the deck last night? No, wrong question. How would Holt expect me to act? The man hardly knew me, after all, and I hardly knew him. I'd awarded him Prince Charming's crown on first acquaintance, just as starry-eyed little Cinderella had. I wondered what my role was, in his private drama. Comic relief, perhaps, or a convenient plot device. "Sure, anyplace will be fine."

We drove on without speaking, through the main street of Enumclaw and out along Highway 410. The road followed the valley of the White River, whose tumbling waters, milky with the fine-ground dust of ancient rocks, originated high up on the glaciers of Rainier. The silence began to stretch thin. *Enjoy the view,* I prompted myself. *It's a beautiful day. You're in love. Say something happy.*

I stretched luxuriously, lifting my fluttering hair from my neck and letting it fall. "It's so good to be out on the road in the sunshine."

"I thought you'd be tired of it by now."

I replied without thinking. "What do you mean?"

"After your drive from Ellensburg this morning."

My heart tripped over, but I recovered. "Oh, this is much nicer, almost like a vacation. Thanks *so* much for coming with me today, Holt."

"I wouldn't miss it."

His smile was relaxed, complacent. I decided to lay it on thicker, and change the subject as well. "I'll be so glad to have you there tonight, for moral support in case anyone's gossiping about me. In fact, if you don't mind, I'll mention that you're the Parrys' attorney, and it'll look like a vote of confidence from them. There were some nasty rumors about Made in Heaven after Grace fired me."

"She should never have done that," he said, with surprising force. The smile was gone. "It was completely uncalled-for. She should have consulted me first."

Why? I wondered. Had Grace inadvertently spoked the wheel of Holt's kidnapping scheme when she replaced me with Dorothy Fenner? But what difference would the replacement make? What would I have done that Dorothy wouldn't? What did I have that she didn't—

The pearls. Before I was fired, I had Nickie's imitation pearls, and even after the kidnapping I still had them. Did Holt go back to St. Anne's that night and look for them in the wastebasket among the shards of my broken mirror? Did he discover, days later, who had taken them away? Could he and Andreas possibly have been searching my houseboat just for the sake of a fake pearl necklace? If so, they didn't find it, because it hadn't been there. The necklace had spent the night safely tucked away in the back of the van, parked over at Lily's house. I'd left it all this time in my tote bag, the one I sometimes used to pack my overnight things.

The one that was now in my suitcase, in the trunk of Holt's car.

"Well, it doesn't matter anymore," I said finally. I had almost lost the thread of the conversation. "Grace did think I was cheating her, after all, and she was angry about it. I just wish she hadn't accused me out of the blue that way, with no chance to investigate and defend myself."

"That's what I mean," said Holt, calmer now. "She should have handled it differently, and not involved the corporate attorneys. But you're right, it doesn't matter anymore."

"And *you're* right. I'll just think about us." I leaned against his shoulder again. I was thinking, all right, but about pearls, trying to fit this new piece into the puzzle. What if they weren't the fakes? What if they were the real ones? Simple enough to switch a gold clasp for a platinum one. But why bother to steal jewelry when—

"Holt, look out!" There was a dead cat ahead of us on the asphalt. At least I hoped it was dead, mangled as it was. "Don't hit it—!"

Holt ran straight over the animal with his left front tire. I cried out, distressed and angry, and looked away from the road. Looked up, in fact, into his face.

"I didn't see it in time," he said, and pulled me to him, as if in consolation. "Sorry."

"It wasn't your fault," I replied automatically. But I had seen, in that upward glimpse, his quick, tight smile as the cat's body made its insignificant thump under the speeding tire, and sent the slightest of tremors through the car to his hands on the steering wheel. It was a smile of satisfaction. Now I knew what Holt Walker enjoyed.

Chapter Thirty-seven

I BREATHED SLOWLY, FEIGNING SLEEP. THE MILES WENT BY. HOLT left his arm curved protectively around my shoulders, shifting only once to free my hair and let it stream up and back in the wind. We entered a stretch of forest, and the tree trunks whipping past sliced the white-yellow sunlight into strobing flashes against my eyelids. A strobe light, or a flickering slide show. Mentally I watched the bright images blink to life and disappear: the dead cat on the road, Gus dead in the roses, Michelle dead behind the wheel of the Mustang. Mary crumpled in the street, Nickie's shorn hair in the moonlight, the pearls in her father's hands. The pearls . . .

The car slowed suddenly, leaving the smooth highway for rattling gravel. I sat up with a start.

"Sorry to wake you." Holt looked at me fondly, with a trace of smugness, a perfectly normal way for a wide-awake man to look at his sleepyhead lover. "I think this is our last chance for a snack till we get to Paradise. If you're still hungry?"

"Yes!" I said fervently. "Calories and caffeine are just what I need." And a telephone, and five minutes alone.

I got the food and the coffee, but that was all. The Trout Pond Café and Gifts was a shabby café with its more cumbersome merchandise—chain-saw carvings of grizzly bears and lawn-ornament ducks with revolving wings—displayed on a sagging front porch. In the shade to one side of the building was a fetid pool of dispirited fish, watched over by a fat teenage boy reading a comic book at a plywood table. A sign stapled to the plywood proclaimed "You Catch 'em We Cook 'em, Our Pole's Or Your's," followed by a list of prices per ounce for a trout dinner.

"Let's skip the seafood," Holt murmured as he opened the holey screen door for me. "I'm allergic to apostrophes."

Inside, flies droned in circles near the ceiling and settled from time to time on the sticky plastic surface of the booth where we sat. A few fishermen nursed beers at the counter, and a pair of exasperated parents sat with four quarreling children at the solitary table. The other booths were empty. A tired overhead fan circulated the heavy smell of French fries and fish. More than a few steps down the culinary ladder from Les Oiseux Blancs.

"Would you order me iced tea?" asked Holt. "Nothing to eat. I see a men's room back there."

He disappeared past the shelves of "gifts," which leaned heavily toward Mount Rainier ashtrays and wall plaques with humorous comments about the habits of fishermen. The waitress appeared, a hefty, breathless woman with a family resemblance to the trout-guarding teenager. I ordered two iced teas and a burger and fries, thinking as I did that Aaron's bagel seemed far in the past. I didn't know what to think about Aaron himself.

"Oh, and is there a pay phone?" I asked as she turned away.

She jerked her head toward the gifts. "Back there by the men's room."

I hesitated, then took my purse and hurried back past the

plaques. If I was quick enough . . . There was a pay phone, all right, just past the door labeled "Gents" in the narrow back hallway. Holt was hunched over it, talking in a rapid undertone. To Theo? To Andreas? To someone shady, or he would have used his car phone. I tried to backtrack quietly, but he looked up and saw me. There was a spark of anger in his eyes, then the familiar warm, photogenic smile as he put his hand over the mouthpiece.

"The Ladies' is that way," he said, pointing back the way I came. He added a shrug of apology. "It's business. I'll be done in a minute. You know how it is."

"Yes," I answered. "I know how it is."

I trudged across to the ladies' room, waited a reasonable amount of time, then came out to find Holt square in the path between me and the phone. He was examining a shelf of toys and trinkets with exaggerated interest, and I had a sudden sense that he, too, was tired of the charade. Did he have nightmares, too, of police in the night and the public shame of a trial and the horrors of a prison cell? Or just dreams of wealth, piled atop his own wealth by a grateful Keith Guthridge?

"Look at this dollhouse stuff," he was saying. I recognized this as well, the brisk, forced chatter to cover the true intention, which in his case was to keep me from that telephone. He held up a tiny teakettle. "This would fit on your little stove."

Then his sea-green eyes widened, ever so slightly, in alarm at what he'd said, and I felt a hot, bright flare of triumph. This time it was Holt who had blundered, for how could he possibly know about my miniature cast iron stove? According to the premise of our charade, *he had never been inside my houseboat to see it.*

We grasped the awful truth at the same instant, I was certain, but on the instant my triumph turned to ashes. In this game within the game, Holt's blunder was a hazard to me, not to him. I had to convince him that he had convinced me of his role, I had to act gullible without seeming to act, or Nickie might never emerge from whatever hole they'd hidden her in.

"Oh, did Nickie tell you about that?" I said brightly. Too brightly, I was talking too fast, smiling too much, but I couldn't stop myself. "She just loved that stove, in fact I almost gave it to her for a wedding present, but I couldn't part with it. I've been keeping an eye out for little pots and things, but I don't think that one is the right scale; it's too small . . . "

I continued to chatter as we returned to our booth. A fly crawled across my hamburger bun, and another squatted on the rim of my iced tea. But I was in no mood to be fastidious. I waved them away and began to eat, filling my mouth with food as a welcome change from lies. Holt kept up his side of the small talk, but there was a sheen of sweat on his face.

"Do you want to wait for me outside?" I asked, without much hope. "It's so hot in here."

"You're almost done."

He took the check up to the cash register, but glanced back at me often as he paid, and I didn't dare try for the phone again. What was there to tell, anyway? Even when we reached the Glacier View, as surely we would, my only reason for calling Aaron would be to reassure him of my safety, or to ask for reassurance. Hardly worth the risk of alarming Holt and, in turn, the men holding Nickie. Holt might already have seen through my chatter; he might be trying to convince me that I had convinced him that he had convinced me . . . The deceptions mirrored each other into infinity. One rash move on my part could smash them all. I'd be left with the truth, and the prospect of being Nickie's executioner.

Resigned and defeated, a prisoner of my own deceit, I followed Holt to the car and he drove me up the mountain.

Chapter Thirty-eight

"HOLT, LET ME GO OR I'LL SCREAM."

I smiled as I said it. Holt was embracing me with every appearance of tender passion, and I was trying to keep up appearances myself until I escaped. The charade was still on. We were in my room at the Glacier View, with its calico curtains and its braided rugs and its little fieldstone fireplace. The lodge went in for rustic luxuries like these, and eschewed modern ones such as telephones and TV sets which might intrude on the atmosphere of romantic seclusion. Seclusion was very much to Holt's taste. We had been apart for hours, and now he was making up for lost time.

The moment we had arrived at the sprawling, log-sided Glacier View, I had dispatched Holt to admire the view of Rainier, from outside on the meadow paths or inside the picture-windowed lounge. I, meanwhile, had plunged gratefully into the business of Anita's wedding. So determined was I to act normally that I didn't even call Aaron—there was nothing to report, anyway. To my relief, there really were dozens of wedding details demanding my attention, including a complicated dispute between the Glacier View's surly kitchen staff and the haughty chef from Solveto's, and a wonderfully time-consuming hunt for the bride's heirloom lace garter, both borrowed and blue, which she planned to wear under her hiking gear in the morning. These feuds and fusses triggered my wedding-day autopilot mode, energetic and efficient, while keeping me safely away from Holt.

Now it was after eight, the summer light growing liquid and dim under gathering clouds, and I'd only just gotten a chance to come up to the third floor to unpack and change. The banquet would begin at nine, to allow for the arrival of far-flung guests. I planned to meet Holt at our table near the kitchen, poised, relaxed, and very much in command of the situation and myself. Instead, just as I had stripped down to bra and underpants en route to a shower, Holt had unlocked my door and walked in. He'd laughed off my feminine indignation at this trespass, and lifted me off my feet to kiss me. As I kissed back, I silently cursed the desk clerk for giving him a key, and wondered if Holt had come to ambush me, or to search my room as he had the houseboat.

"I mean it, Holt. I have to visit Anita one last time before the banquet starts. Put me down!"

He put me down, flat on the bed, and put himself on top of me. We wrestled, laughing, with him using a fraction of his strength and me using all of mine. The hell of it was, I was aroused by the struggle, feeling a lust for the fray and an unwilling, heated response to his hands on my skin and the passion in his eyes. We had fought this way before, and surrendered together, each of us vanquished by desire for the other. After all the righteous fury and creeping fear and simple disgust I'd felt for Holt Walker today, we were suddenly just bodies tumbling on a bed. I wanted to surrender, and to conquer, again.

This insanity lasted only a moment. I dropped the laughter from my voice and put both hands on his chest. We were lying on our sides, and his heart was going like a single, huge piston.

"Seriously, I have to get downstairs. You promised you wouldn't interfere with my work tonight."

"Promises . . . promises." In the split second between the words, he rolled atop me and pinned my wrists to the mattress above my head. I tried to slip them free but he simply tightened the fingers of each hand like manacles, pinching the flesh cruelly. The full weight of his body flattened mine to the bed.

"Holt, stop it."

His eyes were unfocused, his mouth loose. He brought my hands toward each other along the bedspread, twisting my wrists to lock them together under his left hand. He was appallingly strong. His right hand moved to my breasts. The charade was hanging in the balance; the mirrors were about to shatter. I gasped for air enough to scream.

There was a knock on the door.

"Ms. Kincaid? Ms. Kincaid, you have a phone call. You can take it in the library."

The gasp came out in words. "Wait right there, please, I'll be right out! I—I don't know where the library is!"

"OK, no problem."

Holt had freed my hands at the sound of the knock, and now he swung his weight off me and stood up. We gazed at each other, panting and uncertain. And then, to my own surprise, I took command of the scene.

"Come here," I murmured.

Holt came, his eyes locked to mine, and I knew that he could see nothing in them but desire, nothing but what I wanted him to see. No more amateur actress hiding her face, no more faltering lines. I was fueled by lust, and by cold, cold anger. My performance was brief, but it was brilliant. I slid my arms around Holt's neck, and gave him a kiss that promised, that guaranteed, unimaginable delights to follow.

"Get in that bed, mister," I whispered against his lips. I could feel him shudder. "I'll be back in ten minutes, and then I'm going to tear you apart."

Then I pushed him roughly away, and locked myself in the bathroom. First the jade silk dress, pulled on with hands that trembled just a little, then a comb through my tangled hair. No time to correct my makeup, no time for anything except to scrabble through my bulging nylon tote bag until my fingers closed over something cool and coiled and heavy, lying hidden at the bottom like buried treasure. Nickie's "imitation" pearls. I stared at them, at their satiny moonlight glow, then thrust them into the pocket of my dress. No time to think.

I opened the door. Holt was stretched out on the bed, grinning wolfishly, already out of his creamy shirt and his shiny new loafers. His chest and arms were brown against the sheets.

"Ten minutes," he said.

I blew him a kiss, and went flying down the wide wooden stairway to the lobby, my faithful messenger at my heels. The bellboy was a short, bespectacled kid with an air about him that said he knew exactly what had been going on behind Ms. Kincaid's door. What he didn't know, and what Holt didn't know, was that I was on my way to call in the Seventh Cavalry. He might not be John Wayne, but right now I wanted nothing more in this world than a reassuring phone conversation with Aaron Gold.

I stopped short at the bottom of the stairs and the bellboy nearly collided with me. I pulled my change purse from the other pocket and took out a ten-dollar bill.

"Thanks," I said, handing it to him. "Have Reception transfer the call to the kitchen phone, the one by the swinging doors. And then forget where I went. Got that?"

He smirked, the same smirk I'd seen on Lily's face back at the houseboat. "Got it."

The Glacier View's kitchen stretched along the back of the first floor, facing the delivery driveway and the staff parking lot. Instead of vistas of rolling meadow and rising peaks, the few kitchen windows looked out on cars, trucks, and the steep slope of the wooded ridge behind the lodge. Tonight, as I entered from the lobby, the windows reflected back the brightly lit, barely controlled chaos of a banquet in preparation, with Joe Solveto's staff madly unloading coolers and garnishing plates, and the lodge's waiters loading up trays of salads for the first course.

Stout, red-faced Casey Abbott, my liaison with Solveto's, waved at me as I rushed past, but I just waved back and kept rushing, toward the far end of the kitchen where a set of swinging doors led to the dining room. The wall telephone there rang as I reached it, barely audible above the clamor. I picked up the receiver and stepped to one side, stretching the cord away from the service doors to keep myself out of the traffic flow that would soon begin.

"Carnegie Kincaid speaking. Aaron, can you hear me?"

An operator's impersonal tone. "Go ahead, please."

And then a completely unexpected voice. "Carnegie? Speak up! Listen, sister, what the hell have you been playing at?"

"Eddie!"

I sagged against the wall, then pushed myself upright. Through the porthole windows of the swinging doors, I could see rows of white-linened tables, all order and serenity, each with its bouquet of pink heather. Guests were drifting in from the lounge, checking place cards for their names, chatting and laughing. I turned my back and cupped one hand over my ear.

"Eddie, how did you know where I was?"

His growl came through loud and clear. "Where else would you be? We've had it scheduled since Christmas. Listen, I'm calling from Morry's tavern. The police are at the office."

"The police? Wonderful!"

"Yeah, wonderful. They searched the houseboat, too, and now they've got a warrant for your arrest. Kidnapping, for Christ's sake! What's going on?"

My head was spinning. "My arrest? That's crazy! Why would they—"

"Someone named Mariana claims you kidnapped the Parry girl," he went on. "She showed up at the office this afternoon, half-hysterical, saying they were going to deport her but she didn't care, she just wanted Niccola back and that you had taken her. She must have called the police before she came, because they showed up right away and hustled her off, and they've been grilling me ever since. I just now got to a phone."

"But what were you doing at the office? No, never mind that now. Did you tell the police where I am?"

"Are you kidding? I told them you were on the way to Boise to visit your mother."

"Oh, Eddie! You've got to go back there and tell them—"

The line went dead.

I turned, coldly certain of what I would see. Holt, shirt-tails hanging, wolfish grin still in place, had slipped in through the swinging doors. One hand was jammed on the wall phone, cutting the connection, and now the other hand was reaching for me. The charade was over.

With a crazy surge of relief, I brought the receiver cracking down across Holt's knuckles. He swore and lunged at me, his hand catching at my sleeve. I pulled the silky fabric free and whirled to run, but instead I came smack up against Casey. He had a tray of dinner salads in each hand, and the impact of our collision launched them into the air and full into Holt's face. Both men shouted, Casey staggered forward, and as I scrambled out of harm's way on my rubber-soled shoes, the two of them went down in a whirlwind of shattered china and Roquefort dressing. I pushed past the gawking cooks and waiters, heading back for the door to the lobby. If I could just get to another phone—

"Stop her! She's running from the police!"

Holt's voice behind me was commanding, authoritative. Would they believe him? I didn't wait to find out. Pivoting in mid-stride, I rounded a bank of sinks and dove for the exit to the delivery dock. For the moment, no one followed. A small truck was parked there in the chilly twilight, and I took refuge in the shadows behind it to catch my breath. Holt couldn't hurt me with witnesses around, but he could prevent me from calling Eddie back, or alerting Aaron. I could take my case to Mrs. Schiraldi, the manager, but a quick check with the Seattle Police would tell her that Holt was the trusted family attorney, and that I was a fugitive with a grudge against the Parrys. Better to circle around to the front entrance, get to a phone in the lobby—

The exit door swung open, spilling light along the asphalt at my feet. The shadow of a man—Holt's shadow—stretched long and narrow across the parking lot, framed in the oblong of brightness. I shrank back behind the truck, the blood pounding in my ears like surf. If I hid quietly, he might anticipate my next move and head for the lobby himself to cut me off.

And then what? When I didn't appear, what would Holt

do? He would call his henchman, Andreas, and tell him that their scheme had been exposed . . . and then Andreas would kill Nickie, and hide her corpse, and disappear. Douglas and Grace wouldn't even have a coffin to mourn over. And it would be my fault, my burden of guilt for interfering.

There was only one thing to do. I had to stop Holt from calling anyone, just as he had to stop me. Once again we were trapped together, not in a hall of mirrors, but in an outright duel, each of us desperate to silence the other.

I bolted from the shadows, sprinting away from the kitchen. I was clearly visible in the shaft of light from the kitchen door, the mouse daring the cat to follow. Holt's shadow didn't move, and for a dreadful moment I was afraid that he would simply watch me run and return inside. Then the shaft of light narrowed and disappeared, the door clanged shut, and I heard rapid footsteps close behind me.

The charade was over, and the chase was on.

Chapter Thirty-nine

I REACHED THE FAR EDGE OF THE PARKING LOT IN SECONDS. Once I hit the trees I tried to keep sprinting, but the steepness of the slope and the uneven ground made it impossible. Holt's footsteps, echoing mine, changed from distinct raps against the asphalt to a muffled crackling as he reached the carpet of fir needles. Then came a crashing and a string of curses. He had slipped, on those shiny new shoe soles, and yielded me a few vital moments. I didn't even glance back, but scrambled my way through the barely visible tree trunks at a long slant toward the top of the ridge.

My lungs began to heave and burn. Branches like scrabbling hands snagged at my hair and my dress, and one of them, invisible against the dim background, cut painfully across my eyes. Blind and weeping, I pressed on, the noise of Holt's progress drowned out by my own, as the lodge fell farther behind and below us and the crest of the ridge loomed above.

I had no rational plan, no plan at all. The cat was in pursuit, and all the mouse could do was run in terror. Suddenly I came to a break in the trees. A brushy meadow spread out ahead of me, fireweed and dwarf willow and huckleberry dissolving into a single blurred surface in the dying light. The meadow was an old avalanche chute, slicing down from the ridge crest high to my right to the ravine to my left, far below. The top of the chute made a clear gap in the trees silhouetted on the skyline. All the colors of the day were gone, everything was gray on black. But there was just enough light for Holt to see me, if I crossed the meadow.

I moved uphill as quietly as I could, staying in the shadow of the trees. The sweat was cold on my face and down my spine and I knew, with a sickening certainty, that I'd made the wrong decision. I should have stayed in the lodge, confronted Holt in Casey's presence, made a fuss and called the police myself and somehow, somehow, prevented Holt from contacting Andreas. Instead, I'd put myself completely in his power. I couldn't run forever, and once he caught up with me I wouldn't have a hope. The police, when they came, would hear a plausible story: Holt's suspicions, my confession and guilty flight, and then an accident, an ugly fall. No witnesses, except the grave and respectable Mr. Walker.

I halted, breathless and dizzy. The wind had picked up, hissing through the trees and rustling the underbrush, but I could still hear Holt. He had almost reached the meadow's edge. I had to lengthen my lead somehow. The question of Nickie's safety had grown distant and abstract, compared to my own primitive desire to survive. I shoved both shaking hands into my pockets, and had an idea.

Just up the slope from my resting place, a line of firs extended into the meadow like a peninsula into a lake. I crept out along it, using the trees as a screen and peering down between them toward the sound of Holt's advance. Suddenly he appeared, his shirt a soft white shape against the dim wall of the forest, his face turned away from me to scan the lower stretch of meadow.

I pulled my change purse from my pocket and heaved it,

with a wild windmilling motion, across the meadow and up-hill. It made just the right noise, like the inadvertent slip of someone hiding in silence, and Holt spun around and took off toward it, climbing the open slope with the effortless speed of a born athlete. I waited until he had passed my peninsula and entered the woods across the meadow. Then I launched myself downhill, sliding and stumbling through the low, hummocky foliage, making no attempt at quiet or concealment, betting everything on gravity and speed.

I was less than halfway down when Holt stepped out of the trees some ten yards ahead of me. He must have found an easier path downhill, just inside the opposite line of woods. Or perhaps he was a demon, springing out of the ground at will, pursuing me implacably through an endless night. I could never run fast enough to escape him. The nightmare would never end until he caught me, and ended everything.

I fled uphill once more, moving slower and slower with each searing breath, and coldly aware that behind me Holt was keeping his distance, not even trying to close the gap, simply herding his prey up and over the ridge. Farther from witnesses, farther from Eddie and Aaron and Lily, from any lights except this dying twilight and any voices but his own.

Once I stumbled and was still for a moment, crouched against the silvery trunk of a long-dead fir. He called softly to me.

"Carnegie? Come down, darling, I won't hurt you."

I shook my head and continued upward in a trance of ex-haustion and despair. The meadow growth gave way to patches of gravel, and then to larger rocks and boulders, pale as bones. The wind moaned fitfully around them, lifting and flapping my skirt, tugging at my sweat-soaked hair. A few more steps, another stumble, a few more, and then I was standing on the ridge top, gasping, staring at the sky. Giving up.

A full moon glittered far and cold in the darkness, like a dropped dime on a tar-black road. Its light rimmed the racing clouds with silver, and illumined my little clouds of breath against the freezing air. Across the valley behind me, Mount Rainier was a brooding shadow. Holt was close behind, but I didn't look at him. Instead I dropped my gaze to the rocky, almost treeless landscape before me. Just below was a steeply tilted snowfield, a quarter-mile arc gleaming white in the moonlight, with jagged black outcrops rearing up like fangs at the bottom. The wind came howling up the snow, shaking me where I stood, and the clouds covered and uncovered the moon.

But the moon wasn't a dime. It was a pearl. I turned my back to it. Glaring down the west slope at Holt, I reached in my pocket once more, and drew out Nickie's necklace.

"Here it is!" I said. It came out as a shout. "Stop right there, or I'll throw it down the snowbank and you'll never find it!"

"Find what?" Holt was breathing deeply, not in distress, but as if he'd had a brisk, pleasant walk. Even in the faltering moonlight I could see that he was smiling, and I had the sudden thought that he was in a dream of his own, a reverie of pursuit and power that would climax in death. Then he laughed up at me, at the thing I was holding out to him like a talisman to ward off evil. "Costume jewelry? Just what am I supposed to do with that, Carnegie?"

"You were searching for it," I said. "They're the real ones, aren't they?"

He laughed again, smugly, hatefully, and he mimicked my

quavering tone. "No, they aren't 'the real ones.' The real ones are hidden in a flour canister in your kitchen. Or at least they were, until the police found them there and decided to arrest you. You did mention the police on the telephone, didn't you?"

I nodded. I was shivering now, not just with cold. "Mariana called them—"

"I see." He took a step uphill toward me, and I sidled away. "Well, she's a little premature, but we'll handle it. We'll have the ransom soon, anyway."

"The ransom!"

"Signed, sealed, and delivered at midnight tonight. So you and I have to get moving." He took another step, almost up to my level on the crest. One quick leap and he'd have me. I sidled farther, moving gingerly as the rock beneath my feet gave way to hard-packed snow.

"What about Nickie?" I demanded. My voice was shrill, out of control. "What have they done to her?"

"Nobody's done anything," he said. "They're waiting for me to show up with *you*—"

He leaped, but I whipped the necklace across his face, making him flinch away. He recovered at once and grabbed at the necklace with outstretched fingers. An unreasoning determination to yield nothing to Holt, not even this worthless bauble, made me hang on instead of letting go. For one endless moment the double loop of pearls linked us together in a crazy tug of war, our hands separated only by the fragile strands that glowed like living silver in a freakish ray of moonlight. Holt laughed again, his eyes wide with triumph.

The necklace burst.

Knotted fragments sprang into the air, pearls scattered onto the gravel, and we each fell back a step. But while my rubber-soled flats held fast, Holt's feet in his new loafers skidded on the snow and flew out from under him. He pitched backward and sideways, grabbing at the air, a shout rising into a scream as he teetered and went over.

If he had fallen to his left, westward, a brief slide down the gravel would have brought him up against a fallen tree with no harm done. But Holt fell to the right. He plummeted down the icy eastern slope, and there was nothing to break his fall, nothing beneath his flailing arms except the steep, unyielding snow. He skidded and tumbled, faster and yet faster, until he hit bottom with sickening force and fetched up against the grinning black fangs of rock like a scrap of meat and rags.

In the silence, it began to snow.

Chapter Forty

"HOLT? HOLT!" I BRUSHED THE SNOWFLAKES FROM HIS CHEEK. My fingers, numb to the bone, came away with blood on them, and there was blood in moonlit red-black streaks on the cold white surface all around. There had been just enough moonlight to light my way down to him. The wind threw snow at us in gritty, stinging fistfuls, but Holt didn't move. I leaned over him, hesitating and fearful, as I would lean over a dog, hit by a car, that might still jump up to snarl and snap. He moaned, a less than human sound.

"Holt, can you hear me?"

"Carnegie . . . help me."

His eyelids fluttered closed. One hand clawed at the snow, seeking the comfort of a human touch. I took it, and tried to summon up the lessons from a first-aid class years before. Breathing, bleeding, what else was I supposed to look for? Holt's chest rose and fell with a feeble motion, like waves on an ebbing tide. I searched for a major wound but found none, only dozens of shallow gashes from his plunge down the slope. His left leg was clearly broken, and beyond the help of my empty hands. I thought vaguely about shock, and hypothermia, and cradled his head in my bloody palm.

As I knelt there on the mountainside, I thought about making love to this man, and sleeping nestled against his back, and the way he held me as if I were something new and precious. Then I thought about Nickie Parry, brutalized and humiliated, and her frantic parents, and Ray Ishigura's tears.

"Holt," I said loudly, "listen to me. I'll get you a doctor, but only if you tell me where Nickie is."

"Help me!" he croaked.

"Where's Nickie?"

His eyes were wide open now, their sea-green bleached to silver in the half-light. "I'll tell you everything, but first get me back to the lodge. . . ."

He licked his lips. There was calculation in those silvery eyes. Someone I didn't recognize began to speak with my voice, and then to shout.

"I'm going back to the lodge, all right. And if you tell me where Nickie is, Holt, I'll send the Mountain Rescue people up here to get you. If you don't, I promise you I won't say a word to anyone. Not one word. Nobody knows where you are, and if I don't tell them, then you're going to stay right here all night, and you're going to bleed to death or freeze to death or both, right here on this spot, and they won't even find your fucking *corpse!*"

He stared at me, his mouth agape, and when he spoke again he was whimpering. "We didn't hurt Nickie . . . I wouldn't hurt you. Believe me. You won't be convicted—"

"Never mind that. Is Nickie still alive?"

"Yes," he said fervently, "yes, believe me."

"And what happens after what's-his-name, Andreas, gets the ransom?"

His eyelids drooped. "Andreas . . . Andreas will let her go." He looked up again, and I knew that this time he was lying. "Believe me."

"Sure, I believe you. But *where is she?*"

He groaned again, and his voice choked and dwindled to a thread of sound, hardly louder than the scratch of snowflakes against the rocks. "Cabin . . . dirt road . . ."

"What dirt road, Holt? Where?"

"Café . . ."

"What café?" I shook him by the shoulder, desperate not to lose him. The wayward clouds had parted again, and his face was waxen in the sudden clear beams of the moon. "Tell me the name!"

"Trout Pond. Three miles to—"

His eyes rolled back. I could do nothing for him. Holt would have to take his chances, which were still better than Nickie's, and the faster I got going the better everyone's chances would be. Feeling like a grave robber, I fingered each of Holt's pockets until I discovered a smooth snakeskin key case.

"Only one solution," I said out loud, as I began to trudge uphill through the snow. "I'll take the Alfa."

By the time I reached the ridge crest, my world had narrowed to the moonlight, the keening wind, and the knives of pain that were stabbing upward through my sodden feet. When at last I stood panting at the crest, hugging myself in my thin, torn dress, the luminous face of my watch read nine forty-five.

Midnight. I sucked at the wintry air, regaining my strength for the downhill journey. *Signed, sealed, and delivered at midnight . . . Andreas will let her go,* I didn't believe that for a minute. But I did believe that Andreas was waiting for Holt, and that Holt was supposed to bring me along. Why?

"To prove me guilty!" I murmured. What a perfect patsy I'd been. Holt had conned me into bringing him to Mount

Rainier, conveniently close to the scene of my supposed crime. If Nickie had been kept in isolation all this time, how was she—or anyone else—to know that it wasn't her dear friend Carnegie who'd kidnapped her? Especially if her dear friend was there on the scene when she was released.

But that was beside the point. Andreas was expecting Holt and me tonight, and I had to arrive before the ransom did. I almost laughed, as I plunged down the slope in the moonlight. All this effort, this mad scramble to escape in the night, and in the end I was going to keep the rendezvous that Holt intended for me all along. But like a Cinderella reversed through the looking glass, I had to arrive before midnight.

The meadow was easy going, compared to the woods. By the time I reached the moonshadows of the fir trees, I was falling more than running, swinging from one rough, rasping trunk to the next, barely able to keep upright. Again and again I peered at the greenish glow of my watch face. Ten o'clock, ten-fifteen . . . I could make out the lights of the lodge, like clouded stars between the trees, always so far away. Ten-twenty . . . the angle of the slope relented, I ran faster, and at half past ten I was pounding across the parking lot. I came out of the woods near the front entrance with its semicircle drive and its grand, cross-beamed doors. Holt's car was parked here somewhere. As I searched for it I heard music pouring from the lodge along with the lamplight and I realized, with a kind of nightmare logic, that while one bride was dying, another would be dancing. . . .

Someone stepped out from between the cars and grabbed me, a small, wiry man who smelled of cigarettes. I twisted and fought, until I heard him speak.

"Hey, it's me—"

"Aaron!"

"Keep your voice down! Everybody's looking for you; there's this one park ranger who's built like a sumo wrestler. You're in trouble, Wedding Lady."

I fell against him like a shipwrecked sailor falling to kiss the dry land. It wasn't so bad after all, leaning down a little into an embrace. He was short, but he felt so warm, and so safe—

I pulled back. "Aaron, you have to go inside and get someone!"

"What? Who?" He frowned at me. He wore his ugly tan windbreaker, and he still hadn't shaved. He looked wonderful. "Sweetheart, you're hurt!"

"It doesn't matter, just get someone from the lodge. Not the ranger. Get a bellboy or the desk clerk. Don't tell him about me, just get him out here."

"But—"

"Aaron, *please,* just do it."

John Wayne would have asked for an explanation, but Aaron looked in my eyes, nodded, and loped down the line of cars to the lodge. He was back in two minutes with the evening receptionist, a giggling girl in stretch pants and a ski sweater. The snow had turned to rain, and she carried an umbrella with the Glacier View logo.

"But can't you interview me inside?" she was asking slyly. Then she squeaked in dismay. I must have looked pretty gruesome.

"Just listen to the lady, Charlene," said Aaron reassuringly.

"There's been an accident, an emergency," I rapped out. "You've been trained to handle emergencies?"

"Yes, ma'am." Her eyes were huge.

"All right. There's a long meadow that leads up the ridge behind the lodge. Have you got that?"

"Yes, ma'am. The meadow."

"At the top of the meadow, over the top of the ridge, there's a snowfield with rocks at the bottom. A guest from the lodge fell on the snow, and he's lying injured in the rocks."

Aaron's head jerked up. "Walker?"

I didn't answer, but took the girl by the shoulders and aimed her toward the front door. "We're going back up there to help him. You go get the rangers and tell them what I just told you. They'll know what to do. Tell them that we're going back up the ridge, so we'll meet them up there. Now, move!"

She ran off without a backward glance. Maybe they'd find Holt in this darkness, and maybe they wouldn't, but at least I'd steered them away from us.

"We're going to *help* Holt Walker?" Aaron demanded.

I was already walking away, looking frantically for the Alfa Romeo.

"Aaron, how did you get here?"

"I borrowed a friend's station wagon."

"Too slow. We have to hurry—Here it is!" The convertible's top was up, the doors locked. I pulled out the key case and then dropped it, noticing in an abstracted way that while my mind seemed to be working, I couldn't quite control my hands. Aaron picked up the keys and steered me to the passenger's side, wrapping his windbreaker around me as we went.

"I'll drive, you talk. What's going on?"

I told him, about Holt and Andreas and the Trout Pond Café, while he fumbled with the Alfa's gears. The lodge doors opened and a crowd poured out, but they were intent on their rescue plans and didn't notice us creeping away with our lights out. As he rounded the first bend, out of sight of the lodge, Aaron flicked on the headlights and speeded up. The beams cut a tunnel in the night, flashing past the rocky banks and columns of trees, snaking around the hairpin turns that switchbacked down the mountain. We had miles of highway ahead of us, and then an unfamiliar dirt road. What if we couldn't find the cabin, what if—

"Carnegie, you do understand why Walker needed a scapegoat?" His voice, like Holt's earlier in the day, was raised against the noise of the engine. At least now we were protected from the wind, wrapped in the small dim space under the canvas top.

"So he wouldn't be accused of kidnapping. It's obvious."

Aaron shook his head. "No, it isn't. If the plan was to release Nickie safely, without her knowing who kidnapped her, there wouldn't be any accusation. She goes home, Douglas doesn't testify, Holt and Andreas get paid off by Guthridge, and nobody calls the police."

"But then why—"

"I don't think that was the plan, Carnegie. I think they need a scapegoat for murder."

I sank farther down in my seat and closed my eyes. He was right. The same idea had been hammering at my brain and I'd been trying to shut it out. With Nickie safe, Douglas Parry would do as he was bid. With Nickie dead, Douglas would move heaven and earth to find the woman who had cheated him and then stolen his daughter.

"But why—" My voice faltered, and I tried again. "Why kill her at all?"

His fist thumped softly against the steering wheel. "I don't know. I can't figure that part out."

"But at least they won't hurt her until they have the money."

"I hope to God you're right," he muttered. "You said the ransom is due at midnight? What time is it now?"

"Twelve minutes to eleven."

Aaron floored it.

Chapter Forty-one

YOU CAN'T DRIVE FROM THE GLACIER VIEW LODGE TO THE Trout Pond Café and Gifts in one hour and twelve minutes. Not in the dark. Not on a twisting, rain-slicked road. Not unless you're Aaron Gold, hunched over the wheel of an Alfa Romeo and swearing softly but continuously at every curve. I braced myself against the bucket seat and held my breath each time the tires bit into a turn, skimmed a few sickening inches in a skid, and then bit again at Aaron's guidance. The glow from the dashboard lit his features from beneath, but it took a moment for me to register that he was smiling.

"You're enjoying this!"

The swearing stopped, but he waited for a straight stretch of road to reply. A wall of rock rose into the darkness on our left as we hurtled downhill. On our right was a gravel shoulder, then treetops and the vast black abyss of Stevens Canyon.

"It's a sweet machine. I used to test-drive them, but not"—the tires squealed as he fishtailed around a litter of fallen rock— "not this fast."

"You were a test pilot? I mean a test driver?"

"Actually, I was a cab driver, in Boston, summers and weekends during college. But I used to go to dealerships and pretend I was going to buy a sports car."

"Oh. The way you kept mooching rides, I wasn't sure you even had a license."

"No, I just didn't have a car. I keep meaning to buy one, but I've been busy. You know how it is."

An utterly bizarre conversation, under the circumstances, but what choice did we have? I checked my watch: eleven-thirteen. I spread my fingers, front and back, to the whistling heat vent, and then checked again. Still eleven-thirteen.

"We'll make it," said Aaron. "Think about something else."

"Like what?"

"Like what's-her-name."

"Who?"

"Your other bride, up there at the lodge. Tell me about her. What's she like?"

"Anita," I said vaguely. "She's . . . she's nice. She's—oh, for crying out loud, this is stupid! I'm not a child; you don't have to distract me."

"I was trying to distract myself," said Aaron. "I'm scared, too, you know."

"I'm sorry, I just—what's that?"

An urgent wailing, then a whirling blue light that made sapphires of the rain. A state patrol car tore past us up the mountain, and I remembered Eddie's phone call.

"You're aiding and abetting a criminal," I told Aaron, and explained about the police finding Nickie's pearls in my kitchen.

"I'll turn you in later," he retorted. "So that's why Holt and Andreas broke in last night, to hide the necklace. But what about the first time, back in June?"

"I think they were setting me up to get fired. Stealing

invoices, doctoring bills, whatever they had to do to make me look crooked to Grace and Douglas."

"Which would give you a grudge and a reason to kidnap Nickie?"

I nodded. "And I blamed it all on Eddie. He'll never forgive me."

"And of course they didn't use Eddie's copy of your house key," he went on. "Walker must have taken a mold of your house and office keys both. It doesn't take long."

Of course. My purse, with my keys in it, had lain in the Parrys' living room all during the fund-raiser. Right there where I ran into Holt, and he was suddenly so charming to me. And I fell for it.

My chagrin was interrupted by a second siren, an ambulance this time, also speeding up the mountain as we were speeding down. Going for Holt, broken and bleeding in the snow. But what about Nickie? Would she need an ambulance? Would we? Aaron was silent beside me, clenching the steering wheel, and I could sense his thoughts moving parallel to mine. Up that dirt road, at the cabin, Andreas would surely be armed. If our plan failed we might disappear, along with Nickie and the ransom money, and never be heard from until some hunter came across a pile of bones in the woods. . . .

"Anita," I said loudly, and Aaron started. "Anita and Peter are getting married in the morning."

Aaron actually laughed. "Tell me all about it. Every detail."

So I told him all about it, and he egged me on with quips and questions while we raced down Stevens Canyon, shot past the Box Canyon waterfall, rounded the long wide switchback of Backbone Ridge, and finally hit the straightaway of the state highway. The Alfa's engine revved higher, a deer froze and then fled from our headlights, and the glowing hands of my watch hadn't quite clasped together on midnight when we saw the sign: Trout Pond Café and Gifts. The rain drummed on our canvas roof.

"Why are you stopping?" I demanded. "The road must be around back."

But Aaron wasn't looking for the road. He was looking at me. "Carnegie, you should stay here. Call the cops, tell them what's going on—"

"*Now* you turn into John Wayne!" I sputtered.

"What?"

"Never mind. I'm going with you."

"It's too dangerous—"

"Of course it's too dangerous! But they're expecting me and not you, so stop wasting time. I mean it, Aaron. Let's find the damn road and get this over with."

"All right, but I want to ask you—"

"What?"

"Later. I'll ask you later."

The dirt road wasn't hard to find but it was a bitch to drive, two weedy ruts twisting up the hillside, trading off bone-jarring washboard with slippery mud. Lightning flickered. One mile clicked off on the odometer. One point five. Point eight. Two miles. The thunder boomed and echoed, moving into the distance, and the rain slackened, hammered down again in one final burst, and then ceased altogether.

"He said three miles," I muttered, as we rounded another tight curve. "But three miles to the cabin, or to a junction, or what? I should have stayed with him and tried to find out. Maybe—"

"Hang on!" said Aaron, and stood on the brakes.

Pinned in our headlights like another frightened deer was a silver SUV, its front wheels lodged in a ditch, one rear wheel spinning, the other one erupted into shreds. The driver, heading downhill, had kept control during the blowout, and wisely skidded nose-first into the ditch rather than risk the turn. A door swung open and the driver climbed out, sending up spurts of mud as he trotted toward us. A large man, with steel-rimmed glasses and a trim black beard.

"Valker!" he called. "Vere have you been?"

I think I shouted, but Aaron had already put the Alfa in gear. As it lurched forward, Andreas pulled something from his jacket. Aaron hauled at the steering wheel, there was a cry and a thud, and then we were past the SUV and climbing the next stretch of road at a dangerous speed. I wondered, as we passed, if Andreas had heard the same sounds when he aimed his stolen car at Crazy Mary.

"I had to do it," Aaron said hoarsely. He yanked at the steering wheel as if he wanted to uproot it. The car bounced in and out of ruts, the transmission whining, as he drove faster and faster still. "I had to do it, he had a gun, I had to—"

"Aaron. Aaron! Stop the car."

He stopped, and I put my hand over his on the gearshift. We were both shaking. We'd come two and nine tenths miles from the café.

"I had to do it. I'm sure he had a gun."

"Of course he did," I said. "If you hadn't hit him we'd both be—"

"Don't say it." Aaron rubbed at his face with both hands, and when he took them away his voice was almost normal. "All right. I'm all right. Sorry."

"For keeping me from being shot? I forgive you."

He produced a smile. "Well, now we have to find the cabin."

"I think we found it," I said. "Look."

Aaron cut the headlights and the engine. For a single, black-velvet moment the silence and darkness seemed absolute. Then we heard water dripping from the trees all around us, and the gurgle of a creek winding invisibly through the underbrush. As our eyes adjusted we could see, down the slope to our right, a closed door and a shuttered window outlined in splinters of lamplight.

We waited, sure that anyone inside the cabin would have heard our engine. A narrow driveway ran down the slope from our road but there was no other car in sight. We left the Alfa and picked our way down the edge of the drive, keeping to the cushioning earth and away from the telltale gravel, ready at any moment to slip deeper into the trees. I was still wearing Aaron's windbreaker, and the nylon rustle of the sleeves as I walked seemed fearfully loud. I hugged my arms to me and held my breath as we drew closer.

Still no sign of life. I could just make out the squat wooden cabin, its boxy shape broken by a propane tank on one side wall and a chimney pipe rising from the shallow tilt of the tin roof. Two or three rooms at most, but big enough to make a prison. Or a grave. We reached the enormous trunk of a cedar tree, our last cover before the muddy clearing by the front door. Aaron halted me with a touch on my shoulder.

"Wait here," he whispered. "I'll try to get a look through the edge of the window. If anything happens, you run for the car."

"But—"

"Promise me, Wedding Lady."

I sighed. "Promise."

I've never broken a promise faster than that one. Aaron stepped into the clearing, placing each foot carefully, silently. But he didn't get far. Someone leaped out from the other side of the cedar trunk, tackling Aaron between the shoulder blades and slamming him to the ground. Instead of running I stumbled forward, straining to see, while the two figures grappled and rolled like a single huge animal across the clearing toward the cabin. They crashed against the door and then lurched back into the yard, gasping and grunting. The door swung wide but no one emerged.

What did emerge was a flood of white light from a camping lantern, blinding me briefly and throwing up grotesque shadows that leaped and writhed among the trees. Then I saw Aaron's face, contorted almost past recognition with blood and fury as he tried to regain his feet and was knocked down, again and then again. His attacker's back was to me, but his white-blond hair and the overmuscled shoulders straining against his polo shirt were familiar enough.

Aaron, smaller and slighter and taken by surprise, was no match for his attacker. Theo hauled Aaron up by his shirt front and drew back his fist to strike a final blow. I jumped for his upraised arm, but he backhanded me with a casual swat that sent me spread-eagled against the cabin wall, knocking the wind from my lungs and snapping my skull against the splintery wood. I stayed conscious, but just barely. Aaron seized the chance to twist out of Theo's grip and took a pace backward, gasping, raising his fists unsteadily. Theo stood very still.

I never heard the shot. It must have sounded just as I hit my head, for there was utter silence as my vision cleared and the two men came into focus in the light spilling from the cabin door. Then Aaron coughed and staggered, gore spreading down his face and throat from his nose and a gash above one eye. Theo, his back still turned, lifted his head toward the driveway. I stared in groggy fascination as he peered into the darkness, his expression puzzled at first, then sorrowful and almost child-like as he sank to his knees. He swayed, and dropped facedown without even lifting a hand to break his fall.

And still I didn't understand what had happened, until I saw the blood. It seeped out from beneath Theo's chest, an ink black pool spreading to fill the angle between his left arm and his side. The graveled surface where he lay sloped a bit, and the blood swelled and then flowed in a sudden snaking trickle the length of his arm, to puddle around his still, curled fingers.

I wrenched my gaze away to look across him at Aaron. He had one wrist pressed to his face, trying to staunch the nose-bleed with the cuff of his shirt. But he too was peering up the driveway, as out of the shadows came a small neat figure in black slacks and a dark suede jacket, the light flashing off her cornsilk hair.

Grace Parry, with a pistol in her hand.

Relief flowed through me like warm brandy. Grace knew about Theo, then, or at least had guessed at his betrayal of her husband. She hadn't dropped off the ransom and gone meekly home, leaving her stepdaughter to be murdered. I stepped around Theo's body, my eyes averted, and crossed the yard toward Aaron, stammering as I went.

"Thank God you followed him, Grace. Nickie's inside, at least we think she is, we think she's safe. Aaron, are you all right? Let's go in and—"

"Stop it!" Grace snapped, raising the pistol. "Stop right there."

"You don't understand," I said impatiently. Her suspicion was understandable, but I was freezing cold and desperate to find Nickie. "We came to rescue her—we didn't kidnap her! Theo and Andreas, he's the other one, they were working for Holt Walker. They planted Nickie's pearls at my houseboat, to make me look guilty. I'll explain it all later."

"That won't be necessary," said Grace. And she pointed the gun at me. "I know all about it."

Chapter Forty-two

ONCE, ON A HIKING TRAIL IN THE NORTH CASCADES, I CAME face-to-face with a snarling bear. I'd seen bears before, on television and in zoos, so of course I recognized it. What I failed to recognize, for one eternal moment of paralyzing shock, was that I couldn't switch off the drama, that there was no cage, that in this reality the animal was the center of the universe and I might very soon cease to exist. Even after the bear had grumbled off into the bushes, I couldn't believe what I had seen.

I looked at Grace Parry with the same sense of disbelief. Theo had been alive, and now he was dead, and the tiny machine in Grace's hand, so familiar to every American from the thousands of make-believe gunfights that we watch, was now the center of the universe. If she moved her finger, just one tiny movement, Aaron or I or both of us would no longer exist. This could not be reality, but it was.

"I thought—" I began, and had to start again. "I thought Keith Guthridge—"

"I know you thought that," said Grace. "So did Douglas, conveniently enough."

"Two scapegoats," I said slowly, as the pieces fell into place. Suddenly it made sense. First she had directed suspicion at Guthridge, because Douglas Parry would take an ultimatum from him seriously, and not call the police. And because Guthridge really *was* pressuring Douglas about the King County Savings investigation, with threatening letters and phone calls. Then she zeroed in on me, because I was so much easier to maneuver, and incriminate, than a well-guarded man like Keith Guthridge. "But why are you doing this at all? You have money—"

Aaron interrupted me, his voice thick and his words bunching up between gulps for air. "She's been swindling her . . . her clients, but the stock market went against her. Now she's got to pay up . . . to cover her tracks. That's what the ransom is for. . . . She can't get it from Parry directly. He'd divorce her."

Grace cocked her head and narrowed her mismatched eyes at him. "It's the little reporter, isn't it? So you've been working up an exposé on me as well as on my darling husband?"

"Aaron?" I said, astonished. "You knew it was her all along?"

He shook his head and winced at the movement, but his voice had steadied. "I've been turning up rumors about her investment consulting, about elderly windows who don't understand where their money went. And this prenuptial agreement with Parry that keeps her on such a short leash. But I thought it was just a side issue to King County Savings. I didn't know she was linked to Walker."

"Linked," said Grace thoughtfully. "What an interesting word. Yes, Holt and I have been 'linked' since he graduated from law school. The prettiest boy in the class."

"Chicago," I said, half to myself. "Lily said he worked in Chicago."

She looked at me with contempt. "The light dawns. Too bad you didn't figure that out before you fell for him. It's been very entertaining to hear about. Where is he, by the way?"

But the light was still dawning. "Holt wasn't supposed to sleep with me, was he? You told him just to romance me a little, and find out if I'd seen Andreas near the rose garden, or if I really believed Theo's story that I'd fallen instead of being attacked. You didn't like it when you found out we were lovers."

Her laughter sounded forced. "Lovers! He likes his sex a lot rougher than *you* can manage. Now where is he?"

"Was that why you fired me, and made me look like a cheat, because Holt cared about me? Holt didn't fake those invoices, *you* did—that's why Holt was angry about it! You told him I was only there to divert suspicion, that I'd be found innocent in the end, but then you tried to ruin my business just for spite, and you had Andreas kill Mary—"

"*Where is he?*"

"He's under arrest by now," said Aaron sternly, and I knew he was warning me to hold myself together. "He's hurt, he had an accident up on the mountain, but we sent the police after him. And he'll send them after you."

That shook her, but the gun never wavered. She licked her lips. "Holt won't talk. He knows I'll take care of him as long as he follows instructions."

"Just like you took care of Theo," I said.

I thought that would rattle her further, but she just glanced at the body with mild distaste, the way you'd look at a dead bird on your lawn. The cabin door creaked a little in the rising breeze. "He was losing his nerve. He would have given us away to Douglas in the end."

"I thought he was so loyal to Douglas," I said wonderingly. "I thought he was fond of Nickie."

"Oh, he was. Quite the big brother. But he was on parole for assault and drug-dealing, and I had more than enough information tucked away to send him back to prison." She laughed a little, quite naturally this time. "You know the funny thing about big, strong Theo? He had claustrophobia. He would have done anything to stay out of a cell."

"Even kill Nickie?" Aaron demanded. "Or did you tell him the same story you told Walker, that she wouldn't be hurt?"

Grace ignored him. She straightened her shoulders, information assimilated, plans revised. "You, Gold, drag him into the cabin."

Aaron said something odd. He said "No."

She blinked. "Do you think I'm joking? I said get him inside!"

Aaron shook his head, slowly this time. "You're setting me up, aren't you, Mrs. Parry? First the necklace at Carnegie's houseboat, then me with Theo's blood all over me. The police will find us here, the kidnappers with their victim and the corpse of the heroic chauffeur. Why should I help you frame me?"

"Do what I say or I'll shoot!"

But Aaron kept shaking his head, and I could see that the longer he stalled, the more uncertain Grace was becoming. He moved slightly as he spoke, at an angle away from Theo's body, deliberately drawing her attention away from me. His lamplit shadow crept across the trees and disappeared in the darkness beyond the cabin. Grace hesitated, and listened.

"I don't think you want all three of us shot with the same gun, do you, Mrs. Parry?" Aaron continued, his voice turning snide. "How's that going to look? Pretty bad, I *promise* you that. You'd need another patsy who supposedly fired the gun, but Andreas is dead in a ditch, and your boyfriend

Walker is telling the cops about you right this minute, no matter what he *promised*. You've got to do the dirty work yourself, and then what's going to happen when the State Patrol picks you up with blood all over your nice clean clothes?"

"Andreas isn't dead," she blurted out. "He's going to— never mind, just be quiet!"

But Aaron was getting to her, piling one unwelcome fact upon the next. He was also reminding me of my promise to escape to the car.

"You're running out of time, you know." Another step, and the words poured relentlessly from his blood-smeared mouth. "You're supposed to be somewhere else 'delivering' the ransom, aren't you? Then what, Mrs. Parry? You gonna go home and be satisfied with the two million, or is that just a down payment? Is your husband by any chance going to have another heart attack, a fatal one? First your stepdaughter, then your husband. Pretty suspicious, especially if Walker points the finger at you first."

"Shut up!" The gun was aimed square at Aaron now. She'd almost forgotten about me. The wind had grown stronger, and now both their shadows were lost against the backdrop of tossing trees. If Aaron ran in one direction and I ran in the other, if we could only reach the trees . . .

"You were desperate to get rid of Nickie before her wedding," he continued, "so that Ray couldn't inherit. At first you were just going to kill her, but after the plan with the Mustang didn't work you decided to get some cash up front first, with a ransom. But you knew all along that Nickie was never coming back. Jesus, what kind of woman could—*run!*"

And I started to, I really did. But like Lot's wife I looked back, arrested by the crack of the gun going off. Aaron had dodged to one side as he shouted, so Grace's first shot missed, but now as he sprinted for the woods he was moving much too slowly, undone by his fight with Theo. By creating a chance for me, he was giving Grace a clear shot at his back. She lifted the pistol and steadied it with both hands. I scooped up a handful of rough gravel and flung it at Grace, trying to spoil her aim before I ran. I nearly succeeded. A good-sized pebble bounced off her elbow and her hands jerked, but the pistol spat again and at the far edge of the clearing Aaron cried out and fell into the darkness.

Horrified, I watched him fall, but Grace didn't. She just whirled around and pointed the gun at me. No one would spoil her aim this time, and we both knew it.

"Inside," she said.

I went inside, across the clearing and over the cement doorstep. She followed a few careful paces behind, but I had no fight left in me. The most I could do was listen, for a rustle of movement or a single footstep that would tell me Aaron was still alive, that he had faked being hit. But there was only the windy thrashing of evergreen branches, and even that was muted as Grace shut the door.

The cabin stank. The air in the front room was thick with the smells of stale food and unwashed dishes, and the sickeningly familiar scent of clove cigarettes. There was something else, too, faint but acrid: the odor of an open latrine. I looked around. To my right was a card table with a single chair and the lantern, casting its harsh yellow light, and beyond that a wooden counter where a camp stove and a plastic basin made a kitchen of sorts. A trash heap in one corner seemed to be chiefly beer bottles and tuna fish cans. To my left, an ancient propane heater breathed out warmth from beyond a once-green corduroy couch. The single window was shuttered tight, and one of the two interior doors was open, revealing another shuttered window, an unmade bed and a dusty floor scattered with cigarette butts.

The second door was shut and locked, with a big new brass deadbolt fixed solidly in the wood on the right-hand side above the doorknob. Above the deadbolt, too far above for an arm to reach down and unlock it, was a small sawed-out hatchway set with three steel bars. The latrine smell came from that hatchway. I began to cry. For Nickie, or perhaps for myself.

"Take off the jacket," said Grace. "Drop it on the floor."

I obeyed with exaggerated care. Grace was at the breaking point, I could feel it, and if I startled her now I might as well pull the trigger myself.

"Open the door," she said. "Open it and go in."

Her voice was hollow, haunted, and when I stole a look at her she didn't meet my eyes. She just stood there aiming the gun, her gaze fixed on my chest. I understood suddenly that she had never been in this room before, that the fetid air and the bolted door were just as horrible to her as they were to me. It was one thing to instruct Andreas to kill a dog or imprison a girl. It was something else to see the results. She had killed Theo without a qualm, but that was a thrill. This was disgusting.

I stepped to the door. The lock was new and stiff, and I had to strain my fingers against the lever to turn it all the way through its half-circle course. The door swung inward, then Grace shoved me in the small of the back and shot the bolt behind me as I stumbled inside.

"Oh, *Nickie*."

She was lying unconscious on a cot in the tiny windowless room. There was no lantern in here, but a striped square of light from the front room came through the hatchway, and I could see that she was still wearing her Edwardian gown. It was filthy and torn, a mockery of festive elegance, and her dark hair, cut crudely short, was matted and greasy. But she was alive. Thinner and more sallow, but alive. I sat beside her and took her hand, touched her face. Her breathing was slow and uneven.

"Nickie! Nickie, can you hear me? Wake up, honey, come on, wake *up*." I glanced around as I pleaded, hoping for a glass of water. There was nothing, just the cot and an empty bucket set down in the corner just a few feet away. This had been Nickie's whole world for the last seven days, the last room she would ever see.

I flew to the hatchway and wrenched at the slick, unyielding metal of the bars. "Goddamn you, Grace, look in here and see what they've done to your daughter!"

The opening was small, but by craning my neck I could see most of the front room. Grace was seated on the couch with her back to me, concentrating on something in her lap. I heard a clicking sound, and my heart clenched tight. She was reloading the gun. She slipped it into her jacket, then reached into a capacious inner pocket and withdrew a small tool of some kind and a bulky plastic bag.

"*Grace!*" Her head came up then, but still she didn't meet my eyes. "Grace, listen to me. You don't really want to hurt Nickie, do you? You have the money; that's all you need. You can take it and get away."

She stood up, her perfect hair still shining, her stylish clothes unmussed, her face as set and rigid as a mannequin's. Shooting Theo had been a split-second decision, a sudden opportunity to rid herself of a dangerously unreliable underling. What she had to do now was much harder. She had to kill someone who loved her, and do it in very cold blood indeed. I tried for all I was worth to make it harder yet.

"Grace, please, she's your *daughter*. She loves you, you know. She—she admires you, she told me so. You have the money; just keep it and go. You don't want this on your conscience, Grace, do you? Do you?" I tried to speak urgently but calmly, anything to slow her down, make her think. Or feel. And all the while I was wondering if she'd come close enough to the hatchway for me to grab at the gun, wondering if I'd have the guts to try.

Grace didn't come anywhere near the door. With slow, mechanical movements, she pulled on a pair of thin latex gloves and emptied the plastic bag onto the card table. A distinctive gold fountain pen rolled out, and I shut my eyes as I felt the hairs on the back of my neck rising. It was my pen, a gift from Eddie that I hadn't been able to find recently . . . stolen by Andreas, of course. I looked again, to see Grace arranging the other things on the table. A Greek phrasebook that I'd bought once in a fit of optimism and then forgotten about, forgotten so thoroughly that I hadn't noticed it was missing from the houseboat. Some cash, a passport, and a narrow, colorful folder that could only be an airplane ticket. To Athens, no doubt, and in my name.

"This isn't going to work," I told her, wishing I could believe it. "You can't just shoot all of us. The police will never believe it! They'll keep investigating, and sooner or later they'll get back to you, even if Holt doesn't tell them. Grace, *listen*."

Not a flicker of response. Satisfied with the table, Grace picked up Aaron's windbreaker from where I'd dropped it and took it into the bedroom, planting yet more evidence against us. Then she came out and walked carefully around the front room, double-checking the few objects Andreas had left behind. Finally, she went to the heater and turned it off. The wind outside seemed louder now, as the heater's shushing noise died away. Grace knelt on the floor by its base, where a length of jointed copper tubing came through the wall, feeding in propane from the tank outside. She was almost out of my line of vision. I pressed my left cheek hard against the edge of the hatchway and stood on tiptoe. Grace's shoulder and her shining hair hid the tool in her hands from my sight, but she was moving it somehow against the copper tube. Then she stood up. I thought I could hear, in the pauses between gusts of wind, the malicious little hiss of escaping gas.

Without a word, without even a glance at me, Grace Parry picked up a flashlight, turned out the lantern, and left the cabin. She couldn't lock the front door, which had been damaged in the fight, but she closed it firmly behind her, leaving me and her stepdaughter in the dark.

Chapter Forty-three

I'M ASHAMED TO REMEMBER THE NEXT QUARTER-HOUR. BLIND in the claustrophobic darkness, exhausted by everything I'd been through, and panicked by the specter of deadly, smothering gas, I broke down. I wept, I screamed for Aaron, I hammered on the door and pleaded with Grace to come back and let me out. Finally, like a child in a tantrum, I flung myself away from the hatch, tripping against the cot and falling heavily against Nickie.

She and I would die here, and the police would find a plausible tableau: two of the kidnappers shot to death in some kind of thieves' quarrel, the third one asphyxiated by accident along with her victim. Grace would wait for the gas to do its work, then come back and arrange my body outside the bolted door of Nickie's cell, along with a pile of nicely fingerprinted evidence.

Or would she expect Andreas to do that part? No, she would find his vehicle, and maybe his body, when she drove back down toward the café. Unless he was only stunned when the Alfa knocked him flying, and he had come back up the road on foot to meet Grace. The two of them would search the woods for Aaron to make sure he was dead, but I would never know if they found him because I'd be dead too, gassed like a stray dog in a sealed chamber—

Nickie cried out in her drugged sleep and brought me to my senses. She was helpless, but I wasn't. Not yet. I slid to the floor by her side and felt my way down her lace-clad arm for her hand. It was chilled and clammy, so I held it in both of mine, rubbing warmth into her fingers and murmuring wordless reassurances. I closed my eyes, feeling somehow less blind that way, and took a long, steadying breath. I could smell the gas already, a thin rotten-egg odor stealing its way through the heavy atmosphere of the cabin. A utility man in Seattle had explained to me once that natural gas has no smell, that the stink of sulfur is an additive, put in on purpose to alert homeowners to dangerous leaks. They must do the same with propane.

Now *think*, I told myself fiercely. Is propane lighter than air, or heavier? That was simple enough to determine: when I put my face near the floor, the sulfurous smell was not strong, but it was distinct. Then I stood on the wobbling cot, my feet astride Nickie's legs, bracing myself against the wall and stretching my head up high. No sulfur smell at all. So propane was heavy, it would fill the cabin from the floor up. Would it make us cough and vomit first, or just displace our oxygen, pushing me inexorably into unconsciousness along with Nickie? Was it flammable? An irrelevant question, since Grace had extinguished the lantern, and if the heater had a pilot light she must have turned it off as well. But none of this mattered. The gas was coming; that was what mattered. It was creeping across the floorboards and lapping against our door like a slow invisible tide. And there was an inch-high gap along the lower edge of the door.

I sat down again in the darkness and ran my hands down the length of the cot. No sheet or blanket, just the bare canvas stitched to a metal frame that was bolted to the floor. I pulled vainly against the stitching for a moment, then gave up and felt for the skirt of Nickie's gown instead. The fragile satin gave way easily along the waistband with a loud ripping noise, and I thought as I tugged at it that the wind had died down outside. Was Grace stalking Aaron in the hush beneath the trees? Was he dead, was he dying?

I shook off the thought and lifted Nickie up to a sitting position, with the vague idea of keeping her as high as possible. Then I packed the wadded satin into the crack beneath the door. That would buy us a little time, and time was what we needed, whether the cavalry rode to the rescue or not. If it came to the worst, I swore to myself, I'd wake Nickie somehow, just to let her hear a loving voice before she slipped away for good.

But there had to be something I could do before then. On hands and knees, and then on tiptoe, I explored every accessible inch of our lightless cell, letting my hands take the place of my eyes. No eating utensils to pry at the deadbolt, no furniture to break apart and use as a lever against the bars. Nothing but the empty bucket. I carried it to the door and rammed it, over and over, against the unyielding bars, till I drove myself half deaf with the clanging and cast it aside.

Nickie was stirring. She toppled sideways, and I propped her up again, but she wasn't entirely a deadweight this time, and her head no longer flopped over like a broken doll's.

"Ray?" she croaked. "Ray, I'm cold . . ."

"Nickie, it's Carnegie." She began to struggle, like a child caught in a bad dream, so I slipped my arms around her and hugged her to me. It might have been kinder to let her sleep, after all, but it was too late now. "Nickie, you were kidnapped, remember? From the church. But I've found you, and we're, we're trying to get out of this room. Just rest quietly, all right?"

"Carnegie—" She broke off, coughing. I held her for a while longer, until she could sit up on her own, then I went back to the door. She was still groggy, barely awake, and she asked no questions. I was grateful for that.

I leaned my forehead against the bars, and stared toward the invisible front door until my eyes ached. Were those faint lines of moonlight at its edges, and the palest glimmer of reflection on the glass of the lantern, or were they just phantoms created by my blinded mind? Over in the corner the gas leak hissed, like a tiny deadly snake whose poison has almost overcome its prey. I could take off my own dress, and the rest of Nickie's, to stuff into the hatchway, but sealing ourselves into our own coffin would surely be a last resort. First I would try to reach that deadbolt.

I ran my palms along the door, but nothing protruded on this side. I thrust my right arm between one bar and the hatchway edge, glad for once to be long-limbed and skinny, but even with my shoulder jammed against the bars my outstretched fingers clawed at wood and nothing more. I needed a few more inches, and something to press down on one end, or pull up on the other, of the horizontal brass lever.

But which end? I pantomimed the gestures I had used to open the door from the outside, remembering Grace standing behind me, and the stiff resistance as the lever turned. Nickie coughed again, and began to cry and mumble. I ignored her, concentrating furiously. The lever had turned clockwise, in a half-circle, rotating toward the door edge as the bolt inside drew back. To duplicate that motion from the hatchway, I had to pull up on the right-hand end of the lever, or push down on the left. I needed a tool.

The wire handle of the bucket seemed promising at first,

and I found it without much fumbling, my sense of touch and direction heightened by the darkness. But I couldn't pry the heavy loops at either end away from the bucket's rim, and I gave up after wasting several precious minutes. The gas smell was growing stronger; my head was throbbing like a drum. What else was loose in the room or on our persons? My watch band was too short, I had no belt . . . shoes. Nickie was barefoot, but I still had my rubber-soled flats.

No good. Each of my shoes reached the top of the lock when I held it by the toe, but the soft sole of each bent uselessly when shoved downward on the lever, and I lost one and then the other as they dropped from my trembling fingertips. There was nothing else to push with, so I'd have to pull. I needed a loop, a strap . . . of course. I slipped off my dress, undid my bra, and then pulled the dress back on, smiling bleakly at my inane modesty. Light-headed, almost fainting, I sat next to Nickie and tried to tie my lingerie into a noose.

Sitting down was a mistake. I was weary, tired to death; I wanted to give up and sleep forever. Nickie nestled against my shoulder, and I whispered into her hair as the bra slipped from my fingers.

"I'm sorry, Nickie, I'm so sorry. We tried our best, we really did. Don't wake up, honey. You just sleep, we'll both sleep. Sweet dreams, Nickie, we'll just—*shhh!*"

The front door of the cabin was creaking open.

Soft, powdery silver light spilled into our cell, brilliant to my dark-dilated eyes. Moonlight. The storm had gone, the moon had come back. Had Grace returned also, impatient to be done with us? Aching, half resentful that I would ever have to move again before my final rest, I slipped off the cot and leaned dizzily along the door near the hatchway. I was bare minutes from passing out, but I had to know.

I looked through the bars, and I screamed. A huge figure staggered toward me in the shaft of moonlight, bloody and groaning, overturning the chair and table as he came, shattering the lantern and falling full length just short of our door with a crash that echoed through the cabin like thunder.

Theo. It was Theo, risen from the dead. As he fell I thought he was dead again, but his weight lifter's arms twitched and began to move, at random and then with purpose. He dragged his useless body inch by inch along the floorboards and I stared, transfixed, as he reached up for the doorknob. His face and hair were ghost-white in the moonbeams, his arms and clothing black with blood. Grotesque, terrifying, and our only hope, he pulled himself to his knees and rattled at the knob of our prison door.

"Theo?" I whispered. "Theo, turn the lever. Please. Oh, God, please, just turn it."

He fumbled at the brass. I couldn't see his fingers on it, the angle from the hatchway was too steep, but I could hear the stiff metal of the lock sliding, resisting. Stopping. His hand fell away.

"Theo!" His head fell back, his pale eyes focused on mine. "Theo, try again, please. Nickie's with me, I'll get her out, I promise. Just keep trying."

He reached up, he made a small, agonized sound, and the lever turned through its final arc to set us free. Theo slumped against the door, swinging it inward against the wall with a hollow thump. I grabbed Nickie under the arms and dragged her from the cot, yelling into her ears, slapping her cheeks to rouse her and get her moving. We stumbled over Theo's right arm and kept going, Nickie crying and protesting, me grimly set on getting us both into the outside air.

There was a roaring in my head, and my vision was darkening and closing in to a long dim tunnel, but we made it out of the cabin. The trees. All I could think of, half crazed as I was, was getting out of that deadly clearing and into the safe, clean shadows of the trees. I cursed Nickie, I wrenched at her and hurt her more than Andreas ever had, but I got her across that clearing and behind the giant cedar trunk before I looked over my shoulder.

I would have gone back for Theo. At least I think I would have. But as I leaned hidden against the tree trunk, gasping for air, Grace Parry strode out from the woods behind the cabin, the yellow cone of a flashlight beam swinging before her like a broadsword, her dark clothes absorbing the moonlight and her cornsilk hair throwing it back with a golden spark. She must have been searching for Aaron in the woods, unwilling to take a chance that she had only wounded him, and then come running when she heard the commotion. I shrank into the shadows with Nickie silent at my feet. Grace went straight for the open door of the cabin, pistol in hand, raking the clearing as she went with her furious amber eyes.

I saw what happened in the next few seconds, by moonlight and flashlight and in the final flames. I wish I hadn't seen it, and I was glad that Nickie had fainted by then, and would hear only the softened version that I later told her father.

Grace stepped into the cabin. Theo, with one last effort of vengeful will and one last choking groan, reared up at her like a grizzly bear cornering the hunter who has tormented him to death. I saw him in her flashlight beam, and I heard her cry out in horror as she aimed the pistol at his eyes. He fell upon her, the pistol sparked, and together in the same instant came the crack of the bullet and the vast crumpling sound of the explosion as the rooms full of propane blew and the cabin erupted into a torch that seemed to blossom upward and scorch the moon.

Chapter Forty-four

MY HANDS WERE TREMBLING.

I looked down at my bouquet of lacy ferns and lily of the valley and sapphire-blue freesias that caught the color of my gown, and tried very hard to make the damn flowers stop shaking. A wedding is not a scripted performance, I told myself silently, as I'd told every one of my brides. Wedding guests are *guests,* not spectators. Be graceful, but be natural. Smile.

"You look lovely." Dorothy Fenner joined me in the narrow corridor behind the roof garden. She laid a reassuring hand on my arm. "Just relax, and let me worry about the details."

I had to admit, she'd done a marvelous job. The roof garden of the Cortland Hotel had been transformed into a bower of blossoms and greenery, perfect for an intimate yet formal affair. And the reception room inside stood in lavish readiness for the champagne supper to follow. A sideboard with a three-tiered wedding cake, a bit of space for mingling and making toasts, and five tables for eight guests each, in their tuxedos and long gowns. Each table was impeccably correct, down to the last silver napkin ring, crystal candelabra, and handwritten place card.

Sure, I might have vetoed the boysenberry sorbet between

courses, and I thought the chamber quintet now playing Bach
had one woodwind too many, but I'd agreed to give Dorothy free
rein and that was that. Nothing left but to walk down the aisle.

"Go ahead," said Dorothy. "Carnegie, go *ahead*."

I unstuck my cowardly feet from the floor and stepped
outside into the late September afternoon. The Cortland
overlooks downtown Seattle and its harbor from Queen
Anne Hill, a splendid view at any time, and most especially
at this moment. Cloudless and serene, the sky was a tender,
translucent blue overhead, shading westward by impercepti-
ble degrees to warm gold, to apricot, coral, and finally the
blazing vermilion of the setting sun. In the distance the sky-
scraper windows flashed and sparkled, Elliott Bay shone
silver-blue, and the treetops of all the city's parks were a lush
green touched with autumn color. Here on the rooftop in the
golden light, the affectionate faces of the wedding guests
seemed illuminated from within.

I walked, with all the natural grace I could muster, past
Lily James, who had fixed my hair for me, past Julia Parry,
who'd helped me with my dress, and past Eddie Breen, who
hadn't been to a wedding in forty-five years. Eddie had been
remarkably gentle with me, ever since he showed up at the
Pierce County police station where the firemen had taken
me, on the night Grace Parry died.

Grace Parry and Theo Decker. I didn't learn Theo's last
name until I attended his funeral. (Andreas turned out to
have several last names, as the police discovered once they
took fingerprints from his corpse.) The funeral was the first
public appearance Nickie had made since her ordeal, and the
haggard look on her young face as she laid flowers on Theo's
grave was enough to break your heart. I brought flowers myself, and I cried.

Eddie winked at me as I walked past. The night of the explosion he had fetched me from the police station, forgiven me everything, and installed me in Lily's guest room. I stayed with her for much of August, venturing out to the office a couple of times a week. Mom wanted me to come to Boise, but I was just as happy at Lily's, playing with her boys and watching the videos Eddie brought over. Eventually I'd be able to pay him back for the money he sent my mother in my name. He never mentioned the accusations I made, or the tax evasion case in St. Louis, and heaven knows I never did either.

I was very grateful that Eddie had broken his rule about attending weddings, just this once. Grateful to see Joe Solveto, too. He popped out from the dining room to give me a thumbs-up and then went back to his hors d'oeuvres. I kept walking. At the head of the impromptu aisle, marked off by topiary boxwood trees and swaths of white ribbon, stood Reverend Allington. He had agreed to bless this ceremony outside his church, given the unusual circumstances and the publicity-shy guests, and he beamed at me from beneath an arched trellis of ivy and late roses. So did the bridegroom, slim and straight in his tuxedo, black hair combed to perfection, and all the love in the world in his eyes. I beamed back, and tried to look calm.

I should have looked calm. After all, I was only the maid of honor.

As I took my place opposite the best man, Ray Ishigura got his first sight of the bride. Nickie was still thinner than she should be, and after weeks of near-seclusion she was anxious about facing even this small crowd. But the moment her eyes met Ray's she lit up like a candle. Her gown, bought off the rack, was a simple column of smooth pearl-colored silk, lustrous against her olive skin, with a low shawl collar that left her shoulders bare. The silk caught and reflected the rosy glow of sunset, and the short soft curls framing Nickie's face lifted and stirred in the breeze. Circling her throat was the baroque pearl necklace, the real one, that her father had given her as an engagement present such a brief, eternal time ago.

Her father's wedding gift to her was less expensive, but even more precious: an eight-week-old Welsh corgi puppy named Molly, with a face like a baby fox and a butt like a bunny rabbit. Molly was already Nickie's faithful shadow. It had meant a lot to Nickie, just how much I could only guess, to learn from the police that Gus had been killed not by Theo, but by Andreas. The knowledge helped her to believe what she desperately needed to believe: that all along, Theo had never meant her any real harm.

Douglas Parry watched his daughter from a wheelchair, too weak to walk far as yet. He'd had another heart attack, and then a double bypass, but he was recuperating. Nickie paused to kiss his cheek as she walked down the aisle alone. Soon her father would be fit enough to assist with the federal S&L investigation—a far less daunting prospect, now that he was an innocent witness instead of a possible suspect. Guthridge had cleared his old comrade's name in the process of his own plea bargaining, and admitted that the campaign of intimidation had been meant to secure Parry's silence, not to pressure a fellow criminal.

Just now Douglas Parry simply looked like an ailing but very proud father of the bride, and not at all like the central figure of a courtroom drama. Or like a man whose close friend and family attorney, his wife's lover, his betrayer, had died of blood loss and hypothermia alone on a snowy mountainside.

But I refused to think about that. I'd had to shut the thought away several times each day, and more than several times every night. Of all the tangled emotions I'd come away with, pity for Holt Walker was the least expected, and the most painful. Douglas nodded at me, and I smiled back at him and at his niece Gloria, the former maid of honor who'd cheerfully stepped aside for me at Nickie's request. Behind them sat Mariana, Grace's innocent pawn in the scheme to frame me, already weeping happily into a lace handkerchief.

"Dearly beloved, we are assembled here—"

I cleared my mind of everything except good wishes for the bridal pair. Nickie handed me her bouquet to hold, and she and Ray spoke their vows, her voice tremulous, his joyful and determined. Ray would provide the confidence for both of them, at least for now, but Nickie was young and well loved, and would regain her balance soon enough.

The interruption came during the blessing of the rings. The corridor door banged open, there was a muffled giggle, and a short and somehow familiar brunette stepped through. She looked around, young and bubbly in a stylish red dress, then reached back to help her companion get his crutches over the threshold so he could hobble into the garden and take a seat next to Boris and Corinne. (Boris looked like a grizzly bear who'd won the lottery, and Corinne looked like a cat on an all-canary diet. Nickie's ill wind had certainly blown them some good.) A few guests turned to glance at the late arrivals, as they fumbled to put the crutches out of the way, but the clergyman recaptured their attention immediately with a clerical cough. Everyone looked obediently at Reverend Allington, Nickie and Ray looked at each other, and I stood there in the sunset with my hands full of flowers, looking at Aaron Gold and his date.

I missed most of the sermon, though I'm sure it was uplifting. It certainly seemed long. I hadn't seen Aaron since they'd slid him into an ambulance at the Trout Pond Café, and I wasn't sure I wanted to see him now, in or out of a rental tuxedo. He looked terrific in it, though, the black and white setting off his black hair and white teeth.

Aaron had never returned the phone messages I left at the hospital—he was always in physical therapy when I called—and after he was sent home I only tried once. A woman answered, undoubtedly this very woman in the red dress, and I was too flustered to leave my name. *Let him call me,* I thought. And then I thought, *Leave the man alone, he's recovering from a concussion and a shattered ankle.* And then I thought, *What a good thing he hasn't called, because we're obviously incompatible.* In the end I sent him a dumb, jokey get-well card, and he sent an equally dumb card back. End of story.

Only now he was seated in the last row of our little congregation, grinning at the brunette, and soon the two of them would be going inside to drink champagne and eat dinner. Well, as long as we were seated far enough apart—

"I now pronounce you husband and wife. You may kiss the bride."

It was a lovely moment, and Julia Parry was not the only one weeping grateful tears. I returned Nickie's flowers to her, and accompanied Ted, the best man, back up the aisle to the dining room. The warm gold of sunset had cooled to a violet dusk, and it felt good to step inside to the candlelight. While the guests followed us and pressed forward to embrace the bride and admire the cake, I headed straight for Joe Solveto near the kitchen door. I wanted a distraction, and shop talk was my best bet, especially now that my professional reputation had been restored.

"Hey, Carnegie, I finally get to see you with a bouquet instead of a clipboard!" Joe kissed me on the cheek and put a brimming champagne flute in my hand. "It suits you. Now go back and be a guest."

"But I just wanted to ask about the cake-cutting—"

"Would you get off duty, woman! Dorothy Fenner told me you were kibitzing, and I want it stopped."

"But—"

"Now. Go mingle. Go find your place card. Go."

I laughed and obeyed, sipping the cold, fizzing wine faster than I should have. I accepted a refill from one of the white-shirted waiters, and exchanged greetings with Nickie's family and friends as I drifted toward the table where Eddie was already sitting. He wore his natty tuxedo as comfortably as his khakis, and he was deep in subversive conversation with Lily about the obsolete character of the institution of marriage.

"Well, sister," he said, lifting his glass to me, "it's about time you got bossed around instead of bossing. You look pretty, Carnegie."

"It's all Lily's doing," I said, and she smiled. "Am I sitting with you?"

They checked the other place cards and shook their heads, so I drifted on. I didn't see Aaron Gold until I tripped over his crutches. He was seated at an otherwise empty table, with his crutches on the floor, and the brunette was nowhere to be seen. If I'd been in charge I would have known the guest list by heart, and therefore her name. My own name, as it turned out, was on a place card next to Aaron's.

"Well," I said intelligently.

"Well." A pause, and then he said, "I'd jump up to greet you, but—"

"Don't be silly," I said quickly, and sat. Sitting down I was still taller than he was, but not as much. "How's your ankle?"

"Not bad at all, really." He grinned. "The crutches are just for sympathy. Works great on the bus."

"Still no car?" We can do this, I was thinking. We can do small talk.

"Nope, not till I finish rehab. Parry's paying for it."

I had to lean forward to hear him over the babble, and raise my voice a bit in reply. "Well, he should, of course, but it's nice of him to think of it, considering what he's got on his mind."

Aaron nodded in agreement and sipped his champagne. Then he gestured with the glass toward the picture window across the room. On the other side, lingering in the twilight garden above the city, Douglas sat talking to Julia Parry. They both looked weary, worn down by life, but at peace for this one moment. As we watched, Nickie left the dining room and ran out to them, laughing and exhilarated, to urge them inside. We couldn't hear their voices, but her parents looked at her with such grateful tenderness that I glanced away, feeling like an intruder. I lifted my own glass and found it empty.

"More champagne?" I asked Aaron.

"Gail's getting me some. Thanks anyway."

Gail. OK, her name was Gail. Nice name.

"Listen, Carnegie," he was saying, "remember in the car, that night at the café, I was going to ask you something?"

"Um, no, actually I don't."

He shook his head in despair. "It is *so hard* to get women to learn their lines."

I shifted closer, making way for Nickie's very large uncle to sit down on my other side. "Aaron, just refresh my memory, OK?"

He drummed his fingers on the table. The pink linen cloth muffled the sound, and his hand drew back into a fist. "Actually, it's a stupid question. No, it's not a stupid question, it's just jumping to a stupid conclusion, but—" I began to fidget myself at that point, and he pressed on abruptly. "Did you turn me down because I'm Jewish?"

I stopped fidgeting. "Did I *what*?"

"You heard me. On the Fourth of July, at your place, when you said we were too different to get involved with each other, was that the reason?"

"Of course not!"

"Then what was the reason?"

He sounded like a reporter again, badgering me. "I don't know. I mean, I know but I can't explain. Anyway, it wasn't because you're Jewish."

"Why, then? Answer me."

Resentment, and champagne, made me reckless. "It was because you're . . . short."

He cocked his head and stared at the tabletop, his brows drawn together, as if I were speaking a foreign and rather difficult language. "Short."

"Yes, short. I'm very tall, and you're, well, you're not, and I'm just uncomfortable with—"

Aaron opened his mouth wide and laughed, louder than he had laughed that day at the baseball game, loud enough to set the large uncle laughing, and certainly loud enough to irritate me.

"Listen," I said, flushing. "I've got a right to my opinions."

"That's not an opinion," he chortled. "That's just nonsense. And here I was getting paranoid . . ." He wiped his eyes. "Look, Carnegie, it's no problem. You'll get over it."

I stood up and took my place card with me. "I doubt that very much, and even if I did, it's a moot point, isn't it?"

As if on cue, the brunette appeared with a champagne flute in each manicured hand. "What's a moot point?"

"Everything!" he said gaily. "Everything's moot, everything's up for grabs. Gail, this is Carnegie Kincaid, the very tall wedding lady. Carnegie, this is my somewhat short sister Gail, who's been nursing me back to health."

I gazed at her, at her white teeth and her crow-black hair and the look of Aaron Gold she had around her chocolate brown eyes.

She put down the glasses with a mischievous smile. "So *you're* the one he keeps talking about!"

"I am?" I said, with more than champagne fizzing inside me. "I guess I am."

About the Author

DEBORAH DONNELLY'S inspiration for the Carnegie Kincaid series came when she was planning her best friend's wedding and her own at the same time. (Both turned out beautifully.) A long-time resident of Seattle, Donnelly now lives in Boise, Idaho, with her writer husband and their two Welsh corgis. Readers can visit her at www.deborahdonnelly.org.

If you stayed up late with

Veiled Threats,

you'll love

Died to Match,

the next wedding planner mystery by

DEBORAH DONNELLY,

on sale September 2002

Read on for a preview . . .

MASKS ARE DANGEROUS. THE MEREST SCRAP OF SILK OR SLIP of cardboard can eclipse one's civilized identity, and set loose the dark side of the soul.

Trust me. You take a pair of perfectly well-behaved newspaper reporters, or software engineers or whatever, dress them up as Spider-Man and a naughty French maid and whammo! It's a whole new ball game.

Which is why this party was getting out of hand. Free drinks can make people crazy, but free costumes make them wild. Two hundred big black envelopes had gone out to Paul and Elizabeth's friends and colleagues, inviting them to a Halloween engagement party in the Seattle Aquarium, down at Pier 59 on Elliott Bay. And tucked inside the envelope was a very special party favor: a coupon for the persona of one's choice at Characters Inc., a theatre-quality costume shop. So tonight, more than a hundred and fifty reasonably civilized people were living out their fantasies among the fishes. And the fantasies were getting rowdy.

It all started innocently enough: Madonna flirting with Mozart, Death with his scythe trading stock tips with Nero and his violin, Albert Einstein dirty dancing with Monica Lewinsky. And everyone toasting the engaged couple with affection and good cheer. Paul Wheeler, the groom-to-be, was news editor at the *Seattle Sentinel* newspaper; he made a skinny, smiley swashbuckler, sort of Indiana Jones Lite. His fiancée, Elizabeth ("*not* Liz") Lamott, was a tough-minded Microsoft millionaire who had retired at twenty-nine. Dressed as Xena the Warrior Princess, Elizabeth looked both drop-dead sexy and more than capable of beheading barbarian warlords. The Wheeler and Lamott families would all be at the wedding in three weeks—an extravaganza at the Experience Music Project—but tonight's bash was more of a co-ed bachelor party.

And like so many bachelor parties, headed straight to hell. Luke Skywalker was juggling martini glasses, quite unsuccessfully, near "Principles of Ocean Survival." Mister Rogers had knocked over the sushi trays at "Local Invertebrates." Various members of the Spice Girls and Sgt. Pepper's Lonely Hearts Club Band were disappearing into the darkened grotto of "Pacific Coral Reef" and returning with their costumes askew. And at all the liquor stations, masked revelers had begun pushing past the bartenders to pour their own drinks—a danger sign even when the crowd is in civvies.

I wasn't wearing a mask, and I certainly wasn't fantasizing, except about keeping my professional cool and getting our damage deposit back from the Aquarium. It was my hands the party was getting out of: *Made in Heaven Wedding Design, Carnegie Kincaid, Sole Proprietor.* I usually stick to weddings, too, but business had been iffy ever since I'd been a suspect in the abduction of one of my brides. Everybody reads the headlines, nobody reads the follow-up, and now my name, besides being weird in the first place, had a little shadow across it in the minds of some potential clients.

So an extra event with an extra commission had been hard to turn down. And the formidable Ms. Lamott had been impossible to turn down. When Elizabeth wanted something she got it, whether she was launching products for Bill Gates or, more recently, harvesting charity donations from Seattle's crop of wealthy thirty-somethings. Elizabeth asked me to manage her engagement party in person, I explained that I really don't do costumes, and suddenly, somehow, there I was in a long jaggedy-hemmed black gown and a crooked-peaked witch's hat, stationed by the champagne at "Salmon & People: A Healthy Partnership," and reminding my waiters that cleaning broken glass off the floor comes first, no matter how many guests are demanding more booze.

One guest did his demanding in silence: a well-tailored Count Dracula with an especially realistic rubber mask, complete with fangs, that covered his entire head. He pantomimed to the barman with his empty glass, bowed grandly in thanks when it was filled, and disappeared back into the crowd. Nobody—including me—seemed to know who the Count was, and he was steadfastly refusing to speak, no matter who cajoled him, so his voice wouldn't give him away. It was actually getting spooky, watching Dracula move from group to group of party guests, flourishing his cape. I half expected him to morph into a bat and soar away.

"Carnegie!"

"What?" I snapped. "Oh, sorry, Lily. I'm losing my mind here. Are you having a good time?"

Lily James, my best friend, was also my date for the party, because I'd had a spat with Aaron Gold, my who-knows-what. The spat was about Aaron's smoking, which I found deplorable and he found to be none of my business. But it went deeper than that. We were teetering on the brink of being lovers, and life on the brink was uncomfortable. At least it was for me; I kept hesitating and analyzing and wondering if we were right for each other. Aaron's view was that we could analyze just as easily lying down.

Aaron was at the party, of course. All of the *Sentinel*'s reporters were there, gleefully adding to the pandemonium. I could see a laughing, breathless bunch of them now, escorting Paul and Elizabeth up the tunnel from the underwater dome room, where the dancing was. As they headed for the martini bar, Aaron put his arm around Corinne Campbell, the paper's society writer. A handsome couple: he was quite dashing in a Zorro mask and cape, and she made a blonde, bosomy Venus in a filmy white gown crisscrossed with silver cords. I knew Corinne professionally, of course—she often wrote about my brides—and I'd been seeing more of her now that she was one of Elizabeth's bridesmaids. She wasn't the sharpest knife in the drawer, but she could be pleasant enough, in an overeager kind of way. Especially to men. I bet *she* found the scent of cigarettes manly and exciting.

"I said, I'm having a fine time!" Lily's voice broke through this sour speculation. "You're not listening, are you?"

"Sure I am. You're having a fine time."

Lily was certainly looking fine, a statuesque black-skinned Cleopatra, rubber snake and all, with her wide, high-lidded eyes elaborately painted into an Egyptian mask of gold and indigo. By day, Lily staffed the reference desk at Seattle Public, but tonight she was every inch the voluptuous and commanding Queen of the Nile. Of course, Lily could be voluptuous and commanding in sweatpants, I'd seen her do it. Her glittery make-up caught the light as she gazed around and let loose the deep, provocative laugh that often startled the library's patrons. "This is a fabulous place for a party!"

"You bet your asp it is," I said, scanning the crowd over her shoulder. "But it's tough to supervise, with all these corridors and cul-de-sacs. I've got a couple of off-duty cops here as security and I haven't talked to either one in hours except on the two-way radio. Makes me nervous."

I was especially nervous about "Northwest Shores," a dead-end grotto past the martini bar. I'd already had to shoo some Visigoths off the handrail of the shorebird exhibit down at the end. The water in the little beach scene was only a foot deep, hardly a drowning matter, but if anybody tumbled over backwards it would terrify the long-billed curlews and they'd never let me rent this place again. The management, I mean, not the curlews.

"Well, everyone but you is having a blast," said Lily.

I was about to agree when we heard an angry shout from the martini bar. A knot of people tightened suddenly, their backs to us, intent on a scene we couldn't see.

Over their heads, arcing high in the air, rose the scythe of Death.

I shoved my way through the crowd. I'm almost six feet tall, so I can shove with the best. Lunging like a fencer, I parried the scythe with my broomstick just in time to save Zorro from having his hair parted right through his hat.

"What on earth is going on here? Syd? Aaron?"

Death's hood had fallen back, revealing the fat and furious face of Sydney Soper, a big-shot local contractor and personal friend of the bride-to-be. That explained what was going on. Aaron had done an article, the first in a series, questioning Soper's methods of winning state highway contracts. With Seattle and Bellevue booming, and traffic approaching Los Angeles levels, those contracts ran into the millions. According to Aaron, a lot of millions were being misspent, if not actually swindled.

So now Death was pissed off at Zorro, and Zorro was standing his ground and grinning, a lock of raven-black hair flopping down beneath his black caballero hat. I knew from personal experience how infuriating that grin could be, and I felt for Soper. Especially since, unlike me, Soper probably didn't appreciate the sexy brown eyes above the grin. His own eyes, hard and pale as pebbles, were bulging with anger. God knows what Aaron had said to provoke the Grim Reaper, but he was lucky the scythe was plastic.

As I hesitated, wondering how to cast a soothing spell, the scene was stolen from me by a gypsy queen. Mercedes Montoya, another of Elizabeth's bridesmaids, stepped up in a swirl of bright skirts and a chiming of bracelets. She was a classic Castilian beauty, via Mexico City, with a mane of midnight curls framing cheekbones so sharp you could cut yourself. And a mind to match. Mercedes had recently decamped from the *Sentinel* for the headier world of TV news, and she was already making a name for herself. The camera, as they say, loved her.

"Mister Soper," she murmured, with the faintest hint of an accent in her caressing, dark-chocolate voice. "This is a party. Come dance with me."

She held out a slim brown hand, sparkling with costume jewelry. Soper glared at her, breathing hard, but Mercedes' hand never wavered and the smile never left her narrow, aristocratic lips. I marveled at her self-assurance, even as I waited for the burly contractor to snarl her off. We all waited, Zorro and Cleopatra and the rest of us, through a long, uncomfortable moment. And then damned if Soper didn't take her hand and walk away, with a flush rising up the back of his thick neck. Taming the fury of Death, that's what I call magic.

The knot of guests unraveled, many of them following Mercedes and Soper to the dance floor. I saw Dracula bow in silent gallantry to an unaccompanied hippie chick, and sweep her down the tunnel with his scalloped black cape fluttering around her tie-dyed shoulders. Even Lily went off, to boogie with the Visigoths, and I was left with Aaron Gold.

Down below, the DJ cued up "Respect"—Otis, not Aretha. "Look, Aaron, the dome room's next on my rounds, and I'm due for a break anyway. Come dance with me?"

He looked away uncomfortably, straightening his shiny black cape. "I promised Corinne, when she gets back from the restroom. If she ever gets back. She's spending half the party in there."

"Oh. Well, don't let me keep you." Corinne, with her golden curls and her syrupy Southern drawl and her ice-cream–scoop cleavage. I have long red hair, which I'm regrettably vain about, but I'm also skinny as a broomstick, and in my witch's hat I towered over Aaron's middling height. The difference in our statures bothered me, and amused him. He just called me silly nicknames, and insisted that he didn't have to be bigger than me, only smarter and more charming.

"Corinne's kind of my date tonight, Stretch," he was saying. "I'm worried about her. She's been really down since she broke up with that Russian guy."

"She's been looking kind of rocky," I agreed. "But I think it was Boris who broke up with her."

Actually, I knew it was. Boris Nevsky—Lily called him Boris the Mad Russian Florist—had given me the gory details as we planned Paul and Elizabeth's wedding flowers. "She vanted to get *merried!*" he'd announced, mournful and astonished, shaking his shaggy Slavic head over the parrot tulips and the hellebores. Having dated Boris a couple of times myself, I was astonished too, but there's no accounting for taste.

"I wondered about that," said Aaron. "Corinne claims *she* dumped *him*, but she's awfully depressed about it. And I think this wedding stuff is making her feel extra-single. Funny how weddings do that to women. Us bachelor groomsmen are feeling just fine."

"I bet you are. Well, I've got to circulate. If I see Corinne I'll tell her you're waiting for her."

"Thanks, Wedding Lady," said Aaron. "Save a dance for me, OK?"

"I'll save two."

What's wrong with this picture? I asked myself as I pushed open the ladies' room door a short while later. I'm at a party, Aaron's at the same party, and what am I doing? I'm keeping an eye out for his date. What a world. Still, I felt for Corinne. Weddings are hard when you're brokenhearted, and I'm a sucker for broken hearts. That's why I started *Made in Heaven*, I suppose. What better business for a hopeless romantic who likes to throw parties?

Inside the restroom, preening in solitary glory, was Mercedes Montoya. I wondered if Syd Soper was outside somewhere, resting his scythe and hoping for another dance. If so, he was a patient man; a fortune in designer cosmetics lay spilled across the counter, and Mercedes was employing all of it. No wonder the camera loved her. She obviously loved herself.

"The wedding planner!" she announced gaily, shaking back her midnight hair. Her eyes, meeting mine in the mirror, were suspiciously shiny and hugely dilated. Was it only alcohol flying her kite, or a little something extra? I really didn't want to know. "I was just thinking about you! About hiring you."

"Really? I didn't know you were getting married. Who's the lucky man?"

Mercedes clapped a hand to her lips. With the other hand she clutched my arm, tight enough to hurt. "No! It's a secret! You can't tell a soul. Not a single *Sentinel* soul!"

She gave a long peal of melodious laughter, then blinked vacantly and seemed to forget why she was laughing. Definitely something extra. I retrieved my arm. "I won't breathe a word."

"Good," she murmured. "Good. Roger would be furious."

"Roger?"

She gasped again. "How did you know? You have to keep it secret!"

"Keep what secret, Mercedes?"

She leaned close, her ropes of beads clicking and swaying. *"I'm going to marry the mayor!"*

I thought I'd heard her wrong. "Mayor Wyble's already married."

"Not *him*, Roger Talbot! Roger's going to be mayor next year, after I help him beat Wyble." Mercedes was suddenly cold and shrewd. She was cycling through moods like a kaleidoscope.

"We'll have the wedding right before the primaries. The grieving widower finds happiness. People will eat it up."

Apparently the widower wasn't all that grieved, not that it was any of my business. Brides were my business, but I wasn't sure I wanted this volatile prima donna as a client. *And yet*, I thought, while Mercedes went back to fluffing her hair and humming a Motown tune, landing another big-budget, high-profile wedding could put *Made in Heaven* in the news, maybe even in the trade magazines, and definitely in the black. I was still several thousand dollars in debt from starting up my business, and the dock fees on my rented houseboat were killing me. Well, time for those calculations later. I couldn't very well hold her to a decision made under the influence.

"Congratulations," I said, wondering if she'd apply my comment to the engagement or the election. Probably both. "But there's plenty of time to plan. You don't want to choose a bridal consultant on a whim. Think it over."

"You don't believe me," she pouted. Mercedes had a superb pout. She slid a hand down her ragtag gypsy bodice and drew out a long gold chain with twisted herringbone links. Suspended from it, swinging inches from my astonished eyes, was a monster diamond on an ornate platinum band. "You'll believe a girl's best friend, won't you?"

"Mercedes, that's stunning!" I wanted to get away from her and her secrets, but for a moment I was mesmerized. The diamond swung back and forth, like a hypnotist's watch. "It must be nearly three carats! Is it antique?"

"Family heirloom," she said complacently, and lowered the treasure back into its cozy hiding place. X marks the spot. "It was his grandmother's engagement ring, and now it's mine. I told Roger, I'll keep our secret, but I have to have something to put under my pillow, don't I?"

"It's a wonder you can sleep."

She laughed. "I sleep very well. Roger makes sure of that."

I wasn't going anywhere near that one. "Well, like I said, think it over—"

"I don't have to, I want *you*." The kaleidoscope was turning faster; now she was sulky and stubborn. She rummaged in her patchwork shoulder bag and pulled out a wad of bills. "Here, take this. For a deposit."

"Mercedes, you don't have to—"

"Take it!" she said shrilly.

"OK, OK." Anything to calm her down. I took the money; there were twenties, and at least one fifty. "Let's count it and I'll write you a receipt."

"No, no, I trust you. Oh, Carnegie, isn't it exciting? I'm getting married!" Looking suddenly girlish, Mercedes gave me an impulsive hug, laying her head against my shoulder. Her hair was perfumed, sweet and musky. Then she wrenched herself away.

"Just remember, wedding planner . . ." She fixed me with a dark, straight stare, a tiger's stare. "You keep your mouth shut."

Mercedes swept up her paints and swept out of the room. A black and gold powder compact lay overlooked under the balled-up paper towels. I picked it up, but then didn't go after her. I'd had enough schizophrenic gypsy glamour for the moment. Instead, I stood pondering this unexpected glimpse into Roger Talbot's private life. His wife had only been dead a month or so. If Mercedes and Talbot had a whirlwind courtship, it must have blown at gale force, unless they'd gotten involved while Helen Talbot was still alive. A nasty thought. Aaron had mentioned once that Mercedes was constantly in the publisher's office. Maybe she'd been negotiating more than her salary. Maybe her move to television was really part of Talbot's campaign. I hated to be that cynical, but—

A sudden sound, at once revolting and unmistakable. The room had appeared empty, but someone was in the farthest stall being spectacularly sick. I heard ragged breathing, then a moan.

"Hello?" I called, sliding the cash and the compact into the ample pocket of my witch's gown. "Can I help?"

The stall door swung wide to reveal one very unkempt and unsteady Greek goddess. In wordless sympathy, I ran a paper towel under the faucet and handed it to Aaron's long-lost date. Corinne dragged it across her mouth, her long fake fingernails a startling crimson against her pale, trembling lips. How much champagne did it take to drown the memory of Boris Nevsky? A double latte had done the trick for me, but then I never wanted to marry the man.

"I'm going to die," said Corinne. She looked at herself bleakly in the mirror—hairdo in ruins, satiny toga crumpled and soiled—and took a long sobbing breath. "I want to die."

"You'll get over him," I offered. "You'll feel better, really you will."

She glared at me. Her eyes were a weak, watery blue, but the look in them was somehow scarier than Mercedes'. "What do you know about it? How do you know how I feel?"

"Corinne, I just meant that you'll find somebody else—"

Her eyes went wide and rolling, like a panicky horse about to bolt. "I'll never find anyone like him. *Never!*"

Then she pushed past me and was gone. *Aaron*, I thought, *Aaron, she is all yours*. While I waited for the gypsy queen and the drama queen to get a good head start, I belatedly remembered about "Northwest Shores." I radioed Morrie, one of my security guards, and asked him to close it off. Then I left the ladies' and went back to my rounds, checking on each of the bars and food stations. The Halloween menu I'd designed with Joe Solveto, my favorite caterer, was definitely a hit, especially the all-chocolate dessert bar. Good thing we had generous reserves; running out of food is an event planner's highest crime.

Before I could pat myself on the back any harder, I was accosted by a large leprechaun.

"Carnegie, you look glorious! Who are you supposed to be, exactly?"

Tommy Barry, the *Sentinel*'s legendary sportswriter, was also a legendary drinker of Guinness, and when Tommy drank he got very Irish. A shamrock-bedecked hat sat askew on his bush of grizzled hair, and one of his curly-toed leprechaun slippers was missing. I had gently suggested a more reliable best man— and .Elizabeth had demanded a more photogenic one—but Paul was adamant. Tommy was his mentor and his pal, so Tommy it would be. This was my first wedding where the best man went on pub crawls with the florist.

"I'm supposed to be a witch," I told him, "and you were supposed to be here at eight. We had to do the toasts without you. The maid of honor is working tonight, so I was depending on you. You will be on time for the wedding, won't you, Tommy?"

"Of course, of course. Tonight I gave Zack here a ride," he said proudly, as if this were quite a feat. In his current inebriated condition, maybe it was.

Zack Hartmann, the bashful young Internet whiz working

on the *Sentinel* Web site, was Paul's third groomsman. He was usually shy and slouching, but not tonight. Tonight Zack was the Prince of Thieves, with a quiver of arrows over his green-cloaked shoulder and a couple of martinis under his belt. Tall and rangy, with crisp fair hair and long-lashed cobalt-blue eyes, he stood next to Tommy with his shoulders back and his head high. Maid Marion would have been thrilled to bits.

"We were a tad late, perhaps," Tommy was saying, "but now we're raising the roof and showing the girls a good time, aren't we, Zack? You go dance with Carnegie, and I'll just stop by the bar."

"I'm really awfully busy," I began.

"Nonsense!" he rasped. Tommy had a voice that could strip paint. "Too busy to dance with Robin Hood? Off you go, both of you."

I liked Zack, and I didn't want to hurt his feelings. "Sure, just one dance."

As I followed him out onto the dance floor, the DJ ended the Motown set and changed musical gears with the Righteous Brothers, "Soul and Inspiration." I hadn't bargained on a slow dance, but it had been a long night, and if I couldn't have Zorro's arms around me, Robin's looked like a decent substitute. For a few minutes I even relaxed and enjoyed myself. But once the song ended I'd have to go check with Donald, the other security guard, up on the observation deck, to make sure no one had gone skinny-dipping with the seals or feeding paté to the puffins or some damn thing. Not that my presence would prevent them, but—

"Is something wrong?" Zack blurted. I realized he was trembling a bit, and there were spots of hectic color on his cheekbones. What I'd taken for head-high confidence was just a rigid façade. Whether it was the drinks or the awkward social situation, Robin Hood was strung up as tight as piano wire.

"Nothing's wrong. I was just wondering how the rest of the party is going."

"Well, if you're too busy to dance with me, I totally understand." He sounded slightly miffed, and very young.

"Not at all. You dance very well."

Actually, he just danced very tall. Try as I might, slow dancing with a shorter man always made me self-conscious. Aaron had wanted us to go as Rocky and Bullwinkle tonight, for crying out loud. What was he thinking? We were clearly incompatible. Oil and water. Chalk and cheese. High fashion and low comedy. Comedy was the operative word, though. Aaron could always make me laugh. I liked that.

"Tommy was right," said Zack, forcing the words out after a stiff silence. "You really do look beautiful tonight."

Right words, wrong guy. Still, nice words.

"Thanks, Zack. You're pretty gorgeous yourself."

In the shifting underwater light, I couldn't quite see him blushing, but I could feel it. He began to reply, stammered to a halt, then settled for holding me a little tighter. I subtly tried to put a bit of space between us, but the press of bodies kept us close. I peeked over Zack's shoulder, checking the crowd. I didn't see Aaron and Corinne, but Paul and Elizabeth were there, clinging tight, or as tight as they could given the bride's bronze and leather breastplates. She was wearing his Indy fedora on her long black Xena wig and smiling dreamily. Happy clients, that was the ticket. Happy clients who would recommend me to their happy, wealthy friends. My silent partner Eddie Breen, never silent for long, was always pushing me to advertise more, while I favored word-of-mouth among brides and their mothers.

One thought sparked another. "Zack, are you full-time with the *Sentinel* now or do you freelance elsewhere? My partner's been pestering me about jazzing up our Web site."

It was like flipping a high-voltage switch.

"Sure!" Zack's face lit up and he stepped firmly on my foot. "I'd do it for cheap, too, I need more stuff in my portfolio. We could start right away."

"Whoa! Eddie and I need to brainstorm a bit first. Right now the site is just a scan of our print pamphlet—"

"Brochureware!" he groaned. "That is so lame."

"Well, excuse me!"

"I'm sorry, I didn't mean . . . that's what everybody starts with, really. But you can do, like, tons more than that. I'll help you brainstorm. I'll come tomorrow afternoon, OK?"

"Well, OK. Eddie's not usually there on Sundays, but he's wrestling with some new software, so he said he'd be in."

"Oh. Will, uh, you be there too?" He tried to look nonchalant.

"Yes, I'll be there too. So tell me, what could we do that wouldn't be lame?"

The Aquarium's rental rules called for low-volume music in the dome room, which made dance floor conversation possible, and Zack took full advantage of the fact. He regaled me feverishly with the online wonders he could perform for *Made in Heaven*, becoming almost agitated as he raved about JPEG files and animated GIFs and why frames, like, totally suck. Amused but sympathetic—I was shy at his age too—I made fascinated and admiring noises, and kept my feet out from under his.

"You're really interested in this stuff, aren't you?" he asked at one point.

"Sure," I lied. "Why wouldn't I be?"

"Well, some people think it's boring. Or, like, nerdy or something."

"Who thinks that?"

But the song ended and he fell abruptly silent, unsure of his next move in this adult ritual. I could almost read his mind: *Do we just go on dancing, or am I supposed to ask her, or what?* Or maybe Zack had forgotten he was dancing at all, lost in cyberspace.

I took the lead. "That was nice. Now I'd better get back to work."

"I'll come with you!" he blurted. "Maybe I can, you know, help you and stuff."

"There's really nothing for you to do, but thanks." He tagged along anyway, and as we took the stairs to the pier level I privately admired his well-filled doublet and hose. *Hmm. Must lift weights.*

"What made you choose Robin Hood, Zack?"

"Oh, stories, I guess. When I was a kid, we had this book of stories. When I got to that shop and saw the costume, I remembered. Robin Hood was always riding to the rescue and everything. How come you're a witch? I mean, *dressed* as a witch."

I laughed. "I've been feeling a little witchy tonight! But no reason, really. By the time I got around to picking, the glamorous stuff was all taken."

He stopped abruptly at a landing and gazed into my eyes, too close for comfort. "I think you're always glamorous."

It was an absurd situation, made more so by the fact that I was suddenly and warmly aware of Zack's body, and my own. If he'd had a little finesse, I might have forgotten the gap in our ages, at least for the moment. Instead he lurched forward and kissed me, clumsily but with great gusto. It was like being leapt upon by a huge, overfriendly young Labrador retriever. One who tasted like gin.

"Zack, cut it out!" I pulled away and my witch's hat rolled to the floor. When I stooped for it I bumped heads with someone in black: Aaron, coming up the steps right behind us. He returned the hat with a flourish and a barely suppressed laugh.

"Cradle-robbing, Mrs. Robinson?"

I snatched it from him and looked around for Zack, but he had fled. Good, let him go cool off.

"Why didn't you tell me your Web wizard was nuts?"

"Didn't know he was. Must be your black magic working, Wicked Witch. You gonna turn him into a frog? No wait, that comes *before* the kiss."

"Oh, shut up. Did Corinne find you?"

"No. You saw her?"

"In the ladies' room. Aaron, I think she's drinking too much."

"That's funny. I've been fetching her Perrier all night."

"Well, it wasn't Perrier she was chucking up. Do you want to go look for her?"

"No," he said, as we came out onto the pier. He stopped and faced me, and the party guests milling around us seemed to disappear. "No, I want to stay right here and gaze at the city lights and say romantic things to you. For instance, I've noticed that you walk in beauty like the night of cloudless climes and starry skies. Plus, as a bonus, all that's best of dark and bright meet in your aspect and your eyes. I admit you're not quite as dark as Lord Byron's girlfriend must have been, but you know what I mean."

I sagged against the wooden railing and took a deep breath of the damp night air. Elizabeth had insisted that the rain would hold off tonight, and she was right. Maybe she cut a deal with Mother Nature. Far out on Elliott Bay, a ferry was lit up like a birthday cake against the black mirror of the water. Aaron and I had begun our spat on a ferry ride, and continued it back at my houseboat, with encores on the telephone after that. But I never fought with the men I dated, never. What was going on?

"Aaron, I'm working tonight. And besides . . ."

"Besides what?"

"I'm just not sure. About the romantic part." I noticed I was kneading the brim of the witch's hat in my hands, round and round, and made myself stop. "Aaron, I like you a lot, I care about you, but we keep arguing."

"Then let's not, Stretch. Let's do this instead."

He'd been moving closer as he spoke and now he kissed me, one brief kiss and another, and then another, longer this time. He didn't touch me at all except with his lips, warm on mine. He was right, I was the Wicked Witch: melting, *melting* . . .

Then several things happened at once, none of them pleasant. A scream. A splash. A shout of alarm. "Somebody's in the water!"

People surged toward the railing, roughly jostling me and Aaron as we peered downwards. The green-black water of the harbor was dappled with light and dotted with debris: cigarette butts, a paper coffee cup, chunks of sodden driftwood. And one wavering luminous shape, trailing strands of fair hair and edges of pallid cloth that rippled just below the surface, slowly sinking and rising. Two ghostly arms spread wide, the pale fingers parted as if to conjure something up from the depths.

Then the man who made the splash diving in—it was Donald, the security guard, I recognized his crew cut—reached the body, hooked an elbow neatly under the chin, and towed it to a wooden ladder that rose up along a piling. A cacophony of shocked, excited voices filled the night, and people fell over each other in their haste to help him hoist his dripping burden to the pier.

I stepped back from the melee and called 911.